Dreamers, Runaways, and Mysteries

Also by James Sloan Allen

*The Romance of Commerce and Culture: Capitalism, Modernism,
and the Chicago-Aspen Crusade for Cultural Reform*

Worldly Wisdom: Great Books and the Meanings of Life

William James on Habit, Will, Truth, and the Meaning of Life (editor)

Aloha: The Surprising History of an Idea and a Culture

Life Line: A Novel of Romance and Rebirth

Dreamers, Runaways, and Mysteries

A Traveler's Tales and Essays

James Sloan Allen

ISBN: 978-1-7349787-0-4
E-ISBN: 978-1-7349787-1-1

Cover photo "Chinese fishing nets on the bay at Cochin (Kochi), Kerala, India"
    (image is horizontally reversed from original photo for design purposes)
    by James Sloan Allen
Cover and interior design by Rachel Davis

To the Adventures, Surprises, and Romance of Travel

Contents

Prefatory Note

These essays and tales originated in travels to places that affected me lastingly. The essays pretty much speak for themselves on that score. Even so, the essays all arose from curiosity about historical mysteries that enfolded these places and that invited the imagination to probe those mysteries. Consequently, the essays are not just travelogues. They are intellectual and imaginative adventures into places and their pasts.

The tales are akin to this. They were born of places that have stayed with me. But most of them also tell of people I met and of experiences I had in those places. To be sure, I have embellished the telling with imaginative twists. Otherwise, they would amount to mere memoirs. Still, I have tried to be true to the places in every instance, and to the people when I could.

More than half of the people in the tales are real: the dancer with the fish-shaped eyes, the old Chinese man in "Mr. Chan's Tea Time," Ciéla in the story named for her, the crone in "Hadrian's Moon," the lady who goes to the elephant races, the rustic guy on parole in Aspen, Granger (by a different name) in "Safari," the gentle man from Laos, and the happy man in "Livin' the Dream." The other tales put imaginary characters in real places that evoked those characters for me. And nearly all of the tales revolve around characters who dream of living different lives or try to escape from the lives they have lived. There are worse reasons for travel than that.

In sum, this collection of essays and tales claims no literary ambitions. It rather unassumingly celebrates the life-giving experience of travel, along with the unexpected turns that this experience can take when we let it and, in the words of the novelist and prolific travel writer Henry James, "try to be one of those on whom nothing is lost."

Note on Photographs: Unless otherwise identified, the photographs are by the author.

Essays

Cape St. Vincent, Portugal

Reflections at the Edge of the World

It is the edge of the world and looks it. A finger of land crooked into the sea rising two hundred feet or more above the waves. Nature could not have better designed the scene to show that the earth is flat and that its land ends here. The surface is as level as if swiped by a sword, and the cliffs as sheer as if sliced to the water. Little rain falls, the soil is sparse, and incessant winds have ravaged the terrain into a landscape of worn and pockmarked stone resembling nothing so much as the moon, the desolation relieved only by a few scrubby junipers and an occasional asphodel, whose tall spindly stalks and symmetrically looped branches add a whimsically lyrical note to the wilderness.

It is no wonder that Europeans once believed the world to end here, at the southwestern corner of their continent on a remote peninsula of Portugal some three hundred miles west of Gibraltar. Roman geographers called it the *Promontorium Sacrum*, the Sacred Promontory. Since the fourth century it has been known as Cape St. Vincent, after the martyr whose remains were said to have been carried here for burial under the protection of ravens. To the ancients, who had calculated with impressive accuracy the sphericity of the earth, the Sacred Promontory marked the inhabitable end of their hemisphere. Beyond it lay the dark and impassable "ocean," which in legend had been identified with the primordial deity Oceanus and which had swallowed up the island of Atlantis west of Gibraltar and the Atlas Mountains in northwest Africa. Eventually, this ocean would take its name, Atlantic, from the same source as those mountains and that lost island, the Greek god of navigation, Atlas. But for centuries, the Atlantic Ocean was known simply as the "Ocean Sea." To medieval Christians who embraced a moral cosmology requiring the earth to be flat and to be uninhabitable on its underside (albeit not all Christians did, scholars tell us), the world itself ended at Cape St. Vincent, this last point of mainland on the route from the Mediterranean into the Ocean Sea—even though Cabo da Roca north of Lisbon extends a little farther westward. At Cape St. Vincent, it was said, the sun sets with ominous hisses as darkness falls on Europe.

By the time Columbus sailed out into the Ocean Sea, Europeans had long since remembered what the ancients had reasoned about the shape of the earth. Yet, even after Columbus, the world still ended metaphorically at Cape St. Vincent for Europeans who continued to look at the world through European eyes and in the light of European culture. This vision gave us what would become fervently deprecated as "Eurocentrism."

Eurocentrism had its most geographically symbolic home on the stark shores of Cape St. Vincent and Sagres, which names the neighboring peninsula and village with a word signifying "sacred" or "holy," from rituals conducted here in ancient times. For here the

Eurocentric vision gave form to the imagination of discovery that drove the early European explorers who—beset by ancient fears, dependent on weather, sailing fragile ships, and relying on rudimentary navigational implements—ventured out into the Ocean Sea to find its boundaries and to link the lands of the earth. It was here that the great age of European exploration began.

The curtain rose when Infante Dom Henrique, the third son of Portuguese King João I, established himself at Sagres around 1420 and launched the career that was to earn him his reputation as Henry the Navigator. Willful, obsessive, and ascetic, Prince Henry turned his back on court life to pursue, as the court chronicler Gomes Eanes de Zurara reported, "the discovery of things which were hidden from other men, and secret" (this and other quotations from him come from Daniel J. Boorstin's *The Discoverers*). For some forty years, Prince Henry brought together at Sagres the most knowledgeable navigators and cartographers of the time; and using their learning he pressed, financed, and rewarded two generations of mariners who made exploratory voyages for Portugal. At Sagres, and at the principal port of Lagos, the Portuguese were taught to observe and record every landmark and water depth; they learned to prepare and follow accurate charts; they mastered the delicate astrolabe and possibly invented the sextant to fix latitudes with precision; they designed an innovative vessel of exploration, the small maneuverable caravel, which could angle close to the wind to save precious time, and could wend its way through shoreline shoals. They became the leading navigators of Europe, every ship's captain demanding a Portuguese pilot at his helm.

Under Prince Henry's sponsorship, Portuguese sailors did more than wander into the Ocean Sea, which intrepid voyagers had done before them. They systematically extended the known world year by year as they probed the coast of Africa, returning with detailed logs of their sightings and then heading out again. Some returned with tales of endless seas and hopelessness—especially as they neared the terrifying Cape Bojador (now an inconspicuous nub of Morocco), whose churning waters red with clay had cowed unnumbered sailors who believed that beyond this point swelled boiling tides and, as Zurara wrote, that "no ship having once passed the Cape will ever be able to return." This was the preeminent Cape of Fear. But other Portuguese touched land—inching carefully ever southward, searching for a route to the fictional realm of the Christian king Prester John, or a passage east to India, or for whatever lay where no European had gone before—and returned to tell of it. They rounded Cape Bojador in 1434, vanquishing the age-old fears at last and giving a fillip to their secular confidence. They crossed the Tropic of Cancer the next year, and continued on slowly to Cape Blanco in the early 1440s. The following year they reached the westernmost point of Africa, which they dubbed Cape Verde, the Green Cape, almost two thousand miles from Sagres.

By this time, Henry's mariners had achieved more than navigational triumphs in their bold seagoing explorations. On a return to Lagos from Cape Blanco in 1444 they had brought with them not just information about the Ocean Sea and the coast of Africa, and possibly some gold (always on their minds). They had also brought the first Africans to be sold into modern slavery. According to Zurara, Prince Henry looked on in that first slave market in Lagos as families were dispersed amidst wailing and tears, but "he had no other pleasure than in thinking that these lost souls would now be saved" by conversion to Christianity. Whether this account is true or not, biographers do not dispute that Henry the Navigator coupled his scientifically-minded pursuit of geographical and navigational knowledge with creation of the modern African slave trade. That Prince Henry could have considered the slave trade a religious benefaction of exploration illustrates the perverse conscience that clouds the whole history of European exploration. And it should. The evil was not exploration in itself. It was the exploitation of exploration made possible by the European sense of cultural superiority and, perhaps above all, by the imperious self-righteousness that had sanctioned Christian predations since the crusades—and that continued to sanction them through the darkest nights of slavery and racism in America.

After "discovering" Cape Verde, Prince Henry's mariners continued pushing on south—reaping gold and human booty as they went. By the time Prince Henry died in 1460 (characteristically dressed in a "rough shirt of horse hair," noted the aide who attended his body) they had reached Sierra Leone, and maybe even Cape Palmas, where the African coast swings eastward. Nearly three decades later a Portuguese crew led by Bartholomew Diaz finally rounded the Cape of Good Hope (named by the Portuguese king) and entered the Indian Ocean.

Diaz's triumph in 1488 brought Portuguese dominance in the exploration of the seas and the Portuguese era in history close to their brightest hour. But it also foreshadowed their eclipse. The noontide came in 1498 when Vasco da Gama landed in India, fulfilling Europe's venerable dream and crowning Portugal's strategy of sailing southward and then east to Asia. Portugal would later boast colonies or outposts from the Azores and Madeira in the north Atlantic to Goa on India's western coast and Macau on the South China Sea. The Portuguese had even gained the blessing of the Pope to divide the entire undiscovered world with Spain along a line in the western Atlantic—which entitled them to the future Brazil, claimed by Pedro Álvares Cabral in 1500. But, during these Portuguese successes, events elsewhere had begun drawing the curtain on Portugal's glory.

As it happened, those events were set in motion on the very day in 1488 when Bartholomew Diaz was ceremoniously received in Lisbon by King João II. For among the onlookers, so he said, was the Genoese-born sailor Christopher Columbus, who now knew, after a previous rebuff by this king, that the leading seafaring nation was not likely to back his own peculiar westward "enterprise of the Indies." He left Portugal for Spain.

As the world was to learn, Columbus and his "enterprise" were not to be denied. Columbus was nothing if not determined. This determination was among his virtues—and his vices. It had brought him to Portugal in the first place. A twenty-five-year-old common seaman in a merchant convoy bound from the Mediterranean for Lisbon and England in 1476, his ship had been sunk in a battle with a Franco-Portuguese warfleet east of Sagres, but he had plied through six miles of roiling seas to the beach near Lagos. From there he had made his way to Lisbon, where his brother is said to have worked as a chart-maker—a growing profession in those days. Columbus remained in Portugal and its islands for almost ten years, studying map-making, marrying, and reportedly sailing the Atlantic with the Portuguese as far north as Iceland and as far south as the Gold Coast of Africa.

During this time, Columbus probably hatched his notion of a voyage westward to the Indies—a collective name for the regions of Asia associated with India, including Cipangu (Japan) and the kingdom of the Great Khan known from the writings of Marco Polo. After his original proposal to King João II in 1485 for "some vessels to go and discover the Isle of Cipangu by this Western Ocean" was dismissed as "vain, simply founded on imagination," according to the eminent sixteenth-century Portuguese historian João de Barros, Columbus had lobbied King Ferdinand II and Queen Isabella I of Castille to underwrite his "enterprise," with assurances that its potential carried little risk because he was certain (as he had written in some marginal notes) that "the end of Spain and the beginning of India are not far distant, and it is evident that this sea is navigable in a few days with a fair wind." When the Spanish monarchs also rejected the plan, he had returned to Portugal in 1488 with those last short-lived hopes of winning over King João II.

But four years later, in August 1492, Columbus sailed out of Palos, Spain, with two caravels and a flagship, carrying a document signed by the recently won-over Spanish sovereign dispatching him "toward the regions of India," together with other letters from them (in the words of Bartolomé de las Cosas, who originally compiled the Columbus documents) for "the Grand Kahn (sic), and for all the kings and lords of India and of any other region that he might find in the lands which he might discover. He was bound first for the Canary Islands, his last stop in the known world before heading west, as the official charge read, to "discover and acquire certain islands and mainlands in the ocean sea."

There remain ambiguities aplenty about just what Columbus was up to, where he proposed to go, and how he intended both to greet foreign sovereigns and to "discover and acquire" their lands. His traditional admirers, like Samuel Eliot Morison (whose magisterial, if dated, biography, *Christopher Columbus: Admiral of the Ocean Sea*, quotes several of the documents cited here), were not much troubled by them. But nowadays everything Columbian is suspect. And nothing is more suspect, or rather denied altogether, than Columbus's claims to "discovery."

Not only had the Vikings landed and left settlements centuries earlier on what became North America, but, more importantly, the islands Columbus hit upon had long been inhabited. How could Columbus "discover" someone else's homeland? This question has prompted a lot of fuss in recent times, and some thoughtful puzzlement. Kirkpatrick Sale, for instance, concluded in *The Conquest of Paradise*—which generally gives Columbus and the Europeans a pretty rough time of it—that Columbus could not have been aiming for the Indies and the realm of the Great Khan in the first place "since it would be hard to imagine the Sovereigns sending Colón to discover what was already occupied and acquire what was already owned . . . ; they, at least, must have had new territories in mind." This is surprisingly generous. For wasn't that the very Eurocentric arrogance of it all? The Europeans could "discover and acquire" anything they wanted (those first Columbus scholars, de las Cosas and de Barros, showed no hesitation in affirming Columbus's intention to "discover" territories within established kingdoms). And discover and acquire they did.

To "discover" did not mean to them encountering uninhabited lands. It meant encountering lands not claimed by a Christian sovereign. This conception had led the Pope in Prince Henry's day to grant Portugal the right to Africa as far as the purported Christian realm of Prester John. And after Columbus's western landfall, it justified Pope Alexander VI in dividing the entire "undiscovered" world between Portugal and Spain in the Treaty of Tordesillas of 1494. "Since it may happen that your envoys and captains or subjects, while voyaging to the west or south, might land in eastern regions and there discover islands and mainlands that belong to India," stated a papal bull preceding the treaty, "we amplify and extend our aforesaid gift [of Christianity] . . . to all islands and mainlands whatsoever, found and unfound." The explorers clearly made their discoveries for Christ and for His European sovereigns.

Columbus confirmed this upon landing in what he thought was the abundantly peopled East. "I know that you will be pleased at the great victory with which our Lord has crowned my voyage," he wrote to the Spanish monarchs after reaching "the Indies" in just over thirty days. "I found very many islands filled with people innumerable," he went on, "and of them all I have taken possession for their highnesses," and "to the first island which I found I gave the name San Salvador, in remembrance of the Divine Majesty, Who had marvelously bestowed all this." Columbus closed with the exclamation that "all Christendom ought to feel delight, and make great feasts and give solemn thanks" for "the turning of so many peoples to our holy faith, and afterwards for temporal benefits, for not only Spain but all Christians will have hence refreshment and gain." Columbus didn't really know where he was, but had no doubts about what it meant to discover and acquire.

After four voyages to the islands of the Caribbean, Christopher Columbus never abandoned his belief that he had "discovered" for Christianity and Spain some islands off the eastern end of Asia. But he also suffered disappointments, which deepened with every voyage. These were largely of his own making, as his courage fueled his cruelty, and his determination worsened his administrative ineptitude—provoking his return from the third voyage in chains. He blamed his troubles on unpredictable misfortunes, disloyal subordinates, and on what he took to be mistreatment and neglect by the sovereigns who had sponsored his expeditions but who expected greater returns than delivered by the islands Columbus discovered, wherever these were. Finally, ignominiously stranded in rotting ships before he could make his last voyage home, Columbus collected his dejection and self-pity in a letter to the sovereigns. "Weep for me," he begged, "whoever has charity, truth, and justice."

Columbus died embittered in 1506 unaware that he had "discovered" for European Christendom not an inhabited part of the old world but an inhabited "new" world previously unknown to Europe. It was left to his contemporary Italian explorer Amerigo Vespucci to claim *that* discovery. And, as if to legitimize Columbus's sorrows, Amerigo's name stuck to this new world, owing to a widely circulated map published a year after Columbus's death—although, paradoxically, Columbus's misnomer for the native inhabitants, Indians, also stuck (the politically correct name long in use for them, Native *Americans*, was no more native and no less European than was Columbus's term—hence the more recent nomenclature: indigenous peoples).

Columbus and the Portuguese explorers who preceded him, and the many others who followed, treated the "discovered" territories and their inhabitants in ways typical of conquerors animated by the fervor of religious dogmatism and emboldened by the arrogance of presumed cultural superiority, abetted by military power. Far from exemplifying the qualities Columbus wept for, they were ruthless, false, and avaricious (with casual boastfulness Columbus had written from his first voyage that "in the first island which I found, I took by force some of them," and he proudly returned to Europe with natives as property). To be fair, these traits and practices were assailed by many European thinkers, like Thomas More, Francis Bacon, Montaigne, Swift, and Voltaire, who attacked avarice, self-righteousness, and self-deception, and satirized the old world's perceptions and treatment of the new.

But, for all of their self-serving perspective and lamentable deeds, there is no good reason for us to expect the intrepid European explorers to have been wiser, gentler, or more generous than they were. They were, after all, very much of their times: conquistadors, Faustian adventurers ready to deal with the devil (albeit in God's name) to expand the boundaries of their world, to win lands and riches for their sovereigns, and to gain converts for their faith.

These times were, after all, when that wizardly magician the historical Faust lived and became a folk hero by reputedly striking a bargain with Satan to swap his soul for insatiable energies in life. They were also the times when that insatiably curious, boundlessly energetic, and obsessively independent personality type, the Renaissance Man, stepped forth, initiating the distinctive Western cult of the Individual. And they were the times when Machiavelli spelled out the pragmatic rules for exercising political power as an end in itself, then urged everyone to adapt these rules in their own lives to "conquer" what he called "fortune."

We don't use the words *conquer* and *fortune* much anymore, or not as Machiavelli did. The associations of *conquer* are too ugly for us—we who have learned so much (if not enough) about the inhumanities perpetrated in its name. But to Machiavelli, as to the European explorers of the fifteenth and sixteenth centuries—*conquistadors* to the Spanish—conquest signified more than seizure and domination. It marked a victory of will against the dictates of fate and the whiles of fortune, the whims of chance and the forces of circumstance. Machiavelli had this in mind when in *The Prince* (1516) he spurned the belief that "one should submit to the rulings of chance" and asserted, "so as not to rule out our free will," that "fortune is the arbiter of half the things we do, leaving the other half to be controlled by ourselves." And we gain control best by forceful action, he said, since "fortune . . . shows her power when there is no force to hold her in check," adding with a brutishly masculine flourish: "because fortune is a woman, . . . if she is to be submissive it is necessary to beat and coerce her," and "being a woman, she favors young men because they are less circumspect and more ardent, and because they command her with greater audacity."

The language of conquest could be harsh, as were the acts. "Let Africa and the seas beyond begin to feel the weight of your armies and their exploits, until the whole world trembles," sang the Portuguese poet Luís Vaz de Camões to his countrymen in the epic poem that celebrates their explorers, *The Lusiads* (1572). Machiavelli was right. The conquest of fortune, whether of the seas or of anything, took daring, determination, and a dauntless will—as Prince Henry demonstrated when he sent his mariners back a dozen times to Cape Bojador alone before they vanquished their fears of its waters. Although explorations of the uncharted seas were certain to occur sometime, it was the ambitions of Renaissance Europeans bent on affirming their will and conquering fortune (as well as finding wealth and serving Christianity) that made the great age of exploration occur when and how it did.

That age reached its climax with the first circumnavigation of the earth by the Portuguese seafarer Ferdinand Magellan, sailing in 1519 under Spanish flag on what "almost everyone who knows the sea," wrote the eminent naval historian Samuel Eliot Morison, judges to be "the greatest and most wonderful voyage in recorded history." Magellan's voyage, lasting three years and costing Magellan and most of his five-ship crew their lives, brought to a close almost exactly a hundred years of conquests for waterways around the world to the east and west from Europe. The lands of the earth were now linked, if only loosely. And seagoing explorers would never embark with quite the same uncertain ends and pioneering spirit of discovery again. The peerless eighteenth-century seafarer, Captain James Cook, did explore the Pacific Ocean from top to bottom, voyaging, as he wrote in his journal, "not only farther than any man has been before me, but as far as I think it is possible to go." Even so, Cook knew much more of where he was going and of where he was than had those intrepid mariners of three centuries earlier. And not long after Cook's journeys, explorers would yield to travelers, who headed for places already known, however trying their trip might be. Then travelers would become those customers of easy transport, commercial accommodations, and marketable sights and diversions—tourists.

A later-day heir of exploration, tourism is a more immediate offspring of the culture of consumerism and entertainment, which, among its cornucopia of goods, proffers safe trips into the lands of delectable wishes and exotic dreams. So it is that tourists nowadays swarm the globe, aided by an industry that finds it profitable to build sumptuous hotels in steaming jungles and on arid atolls, to lead photographic safaris into the African wilds, to send luxury cruises into every torrid and frozen zone, and to simulate adventures with contrived environments, staged rituals, theme parks, and other pseudo-experiences. Tourism, in the Marxist jargon, has commodified the earth.

I had come to Sagres and Cape St. Vincent as a tourist, yes, but also as a pilgrim, a pilgrim like the many who had antedated tourism. True to a tourist's expectations, it was easy enough getting there, even driving south from Lisbon along treacherous roads infamous as among the most lethal in Europe. And the government pousada, or hotel set in a historic building, overlooking the Sagres promontory was as inviting as promised. But I was not looking for predictable comforts, routine sights, and the standard diversions. I was making a pilgrimage to the past, or rather to an ideal of it.

Sagres and Cape St. Vincent were made for such a tourist. No picture can capture their scale and austerity. Yet more unphotographable than the physical setting is what the mind's eye can see: images of that epoch in history that began unfolding here when Prince Henry and the navigators gathered to start exploring the Ocean Sea and investigate "things which were hidden from other men, and secret."

I wondered what Lord Byron would have made of Sagres and Cape St. Vincent had he come here on his Grand Tour of 1809, which took him and his entourage of friends and servants first to Lisbon. It was Byron's introduction to world travel (tourism was just in the making; Byron is understandably, if dubiously, credited by some with coining the term) and did much to make him the poet he became. Byron had embarked on this tour to escape the constraints of life in England, to relish freedom, and to savor exoticism, which he believed awaited him in the liberating destinations of Italy, Greece, and Turkey. Vividly affected by all he saw—even the disenchanting, uncultured Portuguese—he was moved to write the poetic meditation on freedom and travel that brought him fame, *Childe Harold's Pilgrimage* (begun later in Albania, not, as Portuguese guidebooks say, in the misty mountain village of Sintra near Lisbon, to which he devoted several rhapsodic stanzas of the poem). In its preface he extolled "the stimulus to travel" as "except ambition the most powerful of all excitements"; and at its conclusion he declared: "I am not that which I have been." Between the beginning and the end, Byron had become a revolutionary in sensibility and in aspiration. Fifteen years and many poems of liberation and exoticism after inscribing the first lines of *Childe Harold*, Byron died in that same Albania, where he had returned to join the Greek rebellion against the Turks.

Had Byron gone to Sagres, he might have remarked the ocean and the winds, since, like the seafaring Portuguese of the fifteenth century, he both depended on and welcomed them. Notwithstanding a frustrating week's delay in England awaiting "favorable winds" to fill his sails for Portugal, he would lyricize repeatedly in *Childe Harold* about how "Though the strain'd mast should quiver as a reed, / . . . Still must I [go] on; / . . . on Ocean's foam to sail / Where'er the surge may sweep, the tempest's breath prevail. . . . / I have loved thee, Ocean!" Byron might also have extolled the romance of the Sacred Promontory, so rich in historical fact and lore. But Byron was not making the kind of tour that would likely have taken him to the once-alleged edge of the world. Like Childe Harold he was making a pilgrimage to adventure and to freedom and its ancestral homes. This pilgrimage wanted heroic battle fields and archaic ruins, exotic cities and sublime mountains rather than empty sites reminiscent of the rise of European dominion.

Nor were Sagres and Cape St. Vincent destinations for tourists of any kind in Byron's day. Prince Henry was not yet celebrated— that didn't happen until he gained renown as "The Navigator" after Byron. And it was not until the late twentieth century, when Portugal's southern Algarve coast was "discovered" by sun-worshiping tourists (how nicely our commercial parlance echoes that of the explorers: they "discovered" lands for Crown and Christianity; we "discover" them for tourism) that many people would have thought of traveling to those out-of-the-way precincts.

And even now not many do. A number of modest hotels and the like have sprouted around Sagres since the 1980s, but few tourist attractions exist besides the ocean, a small beach, and the rocky promontory itself. A lighthouse, erected in the nineteenth century and much renovated since then, stands at the tip of Cape St. Vincent, signaling ships that they are approaching land, warning them of its rocky abutments, and bidding others adieu on sailing out from the port of Lagos. And on an adjacent spit of land there is a rebuilt fortress possibly dating to the sixteenth century, which houses a museum of Portuguese explorations. But for the imaginative tourist seeking signs of history, there is one arresting sight. Within the fortress grounds, etched into the flat surface of stone and laid out on it with pebbles, lies a circular form over a hundred feet in diameter depicting a compass rose, with lines radiating from the center marking the four principal directions and points between them. No one knows when this compass figure was created. It precedes any lasting records. So you can only look and wonder. But I like to think it signals that here is indeed where Prince Henry's navigators had come to study.

Beyond this spot, the rocky promontory stretches a mile or more to the lighthouse above the Atlantic. Here perhaps, high above the waves, Henry and his fellow navigators assembled to watch the sun set over Cape St. Vincent, to listen for the water to sizzle, to look for forebodings to rise, and to search the darkening skies for starry clues to navigating the Ocean Sea. But only the silent promontory knows. A pair of weathered cannon point westward toward Cape St. Vincent, a symbol as much as a remnant of the past.

Yet these historical silences say much of Sagres and Cape St. Vincent—and of Portugal itself. For the voices of Portuguese history are hard to hear anywhere: a monument here, a restored fortress there, a church, a monastery, a crumbling castle; but few of them tell detailed stories. There is Camões's *Lusiads*, of course, but that reads today as an elegy no less than as a celebration. And there is the Portuguese language of Brazil, but that now belongs more to Brazil than to Portugal. The earthquake of 1755, which destroyed Lisbon and razed buildings for hundreds of miles (prompting Voltaire to write his satire of optimism and European civilization, *Candide*), still gets surprising notice in Portugal, as if it had occurred recently. In Lisbon the Marquês de Pombal, who rebuilt the city, remains a local hero. But rather than opening a glorious new act in Portuguese history, the earthquake more nearly brought down the final curtain on that history, at least for Portugal's role on the world stage. After the earthquake, the country settled into rather quiet provincial repose—clinging to the territories of Goa until 1961 and Macau until 1999.

Portugal had its glowing historic moment, which lasted about a century. And it was more singular in character than the time in the sun of most world-historic states. Of this, *The Lusiads* stands as the enduring testament. Camões, who had sailed with Cabral, judged the exploits of the Portuguese explorers, especially Vasco da Gama, the central figure of the epic poem, to be supreme in human history. "The heroes and poets of old have had their day," he proclaims at the outset, throwing down the gauntlet to Homer and Virgil, "another and loftier conception of valor has arisen" in "the daring and renown of the Portuguese" who sailed "across seas no man had ever sailed before, . . . exposing themselves to privations and vigils, to fire and sword, to arrows and cannon balls, to burning heat and devastating cold, to the blows of idolaters and Moslems, to shipwreck and the denizens of the deep, to all the uncharted perils of the universe." Yet, even while celebrating those valiant explorers, Camões wanted Portugal to be honored for more than its exploits. His country should also possess and give the world a literature and a culture, which he thought lamentably lacking. Observing, "not without shame," that "never, in short, was there a great warrior of any nation, . . . save only of Portugal, who was not at the same time a man of science and learning," Camões imagined himself to be such a warrior and thinker, who could rouse the Portuguese from being "so uncouth, so austere, so unpolished and remiss in things of the mind." But these aspirations evidently did not avail—as Byron would attest in *Childe Harold*. For just as Portugal gave the world nothing in public life rivaling the explorers' feats, one might say, with only a measure of injustice, it created nothing in cultural life surpassing *The Lusiads*.

To be fair, Portugal has produced numerous distinguished authors, such as the poet Fernando Pessoa and the Nobel Prize-winning novelist José Saramago. And it fashioned the musical genre known as *fado*, whose haunting sonorities carry lyrics of loss and longing and sometimes of deprivation and anger. Still, Camões's epic remains a testimonial at once to the grandeur of Portuguese exploration and to the singular place the explorers staked for Portugal in world culture. As the missionary and author António Vieira re-marked shortly after Portugal's hour had passed—the country it-self falling under Spanish rule in the very year of Camões's death, 1580—"God gave the Portuguese a small country as cradle but all the world as their grave."

So it should come as no surprise that Portugal, particularly Sagres and the Sacred Promontory, where Portugal's chapter in history and the age of exploration itself began, should say so little of its past. That past was out at sea. In Lisbon there stands a proud stone mon-ument to the explorers. But their true monument is history itself, and perhaps the yearning that can still beckon one from the Sacred Promontory into the distance. The Portuguese have a word for this yearning, *saudade*. *Saudade* is not the mere wish for that which is not. It is the more distinct yen to be afar. *Saudade* is said to have drawn the Portuguese seamen toward the horizon, and then to have sum-moned them home again; and, having brought them home, to have called them out again, and then back again, again and again. Many songs of *fado* evoke the yearning qualities of *saudade*. Sagres and the Cape St. Vincent are a place for *saudade* to be sure.

To appreciate Sagres and the Sacred Promontory, therefore, you cannot be a conventional tourist passively taking in conventional sights or sleepily lolling in the sun. You have to be a traveler of the mind, equipped with ideas and mental images invoking the vagaries of history, the curiosities of geography, and the dreams of discov-ery as possessed by mariners who knew not what lay beyond the watery horizon, and for whom every turn of coastline signified for-bidding mysteries and inescapable dangers, and who yet yearned to go. For this kind of tourism one might do well to take Byron as a guide—he who never tired of travel and always saw so much more than the eye could see: "beings of the mind" and "overweening fantasies," as he said in *Childe Harold*, called forth by "my visions" that "flit . . . palpably before me"—or Petrarch, the early traveler who climbed Mount Ventoux in southern France in 1336 with, he wrote, "nothing but the desire to see its conspicuous height," and was then seduced by the majestic view into reveries about his life and his soul.

While sitting beside the rusty cannon on the cliffs of Prince Henry's outpost at Sagres, I recalled Byron and Petrarch. I had come with my wife at the summer solstice for the sunset over Cape St. Vincent, and for whatever hints of Prince Henry's doings I might find or imagine. As the shadows lengthened and a scattering of visitors wandering the rocks departed, we were left alone—with the sunset and with the shades of the explorers. The ocean darkened, but for thin white crests of waves rolling toward the cliffs to crash quietly far below. The promontory rises too high for the sounds of the surf to ascend, so the silence was nearly impenetrable, save the whisperings of the wind sweeping ceaselessly across the barren plateau. Looking along the promontory's ledge, following its westward arc around to Cape St. Vincent, I felt as if I was indeed at the edge of the world, perched above the Ocean Sea. The place was made for *saudade*, but also for reflection, reverie, fantasy—and for all that happens within us when intellect, emotion, and imagination meet to conjure up both insights and fantasies and beget both delights and fears.

Fantasies, some pleasurable, some not, had meant a lot to the explorers of the fifteenth century, as they had to pilgrims and travelers since Gilgamesh, as the historian Eric J. Leed reminded us in *The Mind of the Traveler*. For, in lieu of reliable facts about the nether regions of the world, tales had flourished reporting the wonders of actual and mythical realms. And, real or not, these realms became the aims of exploration. That of the Great Khan was one of them, described by Marco Polo, who had served there in fact for nearly twenty years, but whose accounts were doubted as widely as they were believed—doubts that induced King João II's advisors to dismiss Columbus. There was also the renowned but nonexistent kingdom of Prester John, sought by generations of explorers, including Columbus, who thought he was on John's trail in the

Caribbean. And there were the fantastic regions portrayed in the fanciful fourteenth century travel books of Sir John Mandeville, whose reputation passed from famous traveler to infamous liar owning to adventures of actual explorations. Mindful of the confusion of fact and fiction in travelers' tales, Camões promised readers of his paean to the Portuguese explorers that "there will be no pursuit here of mere national aggrandizement, no praising with false attributions, flights of fancy and feats of the imagination. . . . The deeds I tell of are real." Nevertheless, those deeds originated in medieval fantasies of fabulous lands, and in the Renaissance imagination of discovery.

In all its quietude and desolation, with its evocative panorama of the seascape at the edge of the world, it is easy see why the ascetic Prince Henry chose Sagres as the place to contemplate the Ocean Sea, to ponder tales and fantasies about its distant reaches, and to prepare his mariners to discover whatever the distance concealed. Now as the sun descends there, a tourist—or pilgrim—might find a multitude of fantasies and thoughts arise. Some of these picture Prince Henry's sailors assembled, watching and wondering. Others bear on how, if this is the place where the Eurocentric vision had its most geographically symbolic home, and where the European age of discovery was launched, and where the ignominious modern slave trade had its birth, it is also where an idea of a global culture took form in the desire for a demythologized, unforbidding, and benignly interconnected world.

When the sun sinks beyond the horizon (which it certainly appears to do), silhouetting Cape St. Vincent and its lighthouse against a dimming sky, a visitor might, as tradition says Prince Henry's mariners did, hear hisses and detect rising vapors. Amidst these hisses and vapors, imagined or real, the visitor might also now sense that this is no ordinary twilight. It is nightfall on the reign of the Eurocentric vision of the world itself, on half a millennium of Europe's dominant place in the sun—even as a new Europe struggles to be born. At the same time, remembering the yearnings of those explorers who came here before Columbus to conquer their fears and to master the Ocean Sea, a visitor might today be drawn by a different yearning, another kind of *saudade*—the longing for a time when there were fabled realms and unknown lands in this world yet to "discover" and explore.

A previous version of this essay was originally published in *The Sewanee Review*, Fall, 1992, which awarded it the Monroe K. Spears Prize for Best Essay of the Year.

The Bund with the Peace Hotel and its pyramidal roof in the distance, Shanghai, China

Signs of Shanghai, c. 1996

Walking into the Peace Hotel in Shanghai, China, near the end of the twentieth century, you breathed in the faded chic of an art deco palace refurbished in dour Communist style as the flagship of Shanghai's state-owned hostelries (it got dolled up in a modern renovation from 2007 to 2010, but its past and much of its venerable character seem to have remained). Originally the Cathay Hotel, it had opened in 1929, rising to the dramatic peak of its signature pyramid roof beside the Huangpu River on the broad riverside avenue dubbed the Bund by local Europeans who had constructed its imposing skyline and dominated Shanghai's hundred-year modern history. Built by the cosmopolitan trader, mogul, and baronet Sir Ellice Victor Sassoon (cousin of the renowned World War I poet Siegfried Sassoon), the Cathay had quickly become a glittering gathering place for Europeans in the East. And it had played a starring role in Shanghai's inter-war performance as the Paris of the Orient, a city at once enticing and mysterious, wrapping Western indulgences in Eastern exoticism.

At that time Shanghai was not actually part of China. Or not politically. Thanks to British military incursions of the nineteenth century that had extracted from the Ming emperor not only the opening of Shanghai to Western trade but a grant of virtual autonomy to foreign settlements there. The heart of the original Chinese city was relegated to a walled enclave amidst the International Settlement of British and Americans and the French Concession, both governed by their own laws and beholden to no outside authority. Shanghai was a truly international city.

Owing to its international character, Shanghai was a wide open port requiring no passport to enter. And it attracted fortune hunters, expatiates, travelers on the lam, and affluent cosmopolites seeking adventure or flight from home, as well as aspiring revolutionaries (the Chinese Communist Party was founded in an apartment in the French Concession in 1921) and White Russians fleeing the aftermath of Russian Revolution. Rife with opium dens, fleshpots, prostitutes winsomely known as "sing-song girls," criminals roaming free, and children's sweatshops hidden behind the city's sybaritic façade, Shanghai gave a new name to decadence and intrigue—it had already given a verb to a brash type of abduction. It struck the Sinophile aesthete Harold Acton as a place where "the ordinary had become extraordinary, the freakish commonplace." Here, residents said, "it was assumed that everybody had something to hide."

Amid this maelstrom of urban diversions and exotic depravity, Noël Coward wrote his play *Private Lives* while staying at the Cathay in early 1930. A worldly-wise comedy of misbegotten marriages, piquant regrets, and an ironic meeting of former spouses in a foreign hotel, it fit the Cathay, and it captured the flavor of Shanghai itself with the thematic line: "Very few people are completely normal, deep down in their private lives." The '30s saw many a blithe

Cowardian character drawn to the fashionable Cathay to drink and dance the nights away in its glamorous top-floor ballroom to the ravishing rhythms of the newly faddish and smolderingly erotic tango, the sonorities of boozy jazz, and the sultry tunes and saloon songs of Tin Pan Alley. Crowning the Cathay's scintillating social life were Sir Victor's frequent masked balls, where *tout le beau monde* frolicked in lavish concealment, often going unidentified to each other throughout the night. There the abnormal was on parade, private lives reveling in public disguise.

All of that ended with the Japanese attack in 1937 and retreated into distant memory after World War II and the Communist seizure of power in 1949. Bent on eradicating the toxic fumes of Shanghai's decadence, the Communist regime throttled the city's cosmopolitan vitality and extinguished its international preeminence with the elevation of Peking (Beijing) as China's premier city. No longer the Asian Paris, Shanghai came closer to Russia's post-revolutionary Leningrad, a *grande dame* languishing in neglect for the sins of a dissolute past as promiscuous mistress to the West.

But no more. Shanghai is a burgeoning metropolis again, one of the "Special Economic Zones" assigned to lead a new China under the free-market banner to prosperity and world economic preeminence. At the Cathay, rechristened the Peace Hotel in the 1950s, the cosmopolitan nightlife tradition lives on, if muted, in the nocturnal exertions of the aging Chinese hipsters who bill themselves "The Old Jazz Band." Resolutely banging out every American standard from Cole Porter and Duke Ellington to "Home on the Range" in a pulsing Dixieland style that one wag aptly labeled "wheezy but tenacious." The band nevertheless wins over listeners filling the ground-floor bar, some pairs often shuffling around a diminutive dance area. Sir Victor's glamorous ballroom it is not. Still, late at night, one can almost catch echoes here of the festive Cathay of old, and even of the long-gone, decadently hedonist Shanghai. (Happily, The Old Jazz Band has survived the latest renovations and upgrading of the hotel.)

Sitting in the bar one night absorbing The Old Jazz Band's hearty *gemütlichkeit*, I fell into conversation with a couple of foreign journalists who were writing an article on Shanghai. As we traded China stories—including how we had skirted visa restriction on writers by changing our professions—I grew curious about the odd alliance in this city of Communism and capitalism, authoritarian rule and pleasure-seeking individualism, and about what that alliance portends for China's ambitious future, together with that of Hong Kong, the East's very Western city, re-enveloped by the motherland in 1997.

This curiosity shadowed me later as I wandered the streets of Shanghai, tracking historic sites and taking in the city's tumultuous life. The old Chinese quarter, its tight and tangled passageways overhung with laundry, congested with food stalls, vendors, and craftsmen, and clogged with bicycles and pedestrians, has probably not changed much over time. And the tranquil walled Yu Garden nestled within—constructed during the sixteenth century in thirty cloistered pavilions housing Buddhist shrines, lotus ponds, winding paths, and artfully arranged trees and flowers to provide sanctuary for contemplation and for relishing nature's visual eloquence—can still take you into a serene past. But modern Shanghai snaps you back with a jerk.

The flourishing commercial center extending from the Bund at the Peace Hotel back along the wide thoroughfare, Nanjing Road, could be almost anywhere in the West today, proffering expensive consumer goods from boutique clothing to luxury cars and cluttered with outlets advertising products familiar to every American: Pepsi-Cola, Kentucky Fried Chicken, Häagen-Dazs ice cream, and so on. And across the Huangpu River from the Bund, in the area known as Pudong, a whole new city is rising, led by a soaring futuristic television tower complete with observation deck, followed by a forest of skyscrapers, including the world's tallest building, and a sleek new airport. Pudong is China's Tomorrowland.

But more unexpected to a curious visitor than the striking mingling of old and new in Shanghai was the public atmosphere of pleasant sociability. Bustling, congested, and commercial as Shanghai is, the street life seems quite benign, almost benevolent. Yes, that's the word, I thought, "benevolent," in the sense of that English word often used to translate the Confucian ethical principle of *jen*, meaning general goodness and common humanity. A superficial impression perhaps. Yet unmistakable. Yes, there was a certain Confucian *benevolence* in the air.

"Hello. Hello. Where are you from?" The greeting in clear English reached me again and again as I walked up one street and down another, along the Bund and out through the People's Park where the fanatical Red Guards had once drilled and which now peacefully hosts weekend strollers, kite fliers, and the modernistic new Shanghai Museum. A longtime New Yorker, at first I instinctively clutched my belongings, averted my eyes from the inquisitors, and silently hastened my pace. What did these people want? Pickpockets trying distraction? Black-marketeers hustling deals? Paupers begging? Hookers on the prowl? And yet, none of the stereotypes fit the gentle tone and the quiet withdrawal of the youthful inquisitors. Still, I marched on defensively.

Then rambling down Nanjing Road one Sunday when the street was closed to vehicular traffic and jammed with casually sauntering Shanghainese, I heard yet another "Hello" spoken beside me. The voice sounded so small and chirpy that this time instead of hurrying along I turned to see whom it had come from. There, jauntily pacing beside me in quick small steps, an eight-or-ten-year-old girl looked up brightly and asked, as others had before, "Where are you from?" Detecting no threat, and now curious about the inquiries, I slowed down and replied, "America." And I asked my own question: "Do you live here?" "Yes," she said, adding proudly that she went to school and studied English. She explained that she wanted to practice the language and thought I looked like an American who might talk. A bit startled by the innocence of her wish, I asked if the others who had asked me the same questions had also wanted to practice their English. She answered cheerfully, "Oh, yes. We like to speak English with Americans. They are nice. Where in America do you live?" My reservations allayed, I told her, and we walked together for several blocks talking about our hometowns. Then she abruptly announced she had to go, and with a sweet "good-bye" and a wave, she darted through the jostling pedestrians and vanished down an alley. I made my way back to the hotel thinking how almost unimaginable it would be for a young girl like that to approach a stranger on the streets of New York to practice a language. Free, democratic New York City is not so benevolent as that.

When you sit near the windows in the Dragon Phoenix Restaurant on the eighth floor of the Peace Hotel, you can watch the river traffic of ships and barges, fishing boats and ferries passing silently along the Huangpu's serpentine route below. You also find yourself in the company of a spirited, largely Chinese clientele enjoying the delights of shark fin, abalone, river eel, sea slug, and other delicacies. In the 1990s, the state-owned Peace Hotel belonged very much to the Chinese, unlike the new international hotels sprouting in the city that would cater to foreign tourists and business travelers. Chinese people flocked here to eat, even if not staying in the hotel. Afterwards, many would go down to the expansive promenade that has bordered the river's edge along the Bund since 1986.

Joining this postprandial excursion one evening, I found myself engulfed in another throng now crowding the promenade far into the distance. Chinese tourists mainly, it seemed, and well-dressed young adults socializing. And they all appeared to be taking pictures. Flashes popped everywhere. Couples being photographed against the Bund skyline. Families posing in groups backed by the futuristic tower and rising city across the river. Parents capturing images of their children, who looked like porcelain dolls. The flashes lit the deepening twilight in a minor lightning storm. But the air was calm, the mood convivial, the spirit, well, benevolent.

Through the popping lights and meandering crowds, a large sign in both Chinese and English at the side of the promenade caught my eye. "The Bund Sightseeing Area," read the English heading, followed by a list of rules "to guarantee clean and tidy surroundings." Some of these rules might be found in any large city, forbidding spitting, littering, and so forth. Then came this:

"Any activity or action against social order or repugnant to the eye is prohibited in this area."

My eyes fixed on the words "repugnant to the eye." What is that? I wondered. Sloppy dress? Bad hair? Rude manners? It did dawn on me that New York might benefit from such a code. Street life there would surely be improved if purged of everything "repugnant to the eye." But then, I thought, to whose eye? I reread that edict, dwelling also on the words preceding it prohibiting "any activity or action against social order." Aha, I said to myself. No doubt whose eye rules the Bund. It is that of Chinese political authority. Under that authority, the Bund's peculiar rule reads like an aesthetics of social control, putting in jeopardy not only anyone who violates social order but anyone who does anything that even looks bad. These reflections brought me back to the political reality behind Shanghai's public *benevolence*.

That political reality, so preoccupied with public order, has roots deeper than Communist authoritarianism. Like the air of social benevolence that I felt around me, those roots go back to Confucianism. And to Confucian doctrines that governed China for nearly two thousand years under an almost aesthetic ideal of public harmony embracing all of life, from individuals to civilization. As one of the canonical Confucian classics, *The Great Learning*, puts it: "When the personal life is cultivated, the family will be regulated, when the family is regulated, the state will be in order, and when the state is in order, there will be peace throughout the world." The aesthetic rule on the Bund resonates with this Confucian ideal as much as it states the autocratic demands of the Communist regime for social order. After all, Confucianism insisted that the harmony of all things required that social bonds and respect for authority take precedence over personal interests. So a marriage of Confucianism and Communism should have come quite naturally.

But it didn't. After the overthrow of the Imperial Chinese dynasty in 1911, Confucianism was widely denounced by intellectuals as reactionary dogma anchored in the past and granting too much reverence to tradition. Maoists carried on that verdict and intensified it during the Cultural Revolution of the 1960s and 1970s. Confucianism became anathema. Its shrines were razed, and reading its documents was outlawed.

But future years would see Confucianism return to favor, alongside the courtship of capitalism. Confucian shrines have been restored, and Confucian writings are being read again. The Chinese leader from late June of 1989 to 2004, Jiang Zemin, even warmly recalled learning Confucianism at home when it was prohibited officially. And Chinese politicians, along with many of their authoritarian Asian counterparts—headed by Singapore's longtime political leader and guardian Lee Kuan Yew, who made his squeaky clean city state the model of aesthetic social control—could once again invoke Confucian principles as "Asian values" that set public order above the unruly individualism that democracy can breed and that is so blithely tolerated in the West. Lee Kuan Yew and other Asian spokesmen reacted to the World Conference on Human Rights in Vienna in 1993 by declaring that the Rights of Individuals so celebrated by Westerners should not be taken as the bedrock of human rights. Instead, that bedrock should be the rights of human beings to security and social order, as prized in the East.

This "New Confucianism" has attracted wide notice in the West. But, as China experts have cautioned, just how far China's Communist leadership will go in adopting the humanity of Confucianism remains to be seen. Even so, benevolent social harmony certainly seemed alive to me on the Bund that night, as elsewhere on the streets of Shanghai. And who could deny that feeling safe on a big city's streets is no small freedom?

Mulling these thoughts, I left the disporting visitors on the Bund for the roof garden of the Peace Hotel, where parties are sometimes held faintly evoking the Cathay of old, and where a panorama of Shanghai stretches before you. From there, you see Nanjing Road directly below roaring with traffic from the Huangpu River up into the city center. The Bund bends off with the river the other way, lined by ornately imposing European buildings from a bygone era that glow brightly under spotlights after dark. The Huangpu itself curves slowly past, after coursing down from the provinces, widening through the city as it goes, and flowing eastward to join the Yangtze River a few miles away where they pour into the East China Sea. Across the river, the landmark tower stands like a science fiction movie prop, and the new Pudong extends as far as the eye can see.

On the rooftop of the fabled hotel, among ghosts of its past, you look out upon a great city deeply marked by the contradictions of its history and its present and poised to help shape the future of the New China. In the mid-1990s, the marriage here—or perhaps it was only a romance—of past and present, East and West, communism and capitalism, freedom and order, appeared outwardly happy as reflected in the booming market economy, the gentle citizens on the streets, and the likes of the genial Old Jazz Band. Whether the free-market economy would loosen the Communist regime's resistance to the political rights of individuals, as American policymakers hoped, or domineering political authority continue to reign, none could yet say. But recalling the tragic day of Tiananmen Square on June 4, 1989—when in Hong Kong I had seen a population gripped by forebodings that their Western liberties would be lost with the impending turnover of that city to China (my tailor had trembled and could hardly speak)—I found myself suspecting that of all the clues to the New China, the most poignant may stand there on the Bund of Shanghai in that prohibition of "any activity or actions against social order or repugnant to the eye." For this aesthetics of social harmony and control, woven tightly into Chinese culture for so long, would not likely yield to the clamors of Western individualism any time soon. And it hasn't.

The smiling elephant on Lakshmana Temple, Khajuraho, India

The Mystery of the Smiling Elephant

In the north central Indian province of Madhya Pradesh, the landscape of flat plains and mountainous outcroppings goes dusty brown in the summer months of April, May, and June. Like most of India at that time, it awaits the monsoon, which from June to October washes the land with drenching rain. The cycle is so pervasive in its reach and inexorable in its timing that it holds the country in its thrall. "When the monsoon comes, everything will bloom," my guide assured me in the hot arid wind at the airport of

Khajuraho, a village on these plains. "Then the land will be green again until next year."

But Khajuraho is not a place you come for the vegetation or the climate at any time. You come for the historic Hindu temples that are India's equivalent in artistry and edification of the greatest Christian cathedrals of medieval Europe, their near contemporaries. From about 900 to 1100 CE some eighty-five temples rose from the earth at Khajuraho, the religious capital of the Chandela empire that ruled central India from the tenth to the fourteenth centuries. Only twenty-two of these temples remain, most of them clustered on the few acres of a well-kempt park on the western edge of the village amid scattered shade trees and in sight of the date palms (*kharjura*) that likely gave Khajuraho its name. But twenty-two is enough to awe.

It is not their size that awes. Like most Hindu temples—and unlike Christian cathedrals, which soar magisterially heavenward to be seen from miles around—those at Khajuraho lack grandiose scale. Designed in the Nagara style typical of their era and region, Khajuraho's temples stand on platform terraces rising approximately ten feet from the ground. Narrow steps lead up to the terraces, where small vestibules receive devotees and visitors under two or more domed roofs graduating in height to that of the central sanctums ascending conically to peaks crowned by finials. The finials touch the sky between 75 and 115 feet above the earth; and none of the temple platforms measures much more than that in length or width at the base. Astounding as these edifices unquestionably appeared to Hindu worshipers who first saw them, Khajuraho's temples are pretty modest when compared, say, to Notre-Dame in Paris—erected in the twelfth and thirteenth centuries and accommodating up to 9,000 people in an area approximately 450 feet long and 150 feet wide, under a vault 107 feet overhead, with bell towers surpassing 220 feet and a spire attaining 325 feet. But the temples of Khajuraho were not erected to summon congregations; they housed intimate shrines for sacred rituals and a few prayerful votaries.

Modern Western eyes, used to hugeness, could miss Khajuraho's temples from a distance. In any case, you must come very close to behold their glories. For architecture has not earned Khajuraho its renown. That honor goes to the thousands of sculptures that swarm over the temples' exteriors and crowd the interior chambers. Prodigiously imagined and superbly executed, these sculptures mark, by all expert opinion, the zenith of Hindu temple art. And that art, as the sculptures of Khajuraho more boldly than any others reveal, is an art of human life as much as of religious worship. Or, perhaps, of human life as a form of religious worship.

Before coming to Khajuraho, one might think of Hinduism as a religion of otherworldliness, steeped in the metaphysics of reincarnation, animated by the morality of karma, aspiring to benign extinction in nirvana, and symbolized by hirsute yogis escaping this world by starving themselves and sitting on nails. But that is not the Hinduism of Khajuraho. Here you find a religion of *this* world no less than of the other. Hinduism is, after all, the most ecumenical of religions, uniting sacred and secular, divine and mundane, spiritual and sensuous, infinite and quotidian, and welcoming every form of worship and every god as a manifestation of the one universal deity. "Whoever calls Him by any name," announces the Hindu epic the *Mahābhārata*, "by that name does He come."[1]

This ecumenical theology also entails a primal humanism embracing people in their many reincarnated lives (despite the historically *de*humanizing Hindu caste system and the cruelties it sanctioned). That humanism accepts the facts of nature and admits the varieties of our lives; it encourages pleasures as much as it comprehends pain; and it allows human beings to be mortally imperfect even while idealizing spiritual transcendence. It is, at heart, profoundly tolerant. "Hinduism has a great tolerance of those who strive," explains a contemporary guru, "and a great forgiveness for those who fail."[2] The eminent student of Asian thought Hajime Nakamura went so far as to assert that, thanks to Hinduism, "tolerance is the most conspicuous characteristic of Indian culture."[3]

Hindu temple art gives visible form to this encompassing philosophy. "A Hindu temple is a reflection of life," the guru elaborates, so in it "you can find every variety of humanity."[4] The temples of Khajuraho offer bountiful proof in their panorama of mortal life within a pantheon of gods.

But not even the profusion and artistic splendor of the temple sculptures have by themselves given Khajuraho the reputation it has today. The cause is eroticism. Khajuraho's temples abound with graphic displays of gods and mortals in amorous poses and erotic pursuits. Hindu temples elsewhere in India have a sampling of such sculptures. But none boasts the panoply and spectacle of those at Khajuraho.

Many of Khajuraho's amatory sculptures are aesthetically refined and elegant. Some are rough-hewn and grotesque. Some are subdued. Some audacious. They are unapologetic and sometimes amusing. And together they create a riot of erotic acts: fondling and seduction, coitus and masturbation, cunnilingus and fellatio, voyeurism and exhibitionism, orgies and bestiality, and acrobatic couplings that would be anatomically challenging, if not impossible. Never mind that the erotic sculptures number only about ten percent of those adorning the temples. These are the ones that have made Khajuraho both famous and infamous, touted by hustlers brandishing lurid photographs from Mumbai (Bombay) to Kolkata (Calcutta), Delhi to Chennai (Madras), and without which the temples would be an esoteric out-of-the-way stop on the tourist route across central India. As it is, tourists line up in high season to gawk at the most salacious sex scenes, while honeymoon couples come seeking conjugal inspiration for the sculptures' purportedly eighty-five sexual positions—one winces to think of the injuries conceivably incurred at local hotel bedrooms in the night.

Actually, Khajuraho has not been on the tourist map for long. After the collapse of the Chandela empire in the fourteenth century, Khajuraho was virtually abandoned, left to the pieties of a few resolute monks, the predations of random looters, and possibly the staging of occasional rituals. It fell into disuse, to be engulfed by the dense vegetation that once covered the region owing to a previously wetter climate and to lakes now gone dry. So forgotten did Khajuraho become that the Muslims who repeatedly invaded India from the tenth century onward—ruling most of the country by the eighteenth century—obliterated many Hindu temples and artworks with righteous iconoclasm but let this profuse artistic center survive in deepening neglect.

T. S. Burt, a British engineer posted to India, first described the overgrown site in the 1830s, and another Briton, Alexander Cunningham, followed with archaeological reports. But the reigning Victorian proprieties (if not consistent practices) of their day—which viewed the classical Venus de Milo, unearthed in the 1820s, as chaste and demure—possibly discouraged wide dissemination of the discovery of Khajuraho's sexually explicit artworks. One Victorian who surely would have relished those artworks and eagerly publicized them, and who lived in India for years, evidently knew nothing of them: Sir Richard Burton, the intrepid adventurer, polymath, sensualist, and translator in the 1880s of the Hindu sexual manual *Kama Sutra*, never mentioned Khajuraho. The temples remained obscure until the twentieth century, when diligent scholarly labors finally began reclaiming them.

Khajuraho's sculptures had also brought me here, my interest sparked by references in historical writings and fueled by beckonings in well-thumbed guidebooks. But it was not the eroticism alone that had attracted me. It was a humanistic curiosity about the place of Khajuraho's erotic art in the long cultural history, ecumenical religious life, and peculiar humanity of India. This curiosity had grown from years of studying the arts and ideas, but I did not then know where that curiosity would lead.

After a long journey from New York through Mumbai to Agra for the Taj Mahal and to Varanasi for the welter of life there on the sacred Ganges, I stood before Khajuraho's temples predictably dazzled. Gazing upward from the temple terraces, you see ascending recessed horizontal tiers two to three feet high lined with beauti-fully modeled figures exhibiting, as guides explain, the sublimity and moral authority of the gods, the regal nobility of kings, and the energetic eroticism of "loving couples," or *maithunas*—along with the ritualistic eroticism of a few figures performing such acts as sexual intercourse while standing on their heads. Among these majestic figures of gods and goddesses, kings and consorts, reside others of lower rank, including so-called religious "ascetics" who watch the action or join in, and many voluptuous "celestial nymphs" who perform mundane deeds, like applying cosmetics and extracting thorns from their feet, or who coquettishly expose themselves or coyly shield their eyes while peeking through their fingers at erotic scenes.

Encircling the temples below these tiers of artistically poised and polished figures run friezes containing more rustic arrays of ordinary human beings engaged in worldly activities—farming and domesticity, handicrafts and warfare, schooling and sport, music and dance, socializing and, of course, sex. Raucous orgies appear in some of these friezes. Animals are here as well, sharing in war and work and play and in an orgy or two, or simply standing as orna-mental forms.

It was in one of these lesser friezes that I came across an animal figure that took hold of me more insistently than any other sculp-ture at Khajuraho. As I lingered over it, returning at sundown and in the early morning to see it again and again, I began to ask myself whether this figure was just an anomaly or if it held a telling, off-beat clue to the mystery of Khajuraho.

The frieze was set four or five feet above the terrace of the Lakshmana temple—among the oldest and most bounteously artis-tic and erotically dramatic of them all, its name said to be derived from the king who built and dedicated it to the god, Vishnu—and it held a row of ornamental elephants facing outward exposing their caparisoned heads and their trunks, tusks, and front legs. Two handlers gripped each elephant from the sides. But one of these elephants, tucked away near an alcove corner, didn't fit in. Instead of being firmly held to face outward, expressionless, like the others, it had its head turned in profile to the left. And it had apparently upended the handler on that side, whom it held underfoot to peer at a scene over the handler's flailing limbs. An unmistakable, impish smile curled up its dimpled right cheek at what it saw: a man and woman engaged in an athletic sex act, the male standing and taking the doubled-over female from behind (an unidentifiable object suggesting an extremity, his arm or, more awkwardly, her leg, protruding in the air). Here amid Khajuraho's sacred cornucopia of the divine and mundane, the sacred and profane, of worship and eroticism, stood a quirky icon: an elephant smiling at uninhibited human sexual play.

I saw no other smiling elephants among the many elephant sculptures at Khajuraho. So this one stuck in my mind, nagging me with the questions it raised and the symbolism it must contain—or the symbolism that I imagined it contained. I decided to find some answers, not from scholarly ambition but to satisfy a visitor's imaginative wonder over what that provocative smile might say about the vision of life that Khajuraho embodies, and what this vision might say about the humanity and the humanism of Hinduism, and even about humanity and humanism themselves. This was, at heart, wonder about the intent and meaning of an image.

Sometimes we have a sensation that we dwell on until it settles in our mind's eye as a fixed image, an evocative mental picture. And there it begins to open up, divulging secrets and flowing with meanings that illuminate objects, places, times, occasionally ourselves, and even whole cultures. Forever after, that image carries for us the associations first aroused in us by it.

This has long been a theme, if not a cliché, of literature. The world's first novel, Murasaki Shikibu's *The Tale of Genji*, lavishes a thousand pages on images that signify the metaphysical order and the emotional tenor of existence. Those images reflect how, in

Genji's Buddhist universe, life is but a fleeting passage on a "bridge of dreams," and how human beings should consequently savor the sensations of every moment as they pass—the moonlight on the snow in winter, a line of geese across the sky, the songs of insects, the scent of a flower, and, most emblematic, the cherry blossoms "loved because they bloom so briefly." *The Tale of Genji* is an epic of images savored—and then let go.

So is Marcel Proust's *À la recherche du temps perdu*, except that Proust lets nothing go, clinging to every image of every memory encountered in the search for his past, and for himself. "The meaning of a particular image is but regret for a particular moment," he writes at the end of *Swann's Way*. The taste of a madeleine dipped in tea, the sound of an echoless footstep on a gravel path, the fragrance of a sweet perfume—these and countless other images of sensations and emotions awakened Proust to the moments that shape our lives, consciously or unconsciously, and that dwell in sleeping memories.

William Wordsworth found the latent design in his own life much the same way. Looking back through the landscape of his memories, he discovered certain images—"spots of time," he dubbed them in his autobiographical poem *The Prelude*—so charged with feeling that they would not disappear. Recalling these images revived the original feelings, telling him (as he had promised in the preface to *Lyrical Ballads*) what was "really important" in his life, yet recognizable only from the distance of time and retrospection.

We could add Sigmund Freud to this list as another who found the key to our past and our character in emotionally weighted incidents, real or imagined, locked in recesses of our minds and released only by remembered images of them. Freud made psychoanalysis a science, or rather an art, of interpreting memories.

The likes of Murasaki, Proust, Wordsworth, and Freud remind us how incidents, scenes, objects, and moments residing in memories evoked by mental images give our lives texture, disclose much of who we are, and bespeak value judgments we make extending beyond ourselves. Don't we all cherish certain possessions for much the same reasons? Not just artworks prized for their aesthetic qualities, or acquisitions that bring us pride, or products that we use, but possessions that we keep solely for their quiet resonance in our lives—such as heirlooms descended from our forebears, pictures of people dear to us, artifacts recalling lands visited or times past. These attachments attest to a human love of *things* not for themselves but as vessels of memories, vestiges of experience, tokens of what we wish never to lose. They also attest to our love of images and to a love of metaphors, those fecund creations of mind that coax revealing affinities from disparate ideas and actualities—particularly the metaphors that signal what, as Wordsworth said, is "really important" to us, what we believe is good or true or desired, each having its own story to tell about itself and about us, and possibly about life outside of us. Salman Rushdie nicely captured this notion in a story of India, "The Firebird's Nest," where he has an Indian woman say: "We are caught in metaphors. They transfigure us and reveal the meaning of our lives."

Anthropologists have discerned something close to this in the makings of culture itself. Every object, action, institution, gesture, and idea carries a significance far beyond the literal: food is not just food, manners not just manners, artifacts not just artifacts, religion not just religion. Whatever their purported purposes, the constituents of culture also form a dense pattern of symbolic meanings, or metaphors, that lend mental order and value to experience. Clifford Geertz coined the term "thick description" for the act of penetrating the layers of meaning that each cultural artifact and practice contains. He illustrated the idea with a nice image from India, in the story of an Englishman who asked an Indian to describe his conception of the cosmos. The Indian told him that the world rests on a platform on top of an elephant who stands on the back of a turtle who stands on the back of another turtle. Pressed by the Englishmen to identify what lies under that lower turtle, the Indian explained: "Ah, Sahib. After that it is turtles all the way down."[5]

Geertz tells this engaging story for its *image* of how we must find the turtles, or the layers of meaning, in anything to find the truth in it, whether we get to the bottom or not. It is a good image that does what all good images do: they ignite our curiosity, arouse our imagination, inspire insight, live in memories, and serve as vehicles in metaphors conveying many kinds of understanding.

It is not incidental that Geertz found his illustrative image of "thick description" in India, or that Rushdie selected an Indian character to speak of metaphors as entangling, transfiguring, and revealing. India is a culture openly nourished on images and metaphors, beginning with that supreme, ontologically omnipresent Hindu god Brahman, who expects to be worshiped not just through his chief incarnations as Vishnu and Shiva (a third original member of the triumvirate, Brahma, has faded in importance), but also through every other imaginable deity, as well as through countless symbols and infinite images. "My face is everywhere," this god proclaims in the *Bhagavad-Gita*, the spiritual core of the *Mahābhārata* and Hinduism's holiest text, "there is no limit to my divine manifestations."[6] But when visiting India you need not be a Hindu to feel the tug of images and metaphors. Striking sensations bombard you from every side, tempting you to seize any numbers of them as clues to the culture. These sensations, and sometimes the temptation, can be impossible to resist.

You see people everywhere on the move—crammed into trains, piled on bicycles, spilling out of buses—rushing away from what and to what teases our curiosity. Cars and trucks lie smashed and deserted along every highway, the casual detritus of rambunctious speed and crazed indifference. Shanties lining roads into the large cities resemble human dumping grounds more than dwellings. A flood of movie melodramas pours from the world's most prolific film industry, jejune fantasies of age-old passions and hungry dreams. Sophisticated computer companies sprout from a wretchedly backward economy, oases of efficiency in a land of barely restrained chaos. And yet, hoards of impoverished, illiterate peasants queue patiently to vote in the largest and most implausible democracy, translating their ignorance into hope. These and many other phenomena easily give rise to metaphors of India today—summed up in V. S. Naipaul's metaphor (as he put it in the title of a controversial book) of a "million mutinies" still struggling to create a mature nation in postcolonial India.

Besides the commonplace appearances of contemporary India, you also see abundant tributes to the historic traditions that have long influenced Indian culture, for better and worse. No eye or imagination can easily resist these either. Take, for instance, a sunrise on the Ganges River in the hallowed city of Varanasi. There, while pilgrims perform their dawn ablutions in the sacred waters, and white smoke curls from shoreline crematoria carrying the dead off to other lives after ritual dips in the river, a Hindu holy man floats past in a trance, only his face, toes, and hands breaking the surface, a consummate image of Hindu otherworldliness in the most otherworldly of settings—so unlike Khajuraho. And you can see a different version of religious otherworldliness outside Varanasi in the Deer Park at Sarnath. There, near the spot where Siddhārtha Gautama is said to have given his first pronouncements as the Buddha, monks in saffron robes sit peacefully meditating all day, an image not of hypnotic transport, like the Hindu holy man on the Ganges, but of tranquil Buddhist detachment.

Or take the most renowned historical site in India: the Taj Mahal. Popularly regarded as a peerless monument to love—built by the Muslim emperor Shah Jahan in the seventeenth century to entomb his lamented wife Mumtaz Mahal—the Taj Mahal takes on another aura when seen from Shah Jahan's palace a few miles up the Yamuna River across a low plain behind the tomb. For it was from there, and no closer, that Shah Jahan looked out upon the Taj Mahal during the last seven years of his life, after one of the fourteen children Mumtaz bore him (before dying in her last childbirth) deposed and imprisoned him, and then launched a vendetta against Hinduism that reversed a century of relative religious tolerance initiated by Akbar the Great, who had earnestly tried to syncretize Islam, Hinduism, and Christianity. That vendetta razed innumerable Hindu temples, erected numerous mosques in their stead, and left a hardened legacy of hatred between Hindus and Muslims that wracks India still, and that is nowadays stirring a fervent Hindu nationalism at odds with the ecumenicism and tolerance at the heart of the Hindu religion. For tourists thronging the Taj Mahal's immaculate grounds, the tomb may gleam as a beautiful architectural image of love. From Shah Jahan's prison it is an image of many losses, including a loss of humanity.

This melancholy image of forsaken humanity returns me to Khajuraho, and to the smiling elephant. Khajuraho's temples are as replete with human life as temples can get. And the more I thought about that elephant the more I suspected, or wished, that this amicable creature might be an endearing metaphor of an enduring, benevolent humanism worth affirming in a world prone to divisive ideologies and self-serving ambitions. But when I set out in earnest to learn just how that singular figure might exemplify such a humanism, I met more difficulties than I had expected. I was trying to solve the mystery of Khajuraho and the smiling elephant not through a Wordsworthian or Proustian expedition into a personal past but an excursion of intellectual curiosity into a maze of historical sources and scholarship. This course took me into an unfamiliar intellectual landscape, as well as down several byways to dead ends. But it also lent interest to every step and byway, and in the end it gave the smiling elephant more metaphoric meaning than I had imagined at the outset.

I started with the obvious: elephants. I assumed the smiling elephant must participate in the rich symbolism granted to elephants in South Asian cultures. Asian elephants, smaller than their African cousins, have traditionally played salient roles not only in the economic and political life of these cultures, from physical work to ceremonial performances, but also in art, folklore, and sacred writings. In these artistic and religious contexts, elephants embody contrasting qualities: the grandeur of regal dignity and the service of obedience, the strength to move mountains and the intractability of the unmovable, the stability of sturdy support and the mayhem of rampage, the virtues of self-restraint and the challenge of imposing control. The seminal Buddhist classic *The Dhammapada* (a Sanskrit text of the third century BCE) devotes an entire chapter to the elephant as a symbol of powerful desires that if not tamed will drag us to destruction, but when trained will conduct us safely to nirvana. Yet tradition links none of these qualities, as far as I could learn, to an elephant's smile. A Western book on animals' emotions, Jeffrey Moussaieff Masson and Susan McCarthy's *When Elephants Weep: The Emotional Lives of Animals*, offered no clues either, telling of elephants that cry from sadness but saying nothing of elephants that smile for any reason.

Such silence sent me to the symbolism of the white elephant. I knew that this image also originated in South Asia, where white or albino elephants are highly revered. The early god of India, Indra, characteristically rides one in artworks, and the king of Thailand has historically carried the epithet "Lord of the White Elephant." Thailand also apparently gave birth to the idea of the white elephant as a burdensome gift. As Thai tradition has it, when a warrior or nobleman performed an act of great honor to the kingdom, the king would reward him with a sacred white elephant, together with enough land to maintain the voracious animal. When a warrior or nobleman dishonored the kingdom, the king would also present him with a white elephant but without the land to care for it. Unable to maintain or dispose of the sacred beast, the owner would eventually be ruined. Most of us have had our share of white elephants, if not to our ruin, and we probably smile about them. Perhaps some sacred white elephants smile at their ambiguous efficacy. But I did not come upon any.

In India the sacred elephant, although not white, plays its most prevalent role in the form of the beloved pot-bellied, elephant-headed deity Ganesh (or Gaṇeśa). He is the most popular member of the capacious Hindu pantheon. And since a large figure of Ganesh sits in prominent framed relief on a wall of the elephant-laden Lakshmana temple at Khajuraho, I next thought he might have some kinship to the smiling elephant on the same temple.

The son of Shiva and his consort/wife Parvati, Ganesh got beheaded, according to myth, in a misguided attack by his father, who, as Destroyer of Evil, readily resorts to violence. Alerted to his blunder, and to appease Parvati, Shiva swiftly whacked off an elephant's head and attached it to his son's body. Further atoning for the egregious mistake, Shiva gave Ganesh a host of propitious attributes: he is the god of overcoming obstacles and of fruitful beginnings, good fortune, learning, and wisdom. (The ancient Romans also loosely associated elephants with wisdom, customarily picturing them alongside the goddess of wisdom, Minerva; and the Baroque artist Bernini continued this tradition by fashioning an elephant statue that stands near the Pantheon in Rome over a former temple to Minerva and in front of the church of Santa Maria sopra Minerva, where it supports an Egyptian obelisk and bears an inscription to the "wisdom of Egypt."). Some fables record Ganesh deploying his cleverness to solve problems and outfox rivals; and the *Mahābhārata* credits him with being its scribe (possibly with part of the tusk that he is said to have broken off for that purpose). He is also a merry god who dances gaily—inspired by his father, the god of dance no less than of destruction. No wonder Ganesh is among the most widely worshiped Hindu deities and is routinely supplicated for good luck, successful ventures, wise counsel, and general high-spiritedness.

For instance, Ganesh is invoked (along with Shiva) as benefactor in the immense, epochal collection of Sanskrit fiction compiled during the eleventh century by Somadeva and translated into English under the title *The Ocean of Story*. After beseeching Shiva to spread "prosperity" in the world, Somadeva's formal "invocation" entreats the "Victor of Obstacles" to "protect you" (the readers) and effusively describes Ganesh "sweeping away the stars with his trunk" and seeming "to create others" in "the delirious joy of the evening dance."[7] Such lively devotion to Ganesh has also engendered multifarious religious rites detailed in an enthusiastic literature, like the compendious 700-page volume *Loving Gaṇeśa: Hinduism's Endearing Elephant-Faced God.* The good-natured Ganesh is so fondly venerated and frequently represented that he should have a kinship with the smiling elephant of Khajuraho. And I believe he does. But that kinship does not lie in a notable propensity of Ganesh to smile, for I ran across no clearly smiling Ganesh—although, given his merriment, some must exist. And I certainly saw none smiling at sexuality.

Turning from Ganesh to scan writings on Hindu art and iconography at large, and those on Khajuraho in particular, for depictions of elephants who smile did not help much either. I found no illustration or mention of any. Only the conventional symbolic and ornamental functions of elephants reached the pages I read— the elephants at Khajuraho eliciting merely passing observations in studies of its temples, and the smiling elephant earning not a word. As far as I could tell, elephants who smile must be very rare indeed. Or they have attracted no notice, aroused no interest.

The mystery deepened, and with it my curiosity. If neither the familiar Asian symbolism of elephants nor the Hindu iconography of them, including Ganesh, accounts for the smiling elephant, the explanation must lie in what makes *this* elephant smile: eroticism. I would have to find out why all of that erotic activity at Khajuraho is there.

And that, I soon learned, is a mystery in itself. Combing library shelves, poring through scholarly journals, searching the Internet, I found that no one knows for sure just why Khajuraho's temples teem with erotic acts as they do. It is, of course, easy enough to adduce justifications from Hinduism for visual representations of sexuality. In the first place, Hindu beliefs presuppose sexual congress to be a union of cosmic forces, male and female sexuality forging the very nature of things. As the *Mahābhārata* says, "both the sexes" are "the one cause of the creation of the universe."[8] Manifesting this principle, Hindu art usually portrays the chief male Hindu deities with their consorts/wives, especially Vishnu with Lakshmi and Shiva with Parvati, as pairs that constitute wholeness. Some art even shows Shiva as physically half male and half female. And the gods' sexuality playfully parades through the vast Hindu religious and secular literature—the invocation that opens *The Ocean of Story* formulaically introduces Shiva entwined by "the God of Love" in "the alluring looks of Parvati reclining on his bosom." Some Hindu temple rituals are also said to have once involved public sexual activity, supporting a practice of "sacred prostitution" presumably extinguished by moralistic Muslims in their campaigns against Hindu shrines.

Then there is the *Kama Sutra*. Recorded around 400 CE as a Hindu guide to sexual performance, it begins with the scriptural declaration that "in the beginning the Lord of Beings created men and women" together; and it goes on to detail God's "rules for regulating their existence" according to *kama*, "the ways of enjoyment" of the senses, or the "science of love." (*Kama* is necessary, along with two other sets of precepts, *dharma*, religious duty, and *artha*, social and economic occupations—to fulfill human nature.)[9] Many figures at Khajuraho could illustrate the *Kama Sutra*'s explicit instructions, as observers have pointed out—although the *Kama Sutra* does not sanction all of the sexual indulgences visible at the temples.

And yet, prominent as sexual themes are in Hindu theology and literature, this fact does not answer all of the questions raised by Khajuraho. At least not in the opinion of the experts. That is why ever since Khajuraho got put on the archaeological map scores of scholars have busied themselves with intellectual detective work, erudite speculations, and ingenious arguments, trying to solve the mystery of the temples' striking eroticism.

Traversing this large, unsettled, and provocative scholarly terrain—tracking leads here and there, albeit without trying to probe every corner—I went through several layers of those turtles Geertz talks about. And it became clear that there are almost as many interpretations of Khajuraho's eroticism as there are scholars who study it. The sculptures are said, for example, to be magical icons for fostering fertility, and to be talismans for attracting divine favor and warding off evil. They are said to represent sexual rituals performed in the temples, and to delineate preparations for battle. They are said to commemorate the gods' eternal delectations, and to reflect the doctrines of mystic Tantrism—which demanded a regimen of extreme self-discipline for spiritual purposes, such as sexual exercises that sustain erotic arousal without reaching completion. They are said to symbolize the potency of kingly power, and to prefigure a king's otherworldly joys. They are said to record social history, and to advance secular sex education. They are said to illustrate specific literary, historical, architectural, or religious texts, most obviously the *Kama Sutra*, and increasingly (owing substantially to the industrious Indian art historian Devangana Desai) they are said to exhibit a cornucopia of interrelated sources—myth, theology, literature, technical texts, politics, social structure, and a battery of other historical and cultural influences.[10]

Along this winding scholarly trail I in fact turned up too many of Geertz's turtles. The erotic sculptures of Khajuraho are "overdetermined"—that is, they have more reasons to be there than they need, some of these reasons conflicting (although no one doubts that the eroticism serves the Hindu religion, at least in part, and that it is not mere pornography). But as copious, erudite, and eye-opening as the scholarly interpretations are, they nevertheless largely consist, as they must, of reasonable guesses derived from fragmentary circumstantial evidence. The temples of the long-lost Chandela empire do not give up their secrets easily, however tantalizing the hints they drop. Although not as opaque as it once was, the mystery of Khajuraho's eroticism persists. As one knowledgeable author admitted in a thorough study of the subject, "the perennial bafflement remains: whatever for?"[11]

And what of that elephant who smiles at one of Khajuraho's erotic acts? No scholarly explanation has accounted for or even remarked that amusement. Mystery still fell over it. Then I thought: could this smile be telling us that Khajuraho's much-studied eroticism is all a laughing matter? Could the secret of Khajuraho lie not in sex but in humor, or rather, in the humor of sex?

Who with any sense of humor could deny that sexuality can be pretty funny? It has been a subject of mirth, no less than of ritual, probably for as long as human beings have engaged in it. What would the history of comedy be without it? But in religious art? That is not so easy to understand—particularly in the light of Judeo-Christian-Islamic taboos. Yet at Khajuraho the signs of light-hearted humor pop up everywhere. The peeking voyeuses and the salacious voyeurs, the unlikely couplings and brash exhibitionism, the Rabelaisian orgies complete with animal participants, are the ageless stuff of comedy, whatever the intent here. And although the mien of the sculptures is generally quite restrained—they do not grimace or guffaw—their characteristic expressions approach nascent smiles. The faces of the gods and kings wear sensuous lips slightly raised at the corners in the ingratiating Hindu style, just as their hips tilt in a typical serpentine sway. And most of the goddesses and ladies standing alluringly beside their male companions look up with pronounced suggestions of a smile. These divine and regal smiles betoken, to be sure, more a serene contentment, or an adoring delight, than anything comic. But every trace of a smile at Khajuraho adds to an atmosphere of enjoyment and gives the smiling elephant hospitable company.

The smiling elephant does not have much divine or regal serenity. He is more akin to the smirking voyeurs and voyeuses, and what he sees plainly amuses him. But why? As everyone knows from experience, and as many theorists have argued, humor, laughter, and smiles can mean many things. They can express pleasure, irreverence, ridicule, and malice amid the satisfactions of deflating authority, the *Schadenfreude* of seeing others fall, and the vulgar glee of watching the ideal clash with the real. They can also serve more positive ends, giving joyful release to emotions or energies blocked by restraints, diffusing conflicts, and helping us communicate understanding, reciprocate good feelings, form affinities, and otherwise strengthen human bonds.

Lightly armed with theory, and mustering common sense, I did not need long to find out that Indian humor is a vary large subject, as rich as the culture, but that the humor at Khajuraho has drawn sparse comment. One industrious scholar who noted the comedy evident in the plebeian erotic scenes speculated that this might have made the divine eroticism easier for "the fastidious viewer" or unlearned worshipers to comprehend and to revere—in other words, taking sex lightly opened minds to edification and transformed irreverence into reverence, elevating bawdy humor to a type of sublimation.[12] More plausibly, he and others who have touched on the topic also guess that Khajuraho's humor evinces the universal theme of poking fun at religious piety, specifically by showing "ascetics," clerics, monks, and their ilk in salacious acts—rather like dirty jokes that puncture moral pretentions. Khajuraho's sexual antics would thereby lend religious sanction to irreverence: the religion telling dirty jokes on itself.

The smiling elephant no doubt betrays some of this jokey irreverence. His smile is a bit lascivious, and it certainly makes light of what he sees—while he jovially pins down his handler. Yet, like the rest of Khajuraho, there is more than unalloyed irreverence in that smile, otherwise Khajuraho's eroticism would amount to pornography or make a burlesque of the entire temple complex. Khajuraho's humor is more serious than that. It is divine comedy, we could say. And humane comedy. For it bespeaks a certain affection for human nature shared by the gods and mortals. And for me this idea started bringing together at last a persuasive pattern of clues to the enigmatic elephant.

One of these clues surfaced in the famous tales of the god Krishna (a principal avatar of the triumviral god Vishnu) cavorting with milkmaids—legend says this lusty deity married 1,600 of them! The standard, twelfth-century version by Jayadeva in the *Gita Govinda* describes a Krishna who "disports himself with charming women given to love. . . . He embraces one woman, he kisses another, and fondles another beautiful one. He looks at another one lovely with smiles, and starts in pursuit of another." Amorous and energetic, Krishna is "conducting the love sport, with love for all, bringing delight into being."[13] This is not the severe Krishna whose precepts on rigid spiritual and physical discipline fill the *Bhagavad-Gita*; it is an erotically playful Krishna who would be at home among the temples of Khajuraho.

These loving, joyful qualities of Krishna "bringing delight into being" can be seen all over Khajuraho in the spirited eroticism and blissful faces. As it happens, this atmosphere of felicity has a special connection to the Lakshmana temple itself. For this temple was built to honor Vishnu (Krishna's divine source), and held a treasured central statue of him (now lost but replaced by another) in its sanctum. The temple's dedicatory inscription jubilantly proclaimed that when "the inhabitants of heaven" saw this "charming splendid home" of the god, "which rivals the peaks of the mountain" and sends "the clouds to and fro," they were "struck with wonder" and "filled with increasing delight."[14] Like the elegant representations of Vishnu tenderly fondling Lakshmi, the smiling elephant on that temple surely shared in those divine delights.

A related clue cropped up in the *Mahābhārata*. In one long, vivid episode, a devotee of Vishnu's fellow supreme deity Shiva—whose emblem is the phallic lingam, a sign of prolific life extensively featured in Hindu art, shrines, and ritual—buoyantly describes Shiva as "the parent of all things." Shiva takes on every form, appearing as every god and every animal and every human being, male and female, high and low. And, like Vishnu's avatar Krishna, he brings delight. For "he sometimes laughs and sometimes sings and sometimes dances most beautifully"—occasionally while "an elephant skin forms his upper garment," a costume originating in the myth of Shiva slaying an elephant demon and then victoriously dancing.[15] *This* is the Shiva of Khajuraho, the god to whom most of the temples there are devoted. Not the fearsome Destroyer of Evil, but the patron of fertility, the father of amiable Ganesh, and the divinity of dance, who performs "most beautifully" and "sometimes laughs."

Led by these visions of divine delight, I came upon another invocation of the spirited Shiva that could have been created for Khajuraho. And, in fact, it was. Unearthed in one of Khajuraho's ruined temples. It was an inscription of a Chandela king, dated to the year 1002 CE, just half a century after completion of the Lakshmana temple. It reads: "May the laughter of Shiva, while jesting with his beloved wife Parvati, be for your welfare." One scholar takes this inscription as the epigraph to his book *Divine Ecstasy: The Story of Khajuraho*, in which he ingeniously contends that all of the temple art memorializes the marriage of Shiva and Parvati lavishly detailed in the *Shiva Puranam* (one of the many puranas, or Hindu histories, written between 700 and 1200 CE).[16] But I read this inscription, proclaiming "the laughter of Shiva while jesting" with Parvati "for your welfare," in the light of the elephant's smile. Finally, that smile was revealing itself as apt symbol of Khajuraho, and as a memorable image of much more.

Held in the encompassing embrace of life at Khajuraho, anyone could believe that the temples there do indeed, for one thing, stand as monuments to the universal Hindu deity Brahman, who underlies everything, whose "face is everywhere" and who can be worshiped through any image as "a gesture to God"[17]—including faces that smile. Linking this belief with that skein of clues to the genial spirit of Khajuraho—the disporting Krishna/Vishnu expressing "love for all" and "bringing delight into being"; the gods' "increasing delight" upon first seeing Vishnu's Lakshmana temple; the Shiva who "laughs and sometimes sings," and whose "laughter . . . with his beloved wife" at Khajuraho resounds "for your welfare"; and Shiva's son, the good-natured Ganesh, conspicuous at the temples, who often dances cheerily and brings wisdom and good fortune—I had come to see the smiling elephant as an image at once of Khajuraho and Hinduism and of a venerable, universal, life-affirming humanism.

This is an image primarily of the human attributes and humane virtues that abound at Khajuraho amidst the exaltations of divinity and secular authority: energy and exuberance, appetites and aspirations, desire and generosity, delight and magnanimity. It is an image that invites us to prize the human with the divine and to welcome, as the guru said, "every variety of humanity" with "a great tolerance of those who strive and a great forgiveness for those who fail," and possibility with a bit of humor. This may be a more kindly image of Khajuraho than it entirely deserves—undoubtedly its history, like that of Hinduism, was not invariably benign. But it is an image as true to India as is the beneficent laughter of the gods. And it is an image we can find today in the writings of India's most renowned storyteller, R. K. Narayan, whose many tales of ordinary Indian life draw us into compassionate ironies and warm amusements, leaving us enlightened and smiling. As John Updike remarked, Narayan has not reproached or tried to change his raucous and beloved homeland; he has instead been satisfied "to observe, to invent, to express surprise at the permutations of human behavior, to smile."[18]

We could also say that the smiling elephant is, to borrow from Western literature, an image that evokes some lines of the witty Oscar Wilde, who in a sage moment of the thoughtful comedy *An Ideal Husband* has a character advise: "Life cannot be understood without much charity. Life cannot be lived without much charity." That is to say, fallible as we are, we need charity of heart and mind to live equably with ourselves and compassionately with others, and to share the grace of loving laughter.

And that, after all, is the divine and humane comedy of Khajuraho and of the smiling elephant. It is comedy as a sacred celebration paying homage to very human divinities and to a human nature underlying all religious and cultural demands, a human nature not to be scolded for its earthy impulses and imperfections but accepted with tolerance and charity, and with knowing humor. Khajuraho is a complicated place, but a humane one. The smiling elephant belongs there as its emblem. Or so I concluded.

In the end, I would not claim to have wholly solved the mystery of the smiling elephant. But I found metaphoric meaning in it—akin to the "metaphoric formulations" offered by scholars for most of Khajuraho's enduring enigmas.[19] And that can be enough. For the more we dwell on images like this, the more they exercise their metaphoric power to reveal the meanings of things within and outside ourselves. Anyone can encounter this power and use it. We need only follow the allure of images into the realm of simple wonder and humanistic curiosity, for there images and metaphors flourish, awakening us to both actualities and possibilities. There wishes and inquisitiveness thrive, along with imagination and memory, art and ideas, morals and ideals.

Exemplifying this evocative metaphoric power, the smiling elephant acquired for me still further resonance. Besides signaling Khajuraho's embracing humanity, it became an image of the very humanistic curiosity that had led me to Khajuraho in the first place and had captivated me with an intellectual mystery. This is the curiosity that wakes us up, invigorates our days, and helps us discover metaphors that can, as Rushdie said, "transfigure us and reveal the meaning of our lives." Without such curiosity and its fertile images and transforming metaphors, we risk living passively, dead to the energies of the inner life, inured to prospects for rebirth, and ready prey to the "savage torpor" that Wordsworth diagnosed over two hundred years ago (in the preface to *Lyrical Ballads*), as the insidious malady of our sensorially overstimulated, emotionally undernourished, benumbing modern world. Images and metaphors become antidotes to this torpor, even as they lend new purpose to our lives.

A philosophical tradition in the West passing from Socrates through Nietzsche assures us that the wise are happy because wisdom brings good cheer. I would like to think that the smiling elephant of Khajuraho possesses that kind of cheerfulness. So, among the abundant metaphors and images of India, the one I would most wish to be transfigured by is that singular elephant's knowing smile.

Notes

1. *The Mahābhārata*, trans. William Buck (New York: New American Library, 1979; reprint, New York: Meridian, 1987), 244.

2. Satguru Sivaya Subramuniyaswami, *Loving Gaṇeśa: Hinduism's Endearing Elephant-Faced God* (India-USA: Himalayan Academy, 1996), xxxix.

3. Hajime Nakamura, *Ways of Thinking of Eastern Peoples: India, China, Tibet, Japan*, rev. trans. Philip P. Wiener (Honolulu: East-West Center Press, 1964), 172.

4. *Loving Gaṇeśa*, xlivii.

5. Clifford Geertz, "Thick Description: Toward an Interpretive Theory of Culture," in *The Interpretation of Cultures* (New York: Basic Books, 1973), 28–29.

6. *Song of God: Bhagavad-Gita*, trans. Swami Prabhavanda and Christopher Isherwood (New York: New American Library, 1944; Mentor Books, 1951), 89–90.

7. Somadeva Bhatta, *The Ocean of Story*, 10 vols., trans. C. H. Tawney, ed. N. M. Penzer, Indian edition, 2nd ed. (1923; reprint, Delhi: Motilal Banarsidass, 1968), I:1.

8. *Mahābhārata*, trans. P. C. Roy, in *The Hindu Tradition*, ed. Ainslee T. Embree (New York: Vintage Books, 1972), 236.

9. *The Kama Sutra of Vatsyayana*, trans. Richard Burton and F. F. Arbuthnot, ed. W. G. Archer (New York: G. P. Putnam's Sons, 1963), I:61, 7:220.

10. A survey of scholarly interpretations, with a sustained reinterpretation, appears in Michael Rabe, "Sexual Imagery on the Phantasmagorical Castles of Khajuraho," parts 1 and 2, *International Journal of Tantric Studies* 2, no. 2 (1997, rev. Feb. 1997). Other studies consulted include: Devangana Desai, *Erotic Sculptures of India: A Socio-Cultural Study* (1975) and *The Religious Imagery of Khajuraho* (1996); R. Nath, *The Art of Khajuraho* (1980); S. K. Ramachandra Rao, *The Icons and Images in Indian Temples*

(1981); L. A. Narain, *Khajuraho: Temples of Ecstasy* (1986); Laxminarayan Pachori, *The Erotic Sculptures of Khajuraho* (1989); Hiram W. Woodward Jr., "The Lakṣmaṇa Temple, Khajuraho, and Its Meanings," *Ars Orientalis* (1989); Krishna Deva, *Temples of Khajuraho*, 2 vols. (1990); Shobita Punja, *Divine Ecstasy: The Story of Khajuraho* (1992); Kalyan Kumar Chakravarty et al., eds., *Khajuraho in Perspective* (1994).

11. See note 9, Rabe, 2:1.

12. See note 9, Rabe, 2:5.

13. Jayadeva, *Gita Govinda*, trans. George Keyt, in Ainslee T. Embree, ed., *The Hindu Tradition*, 169–70.

14. Quoted in Krishna Deva, *The Temples of Khajuraho*, 1:346.

15. *Mahābhārata*, in Ainslee T. Embree, ed., *The Hindu Tradition*, 235.

16. Shobita Punja, *Divine Ecstasy*, vi.

17. Mulk Raj Anand, *The Hindu View of Art*, 3rd ed. (1987), 26.

18. John Updike, Max Vadukul, "Malgudi's Master," *The New Yorker* (23–30] June, 1997), 134.

19. The term is Michael Rabe's (see note 9), 2:10.

A previous version of this essay was originally published in *The Georgia Review*, Summer, 1999. The essay was named among the Notable Spiritual Writings of 1999 in *The Best Spiritual Writing 2000*, edited by Philip Zaleski.

*The Djemaa el-Fnaa at sunset, with the minaret of the Koutoubia Mosque in the background,
Marrakech, Morocco*

The Storytellers of Marrakech

In the waning twilight of summer, as a *petite* taxi inches through the tangled, crowded passageways of the medina of Marrakech, Morocco, two passengers from New York City feel almost at home amidst the crushing urban density and barely restrained chaos, at once ominous and inspiriting. The taxi, built to squeeze through the medina's constricted spaces, stops at an unmarked alley, empty until a robed figure steps from its shadows and beckons. Climbing from the car, we follow him into the darkness toward a distant door lit by a naked bulb. The door opens, and we are invited into a dim tiled corridor fragrant with mint and roses. We make our way to a narrow, sharply winding stairway. Around and around we ascend. Then we step through an arch to find ourselves standing under the evening sky, sparkling with stars. Candlelight flickers across a few carved wooden tables surrounded by silk cushions piled on Moroccan rugs. We are on the rooftop of an old villa, or palace, in the depths of the medina. A nobleman once lived here. Now, as is the way of the world, it is a restaurant, where drinks and spiced olives are offered on the roof, to the strains of an African lute, and where dinner is served below in an intimate palm-lined courtyard beside an azure pool on glistening white tablecloths strewn with rose petals. This is a place mainly for tourists. But it can induce even a tourist to lapse into reflections on the life once lived here, on the unexpected beauties hidden from the medina's turbulent streets behind its aging walls, and on the culture that brought this enchanting setting into being.

From the restaurant rooftop, the medina, or original "little city," of Marrakech strikes the eye as a vast interconnected maze, its low horizontal skyline broken only by the graceful towers of minarets, from which muezzins call the Islamic faithful to prayer five times a day. Muhammad had decreed that this call come from the highest point near each mosque. Later that point was constructed with the mosque, and so minarets had spread with Islam, the most visible symbol of Islamic piety and unity. The oldest and tallest of these in Marrakech, dominating the skyline at the Koutoubia mosque (built in the twelfth century and among the most renowned in Islam), now broadcasts its summons to the faithful from loudspeakers, muezzins no longer rising to its balcony because, it is said, the antics of tourists swimming at the nearby Club Med hotel are not for pious eyes to see. Notwithstanding this concession to secular modernity (increasingly common, for various reasons, elsewhere), the echoes of the muezzins' lilting calls in the summer night evoke the spiritual vision of Islam with its peerless devotion to God, or Allah, and its rich feelings for beauty and for life.

Those feelings arise from that devotion. For everything is Islam has its source in Allah and must somehow serve Him. Other religions may make similar claims for their gods. But Islam is different.

The very word *Islam* means submission to God. And this God is not quite like any other.

Of the three great Western monotheistic religions that rejected paganism's polytheistic pantheon, Islam carried monotheism farthest, envisioning a deity of such power and perfection that He (no doubt of the gender, either) transcends everything while remaining only Himself. He is omnipotent and omniscient. Nothing happens without His will. Hence, secularity is tantamount to blasphemy. Allah is the One and Only God, to whom all must be beholden for everything—and Christianity blasphemed Him by regarding Jesus as His son deserving to share His glory. Even the exalted Hebrew conception of God did not match Allah's pervasive role in the universe and in human life.

"Bismallah"—in the name of Allah—is heard wherever you go in Islam, sanctioning all important transactions and social encounters. Nor is it for mortals to anticipate or second-guess Allah's wishes. Even weather forecasters acknowledge that their predictions, however scientific, depend less on science and the caprices of nature than on the Will of God. *"In Sha'Allah"*—if Allah wills it—they sometimes humbly conclude their forecasts. *In Sha'Allah*, a phrase always in a Muslim's thoughts and often on the lips, says more about Islamic culture than do volumes of description.

The one volume that does say more is the Qur'an. Just as Allah is like no other god, so the Qur'an is like no other sacred book. Divine truth and sacred poetry, the Qur'an is the literal word of Allah as revealed to Muhammad by the Angel Gabriel in the Arabic language born almost simultaneously with Islam—purportedly created by Allah Himself, naturally—and as recorded in the exquisite calligraphy that remains Islam's highest visual art form (representational art being prohibited as sacrilege). To read the Qur'an is therefore to encounter directly the thought, the language, and the artistry of Allah.

It is also fundamental to Islam that according to tradition Allah's first word to Muhammad through Gabriel was "recite": "Recite in the name of your Lord who created man from clots of blood. Recite! Your Lord is the Most Bountiful One, who by the pen taught man what he did not know" (Qur'an, 96.1–5, trans. Ahmed Ali). It is understandable that this revelation gave the very name to the book: *Qur'an* means "recitation." No wonder that memorizing and reciting Qur'anic verse is the primary Islamic performance of piety, honoring not just doctrinal orthodoxy but words formed in all of their sanctity and eloquence by Allah Himself. Actually, according to tradition, that act of creation itself took the form of recitation, making Allah's mind and the Qur'an virtually one. Given the Qur'an's lofty status in Islam, it should come as no surprise that many orthodox Muslims consider it futile and even blasphemous for infidels to read, much less to try to interpret, the Holy Book. To be worthy of reading its sacred verse, one must first submit to Allah. For those who do submit, the Qur'an, through Islam, becomes the guide to all things in heaven and on earth.

The atmosphere of Islam is very much in the summer night's air on that rooftop restaurant in Marrakech. But with it are also the aromas of spices and the sounds of romantic song, enticements to sensuous pleasures and inducements to secular fantasies. And these come not from Islam but from something that preceded it and that has survived within it. This is a certain sense of life, indigenous to the territories where Islam later established its empire reaching from Spain and Morocco in the west across North Africa to India and Central Asia. This sense of life, pagan and secular, tribal and proud, engendered many of the attributes associated with Islam. Some of these attributes are social practices, such as extreme patriarchal authority, severe punitive justice, fierce in-group loyalty, and exalted martial honor. But others involve an aesthetic sensibility that relishes pleasures of the senses and the imagination—rich material luxuries, sumptuous flavors, seductive fragrances, and flights of fantasy in tales of marvelous adventures. Europeans took this aesthetic sensibility to be the very essence of the exotic, and the antithesis of Western rationalism and restraint. Attracted to this exoticism for escape and inspiration, many Western artists and writers—among them Lord Byron, Eugène Delacroix, Gustave Flaubert, Richard Burton, Henri Matisse, and Paul Bowles—traveled to its Islamic sources and found what they were looking for.

Nowadays, these Western perceptions of the exotic are derided as condescending Eurocentric "orientalism" (in Edward Said's term). But they are not wholly without foundation. Western perceptions aside, there are indeed distinctive delectations of this ancient aesthetic sensibility. None of these is more conspicuous and enduring than delights of the garden.

Around the medina of Marrakech, gardens can be seen in every direction, their date palms and olive trees bringing welcome shade to summer days. And in the medina, as in the restaurant, private courtyards are gardens, too. No nobleman or wealthy merchant would be without one. Europe, Eastern Asia, and even the Americas may have gardens more lush than those where Islam established its realm. But in this realm gardens are cherished as only a desert people can cherish them. Here gardens are a gift of Allah, growing with the rare blessing of water, like the scattered oases that spare travelers from the desert itself. Here alone is the garden so adored that it gave the very name to Paradise.

Long before Islam, the early peoples of Mesopotamia were the first both to create a literate culture and to conceive of Paradise as a garden. The Old Persian word for a walled garden was just this *pairidaeza,* and most Western languages share in its legacy (as Elizabeth B. Moynihan illustrated in *Paradise as a Garden*). At about the same time, the neighboring Hebrews started recording their worship of a God who crowned His creation of the world with the singular perfection of the Garden of Eden; and for them no fall from grace for humankind could be more punishing than expulsion from it. Then came the Babylonians, who took pride in a fabulous worldly embodiment of the garden paradise: the Hanging Gardens of Babylon, that wonder of the ancient world.

Islam continued this tradition among these people of arid lands with its version of an otherworldly Paradise as a garden of sublime coolness and serene beauty where rivers flow freely and fruits grow abundantly. "This is the Paradise which the righteous have been promised," says the Qur'an. "There shall flow in it rivers of purest water, and rivers of milk forever fresh; rivers of wine delectable to those that drink it, and rivers of clearest honey. They shall eat therein of every fruit and receive forgiveness from their Lord." This Islamic Paradise is no disembodied spiritual realm, like the Christian heaven. It is truly a "garden of delight" in which the faithful, "arrayed in garments of fine green silk and rich brocade, and adorned with bracelets of silver," shall savor all the joys of Paradise. "Reclining there upon soft couches, they shall feel neither the scorching heat nor the biting cold. Trees will spread their shade around them, and fruits will hang in clusters over them. They shall be served with silver dishes, and beakers as large as goblets . . . and cups brim-full with ginger-flavored water. They shall be attended by boys graced with eternal youth, who to the beholder's eyes will seem like sprinkled pearls. When you gaze upon that scene you will behold a kingdom blissful and glorious." This is a garden Paradise such as only a desert people could imagine it, but a desert people imbued with an exceptional aesthetic sensibility as well (Qur'an, 47.15; 5.65; 76.13–21).

"In the garden flows a brook from the River of Paradise," wrote the Persian poet Omar Khayyám in the twelfth century. And "since this garden is enough like Paradise," you should "talk less of the River of Paradise" and just "sit in your [own] paradise with a heavenly-faced girl" (*Rubáiyát*, 232, trans., Avery & Heath-Stubbs). Anyone familiar with the *Rubáiyát* knows that it bears few marks of Islamic piety, and not a little heresy; and you must look closely in it to find Islamic beliefs. But it nevertheless reflects the peculiar marriage in much of Islam between a pre-Islamic aesthetic sensibility and the Islamic submission to Allah. The fruit of this marriage was a certain hedonism tempered by religious piety and fatalism. Khayyám unapologetically envisioned life as a garden of delights for pursuing sensuous pleasures, albeit with a fatalistic resignation to the transcendent will of Allah (if not so named). "One is fetched out and another snatched away," Khayyám writes. "The secret of being is not disclosed to anyone; / By destiny only this . . . amount is allotted to us, / The brief measure of our lifetime . . . / Go and live happily, you did not choose your lot" (169; 154).

Together with the hedonistic fatalism of Khayyám and other varieties of sensuosity, sensuality, and piety, this marriage of aesthetics and submission to Allah also gave rise to a culture in which marvels could occur—genies could materialize, carpets could fly—and where persons could possess astonishing powers to do the most extraordinary things. Among these persons were the whirling dervishes of Turkey and *marabouts* of Morocco.

In Morocco the *marabouts* had wide influence as mystical holy men uniquely bound to Allah—the word *marabout* denotes these sacred bonds. Steeping themselves in spiritual exercises to achieve *baraka*, or charismatic efficacies, they would display these exercises publicly to cultivate and demonstrate their *baraka* by charming snakes, swallowing fire, performing magic tricks and acrobatic feats. These public exhibitions continue today, their origins forgotten, in what is surely the most peculiar public arena in the world, the marketplace of Marrakech, the Djemaa el-Fnaa.

The Djemaa el-Fnaa (or Jemaa el-Fna) is akin to every town square and marketplace in the world, and yet utterly itself. Most historic cities have had central squares or marketplaces, something like it. Ancient Athens had its agora and Rome its forum. Paris has its *places* and Rome its *piazzas*; London has its Trafalgar Square and Piccadilly Circus; Beijing has its Tiananmen Square; Moscow has its Red Square; and New York City has its Times Square. These and others have been the heartbeat of their cities, drawing inhabitants together for marketing, politicking, socializing, and diversion—although modern times have not been kind to the town square and marketplace, rendering them largely superfluous through mass merchandising, electronic technology, and automobiles.

But the Djemaa el-Fnaa is more than a traditional marketplace. Its uniqueness begins with its name, which is uncertain in both origins and import. *Djemaa* is an Arabic word for "gathering" or "assembly" and is therefore related to "mosque." *Fnaa* is more ambiguous, connoting "nothing" or "extinction" or "finished" or "end" or even "death." One account says that a mosque was planned and then never built where the Djemaa el-Fnaa exists today, hence the name signified "the mosque that came to nothing." Another says this was an execution site, and so the name means the "assembly of the dead." Yet another, my favorite, in the words of a poetically inclined guide, says the Djemaa el-Fnaa is "the gathering at the end of the world"—and so it appears.

The Djemaa el-Fnaa is bedlam and civilization as one. Bread makers, fruit vendors, basket weavers, and the like hawk their goods alongside cooks preparing Moroccan fare, water sellers jangling cups, and dentists grinning as they proudly wield pliers beside tables covered with extracted teeth. And scattered among them are performers vying for attention and coins—acrobats balancing on each other and twirling in the air, monkey trainers coaching animal acts, fire-eaters swallowing and breathing flames, magicians pulling bounty from their sleeves, snake charmers enticing serpents into weird dances. Many of these performers could trace their skills back to the *marabouts*. But now they do not stake these claims. They perform for money, mainly from tourists, at least in the daytime.

"Photo? Photo?" invites a monkey trainer as he pushes a costumed monkey into our arms. A photo dutifully taken, his solicitous hand comes forth to receive payment.

A dentist gestures vigorously toward his table of extractions, widens his toothless grin and holds up his pliers. A camera click brings him quickly to his feet with arm outstretched: "Dirhams! Dirhams!" One dirham, the Moroccan currency, elicits only indignation: "Two dirhams!" he insists in English. That is the least his services cost, if not as a working dentist then as a performer, a "photo opportunity" for tourists. One wonders if he has ever pulled a tooth, and shudders to think if he has.

The Djemaa el-Fnaa is the primeval marketplace. Here and in the surrounding *souks*, or shops, in the medina, everything is for sale, and selling is conducted as an art. The actual worth of things is almost impossible to determine with certainty. Price is another matter. Prices are everywhere, and the merchant's art lies in leading the buyer to accept a high one. This is, to be sure, the secret of all selling. "After all," a sage car salesman once explained to me, "a good deal is only the feeling that you are getting a good deal. And some people are willing to pay more for that feeling than others." The merchants of Marrakech excel in giving customers that feeling. Like the magicians and other performers of the Djemaa el-Fnaa, they, too, mingle the real and the unreal in exercises of ingenuity and persuasion. At the same time, they sense that the price paid for an object is ultimately determined, like everything else, by Allah. *"In Sha'Allah,"* hopes the seller, the price will be high. *"Bismallah,"* he mutters when the deal is done.

The Djemaa el-Fnaa saw its first merchants in the eleventh and twelfth centuries when Marrakech emerged from the desert as a well-irrigated center of trade and Islamic political and religious authority. The city was home to Almohad rulers and to scholars like the philosopher Averroes, and it was among the glories of the cultural efflorescence that made Islam the most advanced civilization in the western half of the world. A dozen Islamic cities from Spain to India could boast a hundred thousand inhabitants, illuminated streets, hospitals, and cosmopolitan universities at a time when most of Christian Europe lived in more primitive conditions and intellectual darkness and yet looked upon Islam as a barbarous empire deserving only the crusaders' conquest and pillage. Besides the ravages of the Christian crusades, it was in part to foil and despoil this empire, which stood in the way of Europe's passage to the East, that the epochal European voyages of exploration were later launched in the fifteenth century. And it was typical of the Christian contempt for Islam that, soon after the Europeans' first successful voyage east to India in the 1550s, the explorer Vasco da Gama blithely put to death a shipload of unarmed Muslim pilgrims making their way home from Mecca. "We took a Mecca ship," recorded a crew member, "on board of which were 380 men and many women and children. . . . And we burned the ship and all the people on board with gun power" (quoted in Daniel J. Boorstin, *The Discoverers*, p. 177). By then, of course, Europe was well into its own cultural Renaissance, which would eventually bring the eclipse of Islam's worldly achievements, and those of most of the world, with unparalleled advances in Western science and technology, secularity and capitalism.

But the marketplace of Marrakech possibly remains much as it always was. Although automobiles jam the adjacent streets, camera-toting tourists gawk at the sideshow oddities, and cheap Western goods can be bought there, the Djemaa el-Fnaa still belongs to Moroccans. "It may be for tourists during the day," said our guide, Hassan. "Come at night. Then the Djemaa el-Fnaa is ours." In nothing is this more evident than in those most venerable performers, the storytellers.

How odd to find amidst this welter of merchants, circus acts, and vestigial spiritual exercises figures who simply tell stories. And how surprising that they attract among the largest crowds. But not tourists. Or not non-Arabic speaking tourists. The storytellers tell their stories in the language of their homeland. Non-Arabic speakers can only watch, and then turn away. Even so erudite and captivated a European observer as Elias Canetti confessed in *The Voices of Marrakesh* to doing just that, because, he said, "foreigners were simply not there as far as they," the storytellers, "were concerned." We "did not belong in their world of words."

"I used to have my father bring me here as a child," the guide Hassan said, "just to hear the storytellers. I would stay a long time." He paused and added jocularly, with a cosmopolitan flair: "They were like your American television shows—their stories went on and on and on." I wondered if that were really true: are the storytellers of the Djemaa el-Fnaa just entertainers, or, like the acrobats and the snake charmers who could trace their lineage back to the *marabouts*, are they also something more?

As I watched and listened to a storyteller weave his spellbinding tales, whispering and shouting, crouching and prancing, beckoning the crowd closer and closer, I thought of storytellers of other times and places, and how theirs is by all odds the oldest entertainment, if not profession. Nowadays storytelling has acquired a certain fashion in American intellectual life, bringing storytellers to college campuses and making narrative—even narratology, as academia dubs the study of it—a hot topic among professors. But what culture has ever existed without storytelling? Intellectual culture begins with it in myths of creations and divinity. Many of the world's sacred scriptures—think of the Bible or the *Mahābhārata*—are oft-told stories of peoples and their gods, as are the earliest literary epics like *Gilgamesh* and the *Iliad*. In their origins all of these belong to the same tradition as the storytellers of Marrakech today: the oral tradition. And in this tradition, stories possess an authority lost to print and other technologies. This is the authority of truth. For where all knowledge beyond immediate experience comes from the spoken word, not only diversion but truth is transmitted by tellers of tales.

The Peruvian writer Mario Vargas Llosa wrote a novel on this subject called none other than *The Storyteller (El Hablador)*. It records the life of an educated man who abandons his profession in Lima to become a storyteller among a scattered and illiterate people of the jungle held together only by their common language and their stories. He wanders from tribe to tribe repeating these stories and embellishing them. They are not merely entertainments either. In an oral culture, stories could never be only that. They are true. Or, rather, there is always some truth in them. Vargas Llosa's storyteller assures his listeners of this with the words that end his every tale, however strange: "Well, that, anyway, is what I have learned."

Watching the storyteller in Marrakech play this same venerable role, my mind passed from this novel to some lines in two other novels bearing on storytelling. In Salman Rushdie's *Haroun and the Sea of Stories*, Haroun asks his father, who is a storyteller, "What's the use of stories that aren't even true?" He eventually learns they have uses that make them essential to life and therefore, in effect, true. As if in reply to Haroun, Chinua Achebe has an old man say to a young man in *Things Fall Apart*: "There is no story that is not true." It struck me that Achebe's old man was right. He was surely right for oral cultures, but he might be right for literate cultures, too. Even there stories can be carriers of truth, just as they are essential to human life.

Aristotle thought so, as he said in an observation that resonates through all of literature and the truths it tells. "History treats of particular facts" or "what has happened," he wrote in the *Poetics*. By contrast, "poetry [or literature] is concerned with universal truths" or with "things that might happen." "For this reason," Aristotle concluded, "poetry is something more philosophical and more worthy of serious attention than history."

A questionable proposition, perhaps; but Aristotle wanted us to see that the purpose of literature is to deal in the "universal truths" of the *possible* rather than the "particular facts" of the *actual*. Aristotle looked for these truths in imaginings, as he said, of what "a certain type of person will probably or necessarily say or do in a given situation." But the truths of "what might happen" can also live in imaginings that take us altogether beyond ourselves and our experience. That is what Achebe had in mind.

In asserting that "there is no story that is not true," Achebe's old man was chastening those who disbelieved as incredible the first reports of white men and their slave trade in Nigeria. We dismiss seeming impossibilities only at our peril, he cautions. The folly of comforting disbelief was also the theme of Elie Wiesel's narratives about the Nazis' attempted extermination of the Jews. Nurtured on the horrors of "what has happened," Wiesel tirelessly dwelled on the potent image of the Holocaust to teach us the storyteller's "universal truth" that in the realm of "what might happen," as Wiesel said with knowing sorrow, "anything is possible."

But the truths of "what might happen" are not all bad. Far from it. Nor are they confined to imagined possibilities. For literature not only imagines possibilities, it also induces us to act, transforming fiction into fact, the possible into the actual. This potency has led many moralists to censor literature for undermining orthodoxy and social stability. Plato set the model in the West by banishing poets from his ideal state to guard against their irresistible emotional powers (while nonetheless exploiting these same powers himself in dialogues abounding with vivid scenes and images showing Socrates discussing the beautiful, the good, and the true). Miguel de Cervantes emblematically stated these moralist fears in the words of a cleric condemning the books of chivalry that had influenced Don Quixote: "I would pitch them into the fire," he cries, because they inspire "new ways of life." As the cleric knew, by embracing the essential truth of stories, which is that anything is possible, we help bring possibilities to pass in "new ways of life."

The storytellers of Marrakech know this, too. And yet an irony, or paradox, lies in their knowledge, and in their very existence. For Islam should have no storytellers. The Qur'an would have none of them. Although it contains arresting and poetic images—like those of Paradise and of Allah Himself, who is invoked rather than described—unlike many other formative religious documents, the Qur'an is not a narrative. It is above stories, being the sacred word of Allah, conveying His nature and prescribing His law. It is to be memorized and worshipfully recited, not read as literature. Consequently, the Qur'an denounces poets and storytellers as fabricators and deceivers alien to the truths of Allah and capable of doing harm: "Among men are also those who spread frivolous stories to mislead from the way of God, without any knowledge, and take it lightly. . . . As for poets, only those who go astray follow them." (31.6; 26.224). Like conservative moralists everywhere, the Qur'an denies that stories bear truths; stories subvert orthodoxy and lead to "new ways of life."

Yet the irony is that, even as it repudiated storytellers, the Qur'an unwittingly encouraged them. For one thing, the very absence of narrative in the Qur'an actually nourished in the Islamic imagination a penchant for stories purporting to illuminate and honor the holy book. Tradition tells us that the first Islamic storytellers were literary fantasists who imaginatively amplified upon the Qur'an with narratives to render it more readily comprehensible and inviting to the uneducated. Orthodox theologians, protectors of the divine truth, sought to discredit them. But despite the official distrust and disdain, these and other storytellers thrived in Islam. And they thrived not only by compensating for the Qur'an's want of narrative. They also found something in the Qur'an itself to inspire them. This was Allah's Omnipotence. His absolute Will. Although the demand for submission to this omnipotence has curtailed much artistic expression in Islam, it has also bred the opposite: the imagination of possibility. For if Allah's will is unbounded, anything can happen that Allah wills. Hence Islamic storytellers have taken license to mingle fact and fantasy, morals and marvels, the possible and the seemingly impossible more exuberantly perhaps than any other storytellers in the world—while always honoring Allah. That's why their carpets can fly.

Consider that most renowned Islamic collection of stories, *The Thousand and One Nights* or *The Arabian Nights*. Although scholars tell us that the original compilation from diverse sources made in the ninth century probably differed greatly from later versions, the modern authoritative edition by Muhsin Mahdī (as translated by Husain Haddawy—who recalls being reared on these stories in Baghdad) shows *The Arabian Nights* to be classic Islamic storytelling.

Prefacing the collection with an obligatory Qur'anic tribute to Allah—which heads every sura in the Holy Book: "In the Name of

God the Compassionate, the Merciful"—the narrator proceeds to explain that "the purpose of writing this agreeable and entertaining book" is not only to "delight and divert" readers "burdened with the cares of life" but also "the instruction of those who peruse it" for its "edifying histories and excellent lessons." Above all, it will "teach the reader to detect deception and to protect himself from it" while also enabling the reader "to learn the art of discourse," which is the art of storytelling itself. So it is that deception and storytelling are central subjects of *The Arabian Nights*. Finally, lest the narrator claim to know too much, the preface ends with a pious demurral to Allah's authority: "It is the Supreme God who is the True Guide."

The narrative itself opens with more deference to Allah's omniscience, as this extends to storytelling: "It is related—but God knows and sees best what lies hidden in the old accounts of bygone peoples and times—that long ago. . . ." The Islamic storyteller must not presume to know the whole truth of the stories he or she tells. Only Allah knows that. But anything is possible.

Then comes the famous tale of Scheherazade (or Shahrazad), which frames the collection. More than a literary device, this framing tale is the narrator's and Scheherazade's testimonial to the power of stories to transform listeners through curiosity, imagination, emotion, and discovery.

Wishing to save her people from the vengeful bloodlust of King Shahrayar, whose betrayal by his wife has driven him to marry a new woman every night and then to execute her in the morning, Scheherazade requests that her father arrange her own marriage to the king. She has a plan, ingenious and simple. Before the fateful morning comes, she explains, "I will begin to tell a story, and it will cause the king to stop his practice, save myself, and deliver the people." Scheherazade is confident she can succeed because she believes stories can be more powerful than passions or principles. She will wield this power by enticing Shahrayar to listen to a story; once its pleasures, suspense, and enlightenment have taken hold of him, she will never let it end until he is transformed by the story—or the stories within the story—itself.

The gambit works. "Morning overtook Scheherazade and she lapsed into silence, leaving King Shahrayar burning with curiosity to hear the rest of the story." She assures him that "tomorrow night I shall tell you something even lovelier, stranger, and more wonderful if I live, the Almighty willing." He muses: "I will spare her until I hear the rest of the story; then I will have her put to death the next day." And so it goes for a thousand and one nights, the same seductive invitation, the same hesitant concession. Tradition has it that through those nights Scheherazade's stories achieved their desired effect. King Shahrayar abandoned his misogynistic vengeance and remained happily with Scheherazade thereafter.

But Scheherazade's stories succeeded not by fictional fascination alone. Their plots also played upon her own belief in the beneficent effects of storytelling, the "art of discourse." Scheherazade's stories show these effects to be not only "how to detect deception" but how hardened hearts can be softened and how a listener's humanity can be awakened. For instance, in her stories, a caliph loses his ruthless sense of justice after tasting the emotional pleasures of stories; a king of China grows merciful after hearing a sequence of stories within stories within stories, each more beguiling than its predecessor; demons are pacified, monsters quelled, genies bewitched all by good storytellers. Scheherazade herself so deftly demonstrated the humanizing efficacies of storytelling that she did more than win over Shahrayar, saving her own life and her people—never mind that she had deceived Shahrayar to do it. She became the prototypical storyteller—in Islam, and in the world.

You cannot fail to think of Scheherazade while listening to the storytellers in the Djemaa el-Fnaa. You suspect their stories contain many fantasies and probably a bit of deception. You can see that they yield much pleasure, and perhaps they proffer some truth. But not understanding the language, you might ask yourself: Do these stories resemble Scheherazade's? Are they mere entertainments?

Or, like hers, do they also have a moral purpose? Do they have useful truths to tell, and if so what are they? Do they say anything of value about the world and about human life? And whatever the tales they tell, how did the storytellers of Marrakech come to be who they are?

Unanswered, such questions went with me as I left the sights and sounds of the Djemaa el-Fnaa and the medina of Marrakech to return to the more familiar chaos of New York City. Idle questions at first, they would not go away. They kept asking themselves, and they wanted answers. Then, during the long languid hours of the westward flight across the Atlantic, they called forth an idea or, rather, an image.

It was of a young man living long ago in a village near the Atlas Mountains that rise to the east of Marrakech. He was agitated, like the Faust of European lore, by a great curiosity to know all there is to know, to possess the absolute truth. But, unlike Faust, he was a faithful Muslim. So instead of consorting with the devil to satisfy his desires, he prayed to Allah. Allah, being who He is, chastised the young man for his blasphemous ambitions. Only Allah can know everything. But, also being the Ever Merciful and Compassionate, Allah gave the young man something instead of knowledge. He gave him the imagination of possibility, and He gave him the "art of discourse," with permission to tell others whatever he imagined, as long as he honored Allah. With Allah's blessing, the young man could imagine and portray *possible* truths without claiming to know anything for sure. And what he imagined was full of wonder and mystery. And he began to tell others these things. And he was so gifted in the "art of discourse" that people gathered around to hear, seeking diversion and perhaps some wisdom. At first some thought he was a prophet speaking for Allah. Others thought he was a philosopher explaining the ways of the world. Others thought he was a historian reporting the past. But he told them, "No. I do not speak for Allah, although I honor Him, or of philosophy or of history. I have no actual truths to give you. I have only tales of what might have been and of what might yet be." And because the people got such enjoyment from his tales, which showed them marvelous possibilities, and because they also discovered in the tales many things about themselves and each other and the world, they urged him to tell them more and more. They began to come from other villages and to bring him gifts and money for his stories. In time, the listeners grew too numerous for his cottage and his yard to hold them. Finally, encouraged by his listeners, he decided to go to the city to tell his tales in the marketplace alongside the merchants and the *marabouts*. And intoning *"In Sha'Allah,"* he went to the Djemaa el-Fnaa and became the first storyteller of Marrakech.

A trite fantasy. Still it reminded me how infectious storytelling can be—especially in a place where, not overwhelmed by electronic technology and mass entertainments, storytelling survives as the elemental diversion and education. The little fantasy roused my curiosity anew. By the time I reached New York, I had to know. Who are the storytellers of Marrakech, and what are the stories they tell? Before long, I went back to Djemaa el-Fnaa to find out.

There, led by one guide after another—"interpreters' or "informants" to anthropologists, although most of them, who foist their services on visitors whether you want them or not, hardly live up to such titles—I trekked the mile from La Mamounia Hotel to the Djemaa el-Fnaa again and again. I cannot vouch for the truth of what these guides told me, and they were not very consistent. But, to echo Vargas Llosa's storyteller: this, anyway, is what I learned.

"Where do the storytellers come from?" I asked Amin, an educated native of Marrakech and probably the most informative guide I talked to.

"Oh, that is a big question," he responded gravely. "No one knows. Storytellers have been in the Djemaa el-Fnaa since before anyone can remember, or anyone can remember anyone remembering."

"But how do they become storytellers?" I pressed on.

"The young learn from the old," he said. "I know one storyteller who is the son of a storyteller who was the son of a storyteller."

Recalling the Hindu cosmology that says the world rests on a platform on the back of an elephant that stands on the back of a turtle that stands on the back of another turtle, and from there it is turtles all the way down, I thought, in the Djemaa el-Fnaa it is the storytellers that go all the way down.

"Are there storytellers like this in other Moroccan cities?" I continued.

"In some Berber villages," Amin replied. "But the storytellers in Marrakech are Arab, not Berber. Arabs are more educated." Being an Arab, Amin was bound to prize his own. "Some people come from far away to hear them," he went on. "When I was a boy we came in groups and listened for a long time. The stories never ended."

Maybe, I mused, that little fantasy of mine about the first storyteller was not far off.

"And what are they about?" I asked with the nagging question that had brought me back to Marrakech.

"Some are about Arab history," he began. "They tell of heroes who kill many enemies, sending their heads rolling on the ground. These make us proud of our past. But mostly they are like *The Arabian Nights*."

I jumped at this. "How so? What is the similarity exactly?"

"They tell of kings and romance and adventure and often of trickery—how a clever person can win out in the end."

"Give me some examples," I implored.

"Well, there is a story of a magic ring. Those who wear it can get anything they wish, if they know how to turn the setting just right. If they don't know this, the ring is ordinary and worth little."

"And what do they wish for?"

"Oh, first they wish for a palace, always a palace. Then often for a princess. But if they lose the ring, they can lose everything, because someone could use it against them. The adventures of the wearers of the magic ring are many."

I had earlier encountered a wood-carver in the medina who must have known such a tale. Fetching a little wooden box and cradling it close to me, he had confided that it was unlike any other. Carefully he had slid one panel up and another down, twisted a segment around, pulled out a hidden drawer, fingered inside for an imperceptible handle and lifted a tiny door. "Here is a secret chamber," he had whispered, "where you can hide your magic key."

"What magic key?" had come my retort. "What if I don't have one?"

"Everyone has a magic key," he had said with a wink.

The story of the magic ring and the ingenuity of the box for the magic key revealed anew the penchant in this culture for secrets and wishes, trickery and enchantment. Objects of all kinds are devices of concealment, women's veils and garden walls, jewel boxes and finger rings—all masks of appearance and enticements to fantasy and imagined possibilities.

"I have also heard a story of the chess player," Amin went on. "The chess player challenges the king to a game. If he wins, the king must grant him anything in the kingdom. If he loses, he must yield his freedom to the king. But to win he must capture every square of the chess board, covering it with kernels of wheat. He knows all the tricks of the game. Even better, he distracts the king with stories of his adventures, like Scheherazade in *The Arabian Nights*. So he wins. Then he demands a palace."

Of course! I thought. Games and tricks and stories, the natural companions of secrets and magic. As Amin had said, the tales in the Djemaa el-Fnaa are indeed like *The Arabian Nights*: they not only imagine wondrous possibilities, they also teach the "art of discourse" and how to "detect deception," highly valued truths and skills in a world of concealment and marvels.

"Many of the stories are about journeys," Amin resumed. "They tell of hardships and terrors, but they all end in the victory of the hero. Like the one about the young man who travels throughout the world looking for a magic flower to cure a princess of a mysterious disease. He must go into dangerous caverns and across snowy mountains and fight horrible creatures and terrible villains. It is a story that can go on forever. But always the young man conquers whatever threatens him, sometimes by bravery, sometimes by cunning. He learns a lot, too. He learns how to survive in wild nature and how to outwit enemies. And he gets the flower and saves the princess."

In the Djemaa el-Fnaa, Amin pointed out a storyteller telling a similar story. "He is speaking many languages, playing the parts of every character he meets on the journey. He is also very philosophical, telling how the hero has to be clever to escape dangers on his way."

"These stories of journeys resemble the *Odyssey* of Homer," I remarked.

"Yes," he said, "but they are also different. These heroes live in a world of miraculous things, and they know that they cannot prevail without Allah. He helps them if He wishes. You see," he explained pensively, "we are what you Americans might think of as a superstitious people. We believe that everything happens according to Allah's will. And Allah can will anything. So, since we do not know Allah's will, we often say *In Sha'Allah*, if God wills it—sort of like you say 'good luck,' but with more conviction." He smiled.

In Sha'Allah. No story in the Djemaa el-Fnaa can be told without it. But, as I kept returning to learn more, no two of my "informants" gave quite the same version of the stories told there. Amin was the best educated and most articulate of them, but others also shed light on the storytellers—and on themselves and their world.

"The stories are about animals and magic," said one of the several Abdullahs I met.

"They are about romance," said Rashid, with a glint in his eye.

"They are about Muhammad and the Qur'an," said Abdul, with

assurance. And he insisted that the stories do not just acknowledge the will of Allah, they revolve entirely around it and Islam.

"They all tell of Muhammad's life and his victories," he declared, "and about the Qur'an and the *Shari'a* [Islamic law or way of life], and about how Allah's enemies will all be slain and believers will go to Paradise."

"Don't they tell of romance and adventure and trickery, like *The Arabian Nights*?" I blurted.

"No," he replied emphatically. And he proceeded to identify one after another of these Qur'anic storytellers in the Djemaa el-Fnaa, Arabic texts spread before some of them, their audiences in hushed attention. But I wondered if he could be telling me only what he wanted me to hear.

"Aren't these really teachers, not storytellers?" I asked.

"They are all the same," was his pat answer.

Perhaps Abdul was right. Islamic storytellers and teachers are the same, or at least they are difficult to separate, as it has been from the beginning. I put the question to Hatim, a cultured Casablancan who had lived in New York and Los Angeles and now resided in Marrakech.

"What stories do the storytellers tell in the Djemaa el-Fnaa? Are they all about Islam, or are they about adventures and romance and so on?"

"I don't believe in storytellers," he snapped. "Some people do, but they are fools."

Taken aback, I responded, "What does it mean to *believe* in storytellers?"

"It means to believe that storytellers tell the truth. But they don't. They just invent things." Hatim was an orthodox Muslim like Abdul. The Qur'an was his truth, and he accepted its judgment of storytellers as liars who "mislead from the way of God." "To understand the Qur'an is very difficult," he continued. "You must know Arabic well. But people want things to be easy, so they listen to storytellers and believe their lies about Allah and everything."

The words of Rushdie, Achebe, and Vargas Llosa echoed in my mind: "What good is a story that isn't even true?"—"There is no story that is not true."—"That, anyway, is what I have learned." And it occurred to me that Islamic storytellers do indeed have an unusual relation to truth. For whether their stories are about the Qur'an or not, those stories tell of a world guided by Allah's will, and about what might have been and what might yet be in that world. There can be no other subject or mere secular invention. To Muslims like Hatim stories or narrative creations are misleading, even pernicious. And they should not be believed. But to others, stories are at once entertainment and instruction in the possible ways of Allah's universe. As the narrator of *The Arabian Nights* says at the outset: "It is related—but God alone knows. . . ."

Back I went with Hatim to the Djemaa el-Fnaa to get his account of the storytellers in action. We first came upon an animated figure crouched on the ground surrounded by a crowd. "He is talking about life and suffering," Hatim explained, "and how he learned about it." Hatim hesitated. "Oh, he is only a medicine seller. Never mind him."

We elbowed our way toward another gathering around yet another earnest talker. A murky adventure seemed to be unfolding. Then . . . more medicine! The talker had found a secret cure, for what Hatim could not discern. As we moved away, I recalled the story of the magic flower, and I suspected that it was believed, and probably purveyed by medicine sellers.

The medicine sellers were many in the Djemaa el-Fnaa that evening, carrying on like snake-oil salesmen in the American Old West. And their narrative performances were not readily distinguishable from those of the Qur'anic teachers and storytellers. But then neither were those of the spice merchants who lured buyers with reports of distant places and the salutary properties of the spices.

There was also an animated musician, whom Hatim identified only by the stringed instrument lying beside him. He was, Hatim explained, dramatically depicting the history of the music he was going to play and sing and the sad import of the song's lyrics. Singers and minstrels have ever been the twins of storytellers. Homer was a singing poet. In Australia, as Bruce Chatwin recorded in the *The Songlines*, songs set forth the original narrative and mnemonic images of the earth, describing the landscape and guiding aboriginals across it. In the Djemaa el-Fnaa, the musicians and storytellers no doubt descend from shared pre-Islamic forebears, and draw upon both pre-Islamic and Islamic traditions in plying their trades.

We left the musician talking his way toward his song and passed a crowd laughing at a pair of comedians, one rigged up in donkey's ears. "They are playing the parts of master and servant," Hatim said, "and making fun of people from different places."

From there we moved on to a large group encircling a character shouting and leaping. "He's telling them about a very bad man who was cruel to everyone," Hatim observed. "This guy taught himself to fight against the bad man with his fists. Eventually he defeated the man and drove him from the village. See his boxing gloves? He is going to fight that fellow over there," Hatim pointed to a youth cowering histrionically. "They are only boxers. You won't be interested." We turned away. Darkness was descending, and the crowds were growing so dense we could hardly move. It was time to leave.

Pushing through the jostling hordes, Hatim led me to a café on the edge of the square, where we passed through an unassuming doorway, climbed a long flight of stairs, and stepped outside onto a broad veranda. Below us lay the Djemaa el-Fnaa, stretching out for acres and roiling with activity. Smoke curled up from dozens of fires where food was being prepared—lamb, chicken, fish, vegetables, snails, couscous, and all the cornucopia of Moroccan dishes being consumed by hungry eaters at makeshift tables. Acrobats were turning somersaults. Fire-eaters were tossing torches and swallowing their flames. Snake charmers were banging drums and blowing pipes to coax their serpents to sway. Musicians were talking and singing and playing instruments. Magicians were making things disappear and reappear. Comedians and boxers were acting out their staged routines. Monkeys tethered to their trainers were bounding about and posing for tourists. Medicine sellers and spice merchants and countless others were enticing potential buyers. Qur'anic teachers were instructing votaries.

And the storytellers. Here and there I could see them vigorously speaking and gesturing amidst captivated audiences. But from the café veranda, I could not with assurance distinguish them from the other performers and merchants. Then it dawned on me that in the Djemaa el-Fnaa it's not just teachers and storytellers who are the much the same, as Abdul had said. The teachers, the performers, the merchants and the rest are all storytellers of a kind. For they all embellish their activities with narratives: fanciful histories, fabulous adventures, wondrous promises, Qur'anic extrapolations, images of marvelous possibilities. The Djemaa el-Fnaa is not just a marketplace with storytellers. It is *a marketplace of storytelling*, an arena of narrative ingenuity where the storyteller's "art of discourse" pervades everything, and where storytellers themselves have their most exemplary home.

As I looked across the swarming Djemaa el-Fnaa for the last time, its fires and lights glowing in the deepening dusk, the Koutoubia minaret silhouetted in the distance, I thought again of how this place invokes the origins of civilization: the city square where buying and selling, performing and mingling, teaching and storytelling create society.

Then my eye caught something I had not noticed before. And it brought me back to the moment. Along the roofs of the medina stood an array of metal rods perched at all angles. Looking more closely, I recognized what they were—television antennas. How anachronistic they seemed. How wrong in this timeless place. And I asked myself: Do they betoken a decline in the exuberant culture—for that is what it is—of the Djemaa el-Fnaa? Do they foreshadow the end of the storytellers of Marrakech? A melancholy thought.

No culture has stayed the same once those rods have risen in its sky, luring people from public activity to private diversion.

But maybe not. Perhaps the Djemaa el-Fnaa and its storytellers will not wholly succumb to the seductions of modernity. For what other place serves such a variety of spirited human interactions and—thanks to Islam and, albeit ironically, its storytellers—is so alive with the imagination of possibility? I would like to think that the Djemaa el-Fnaa and the storytellers of Marrakech will endure, exemplifying as they do the benign interplay of urban life and the vitality of culture itself. They might even outlive television. But that, *In Sha'Allah*, will be another story.

A previous version of this essay was originally published in *The Sewanee Review*, Fall, 1996.

Tales

Raffles Hotel, Singapore

Raffles

Stuart Murphy swung his car onto the highway, joining the daily throng into the city. Horns honked. Fumes swirled. Traffic crawled. He peered emptily through the windshield.

"The world is too much with us," he sighed, "late and soon, getting and spending, we lay waste our powers."

Stuart knew his Wordsworth. And cherished nice literary phrases. A middle-aged former literature professor, he was driving from his Scarsdale home to the office in New York City where he now edited scholarly books and *The Journal of European Literary Traditions*. Favorite lines of literature often got him through the day, punctuating the tedium of work—reading dull manuscripts, writing dull letters.

"But what did Wordsworth know about the world being 'too much with us'?" he mused, oblivious to the sea of cars ebbing and flowing around him. The question stirred his professorial imagination, and he went on earnestly: "Wordsworth's world was so much simpler than ours. And yet it had so much more—what?—weight to it. Everything nowadays is so ephemeral. Novelty. Fashion. Celebrity. They're all our world cares about. It's all so . . . inconsequential."

These complaints were not new to Stuart. They were kind of a litany. But today they struck him harder than usual. He went on, talking to himself: "People used to care about real things. History. Society. Philosophy. Literature. They knew their literary lines, too. Clichés, maybe. But who today even knows what a good literary cliché is?" Stuart paused to absorb the idea. "A good cliché, a really good cliché," he continued, pleased with his unfolding insight, "is more than a worn-out phrase or a bit of familiar movie dialogue. It's more like an epiphany. It reveals, or at any rate reminds us of, something every time we hear it."

The blaring horns of cars behind him jolted Stuart out of his meditations. He propelled the car forward, lost his train of thought, and, after a mentally vacant drive and habitually parking his car in the usual garage, arrived at his office bracing for another day of routine. Closing the door behind him, he sat down at his desk, leaned back in his chair, and again let his mind drift.

"I would prefer not to."

The passively defiant words of Melville's Bartleby rose to Stuart's lips. He chuckled.

"Now, that is a *good* cliché. A life-affirming idea. It signals something important."

The words took hold of him.

"I would prefer not to," he repeated. "And maybe," Stuart whispered through clenched teeth, "I won't! I'll just walk away. Go someplace where the world isn't 'too much with us.' But where?"

I could just get in the car and drive, he thought. But that would be no change. Europe? No. That's too commonplace. It has to be farther away. The other side of the world.

Hong Kong? Too commercial.

Bangkok? Lethal traffic.

Bali? Tourists.

Singapore? The sound appealed. And so did the image formed by fiction and movies. The Crossroads of the Orient, and all of that. "But it's modern now," Stuart reflected. "And it's got a repressive political regime. Still, it is as far away as I could go. And there's a great old hotel where famous authors have stayed."

But could I really do it? he asked himself. Can I really leave? Just like that, if only for a while?

He had no family. Only a career. But what, he questioned dismissively, is that? He also had enough investments to live on for a while if he needed to. That emboldened him.

Within the month, Stuart Murphy was on his way. The twenty-four hour flight through Tokyo left him drained. Even so, as the plane touched down, he felt exhilarated. He was on the other side of the world.

"Welcome to Singapore," came the pleasing voice on the plane's loud speaker. "The local time is 6:00 p.m."

Stuart had heard that Changi airport is perhaps the best in the world—large, clean, efficient. But he was not prepared for the futuristic setting that greeted him.

Vast expanses of glistening cleanliness. No crowds. Polite service personnel. An electric monorail to whisk him from the plane to the baggage claim where the bags were already waiting. It was not exactly exotic. But it felt fine.

The drive into town flowed peacefully along a wide uncrowded highway through a lush and manicured landscape. The calm and beauty were idyllic.

Then the city came into view. Stuart's heart sank. It looked like Seattle. Or Houston. If not New York. A skyline of towering mirrored-glass buildings designed by Western architects.[*]

____

[*] Singapore would in time get some more fanciful and even grandiose architecture in the Marina Bay section.

My God! he thought. Did I make a mistake?

Once in the urban maze, the taxi soon wheeled into the broad driveway of Raffles Hotel. The hotel looked strikingly like the photographs taken a century earlier, not long after the hotel opened in the 1880s—the gracefully ornate three-story Victorian façade distinctively angled at each end toward the entrance and capped by a classical pediment in the center, with a broad welcoming portico stretching across the front. But the hotel had recently been restored to appear almost new, pristine, and whiter than snow. Remembering that in the early photographs Raffles had stood on the harbor, Stuart surveyed the scene. No harbor. Only glass-and-steel behemoths surrounding the picturesque nineteenth-century hotel like predators closing in on a prey. They had pushed the harbor out of sight.

Spurning the blight, Stuart turned toward the hotel's imperial entrance, where a resplendent red carpet, extending from there to the driveway, glowed against the white surroundings, and where liveried doormen were poised at attention. They drew open the doors, and he strode into the lobby. The red carpet led across a bright marble floor to an imposing mahogany staircase. An atrium rose with the stairs and its landings to the height of the building. From the base of the stairway to the walls he saw, to his delight, the chairs and tables, flowers and potted palms of the "Authors' Lounge," which had long enticed visitors for refreshment amidst the ghosts of renowned guests like Joseph Conrad, Noël Coward, and Somerset Maugham—especially Somerset Maugham, who, so the hotel liked to imply, had made Raffles an Asian retreat, even if he had visited only once. Stuart knew all about them. He began to feel that he had come to the right place after all.

"Greetings, Mr. Murphy," said the desk clerk graciously. "We have been expecting you. The Somerset Maugham Suite is ready as you requested."

He signed the register and followed the bellboy outside along a covered corridor encircling a courtyard. The heat now hit him for the first time. Heavy, wet, tropical heat that evoked images of explorers slashing through jungles and colonial bureaucrats sweatily conducting the affairs of empire. He liked that.

They reached their destination. "Somerset Maugham Suite," read the plaque on the door. "This was Mr. Somerset Maugham's suite when he stayed here," announced the bellboy with a smile. Stuart doubted the claim considering the passage of time and periodic renovations, but that didn't bother him. The bellboy undid the latch. Stuart stepped into a small sitting room as cool as mountain air. A chilled ice bucket holding a bottle of champagne rested on a dining table beside a bowl of tropical fruit. An archway opened from there into a spacious room where oriental carpets lay on a dark hardwood floor leading to a massive bed at the far end. A ceiling fan rotated noiselessly. Photographs of Somerset Maugham hung on the wall. Nearby stood a desk and a bookcase studiously arrayed with Maugham's books and some memorabilia.

Stuart tipped the bellboy, who quietly vanished. He approached the desk, fingering its surface, and sat down in its worn leather chair. He picked up a sheet of stationery and read the letterhead: "Raffles Hotel. Somerset Maugham Suite."

Stuart smiled, drank in the atmosphere, and thought, "Yes. I have escaped."

He sat there for a while then went to the bed and lay down, his yearning to explore the hotel fighting with his exhaustion. Exhaustion won out, and he dozed off. But it was a brief victory. Abetted by thirst and hunger, the yearning to explore reasserted itself. Opening the hotel information guide, Stuart noticed an entry for the Long Bar, birthplace of the Singapore Sling. Perfect.

A winding stairway on the far side of the hotel delivered Stuart to a barroom that could have been a stage set for a 1940s movie set in Singapore—smoky air, rattan furniture, ceiling fans, cages of tropical birds, languorous patrons sipping tall fruit-adorned beverages. Stuart sank into a chair along the wall and ordered a Singapore Sling. It came in no time, and was gone just as fast, the sharpness of the gin enfolded in pink sweetness. He ordered another. Feeling the spirit of the place, he craned to hear what other patrons were saying. The indistinctness of their covert voices fed his curiosity.

The second drink went down as easily as the first. And then a third. The room began to grow a bit hazy, the figures in it distant, the sounds of voices, the clinking of glasses, the squawking of the caged birds, grew muffled. It was all taking on an air of unreality.

"No. This *is* reality," Stuart assured himself. "A fiction come to life. All that Somerset Maugham and Hollywood movies had portrayed. The old Singapore, where intrigues were hatched, liaisons were hidden, and forlorn souls came to lose themselves. It's delicious."

Delicious. The word awakened Stuart from his reveries. Hunger gripped him. Recalling the hotel's Tiffin Room, where, he had heard, you could get the best Indian food in southeast Asia, he signed the check and went out into the night. The air was torpid and fragrant. Stuart breathed it in voluptuously as he made his way through the palms and hibiscus.

The Tiffin Room's lights radiated welcomingly through the windows, beckoning Stuart like a moth to a flame. Entering, he was engulfed in the scents of curry and countless other spices rising from the buffet of pakoras and samosas, chutneys and naans, biryanis and kormas. He piled his plate high, seated himself beneath a fan near gently wafting palm fronds, ordered an Indian beer, and feasted. As he scanned the room, he was amused to see other patrons dressed in their natty whites playing the role of colonials, casually snapping their fingers to summon the crisply uniformed and obedient waiters.

A colonial theme park, he said to himself. That's what Raffles is. Renovated to recapture the past as pictured by writers and movie makers and tourists. And yet possibly better than the original.

By the time Stuart returned to his room he was drifting along blissfully on the sensation that he had found the world he had been looking for. He stretched out on the bed and reached for a volume of Maugham's stories on the night table. Flipping through its pages, he paused at "Rain." He knew it well. The tale of Sadie Thompson, a harlot from Hawaii who seduces a scolding Christian missionary in Samoa and drives him to suicide. The tropics had vanquished the missionary's repressions—and him.

Thumbing farther he came to "The Fall of Edward Barnard." Stuart had read it years ago, and it still resonated in his memory. Now he followed its tale of a young man who abandons a promising commercial career and a fiancée in Chicago for the seductive allure and delectable idleness of Tahiti. A friend seeks him out to save him. But the friend fails. Edward Barnard will not go home. *"You can't think with what zest I look forward to life,"* Edward explains, amidst *"the infinite variety of the sea and the sky, the freshness of the dawn and the beauty of the sunset, and the rich magnificence of the night."* Stuart lingered over the story's closing line, ruefully spoken by Edward's fiancée back in Chicago when she learns of his decision to turn his back on the future he might have had: *"Poor Edward."*

"Poor Edward, indeed," Stuart thought as he smiled and closed his eyes and let sleep sweetly overcome him.

Stuart got up the next day still fatigued from jet lag. But breakfast in the courtyard outside his suite energized him, and he set out to see the old Singapore.

"Bugis Street," he instructed the taxi driver, naming the street where generations of male travelers had sampled the bawdy pleasures of the exotic East.

"And I'd like to see the Arab quarter."

"Very good," said the driver in barely accented English.

They drove through block after block of new office buildings. Pedestrians in Western business clothes crowded the sidewalks. A modern city on its way to work. But something seemed odd. The traffic. There were actually few cars on the streets. No honking horns.

"Where is all the traffic?" he asked.

"Restricted zone," came the reply. "At certain times of the day you have to pay a fee to drive into the center of the city."

The driver pointed to a permit attached to his windshield. "You get one of these when you enter the zone. The government does this to keep traffic out."

Stuart wondered if that would work in New York and doubted it. The car pulled to the curb at a roadside police station, where an official removed the temporary permit. Above them an arch spanned the wide avenue, emblazoned with the words: "Restricted Zone."

"The government is very strict," the driver continued as they resumed the trip beyond the city center. "But people benefit. The streets are clean. The schools are good. Everyone owns their own apartment, with government help. We all save money. And there is no crime. How can anyone live in America," he added, "with so much crime and violence?"

Taking the bait, Stuart spoke up, drawing on his newspaper knowledge of Singapore. "But are you free to do and say what you want? Here you can be put in jail for all kinds of things, can't you, even for just buying chewing gum or dropping paper on the street or criticizing the government? And you can get officially caned for an adolescent prank."

"You Americans have strange ideas of freedom," the driver responded soberly. "Here we are free to live a good life in safety and to have respect for authority and for everyone. In America you are free to show disrespect for everything and to be poor and to be robbed or killed. Who is better off?"

Stuart sat back in silence thinking of New York City where crimes can occur every few minutes and random bullets can strike down children at play. Maybe you can invent a world, he said to himself. Just as Raffles is a colonial theme park, Singapore is an urban theme park, a perfectly ordered city. An adult Disneyland with people living in it. What kind of freedom is there in Disneyland, anyway?

Isn't Disneyland a model of what people think the world should be? Clean? Safe? Prosperous? Fulfilling every fantasy? And fun?

Unsure of his own conclusions, Stuart gazed through the taxi window. The modern office towers had yielded to low older buildings. The pedestrians were less Western-looking now than those earlier, but nothing he hadn't seen at home. Finally the taxi came to a stop in front of an open market. Stalls filled with oranges, pomegranates, melons, durian, and other fruits and vegetables extended far from the street.

"This is it," said the driver.

"What?"

"Bugis Street."

"This? What do you mean? It's just a marketplace."

"The old Bugis Street was torn down," explained the driver. "The government didn't like it because it attracted trouble. Now it's a market for everyone."

"There is nothing here to see," Stuart said disappointedly, having anticipated an exotic locale of hidden pleasures. "Let's go to the Arab quarter."

"Oh, you have seen that already. We drove through on the way here. Muslims were selling goods on the sidewalk. You want to go back to the mosque?"

"No." Stuart had seen mosques. He had hoped for an ethnic enclave with picturesque native customs. "Let's go to the Chinese quarter."

"OK."

The taxi went off toward the other side of the city, circling the Restricted Zone on a broad avenue that rolled through residential neighborhoods and landscaped hillsides. Eventually they turned down a narrow street and entered a section of rather tawdry-looking shops. Chinese people were everywhere. The taxi eased around tight corners and came to a stop.

"This is the oldest Buddhist temple in Singapore," said the driver. "You can go in."

Climbing from the car, Stuart saw a weathered wooden doorway squeezed within a block of shops. Through it he could see an open courtyard clouded with incense. He stepped inside tentatively. Votaries were performing their obeisances here and there, and Buddhist priests were conducting rites. A few tourists were viewing artifacts of Buddhist piety. Stuart sensed an atmosphere of Buddhist detachment from the world, the temple an island of contemplation and transcendence—except for the intrusion of tourists.

Outside again, raising his eyes to the sky above, Stuart caught sight of dragons curling from the corners of the temple roof toward the heavens, warding off evil spirits. They signaled the confidence of faith and the endurance of tradition. Then beyond the dragons, Stuart's eyes focused on other forms. The skyscrapers of modern Singapore rose just blocks away, piercing the heavens with indifferent secularity and overwhelming all around. Against this backdrop, the temple dragons' soaring defiance of evil fell into a theatrical gesture, a quaint dumb show.

Could any Buddhist believe in the efficacy of temple dragons after seeing this? he wondered.

"How old is this temple?" Stuart asked one of the priests who was doubling as a guide.

"It is the oldest in Singapore," he answered proudly. "A hundred and fifty years."

"But Buddhism is many hundreds of years old," Stuart retorted. "Weren't there Buddhists here before that?"

"Who knows? Before the British came there were only fishermen."

"Uh, huh," Stuart responded uncertainly.

Maybe that is the clue to Singapore, he thought. It's not an Asian city at all. It has no history before the British. It's a colonial city. A creation of old Stamford Raffles himself, who, as Stuart knew from his tourist researches, had established a British outpost around 1820. So Raffles Hotel is almost as historic and authentic as anything here." Gratified, if a tinge disillusioned, at this discovery, Stuart returned to the taxi.

"Is there a *real* Singapore?" he asked the driver.

"What do you mean?"

"I mean what Singapore really is. The essence of it."

"That is probably Orchard Road," the driver replied with a hint of hesitation.

"Let's go there."

Back again onto the wide avenues. Up and down the rolling manicured hills. In twenty minutes they arrived at the top of a busy commercial thoroughfare.

"Orchard Road," announced the driver.

Stuart's eyes took in the *real* Singapore. Garish hotels and glittery shopping malls, chrome storefronts and neon signs, movie theaters and fast food outlets lined the street as far as Stuart could see.

"You can buy anything here," the driver boasted. "Clothes. Jewelry. Carpets. Cameras. Televisions. Cars. Anything. Do you want to get out and walk?"

"No," Stuart sighed. "I think I'll just go back to the hotel. 'The world is too much . . .'" he grumbled.

Back at Raffles, Stuart closed the door of his suite behind him with relief. The coolness and quiet isolation were a balm. He poured a drink and stretched out on the bed. The overhead fan softly stirred the air with its silent, hypnotic rotations. Taking up the Maugham volume again, he let it fall open to any page. *"I was in Pagan, in Burma,"* the narrator of the story "Mabel" began, *"and from there I took the steamer to Mandalay."* Stuart was again in the world he had come to find. That mood went with him to the Tiffin Room for dinner. Then he returned to read more tales of colonial South Seas adventures.

He could not remember just when he fell asleep, but when he awoke the next day he could hear the sound of rain on the leaves outside. It was a comforting sound, assuring him that he could avoid the "real world" for a while.

"I'll just stay in the hotel today," he decided firmly.

After ordering breakfast he studied the hotel plan again to chart an itinerary. Restaurants. Shops. Pool. Bar. The usual.

But what's this? he exclaimed silently. A museum? A hotel museum? That could be intriguing.

Breakfast arrived promptly, served on the parlor table from where Stuart watched the rain outside. It was coming down so densely that he could hardly make out the main wing of the hotel across the courtyard. And yet it was more gentle than harsh.

Ah, good tropical rain, he said to himself. Drenching, maybe, but soft and warm. Not like the claustrophobic and foreboding downpours of Maugham's "Rain."

After finishing the mangoes and croissants, Stuart left for the museum. The rain had eased some, and the canopied corridor sheltered him while letting the moisture permeate the air. It led him past hotel shops—Oriental antiques, Asian carpets, tropical attire, dozens of others—until it took him up a flight of stairs to Raffles Museum. Walking in, he found himself amidst memorabilia of Singapore's history as an outpost of empire and a stopping place for wayfarers. Photographs, decals, correspondence, newspapers, as well as emblems of other colonial hotels which, along with Raffles, had "civilized" the East for Western travelers long ago—the Oriental in Bangkok, the Grand in Rangoon, the Continental in Saigon, the Peninsula in Hong Kong, the Cathay in Shanghai.

Those were the days, he thought as he examined the artifacts. The days of real travel, when the East was far away.

A framed newspaper story caught his eye. "Tiger Shot at Raffles," blazoned the headline of *The Straits Times*. The year was 1902. He leaned forward to read the harrowing account in the mock melodramatic style of the day:

A day or two ago, Stripes, a tiger belonging to a native show broke from captivity and to all intents and purposes disappeared. The watchman alleges that the tiger interviewed him and after giving him

A Few Friendly Scratches

made off, presumably swimming gaily up the Singapore river. From this point he was missed until the closing hour of the Raffles Billiard Room last night when, Lo and Behold! he stared through the veranda railing of the Billiard Room and gave the bar "boy" a stiff shock. This was rather

Too Much For The "Boy"

who promptly secluded himself and awaited developments. Finding the tiger did not seek a personal interview with him, the "boy" stealthily emerged, and "scooted!", hurried by sundry scratches from under the floor beneath the billiard table. Mr. Phillips of Raffles Institution was roused from his bed and, taking his rifle, proceeded to the scene of the action

In His Pajamas.

The tiger was still under the floor. There was no doubt about that. Yet no amount of peering into the gloom could discover his presence. At last the hunters got sight of the tiger. That is to say, they

Saw His Eyes Gleaming.

Mr. Phillips put one of those nasty hollow-nosed bullets right between the pair of eyes, and Stripes laid down and died

Dead As A Nail.

A museum note somberly reported that this was the last tiger killed in Singapore.

A rather sad story, Stuart thought. Hardly fair to poor Stripes. But he liked its style. And the museum. He bought some reproductions of old photographs and some luggage stickers and went to find the Billiard Room where the historic Stripes had met his doom.

The rain had picked up again and was now coming down in sheets. Stuart was glad. It gave him a pleasant feeling of tropical isolation.

Shortly after leaving the museum, he passed before a shop window where a male mannequin stood in a dashing white double-breasted linen suit and white fedora adorned with an aqua colored band. He eyed his own nondescript American outfit and said, "I must have it."

A few minutes later, Stuart Murphy emerged transformed. The suit, the hat, a silky white shirt, a floral tie, and woven leather shoes made him into a character out of the stories and old movies he adored. In his late fifties, slender and a bit over six feet tall but slightly stooped, his aging faced lined more from thought than from experience, Stuart now floated along the corridor with a newborn panache. Admiring his reflection in the shop windows, he was all he imagined himself to be. A man of the world, thriving on adventure and alive with exotic tales of his own to tell.

He found the fabled Bar and Billiard Room standing a few yards from the main building near the front. It had not changed since the early photographs—or it had been changed back again.

"I would like to sit near the billiard table, if I may," he asked the waiter with decorous politeness. They circled around the bar to the far end of the room. There stood the table, its green felt gaming area brightly lit against the rich dark wood of the room. Shuttered windows let in a soft illumination from the gray day outside. Rain pelted the roof.

Stuart sat down and ordered a drink, conjuring up visions of the hapless tiger and the ferocious hunter in his pajamas who had made history here. Not world history, but history all the same.

Looking around the warm convivial room, he saw the usual tourists and businessmen who had made modern Singapore an economic boom town. Yet they all seemed rather like bit characters in the drama he was living. He felt at home. He belonged here more than they did.

The rain continued intermittently for days. Stuart stayed in the hotel.

Finally, the weather changed. Stuart did not leave.

A week went by. Then another. Stuart stayed on. He was often seen in the public rooms. The Long Bar. The Tiffin Room. The Bar and Billiard Room. The Authors' Lounge. The Museum. The shops. His white suit and fedora became a familiar sight. As did the dog-eared copies of Somerset Maugham that seemed an inseparable part of his attire.

Most of the staff came to know and like him. He was always polite. And he left good tips.

"Good morning, sir. What will you be doing today?"

"Oh, I think I'll just stay in and do some reading."

"Good afternoon, sir. What are you reading today? More of the same?"

"Ah, yes."

"Good evening, sir. Will you be with us much longer?"

"Indeed, I will."

One morning as Stuart was preparing for another of these irresistibly repetitious days, the telephone rang.

"Good morning, sir. This is the manager. I am calling about your bill. I am afraid your credit card will no longer the accept charges. I'm sure there is some mistake that can easily be cleared up. Would you be so good as to arrange to settle your current bill which, as you know, we must process from time to time for long-term guests, and arrange for future payments to be made so that we can continue to provide you services?"

"Good heavens!" Stuart exclaimed. "I am terribly sorry. I don't know how this could have happened. I will take care of it immediately."

Stuart promptly sent a message to his accountant, who handled his financial affairs, in New York: "Please wire me $100,000 at once and see that my credit card charges are covered from now on. Do whatever you must.—SM"

The transaction completed, Stuart informed the hotel manager that everything would be straightened out within a day or two. He apologized again, then he lay down on the bed and reached for Maugham.

When the money came, accompanied by a laconic note from the accountant—"What the hell are you doing?!"—Stuart paid his balance and assured the manager that there would be no further misunderstandings.

More weeks went by. He had to move from the Somerset Maugham Suite occasionally to accommodate other guests who had booked it long in advance, but he always came back. And he gave no thought to the cost.

His accountant did. Communications from him to Stuart became more urgent and exasperated.

"Your resources are dwindling. Come to your senses!! I take no responsibility for the consequences!"

"Just do what I ask!—SM"

"The cash is nearly gone. What are you going to do?! Are you crazy!"

"Sell! Stocks. The art collection. The house. The car. Everything. It means nothing to me!—SM."

All the while, Stuart never strayed from Raffles.

But a change was coming over him. He receded almost completely from the world outside the hotel's walls. He never read a newspaper or a magazine. He wandered the hotel, sometimes exploring undiscovered precincts, sometimes aimlessly. And he would sit for hours in the Authors' Lounge reading Maugham and watching people passing through the lobby.

In time, the change took another turn. Stuart evermore thought of himself as a great traveler and wanted to share his adventures. Tentatively at first, then with accumulating confidence, he would collar waiters, linger with shop keepers, and even approach hotel guests as if to offer a confidence. Once he had their ear, he would tell them of his exploits and of the peculiar characters he had known.

"When I was in Chiang Mai before the war," he might whisper to a waiter, "I knew a man not unlike that one over there," pointing to a lone diner hunched over his plate at a neighboring table. "He wanted to sell me his business there because his wife had run off with a missionary and he wanted to leave. I declined, knowing how bad luck clings to things in the Orient. He died soon after that from an excess of opium."

And drawing close to a guest in the Authors' Lounge or the Long Bar he would tell of intrigues in Jakarta and loves in Papeete, of mysteries in Denpasar and discoveries in Calcutta, of dangers in Macau and seductions in Shanghai. Listeners usually grew curious. Some would relate incidents of their own. In time, they would excuse themselves and drift away.

Eventually, Stuart added another feature to his behavior. He started to write. At first he appeared to be idly penning letters. Then his concentration deepened. With heated intensity he began filling page after page of stationery from the Somerset Maugham Suite. The waiters could not have failed to notice.

"You write a lot these days, sir," one of them observed while serving him a drink in the Authors' Lounge. "If I may ask, are you writing a book?"

"Oh," Stuart replied, "I am writing about many things, places I have been, people I have known. Human nature is so peculiar, you know. Let me tell you about a time when I was in Kathmandu. . . ."

"Uh, excuse me sir," interrupted the waiter, "I am being called."

Stuart picked up his pen again. *"Kathmandu in winter,"* he began, *"was the perfect place for a hunted man to hide. . . ."*

As more time went by, Stuart steeped himself ever deeper in his work. Each day brought a new outpouring of creative energy. The pages piled up. His life brimmed with purpose. And he moved among his hotel haunts with a manner mingling authorial curiosity with preoccupied distraction. Meanwhile, his white suit grew yellowed and wrinkled, his fedora stained and floppy.

Early one morning a knock came at his door at the Maugham Suite. Stuart opened it.

"Mr. Murphy. I am the manager."

"Ah, yes. How nice of you to visit," Stuart responded cordially and invited him into the sitting room. The manager declined to sit saying this was not a social call.

"Mr. Murphy," the manager went on rather sternly, "I'm afraid you have another unpaid bill. And all of your credit cards appear to have been canceled. The accountant you told me to telephone whenever I needed to do so informed me he no longer represents you because, well, you have exhausted your funds."

"I beg your pardon?" Stuart reacted with a puzzled expression.

"Mr. Murphy," the manager repeatedly emphatically, "you evidently cannot settle your account anymore, and you seem to have no one to assist you. And quite frankly, Mr. Murphy, I regret to tell you that you have become . . . something of an embarrassment to the hotel. I have no choice but to tell you that you must leave Raffles."

"Oh, there is some mistake," Stuart said with assurance. "You are looking for someone else. Surely you know me. Somerset Maugham. My name and initials and books are everywhere. You see." He pointed to the plaque on the door: "Somerset Maugham Suite." And he displayed the SM sown into the frayed cuffs of his shirt and engraved on the cuff links clasping them. He went into the bedroom and displayed the similarly marked luggage stacked in a closet. "And here are my books." He gestured toward the desk and the bookcase full of them. "I would be happy to autograph one for you, if you would like. After all," he went on, "I do a lot of my writing at Raffles. On my personal stationery." He plucked a sheet of it from the desk and brought it to the manager.

The manager started to protest Stuart's behavior then thought better of it. After a pause, he simply said, "I will look into the matter further. Forgive me for disturbing you."

Stuart closed the door satisfied and prepared for another day of work and meandering. He made a feeble attempt to straighten his suit, donned his disheveled hat, gathered up a batch of stationery and a book of Maugham's stories and departed for the Authors' Lounge.

He settled into his usual chair advantageously situated at a small table in a corner from where he could view the comings and goings of hotel guests. It belonged to his home now. Placing the stationery on the table, he leaned back and let the book fall open in front of him. The pages fanned. He looked down as they rested at the story "Honolulu."

"The wise traveler travels only in imagination."

Stuart knew this opening line well. He often thought of it. He could almost remember writing it. He positioned some stationery, took out his pen, and began to write:

"The tramp steamer cast off as the dawn came up in a summer haze, and a blanket of stifling heat descended upon Singapore. We were headed for Pago Pago. But where didn't matter. We were on the sea again. . . ."

Stuart's concentration was broken by the voice of the bellboy: "Mr. Maugham. Paging Mr. Somerset Maugham."

Patrons in the lobby and the Authors' Lounge looked quizzically at the bellboy walking toward the odd figure in the rumpled white suit and floppy fedora sitting in the corner, his arm waving to attract the boy's attention.

"Mr. Maugham," the boy said in a hushed tone, "the manager would like to invite you to his office. Would you be so kind as to accompany me?"

"Certainly," Stuart said graciously. Maybe he wants to make up for the misunderstanding, he thought, and plan a reception for some of the guests to meet me. That's always good public relations for a hotel.

Stuart got up and, affecting an urbane air, followed the boy through the lobby. He nodded at curious guests, pleased to be known and admired. From the lobby, the boy led Stuart on a circuitous path toward the rear of the hotel. It brought them to a hallway leading to a door at the end. As they reached the door, Stuart wondered how this area had eluded his explorations before, and he concluded that the door must open into a room confined to especially important, possibly secret, meetings.

The bellboy knocked. The door opened. "Come in," the manager said graciously, as he ushered Stuart into a modest room furnished with a small desk and several rattan chairs. There, under a lazy ceiling fan in the soft light filtering through slatted blinds at the windows, officers of the Singapore police were waiting.

Seasoned tango dancers in a café, Buenos Aires, Argentina (vintage magazine photo)

Tango

My bottle of cheap *vino tinto* cast a wispy, ragged shadow over the graffiti scratched into my tiny wooden table at the Café Dorengo deep within the old San Telmo section of Buenos Aires. Shelves of empty, dust-covered wine bottles lined the neglected walls. Unwashed windows wore the grit of time; some, like the etched-glass panes of the swinging entrance doors, were pieced together with tape. Ceiling fans creaked overhead.

Yellowed light fixtures sent a sepia tint into the haze of cigarette smoke and on down upon the scarred tables and the scuffed black-and-white floor tiles. Here and there, clusters of patrons were drinking and talking. Lovers huddled in corners sharing whispers and hiding kisses. A smattering of loners like me were whiling away hours by themselves. And through the cloudy air pulsed the thin, grainy sounds of old recordings playing the aching, angry, sensual songs of the tango.

A young couple got up from their table and sidled through the chairs to an open space at the center of the room. They struck a sultry pose and stepped into the dance. Hands linked. Feet crossed. Legs entwined. Thighs pressed. They twirled apart and spun back together. Again and again. Again and again. Then they slowed and, weaving sensuously around each other back to front, front to back, they oozed off the dance floor, wended to their table, and looped balletically into their chairs. Scattered applause crackled. And a ragged voice from a nearby table said, "Tango eeess muueee pelee-groooso."

I turned to see the craggy features of an old man facing me from the next table.

"Pardone?" I stammered, trying to sound Spanish.

"Ah," he nodded, sensing an American, and leaned toward me. "Tango eeess verrree danngerrrusss."

I squinted to see him clearly. He could have been sixty years old or a hundred-and-sixty. His face carried more than lines of age. It bore shadows of a buried life and ancient sorrows. My curiosity teased, I asked what he meant about the tango.

"Tango ees no onlee danz," he rasped, his voice deep with age and years of smoking. "Some peeple say eet ees, 'sad song made eento danz.' But eet ees more. Tango ees 'La danza de amor e muerte,' says a poet, 'The danz of luv and deth.' Ees true. Tango can deestroe you." He puffed on a stumpy cigarette, and gulped from the glass of wine in front of him. He held me with his arresting, rheumy, plaintive eyes. This was a man with a story. A story he wanted to tell. And I wanted to hear it. I beckoned him closer.

"Eet beegeen heer," he confided, gathering his wine and cigarettes and dragging his chair over to my table. "Een thees café." He went on in his thick accent, but with a fluency that quickly captured me and lost to my ear almost all traces of foreignness.

"Eet wass hard times een Buenos Aires," he explained. "Leetl work. Mucho truuble. San Telmo and La Boca had riots. Wee beecame socialeests to change theengs. And wee went to cafés to dreenk and to forget, and to dreem and to danz." He paused and looked around the smoky room then leaned toward me.

"They met here one of those nights. Museecians played, over there een that corner," and he gestured with his glass. "A bandoneeon—you call it accordeeon—a violeen, a geetar, a seenger. Tango. Always tango. Not like een fancee danz halls or toureest shows today. Een those days eet was *our* museek. *Our* danz. The danz of our dreems and sadness. The danz of luv and deth.

"She came een weeth a man," he went on, picking up the thread, "and sat faceeng thees way. Her black hair gleemed een the candle light as eet fell to the shoulders of her shinee black dress. Her face een that light had the beeutee of the angels. Skeen of gold. High round cheeks. Leeps full and red, openeeng to a wide smile. Large, dark, enticeeng, and posseeblee dangeruss eyes. Madreelena was her name. But Eduardo deedn't know that then.

"Eduardo had sat alone, smokeeng, dreenkeeng, leesteneeng to tango. Then he saw her come een and watched her hair gleesen, her face glow, her leeps part to speek and smile and seep from her glass and to purss around seegarettes. Suddenlee shock and anger came over her. Eduardo heard her voice rise, and he saw her jump up, grab her glass, and throw veeno on the man, shouteeng, 'Mierda! Merrrda! Salió! Sal!! SAL!! [Sheeet! Get out!!]' The man tried to quiet her, but she ran to the bar and bent over eet, covereeng her face weeth her hands. The man followed. He spoke and touched her on the shoulder from beehind. She spun around screemeeng, 'Nunca!! Bastardo!!' and weeth an open hand slapped the side of hees face and clawed bloodee streeks down hees cheek weeth her nails. He staggered back and raised a feest to crush her. But he held back. She stood strong, deefiant. The man growled a curse and stalked out of the café.

"Eet all happened so fast that Eduardo could onlee stare. While she remained standeeng at the bar, sometheeng told heem to go to her. And that was how they met.

"Madreelena was steel hot weeth rage, but she agreed to seet and have a dreenk weeth Eduardo. She said the man had betrayed her luv, and weeth her own friend. She wanted heem to die. They drank and smoked and talked of hate and luv, heartache and pain. And leestened to the museek of their mood. They had many feeleengs to share. Many hurts and many yearneengs. Eet was veree late when Eduardo asked Madreelena to danz weeth heem. She deedn't answer. She sleed her hand across the table. He leefted her feengers weeth hees. They both rose, drew together, and slowlee stepped eento the museek.

"They moved around the leetl floor carefullee at first. But graduallee the tango freed them. Their bodees felt the rheethm, their feet found a pattern, their eyes met, then weeth a whirl they spun apart and came back een a clasp where their eyes met again more closelee. Een time the tables and chairs and voices and people around them faded away eento the smokee haze, leeveeng Madeelena and Eduardo danzeeng alone to the museek of the bandoneeon, the violeen, and the geetar, and to the seenger sobbeeng of cruel deespairs, broken hearts, tattered dreems, and tango."

In his low raspy voice, my companion softly sang:

O, my sorrowful night. . . .
I'm drowneeng een my sorrows
To try to forget your luv.

So, sell the soul
Raffle the heart
And danz the tango.
Feel the blood rise to your face
Weeth everee beet,
While an arm winds like a snake
Around a waist
About to break.
Thees ees how to danz the tango! . . .
Sad seveer tango . . .
Danz of luv and deth.

After a swallow of wine, he resumed his story. "Lost een the museek, stung by the songs, they danzed unteel the last note faded. Then, weethout word or glance, Madreelena said she had to go and sweeftlee walked away. Eduardo called out to her. She pushed through the sweengeeng glass doors to the street. But he thought he heard her say over her shoulder, 'Mañana en la noche.' 'Tomorrow night.' He started to go after her, but stopped. He knew eet would be no use.

"Eduardo waited the next night at the same table, uncertain that she would come. But she deed. The same black, gleemeeng hair. The same shinee black dress. The same gloweeng face. The same dark, enticeeng, dangeruss eyes. She stood eenside the door. He went to her. The first night repeeted eetself. Talkeeng, dreenkeeng, smokeeng. And tango. But thees time the talk was shorter, the veeno sweeter, the smoke theecker. And the tango more sure and more eentense. Eduardo led weeth a firmer hand. Madreelena did her turns and bends, ochos and boleros weeth touches of flair. They were beegeenneeng to know eech other's moves, feeleeng muscles tense, senseeng moments for feet to cross, tap, kick, and speen as they danzed feegures of their own to the pulseeng museek, while their eyes locked together more and more often, their steps queeekened, and their holds tightened as if poureeng fuel on a fire een their hearts. The café vaneeshed for them as beefore, leeveeng them alone weeth the urgent museek, and the sad songs that cut through the smokee air like poems of greef from tormented souls.

"Then eet was over. She left. And again 'mañana en la noche' echoed een Eduardo's ears. She came back the next night. And eet all happened again. The next night, too. But now their talk was leetl. The veeno went down fast. Half-smoked seegarettes burned een the tray. Eduardo and Madreelena were here to tango.

"Their earlier heseetations had deesappeered. They greepped eech other weeth strong hands, their eyes eentent, their feet knoweeng what to do. Others een the café sat back to watch. And what they saw was not just danz. It was passeeon. A passeeon made of sadness and pain, fire and lust. A passeeon the tango knows well.

"And that night, after swirleeng and keeckeeng and deeppeeng and clencheeng weeth a careless preecision and a riseeng heet, the last steps of a spinneeng, entangleeng embrace brought Madreelena's and Eduardo's faces together een a breathless keess. They held eet and eech other for seconds, like a tableau. Then they eezed apart, and, weeth the museek steel playeeng, they tangoed gracefullee through the crowd to the sweengeeng doors and went out to the street together, arm een arm.

"What happened next, onlee they could know. Peeple told manee storees about them. But notheeng is as true as what I tell you now.

"Een Madreelena's cramped room on a narrow street of San Telmo, the passeeons of their tango beecame a tango of passeeonate lust. And like their tango, there was notheeng tender een eet. They keessed weeth fire and threw themselves on eech other, wrestleeng, squeezeeng, heeveeng. It was feerce, ferocious. And ecstatic. They said notheeng, but for the sounds of excitement that sprang from their throats. Their language had beecome passeeon itself, beyond words. The passeeon of the tango, and of their flameeng deesires. When the night ended, they were no longer themselves.

"From then on, Eduardo and Madreelena came not just heer to the Café Dorengo. They went to tango bars all over Buenos Aires. The cafés of San Telmo, the dives of La Boca, the danz halls of Central where the tango was weenneeng the fashionable set. They danzed to small groups of players like heer, and to whole tango orchestras, to everee song and everee seenger, old men weeth ravaged memorees, young men weeth anguished hearts. She always wore a shinee black dress, sleek, sleet up the side; he wore black, too, peenstriped pants and an open shirt for the cafés, a suit, sometimes a hat, for the danz halls. They had leetl money. But what monee they had went to the tango.

"Before long they were known evereewhere. Not onlee beecause they danzed often. But beecause their tango was the most flamboyant, and the most dareeng. Their steps raced, their thighs twined, their heels flashed. Madreelena's tweests and keecks flared and her high leeps soared eento Eduardo's steelee catches. Hees arms leefted her like a feather and tossed her like a leef, deepped her like a flower and greepped her like a vice. Other danzers started draweeng aside when Madreelena and Eduardo took the floor. They watched and murmured that thees tango was the pure 'danz of luv and deth.'

"When Madreelena and Eduardo were by themselves, their passeeons, like their tango, possessed them weeth a mounteeng furee. Hungreelee, their bodees sought out everee sensation. The stronger the better. And the stronger the sensations beecame, the stronger they had yet to beecome. Old pleasures went numb. Old feeleengs dulled. New sensations deemanded brighter flames, hotter fire. And the violence beeneeth the surface of their tango and of their deesires beegan breakeeng through.

"You could see thees happeneeng een the bars and danz halls. Everee week Madreelena and Eduardo's movements beecame more exaggerated, the keecks higher, the speens faster, the leeps farther, the bumps harder, the deeps deeper. Cries of shock and sighs of awe burst from the crowds gathered around them as they danzed weeth an aneemal ferocitee and terreefyeeng energee that came closer and closer to catastrophe. Eet was as though they were tempteeng eech other to reeskieer threells, sharper pains, greater dangers, a contest of appetites and endurance, a mateeng danz een the wild that grows more exciteeng as eet grows more violent.

"One night, after the tango had left them more eentoxeecated than ever weeth passeeon, they went home and made a shambles of Madreelena's room, rolleeng and crasheeng about, eech clutcheeng at the other's body, pulleeng hair, scratcheeng flesh, proddeeng themselves to feel more and more and more, upendeeng chairs, crusheeng tables, shattereeng deeshes, teareeng the bed sheets, and reeppeeng the peellows, speweeng feathers eento the air to flutter down over evereetheeng, steekeeng to their soakeeng naked bodees that lay steell at last, panteeng een a queevereeng heep on the floor. They had found new heights, or depths, to their savage deelights. New freedom. New feeleengs. New exheelaration. The violence threelled them. Their passeeon was sheer erotic obsession now. Its taste a beetter-sweet eleexeer they had to dreenk. They had never felt so alive. Or so close to deth.

"The ravenous hunger was consumeeng them again when they went late one night to La Corrientes een Central. The summer's heet hung een the air. The hall was feelled weeth danzers and luvers and porteños out to see tango een a safe place. The puncheeng beet of four bandoneeons surged through the large room, while four violeens traded skeettereeng melodies weeth the bandoneeons and weeth a throbbeeng piano, all pumpeeng tango eento the air, and the blood. One after another, seengers young and old, cried their acheeng songs of pain and sorrow.

"Madreelena and Eduardo beegan circleeng slowlee around eech other, like jungle cats, their feerce, menaceeng eyes pierceeng eento eech other. Those who had seen them beefore, and many had, could tell they were entereeng a world of their own, where no one else could go, or would dare. Graduallee they moved eento their tango as eef een a slow-motion feelm, restraint addeeng tension and energee to their movements. Their entire first danz went like that, a pantomime of tango een slow motion. But you could feel the fire een eet. Like the foreplay of sex, but not tender. Never that for them. White hot. Close to exploseeon.

"Weeth everee danz their flame burned hotter and hotter, riseeng like an awakeneeng volcano, breakeeng out een veeciouslee fla-sheeng keecks, frighteneeng leeps, bruiseeng embraces. Other dan-zers backed farther and farther away, as eef to keep from getteeng singed. Step by step, spark by spark, Eduardo and Madreelena con-quered the floor unteel eet was theirs alone. The museecians played onlee for them, faster and faster the pace, louder and harsher the sound. The bandoneeons' rheethms stabbed, the violeens' cho-rus cried, the peeano's bass shook, and melodees raced and gal-loped and tumbled een a frenzeed crescendo of heart-poundeeng, soul-wrencheeng tango. Urgeeng the museek on, Eduardo and Madreelena swirled and tweested and keecked and skeepped and leeped and sleed and deepped and clenched. They seemed unable to stop. Everee pause onlee fueled their fire, launcheeng ever more extreeme and perilous movements. No one had seen anytheeng quite like eet. Even from Eduardo and Madreelena.

"Finallee the volcano erupted. Weeth the tango at a peetch no bandoneeonist could sustain, no violeenist could continue, no pee-anist could endure, and no danzer could long survive, Madreelena unwound herself from a long speen, coiled again, and threw herself through the air at Eduardo as eef hurled by the weend. Her spleet skirt pulled high, she curled one leg beneeth her and pointed the other out straight, her feesh-net stockeengs gleesteneeng from her heep to her spiked heel. Braceeng for the catch, Eduardo spread hees legs and anchored hees feet, bent hees knees, and reeched out hees arms. Flames arced from her eyes to hees as she flew. The eenstant he grasped her he knew. He saw her teeth cut through her lip and felt a blindeeng pain where her heel tore through hees trousers and slashed eento hees flesh. At almost the same een-stant, Madreelena's hand clamped around the back of hees neck and pulled their mouths together een a hard, biteeng keess, while Eduardo wrapped an arm tightlee around her waist, and grasped Madreelena to heem weeth a powerful sudden force that drove a cry from her throat and made her legs go leemp. Her feengernails etched deep red lines down hees cheek as the two bodees crumpled to the floor. Eduardo groaned. Blood oozed from hees face and spread from the tear between hees legs. Madreelena moaned but deed not move. The crowd gasped. The museek stuttered to a stop."

The old man's voice trailed off. He downed the last of his wine. I waited. He dragged on a cigarette and let the smoke drift from his nose and mouth. He tapped the ashes onto a pile spilling over the ashtray.

At last, I asked haltingly, "What . . . What happened to them?"

Releasing another chest-full of smoke, he sighed, "Madreelena. She could not walk again."

"My god. . . . And Eduardo?"

The old man took another deep pull on his cigarette. Exhaling heavily, he wheezed, "Eduardo could never . . ." He coughed gruffly, phlegm thick in his throat. Then, peering past me as though seeing someone in the distance, he smothered his cigarette butt in the ashes, flicked the discarded pack toward me, and shoved his chair from the table, scraping the tiles. Standing up stiffly, he muttered, "Eet ees feeneesh. Adeeos ameego." And he shuffled away.

I sat bewildered. Who was that? A storyteller? An old dreamer bewitched by the tango? This is a good place for such stories, I had to admit. Spend enough time here, and anyone might start to tell 'em. I drained my wine and turned around to watch the old man leave. I could see him near the entrance laying a shawl around the shoulders of an old woman in a chair. She must've just come in, or maybe she'd signaled to him to go out with her. He patted her back. She lifted a frail hand. He placed his fingers under hers. And, slowly circling her like a dancer, he gracefully swung her chair around on its wheels and gently pushed her out through the glass doors.

My mouth fell open. What the . . . ? He . . . ? She . . . ? Was it possible? I was still gaping at the flapping door panes held in place by their fraying strips of tape when a skirt brushed my arm. The young dancers from earlier swept past me into the center. My gaze involuntarily followed them. He gripped her tight around the waist, they cocked their heads, and they flowed into a tango that seemed more intense and sensual than before. The sobbing baritone on a tinny recording sang,

Feel the blood rise to your face
With every beat;
While an arm winds like a snake
Around a waist
About to break.
This is how to dance the tango! . . .
Dance of love and death.

Yielding to an obscure yearning, I ordered another *vino tinto.* Idly fingering the rumpled cigarette pack, I felt one left inside. I slipped it out, put it to my lips, lit it, and inhaled deeply. Propping my elbows on the table and resting my chin on my open palms, I let the smoke float mistily from my lungs. And, with the music of the tango pulsing in my ears, and a throb in my heart, I began searching the room through the haze for a pair of dark, enticing, dangerous eyes.

[Tango lyrics and the lines from the poem "Tango" by Ricardo Güiraldes come from Simon Collier, et al., *Tango: The Dance, The Song, The Story* (London: 1995).]

Hot air balloon rising from the grounds of chateau, with spires of Saint-Remi in background, Reims, France

A Bon Vivant's Dream

You might think of April in Paris bursting with "chestnuts in blossom" and adorned with the "charm of spring," as the familiar song says. But the reality is often closer to T. S. Eliot's lines: "April is the cruelest month," wrenching "dull roots" from the "dead land" in a chilly "spring rain," cold and rainy, bringing barely a harbinger of summer days to come. I'd take October in Paris over April any day. It has the pleasures of waning summer. Some tourists may still be there, but not in hoards, and the colors are out, the air is clear and fresh, and the gaiety of children frolicking after school in the Luxembourg and Tuileries gardens on sunny autumn days brings a smile to your lips and youth to your heart. When Ernest Hemingway complained that in October the rains come and the wind beats fallen leaves against the window panes, he was slanting his memories. October in Paris is usually just fine. Never mind the rain that does come eventually.

We had lived in Paris for five years in a flat on the rue de l'Odéon. My wife, Martine, was a journalist, and I was trying to write—what else?—a novel. We loved every minute of our Parisian life—the morning *café au lait* and croissants down the street in the Carrefour de l'Odéon or on the nearby boulevard Saint-Germain, fresh fruits and vegetables from the open market in the rue de Buci and crisp baguettes from any boulangerie, strolls through the picturesque streets of the left bank, browsing among the book stalls along the Seine, dining at the ubiquitous sidewalk brasseries. Yes, life in Paris was good, especially in the early autumn between the tourist inundation of summer and the long winter nights that descend in mid-afternoon.

The end of summer also brought the grape harvest and our annual visit to the champagne country, ninety minutes east of Paris. We'd gone there for years, always staying in the same room of a former château, now an elegant hotel, on the outskirts of Reims set on a hill with manicured gardens rolling down toward the delicate spires of the sixteenth-century Basilica of Saint-Remi rising in the middle distance beyond the garden's surrounding trees. We'd been told of this château by Jacques Sevinchy, an acquaintance who had said it had one of the best restaurants in France, given three stars by the Michelin *Red Guide*. And he should know, since he had long been one of the Michelin judges. What a life Jacques led, we often said to him a bit enviously. He lived a bon vivant's dream, traveling around France, staying in the best hotels, high and low, and dining in the best restaurants, lavish and modest, rating them all as he saw fit. By now Jacques knew many of them like family or friends, whom he nonetheless didn't hesitate to chastise for disappointing him. He was an especially harsh judge of the most celebrated restaurants. He said their pretensions demanded it. Twirling the impressive curl of his long mustache, he could distinguish a dozen types of duckling served in Paris's oldest restaurant, La Tour d'Argent (from which he had voted to strip one and then two of its three Michelin stars for growing tired and failing to keep pace with the inventiveness of new culinary trends and lighter cuisine); he could question a quenelle at Taillevent for being a gram too heavy; he could tut-tut a truffle soup at Paul Bocuse for being insufficiently earthy; he could fault a pigeon at Alain Ducasse for missing a precise balance of crispness and succulence; and on and on. But we never heard him murmur a sound of dissatisfactions with the food at the château in Reims.

As it happened, unbeknownst to us Jacques was staying there when we arrived, completing his latest round of visits to the twenty or so three-star restaurants of France. We had come to know him after Martine had written an article on the Michelin Guides during our first year in Paris, and he had graciously, but discreetly, served as a resource and then equally graciously and discreetly befriended us, despite Martine's husband being a vulgar American. I know it was Martine's beauty and elegance that attracted him, but he had always showed me a friendly courtesy and even seemingly genuine curiosity about my work.

We ran across him sitting on the veranda that overlooks the garden. He had just finished his lunch and was sipping champagne and gazing toward Saint-Remi. Exchanging surprised greetings, we offered him our usual envious sighs. He smiled, rather wanly, I thought, and we talked briefly about his latest culinary explorations, which he reported with his customarily sardonic wit about sauces gone awry and waiters gone missing and wines that could fuel machinery, but with somewhat less of his customary panache. I wondered why but said nothing of it. Always enjoying his company, we invited him to take a drive with us that afternoon into the countryside to see the late grape harvest. He graciously declined, pleading a need to finish some work and to take a nap, but he amiably asked us to join him for dinner. That was an invitation we would never refuse. We agreed to meet for champagne in the conservatoire, an airy glass-enclosed space off the dining room overlooking the garden.

He left us, and we had a light lunch ourselves. Afterwards we decided to put off the countryside venture until tomorrow and drove instead into Reims along tree-lined streets that showed off the city in radiant fall colors and that were home to many a champagne maker. We paused at the Basilica of Saint-Remi, which always seemed larger and farther away as seen from the terrace of our room at the château than it proved to be up close. From there, we went on into the old part of the city to visit the historic thirteenth-century cathedral of Notre-Dame, where the truce of World War I was signed, and where in an earlier chapel on the site, Charlemagne was crowned Emperor of the Holy Roman Empire. It wore its age well and still overwhelmed with its monumental size, which dwarfs the rest of the city from miles away. But it hardly seemed suited to the modern metropolis that has smothered most remnants of medieval Reims around it. The cathedral stands as a reminder of an age that had patiently taken centuries to erect such monuments to the eternal life, unlike the modern city born of times when temples of business get built in a hurry and might be torn down in mere decades to make way for new commercial edifices. Here we could see the poignant historical passage from the eternal to the ephemeral.

We wandered meditatively through the cathedral and browsed the neighborhood searching for traces of long ago. We found some along a few cobbled streets and shadowed alleys, but they were only vestiges of the past. After exploring the "old" city for a while, we got back in the car and headed for local champagne houses to sample the finished product of what we would see being harvested the next day. We stopped briefly at Mumm's stately home to sip some varieties of their signature Cordon Rouge, which Martine found to be a trifle sweet, and we paused at Taittinger's nondescript tasting room to sample the dry Taittinger brews, more to Martine's liking, although I enjoyed them both. Then on to Pommery, a palatial historic establishment just across the boulevard from our château. There we followed an old stairway underground to the massive caves carved through chalky stone and traversed the maze of corridors lined with thousands of bottles, each given a quarter turn daily by a dutiful caretaker while the champagne ages. After tasting a few of their rather floral styles, we bought a bottle of vintage Pommery to take home. Having sipped about nine champagnes altogether that afternoon, we were ready to return to our room for a rest before dinner. It had all been a suitable prelude to one of the best meals to be had in France, with a man whose esteemed imprimatur vouched for it.

Martine and I arrived in the conservatoire early and sat on a plush sofa to await our companion for a glass of champagne and to choose our dinner selections from the menus brought by the waiter. While we were taking in the place, I noticed in the waning daylight outside some workmen unloading a brightly colored object from a truck onto the lawn. As they laid it out, it looked like a carousel canopy, and I wondered if they were preparing for a carnival to celebrate the harvest, or to stage a party for a guest. I flagged the waiter and asked what was going on in the garden.

He glanced outside and replied in softly accented English, "A balloon. Someone arranged it to sail over the countryside tomorrow."

"Nice idea," I responded and thanked him.

Jacques arrived moments later, and we toasted the occasion with the featured champagne of the night, a delicate Billicarte-Salmon produced in a village north of Reims. We exchanged reminiscences of previous meetings and summaries of our activities since our last encounter. We told him of our work and the pleasures of our Paris days, and we probed him for culinary explorations and discoveries.

He complied with good stories in his usual charming manner but with, it struck me, more than a trace of cynicism. Browsing through the sumptuous-sounding menu, we ordered dinner, and a few minutes later the waiter returned to say that our table was ready whenever we would care to go in. We finished our champagne and followed him through the elegant ersatz Louis XVI dining room and on into a more intimate space on the far side matching the conservatoire. We were led to a table with a nice view of the garden. Dinner unfolded as wonderfully as we had come to expect. The Salade Père Girard, mingling greens with morsels of foie gras and lobster lifted us from our seats; the langoustine melted on the tongue; the pigeon with quince sent us soaring; the peach soufflé took us to heaven. And the orchestrated champagnes made us not want to return to earth.

But for some reason, Jacques did not seem quite as animated as usual or as taken with it all as Martine and I were. He nodded approval and made some notes, and he chatted cordially as always, but the normally serene smile on his face that we liked so much was fleeting. Perhaps he was disappointed with the food after all. Or maybe just tired. Or even bored. But can a bon vivant living a dream suffer boredom, I asked myself, or what the French bewail as *ennui*?

When we inquired where he was going from here, he paused and said he was leaving early the next day on his way to Burgundy and then Provence. "Ah," I sighed. "What a life you lead. Driving south from here will be a marvelous trip. The countryside is so beautiful right now." I thought of the balloon and drew their attention to it still being assembled in the garden. "We should take a balloon from here some time," I said to Martine. "How lovely that would be, sailing over the champagne country. Have you ever done that, Jacques?" I asked.

"*Oui.* I've ridden balloons a few times, but not from here. *C'est très jolie.* Floating over the countryside, above it all and seeing everything from the sweet silence of the sky. You feel that you could go on *pour toujours, sans cesse* [forever, without end]." He let his words trail off as though he were losing himself in the thought.

"Sounds divine," Martine said.

"I wish we could go tomorrow," I put in. "Maybe next time. We could all go together. Would you be interested?" I asked Jacques. He was still kind of lost in thought. Then he looked at me, and for the first time since we had met him yesterday, his eyes appeared to brighten and a happy smile broke across his face.

"Perhaps," he said softly.

We exchanged more reminiscences and reflections through the rest of dinner down to coffee and cognac and the heavenly peach soufflé. Finally, Martine and I said goodnight, looking forward to our drive through the country tomorrow and hoping for blue skies. Jacques echoed our hopes, with regrets that he could not join us, and bid us *bonne nuit* with a nice smile. We would see each other again at breakfast before going our separate ways.

The sun was gleaming when we got up the next morning. Stepping out on our private terrace in the fresh clear air, we were greeted by the spectacle of a resplendent autumn day in the garden of the château. The reds of the maples, the oranges of the oaks, the yellows of the locusts all engulfed us in a kaleidoscope of colors framing the spires of Saint-Remi. And spread out on the broad green lawn in the center lay the equally colorful hot air balloon being prepared for flight.

We dressed and went down to the dining room and sat at a table by the window. When Jacques didn't appear, we concluded he would arrive in due course or he might have left earlier than expected, and we proceeded to order. We savored omelets, buttery croissants, and *café au lait*, while looking out the tall windows to where workmen were now inflating the balloon in the middle of the expansive lawn. Its buoyantly multicolored panes swelled slowly with hot air from the burner. As its folds unfurled, it gradually bobbed off the grass and swayed in the breeze, a gigantic colorful bubble amid the autumn leaves under a clear blue sky, its basket tethered to the ground by a couple of lines and weighted down by bags of sand hefted in by workmen before igniting the burner. Wishing we could take the flight, we watched the workmen finish their job and withdraw. We resumed our breakfast speculating on what had delayed Jacques.

A few minutes later, Martine pointed outside. "Look!" she said with an urgent tone.

A workman was racing down the lawn toward the balloon, waving his arms and shouting. The balloon's basket had been untethered, and someone was tossing bags over the side. The basket was waggling. A pillar of flame was rising brightly from the burner, sending more hot air into the balloon. By the time the workman got there, the balloon had lifted from the ground. They could not reach it.

Half a dozen people were now running from the château in the direction of the ascending balloon. We quickly signed the check and went out to the garden to see what the commotion was about. The crowd stood helplessly looking upward as the balloon bobbled, rose above the tree tops, and drifted toward the spires of Saint-Remi. A man and woman left the group and hastened toward the château ranting at a manager, who had come out to handle the situation. While he was trying to calm them, a workman approached from the lawn and handed the manager a thick envelope and a note of some kind, gesturing back to where the balloon had been. The manager read the note and opened the envelope. He drew out what looked to us, standing a few yards away, like a handful of Euros. He examined the note back and front and shook his head in puzzlement. Then he cast a final look at the departing balloon and invited the animated couple to go with him into the château.

Curious, Martine and I walked over to the workman who had brought the envelope and asked him what had happened. He was still a little agitated, and my French wasn't good enough to make out all he said, but I gathered that the couple we'd seen had rented the balloon, but someone had taken off in it. The workman had found an envelope and a note left behind on the ground and had given these to the manager.

"*Qu'en était-il dans l'enveloppe?* [What was in the envelope?]" Martine asked.

"*Argent.* [Money.]" he answered.

"*Qu'est-ce que la note disait?* [What did the note say?]" she added.

"*Il disait, 'Veuillez me pardonner. Adieu.'* [It said, 'Please forgive me. Goodbye.']"

"*C'est tout?* [That's all?]" I prodded.

He shrugged and said, "*Eh bien, il y avait les mots 'Guides Michelin' imprimé dessus.* [Well, there were the words 'Michelin Guides' printed on it.]"

"What?!" I gasped and turned to Martine. "Could it be? Jacques? He never said he could fly a balloon. And why would he go off like that?"

Spontaneously our eyes looked to the sky beyond the trees at the end of the garden. The balloon, its colors radiant in the morning sun was now floating off over Saint-Remi. We watched it go, gently levitating up over the city and out of sight on a peaceful, inexplicable journey to the champagne countryside, and who knows where else.

I asked the workman how far the balloon could go. He shrugged again and said it could go as far as the air currents could take it until it ran out of fuel, and if the guy in it knows anything about flying balloons, that could be a very long way. To the Alps anyway, or the Mediterranean.

Shaking our heads, Martine and I went inside and inquired about Jacques at the desk. We were told he had packed his bags and paid his bill but had left the bags in his room. He was nowhere to be seen.

"He did it!" I exclaimed. "He's in the balloon. But why? To where . . . ?"

Mystified, we decided to make our drive into the countryside as planned, thinking that we might just find the balloon on the ground and Jacques seated in a village café, sipping champagne and smiling at his adventure.

We didn't find him or the balloon. And in the late afternoon, we returned to the château, checked out, and drove back to Paris, talking about the mystery and what Jacques had had in mind. Surely he knew what he was doing. But where was he going? Did he fly off to pursue a bon vivant's dream, or did he do it to escape from *ennui*?

A couple of months later, I read in a Paris newspaper that a long-time Michelin judge named Jacques Sevinchy was being replaced. The article gave no explanation except to say that he was last seen at a hotel in Reims. My mind's eye saw the balloon drifting away, and I could faintly hear his wistful words: *Pour toujours, sans cesse.*

Lighthouse on Penobscot Bay, Mid-Coast, Maine

From the Lighthouse

For the last ten years Rosalind Ransom had spent summers at a small house she owned on the coast of Maine, where the rocky shoreline rises high to forests of pines, and the tides rise almost as high, and colorful buoys of lobster traps dot the coastal waters, and picturesque coves shelter bobbing sail boats, and photogenic lighthouses stand watch over the treacherous coastline blinking signals to approaching vessels. Childhood memories of summertime visits to this coast had stirred her desire to have a house here someday so she could listen to the waves crashing against the rocks and hear the seagulls singing as they swoop through the sky and dive for fish, and she could watch the tides come and go and boats sail to and fro and see a lighthouse blinking on the horizon.

The tides were the first thing that had struck her. On a summer afternoon many years ago, as she and her parents and sister had first driven down a long winding road to their rented cottage on a cove near the end of a peninsula, she had thought a terrible drought must be afflicting the area. No water could be seen in the inlets along the road, only empty mud flats and protruding rocks. When they reached the cottage, perched with a few others above the cove, the cove itself had also looked largely drained of water. The ocean came no closer than a hundred yards to the shore so that much of the cove, down some thirty feet of rocks from the cottage, lay waterless. Here and there small boats rested on the mud and steep piers descended toward them, stopping short in the air above them, while other piers extended farther out but still ended over land. The water had withdrawn so far from the back of the cove that acres of rock and mud lay bare.

Troubled by the desiccation, Rosalind had asked her father about it. He had laughed and told her to wait. And she had seen it happen. Ripples had soon begun rolling in, lapping up the stony slant below the cottage and inching into the vacant back of the cove. An hour later the water had risen three feet. The family watched in awe as the high tide returned almost in a rush. In five more hours the "drought" was over. The ocean had re-filled the cove, covering the barren acres all the way to the back, lifting the sail boats and fishing craft and claiming nearly twenty feet of the rocky height between the floor of the cove and the cottage. Rosalind's father had explained that the high tide would start ebbing soon and be gone again in about six hours, leaving the cove bare again, then return in about six hours after that. It had been too late at night to wait, but she had gotten up the next morning to see. It looked as though nothing much had happened since the evening before. The cove was still full. Her father told her she had missed the late night ebb and flow and to watch more closely. As she stared at the water, she could detect it starting to ebb out, at first inch by inch, then foot by foot. By noon, when the family gathered for lunch after exploring the terrain, the ocean was nearly gone. Rosalind could hardly believe the tides could move so fast and rise so high. She had wanted to see it every day.

Her father had bought her a tide chart at a local store to time the roughly six-hour cycle, and she had followed it religiously. The tide had become a preoccupation. She had started reading about how the tides vary around the world, and rise with gravity and the moon and local conditions, and that the highest tides anywhere occur along that same coastline to the far north in Canada. There, she had learned with fascination, in some parts of the Bay of Fundy the tide rises fifty feet up cliffs, occasionally catching unwary tourists who wander too far out on the sand at low tide and find themselves in peril as the tide comes back in a hurry, and that in other places the tide flows in through river channels from the bay with the current of a rapids and then, after falling slack for a few minutes, reverses itself and rushes out in reversing tides, as they are known. Rosalind had wanted to see these things, and one summer her parents had obliged with a weeklong trip all the way up the coast through Saint John, New Brunswick, for its dramatic reversing tide on an estuary that reaches into the city, and on to Moncton at the top of the Bay of Fundy, where they had joined other tourists to watch the famous tidal bore roll up the riverbed in a wave—although it had turned out that day to be more of a ripple. In later years, when she was able to get a summer house of her own on this coast, she had picked one where she could see the tides rise and fall. She had never lost her fascination for them.

And there were the lighthouses. She had loved them from the beginning, too, and had learned that no two are alike. Their lights blink in unique patterns giving them individual maritime "addresses" to direct passing mariners. Most of all, she had been drawn to the romance of the lone lighthouse dwellers, living at the lights on remote islands or isolated promontories. How pure their lives must be, she had thought. How solitary. How free. How spiritual even. Rosalind was that kind of person. She had always needed her solitude, away from everyone. She was sorry to learn that now this romance of the lighthouse had largely passed, outdated by technology that had mechanized the lights and sent lighthouse dwellers to other lives. But she had visited many a lighthouse over the years with that romance in mind. And she had vowed to get a summer house one day with a view of a lighthouse out there over the tides. Which she did.

Rosalind had not married. Perhaps she was too solitary. Too inward. She needed too much time alone. Like a lighthouse keeper. For her, romance was more a state of mind than a human relationship. Human relations tended to clutter and dim the beauty of pure romance. The romance of imagination, the romance of the soul. She did have people in her life, of course, and some of them kidded her about being a Platonist, preferring her ideals of reality to reality itself, to which she jibed that theirs was merely an unimaginative realist's bias against ideals. Not that she was doctrinaire about this. It was more of a temperamental bent than a philosophy. Rosalind was, after all, not a philosopher. She was an artist. By temperament first. That is how she saw herself and the world. She lived in a realm of aesthetics rich with sensations, images, and emotions born of art and nature. She would rather look at a painting than run a company, listen to a string quartet than make millions, read a poem than attend a state dinner, watch a sunrise over the ocean than win an award, see a lighthouse blinking across the water than live in a palace, observe the tides rise and fall than decide the fate of nations.

She was also an artist by profession, more or less. A painter. She was lucky in that, and she knew it. She managed to live in the "real world" on a respectable income from her art, or rather from that and teaching. The teaching was a concession to the "real world," she granted, but she also took a measure of pride in getting students not so much to paint well—that was usually futile—as in getting a few of them to perceive and prize aesthetic form. This was what made art and life worth while for her. The beauty—no, not that exactly, she would say; the pleasure of beauty was not enough; it was, what? . . . the power, yes, the power of aesthetic form to animate and sometimes transform us. Was this art for art's sake? she was sometimes asked. No. It wasn't, she would say. It was art for life's sake.

This is what she had long told herself anyway. And she had always felt it when painting. She thought of herself as awakening people to the power and joy of aesthetic form. What could be more important in art or life than that?

Maine was the place to make it happen for her. Possibly an odd choice. She was no Maine painter in the traditional mold. She knew all about that tradition, from Winslow Homer to the Wyeths and the many other less-renowned artists who had found inspiration in the light and water and weather and life on the Maine coast with its fogs and fishermen, lighthouses and storms, rugged shore and hardy people. She didn't care for much of that art aesthetically, but she admired Andrew Wyeth's evocative depictions of people and places, and she remembered seeing his most famous painting, "Christina's World," at the Museum of Modern Art in New York when she was young and being moved by the mystery and melancholy of the woman in the foreground sprawled on the grass at the bottom of a hill propping herself up on her arms and looking, it seems forlornly, toward a house far away at the top. She is so alone. Why is she there, and in that position? A metaphor of isolation and loneliness and alienation? An existentialist painting. That is what Rosalind, like many other people, had thought anyway. And this had appealed to her nature. But later, in Maine, she had gone to that very house on that hill, which had become a Wyeth shrine, and had learned the more prosaic truth. Christina's world was not that of the alienated human condition but that of a girl who couldn't walk and who often crawled down that hill and back from the house where she had lived quite happily with the Olsen family. Wyeth had known her and the Olsens well and had often painted in that house on the hill. Rosalind accepted the prosaic truth, but she never lost her memory of the painting as a work of ambiguity, alienation, and mystery.

That is what she painted. Ambiguity and mystery, with hints of alienation, or at least isolation. Her paintings were inward and abstract, gentle brushstrokes and soft colors with a sparing use of paint. Critics labeled her a lyrical minimalist, praising the subtlety and suggestiveness of her canvases. But for all of their ambiguity and mystery, her paintings weren't wholly removed from the world. The world must always be there, Rosalind said, or some semblance of it, if only as form. That was part of her aesthetic sensibility. She experienced the world as aesthetic form. And sometimes when she was at her own house on the coast of Maine starting work on a new painting, her thoughts of art and life led her to Lily Briscoe.

Lily Briscoe, in Virginia Woolf's *To the Lighthouse*, who had tried and failed to paint Mrs. Ramsey sitting in the window at the seaside house where Lily had spent summers with the Ramseys before the war. And where, years later, after Mrs. Ramsey had died and Lily had returned for a visit with Mr. Ramsey and his grown children, when she had then stood before a blank canvas watching them rowing out to the distant lighthouse she had at that moment discovered how to paint. A slash of blue sea here, a swath of green grass there, a patchwork of blue and yellow for the sky, flicks of white for sunlight glistening on the water, and a faint and obscure and all-important daub as the lighthouse on the horizon. Then it was finished, and Lily knew she had found her way.

Now, here in her coastal Maine home, Rosalind again thought of that scene at the end of the novel and imagined herself as Lily, whose art could have been rather like her own. But on this occasion, Rosalind felt she had more than this in common with Lily. Her own mother had died ten years ago today, and memories of her flooded Rosalind's mind and emotions, the way memories of Mrs. Ramsey had absorbed Lily Briscoe. Mrs. Ramsey had been a surrogate mother to Lily, and the dominant figure in the lives of all around her. Mr. Ramsey had demanded attention and intellectual respect, as Virginia Woolf's own father had. But Mrs. Ramsey won everyone's heart and shaped their souls. Rosalind's mother had been like that. She had shaped Rosalind's and her sister's souls, even while giving Rosalind's father the attention he needed as an ambitious academic. She had died when Rosalind was going off to college. Her mother had kept on her dresser a couple of framed quotations that Rosalind had wondered about in childhood. They hadn't made much sense at first, but in time they had stayed with her. One, from Walter Pater, read, "To burn always with a hard gem-like flame, to maintain this ecstasy, is success in life." The other, from Henry James, said, "Try to be one of those people on whom nothing is lost." Rosalind had never been quite sure how her mother had lived out these lines herself. But her mother had communicated them to her daughters as a kind of creed. Perhaps it had been compensation for living a more conventional life than her nature had desired. Or perhaps she had lived those lines inside. The flame, the ecstasy, the sense of letting nothing be lost on her. She did have that, Rosalind reflected, in her way. A kind of intensity of being in her inner life. But why hadn't her mother done more with it? Why had she lived so conventional a life if that was how she felt? She had let it remain a state of mind. Or so it seemed. Some of this was generational, Rosalind understood. If her mother had lived later she would likely have lived differently. Possibly she would have become an artist. Her creed was, above all, that of the artist.

On this day, the tenth anniversary of her mother's passing, as Rosalind found herself awash in memories of her mother, she remembered something in particular that Lily Briscoe had learned from Mrs. Ramsey. It was about something that could be pretentious but in her was not, namely, the meaning, or meanings, of life. Mrs. Ramsey had told Lily that these meanings don't come in any dramatic revelation. They come in little things, tiny illuminations from "matches struck in the dark." Rosalind's mother would have agreed. The meanings of life could surprise you in their seeming triviality. A sight, a sound, an incident, a feeling, an idea. A match struck in the dark. Anything might turn out to show us one of the meanings of life that can change us if we get it right. Her mother's life had surely been made of such things, letting nothing be lost on her. That had given her the quiet intensity. A silent ecstasy. Rosalind had wanted to be like that. But not just as a state of mind, inside. Rosalind had been determined to live it out. As an artist. She had become rather successful, too, with occasional gallery shows in New York, laudatory reviews, and periodic sales to collectors.

But today, while she stood at her easel outside in the sunlight facing the blank canvas and looking toward the lighthouse on its lonely promontory near the horizon beyond the mouth of the cove, she wondered why she felt so . . . off. The melancholy anniversary was part of it. Rosalind missed her mother. She wanted to talk to her. There were so many things left unsaid ten years ago. Rosalind had been thirty years old then, just starting out, really. And so many things had happened since then. She wanted to talk with her mother about everything. The past. The future. Art. Life. They hadn't always gotten along, of course. All strong mothers and daughters have some tensions. But Rosalind had identified herself with her mother in many ways, and the bond between them had gone deep. Then that bond had been torn from Rosalind's heart when her mother had died. And she had felt that part of herself was gone. It was. That's what mourning is about, isn't it? she had told herself. You lose part of yourself when a loved one goes. And it takes time to heal the wound, whether you go through Kubler-Ross's five stages of grief or not. But later she had asked herself, do some wounds of mourning hurt too much to ever heal? She wondered that again today. Was that why she felt as she did?

To escape the feeling, she picked up her brush. She thought again of Lily Briscoe doing just that while thinking of Mrs. Ramsey and watching Mr. Ramsey and his children row away out to the lighthouse. Rosalind had kind of a déjà vu as she roughed in a foreground of green, then beyond it painted a wide horizontal line of blue and on top of that at one side added a small patch of brown, and finally put into the background a short, vaguely shaped, vertical white line. She paused. Lily Briscoe's lighthouse? She wasn't trying to do that. She wasn't very consciously trying to do anything except keep melancholy at bay.

As she studied the canvas, her hand and brushes mysteriously seemed to take on a will of their own. They started painting ovals and lines and planes and dots and areas of light and shade and colors and unintended forms. She was hardly there. The painting was taking form without her. When the work was done, Rosalind stepped back. Her mother looked out at her from the canvas. Not crystal clear, but it was indisputably her mother sitting in the foreground. At about the age, ten years ago, when she had died. Her graying hair cut just above the shoulders. Her gentle features and winsome mouth. The quietly intense, inwardly vibrant, softly affectionate expression most typical of her. Looking more closely, Rosalind saw something else. The lips did not smile, and a few lines at their corners suggested concern. And the eyes. They seemed to have an unusual trace of sorrow in them and to be searching, asking.

As Rosalind focused on those eyes, she felt the world around her dissolve, and she was alone with her mother. Her mother's eyes were looking at her searching, asking her . . . what? Gradually Rosalind thought she could hear her mother's voice quietly saying sadly: "Did you not understand what I meant?" About what? Rosalind answered silently. "About life. The gem-like flame, and letting nothing be lost on you." Yes, I did, Rosalind thought. "But," her mother replied, "you have lived for art and aesthetics and beauty and form. That's not what I meant."

But what . . . ? Rosalind started to ask. Then it came to her. Could it be that for all of her mother's suppressed artistic sensibility, and her inward intensity, she had chosen to live not for art and beauty but for other people and love and beneficence? Could it be that this is why she had never tried to be an artist? Because she had found her ecstasy in her conventional life? And that Rosalind had misunderstood by living an artist's life that was even more inward than her mother's? True, Rosalind had to admit, she had never given much of herself to anyone or sacrificed anything that she cared about for someone else. She had loved her life with all of its sensations and feelings and artistic creativity and "gem-like flame" of aesthetic intensity. She had thought her life had been full. But was it? Had she really let nothing be lost on her? Maybe she had let that happen after all. Maybe she had missed some "matches struck in the dark." Maybe that's why she had felt so strange as she thought of her mother today.

But if she had misunderstood her mother, why hadn't her mother told her? Perhaps she had tried. Or perhaps she had thought Rosalind would see it for herself. Or, could it be that this is what her mother was doing now? Through the painting?

As Rosalind looked closely at the painting again, she thought she saw the expression start to change. A little warmer in the eyes. A little softer at the corners of the mouth, hinting at a smile. She had the sensation of being like Dorian Gray seeing the portrait of himself monstrously transformed before his eyes. But this portrait seemed to be changing before her eyes for the better not the worse. She stared at it. Was her mother telling her something more? Or was it all in her mind? She felt even stranger than before. She stepped back again. The picture retained its softness. What was she to make of that? What should she do now?

Confused and distracted, she packed up her paints and brushes, folded the easel and carried them along with the picture into the house. There she stowed the painting materials in a closet, and took the picture into the living room. She removed one of her abstract paintings from the wall next to a window with a view out across the water to the lighthouse and placed the new portrait of her mother in its place. The painting's image of the lighthouse in the distance behind her mother faintly mirrored what Rosalind could now see in the distance out the window. Looking at the picture once more, she said to herself that it was a pretty good portrait. But not one she wanted to see again for a while.

She prepared the house for a long absence and packed her bags and put them in the car. Returning to the living room, she went to the window and stood pensively looking out at the tides and the lighthouse. She said goodbye to the scene. Then she turned to the portrait and said aloud: "I'll be back mother. But I don't know when. I hope I'll see you still smiling."

She locked the door behind her and left.

Classical Indian dancer (Wikimedia Commons)

The Dancer with the Fish-Shaped Eyes

It had been several years since I had first come to Madras—or Chennai, as it is now officially called, expunging another remnant of the Raj. I had liked it. Yes, it had the same air of barely constrained chaos that typifies Indian cities. Its crumbling sidewalks teemed with people, traffic-clogged streets streamed with honking vehicles, gypsy-like women clutching infants swarmed amidst cars at stoplights begging from captive drivers, hovels of the poor were strewn like rubbish along thoroughfares, modern offices and fanciful Victorian buildings from British days stood shoulder to shoulder with ramshackle huts, and garish billboards boosted the melodramatic movies made in abundance here and in Bombay—now Mumbai. But Chennai also has a magnificent sea shore where wide sandy Marina Beach runs for miles along the Bay of Bengal, which gives reprieve from the heat to sweaty bathers, although sharks have claimed much of its waters as home. In all, this southern Indian city by the sea has a beauty and vitality and southern charm that can win you. It had won me. And it hadn't changed much to my eyes.

I had come back to consult with an editor about an article I'd agreed to write for her magazine. And I was planning to visit an acquaintance in the shipping business here whom I had met in Montevideo, Uruguay, when I was there researching an article on a prominent Uruguayan artist and he was there trying to buy a used tanker. He and I had found ourselves sitting together one night in Montevideo at a tango show.

"The tango is very intense," he had said to me as we walked out returning to our hotels. "Full of passion with stories to tell. Indian dance has that, too. But classical Indian dance is not about ordinary people. It is about myths and religion. Have you seen Indian dance?"

I had told him that I had indeed seen it and had even met an Indian dancer in old Madras.

Delighted that I knew his city, he had invited me to visit him on my next trip to India. And he had promised to take me out for the best food in southern India and to see some of the best dancers in the country. Now I was here taking him up on his offer the night before meeting with my editor.

He was as good as his word. We went to a luxurious restaurant where we dined on dishes from the four south Indian states, Tamil Nadu, Kerala, Karnataka, and Andhra Pradesh, sumptuously mingling an array of spices, familiar and unfamiliar, in irresistible ways, reminding me why the early Europeans had hungered to find a swift trade route to India. And the dancers were all that he had promised. Sometimes in pairs, sometimes alone, the gracefully sensuous women, adorned in gilded silks, riveted every gaze on the small polished marble stage where, to the music of a sitar and tabla drums, they performed movements and gestures and expressions that had descended through centuries, wordlessly depicting the epic stories of Hindu mythology. Angling their feet sideways and slapping them on the shiny stone, crooking their lithe arms and curving back their long fingers, alternately smiling and frowning while arching their eyebrows and widening their flashing eyes, they portrayed tragedy and comedy, defeat and victory, violence and love, fear and tenderness, sorrow and joy. Watching them took me back to the time in Madras when I had met, and had then seen perform, the dancer with the fish-shaped eyes.

Her name was Samya. I had met her at lunch with the same magazine editor I was here to see again. Samya was the daughter of a friend of that editor. I had guessed Samya was in her early twenties. She had wanted to be an Indian dancer. But, as she had explained, Indian parents are very protective of their single daughters, even when those daughters are grown up, and even when those parents are highly educated, like hers. They had wanted her to have a more secure life than that of a dancer and to marry well. She had insisted that dance was her true love. Finally they had struck a compromise. Her parents had arranged for her to learn the profession of magazine editing under the tutelage and protective wing of this editor, a friend of the family, and Samya had consented to go along if she could continue to study dance and to perform. She had been grateful to the editor for her care and instruction, but she had hoped that her determination to dance would eventually exhaust her parents' resistance. My editor had filled me in on this story before I had met Samya, whom she had thought might be helpful with the article I was writing on Hindu temple art for her magazine.

At lunch that day the three of us had talked about writing and magazines, art and Hinduism. And I had asked Samya to tell me about Indian dance. She had said something like this:

"Indian dance is not just art. We're not like you in the West. Our dance is more than dance. Our art is more than art. It is an act of ritual and spirit and tells stories of legends and life. Like the sculptures on Hindu temples. Most of them depict gods and goddesses, often swaying their hips and using their hands as in dance. Our most important god today, Lord Shiva, who is the Destroyer of Evil, is also the God of Dance. He is often shown encircled by a ring of flames dancing in victory over demons. His son Ganesh, the cheerful little elephant with a broken tusk who brings good luck, often dances too. To understand Indian temple art, you must understand Indian dance, and to understand Indian dance you must know Hinduism."

"What makes a good Indian dancer?" I had asked. She had said that Indian dance may not be as difficult as Western classical ballet because it is not so acrobatic, and the footwork is simpler. But the art of Indian dance isn't in leaps or in the feet. It is mainly in the hands and arms and face. You have to get every gesture and expression right. Then she had gone on to say something that particularly stuck in my mind.

"A female dancer must be like a temple sculpture," she had explained. "All very sensuous and sensual and full and round, not like skinny Western dancers." She had unabashedly patted her cheeks and hips. "And the dancer must learn to move her body in different directions at once and to bend her fingers way back. And"—this is what I will not forget—"she should have large fish-shaped eyes." As she had said this, she lifted a hand to one of her eyes, opened her long fingers and pinched her thumb and forefinger together at the top of her nose, creating a wide elliptical space between them in front of her eye, while splaying her other fingers upward. She had created a large fish-shaped eye. When she had lowered her hand again, I could see, as I had noticed when I had first seen her without putting a name to it, that her own eyes were like that. Especially when she opened them full. They were fiery dark and unusually large and wide, the lids arching high in sensuous curves from beside her delicate nose and sloping away down to soft points near the edge of her face like a long fish tail. Yes, I could see. Hers was an Indian dancer's face with large fish-shaped eyes. I had asked where I could see her perform. And I went there the next night.

She had danced like a temple sculpture come to life. Draped in radiant red and gold silks, her rounded form moved simultaneously in several directions as though born to it, while her bare feet pranced and slapped the floor and her arms and hands fluidly told epic Hindu stories, accentuated by dramatic expressions on her face. But arresting my stare were those large fish-shaped eyes. On stage, with Samya in costume and makeup, those eyes had burst forth like none I had ever seen before. Their preternatural size, blazing energy, and beautifully sculpted form had dominated her every expression, enhancing every move. In her, I had said to myself, Yeats was right: you could not tell the dancer from the dance.

In the years since then I have seen Indian dancers in other places. Many have been quite wonderful. I have always looked closely at their eyes, but I have never seen any as remarkable as Samya's. Now, back in Chennai, watching Indian dancers with my Uruguayan friend, I thought of Samya and hoped I could see her dance again. I wondered if she was living the dancer's life that she had wanted to live, or if she had become an editor. Or if had she gotten married and settled into a different life altogether. Surely, I said to myself, her devotion to dance and her talent for performing it could not have been cast aside. Since I was having lunch with my editor the following day, I would ask. She would know.

When the evening ended, I thanked my generous host for a memorable Indian experience, and I was already looking forward to that lunch. There, as soon as our business was done, I asked my editor about Samya. Had she prevailed with her parents and become a full-time dancer, or had things gone another way? This is what she told me:

"Well, it is kind of a long story. Yes, Samya finally convinced her parents that she could be a successful professional dancer and that she would never be really happy doing anything else. Before long, she became one of the best classical dancers in Madras, if not *the* best. She was known to lovers of Indian dance all over the city and was getting known in Mumbai and elsewhere as well. Then one night there was an accident. She fell down some stairs back stage following a performance. No one saw it happen. They found her with a fractured hand and a leg badly broken. She later explained that she had lost her balance and slipped when she had stepped on something sharp in her bare feet. She had been thinking happily of the evening and had been unprepared for the mishap. She was devastated, of course. After an unhappy stay in the hospital, she had worn casts for many weeks. And she had feared she would never be able to dance again, not in the way she wanted to. After the casts came off, she had physical therapy and worked to get her agility back. But she couldn't bend her knee completely or balance on that leg. And her hand wouldn't do all that she wanted it to do. Her fears had come true. She knew her dancing career was over. Reluctantly, she started teaching young dancers. And I invited her to help edit the magazine and write articles about dance, which she did. But her heart wasn't in it. Any of it. You could see that in her face. It was as though she felt that her life, her *real* life, or maybe her dream of a life, was over.

"Then one day she didn't come to the office as she had said she would. She left no message, which was very unlike her. She had a professional's discipline in everything she did. She wasn't at home, either. No one knew where she had gone. She had said nothing to anyone. She had seemingly disappeared."

My editor paused, and I stammered, "Is that all?"

"No," she went on in a subdued tone. "It was about a week afterwards that I got a call from a police officer I knew whom I had informed of Samya's disappearance. He asked me to come down to the medical examiner's office. They had recovered the remains of a woman washed up on Marina Beach, and he thought I might be able to identify her. She had drowned, he said, probably after walking, for some unknown reason, out too far into the ocean, before the sharks had got to her. But they been surprisingly kind to her. They had left her mostly intact. A couple of other things were also unusual, he went on. 'She is dressed in a dancer's silks. And,' he added with a kind of awe in his voice, 'she has the most remarkable fish-shaped eyes.'"

*Looking up the River Thames from Waterloo Bridge toward Big Ben and Parliament
with the Millennium Wheel on the left, London, England*

London Millennium

The Thames was choppy on this dank December day, and spray flew up over the bow of the ferry plowing downriver from Westminster Bridge at Parliament to Greenwich. A handful of bundled-up passengers huddled inside drinking hot coffee or tea and wiping steam off the cold wet windows to catch the sights along the shore, while a cheery boatman with a raspy voice kept up his tour-guide patter for the forty-five minute ride. Boasting that this boat had been one of those that had valiantly evacuated British troops from Dunkirk during the war, he exuded British national pride and reverence for the past, and he cast a questioning eye on the present. The present happened to be December 31, 2000, a year after the celebration marking what the world had come to accept as the birth of a new millennium when December 31, 1999 passed to January 1, 2000.

Across the river from the stately government buildings of Whitehall, he observed in a slightly mocking tone as they chugged along, stood the "Millennium Wheel," the gigantic Ferris Wheel erected to ring in the new era with an inaugural spin at midnight on December 31, 1999. "They proudly called it the 'London Eye,'" he said with a chuckle. "But right off it ran into trouble. First, the bloody thing collapsed when they tried to hoist it onto its frame. Then, after they got it up and ready to run, the government blokes wouldn't let it pass inspection for passengers at the last minute. Missing screws or something. They decided to give it a ceremonial spin at midnight anyway without passengers. Then it wouldn't go 'round. All that fanfare for a dud. But it's running now, as you can see. A right fine view from the top they say. But it makes London look like a bloomin' carnival."

He laughed good-naturedly and went on to other sights, new and old, as the ferry sailed onward. The new Tate Gallery of Modern Art approached, set in an old power plant adjacent to the fanciful Millennium Bridge, designed for its namesake occasion, the boatman pointed out, by the renowned British architect Norman Foster. "You see it leads from the Tate Modern, as they call it, over the Thames to old London near St. Paul's Cathedral, by Britain's greatest architect ever, Christopher Wren. St. Paul's has been there for three hundred years. Came through the war standing firm. But the bridge, well, like the Ferris Wheel, it didn't work when it opened. It swayed like crazy and had to be closed. Still closed a year later. Can't have folks flying about into the river can we? Even for art and the millennium." He laughed again. "Ah, modernity," he sighed theatrically.

Just beyond the Tate, he directed everyone's eyes toward an inauspicious low structure that he identified as the New Globe Theater set in the old Elizabethan neighborhood where actors and other lowlifes had lived. "An exact replica of the original one Shakespeare put on his plays in, down to its wooden nails." He seemed pleased with that homage to the past. And, as the ferry passed under the non-descript London Bridge—which, he laughingly said, had replaced an earlier version in the 1960s bought by an American who had thought he was buying the Tower Bridge—he welcomed the sight not far away of the picturesque Tower Bridge itself and the nearby castle, the Tower of London. He happily told the colorful, some-times bloody, story of the castle, going back to Norman times, and of the Tower Bridge as a monument to the grand Victorian era. But he did not warm so much to the recent commercial development at the foot of the bridge across the river from the castle—warehouses and workshops converted into a stylish apartment complex, a clus-ter of restaurants by the trendy designer Terence Conran, and a Museum of Design. "Livens things up, sure enough," he said. "Very fashionable today. But you've got to have a pile of pounds to enjoy it. Fashion is fashion. Its time will pass." And he was not pleased at all, a few minutes later, with the new Canary Wharf buildings rising above the rest of London on a bend in the river. "London's version of New York," he sighed. "Doesn't belong here. No history to it." Then around that bend came "one more millennium folly," he declared. "The Millennium Dome, designed by another famous British architect, Richard Rogers. Looks like a giant tennis ball stuck with pins. Could house a city. Cost a million-and-a-half pounds. It was supposed to be a big hit when it opened last January 1 with exhibits and events and I don't know what all. But not many folks went there. They're going to sell it, if they can, hoping somebody will turn it into an attraction of some kind. Or maybe they'll tear it down. You could say the millennium celebration wasn't Britain's finest hour," he chuckled. "But then, flashiness and looking to the future aren't our strength. We're better at resilience and respect for the past. You can depend on these things."

Half-listening to this patter, Jeremy Squithers peered through the foggy windows at the past and present, and possibly some of the future, passing by outside. He had seen it before. He was no tourist. He was a retired professor of history at the University of London. And he was heading to the Greenwich Observatory to give a lecture as part of England's year-long celebration of the new millennium, which purists like him insisted would begin tomorrow, January 1, 2001.

In matters of time, Professor Jeremy Squithers was a perfectionist. And an expert. He had written scores of articles and some books about time and its measurement, earning him high repute in the scholarly world, at least his corner of it. So it seemed to him only appropriate that he should play a role in Britain's millennial celebrations and put people straight. Why not, he had thought, give a lecture for the general public on *time*? (He always italicized the word in his mind.) And do it on the true eve of the new millennium at the place that established the standard of the world's *time*, the Royal Observatory in Greenwich. And tell them how Greenwich got that distinction thanks to the invention of a particular clock. But that topic would just be one of many. He would talk about *time* in many learned and provocative ways. He had written to the director of the Observatory with the idea and had received an invitation to speak at the Observatory on the afternoon of December 31, 2000, in recognition of his scholarly reputation in matters of clocks and *time*.

Jeremy Squithers was feeling good as he sailed down the Thames, clutching his briefcase and watching the shoreline roll by in the misty rain. He thought about how the journey was in a sense taking him back in *time* from the nineteenth-century London of Parliament, Big Ben, and Westminster, which had been the center of the world, on downstream to the London of the seventeenth century and the "City" where the great fire had started in 1666 and where Christopher Wren had then started giving London a new and grand architectural identity crowned by St. Paul's, and on past the still older London of the Tower where kings and queens had once lived, and some had lost their heads. It was a poignant historical journey through the centuries, he mused. *Time* travel down the Thames—

interrupted here and there by jarring additions of the twentieth century. A voyage in space through *time*. Perhaps, it occurred to him, he should have put that colorful observation in his talk. He liked the idea.

He had relished the prospect of lecturing on *time* where the keeping of *time* had been so important to history. And he planned to perform as he'd never done before. He would be entertaining yet substantive. Dazzle with knowledge and flair. He'd start off with the idea of the new millennium itself, then build to ever more surprising ideas about *time*, weaving together culture and calendars, clocks and consciousness, *time* and space, truth and illusion, life and death. Tom Stoppard's intellectual acrobatics on stage would seem stuffy by comparison. And he'd change the way people look at the world and how they think about *time*. It was *time* that he gained the renown he deserved, beyond mere academic recognition among tweedy types. He deserved it more than the popularizers who rehash other people's work and contribute nothing to the understanding of *time*. He was the real thing. And now he'd do himself and *time* justice. He might get a lucrative book contract out of it. Television appearances for sure. Possibly even a movie deal. Yes, he would make *time* pay off for him. The title he had chosen for his lecture struck the tone: "As *Time* Goes By: What Is *Time*? What *Time* Is It?"

When Jeremy Squithers reached Greenwich, he was growing ever more enraptured with his subject and his ever-expanding insights into it and expectations for his own future. And he was feeling younger than he had in years. Scholarship had cost him. It took so much *time*. Hours and days and weeks and months and years researching the history of clocks in culture and steeping himself in the nature of *time*. Now in his twilight years, with *time* taking its toll in every molecule of his body, he was going to try something new. If he couldn't stop *time*, maybe he could at least use it to launch a new life for himself in the new millennium as an intellectual star.

When the ferry docked at Greenwich, Jeremy Squithers disembarked with others who were braving the dreary weather to see the home of Greenwich Mean Time and the Prime Meridian at the Royal Observatory up the hill. He knew that they would learn about how the Observatory had been built in the late seventeenth century for the first Royal Astronomer to map the night sky with his twenty-foot-long telescope, hoping to enable British sailors plying the seas to find their distance from port sailing west and east—that is, their longitude—which they could not otherwise do, and how a clockmaker, not an astronomer, had eventually solved what was known as the "problem of longitude." But he would tell his audience much more than that.

Jeremy Squithers trudged up that hill toward the hall adjacent to the Observatory where he would give his lecture, admiring along the way the distinguished Royal Naval College by the river, another of Wren's fine buildings, and feeling very good about himself indeed. He was going to breathe new life into old ideas and into himself.

He stood on the promontory near the Observatory under his umbrella in a light drizzle to look out over London stretching westward below. The Millennium Dome with its pin-cushion roof lay in the near distance, and just beyond it the skyscrapers of Canary Wharf dwarfed practically everything else in sight. In the far distance he could just make out St. Paul's, and he knew that on a clear day he might even see Big Ben and Parliament from here, but not today. Braced by the sight of his beloved city laden with history and embodying civilization—despite the intrusion of modern obscenities, and whose *time* in the sun he granted had rather passed—he turned and strode to the lecture hall beside the Observatory. Outside he saw a large sign announcing the event and glowed at what wonders that portended for his future.

He entered about fifteen minutes early and found a modest audience already gathered. Fellow scholars, journalists, tourists, and the idly curious, he assumed, who would all be enthralled. And the press would report his performance, and his public career would take off. As he reached the front of the hall, Algernon Mahoney, the director of the Royal Observatory, came up and politely addressed him, "Professor Squithers?" The professor nodded, and the director introduced himself then escorted his guest to the dais, making gracious small talk about how pleased he had been to receive the professor's offer to speak, although he did not disclose his surprise upon receiving the offer that Professor Squithers—known to Mahoney through scholarly writings of long ago—was still alive. Once seated, they chatted on about the professor's works and the hoopla over the millennium. Then the professor took a few minutes to consult his written notes, cocking an eye toward the audience, which he had expected to fill the hall, but which he was gratified to see now at least covered much of it. When the moment came to begin, Mr. Mahoney went to the lectern. He remarked the unique occasion for this event at the genuine turn of the millennium, and, after ticking off some of the noted speaker's scholarly accomplishments, he hailed him as a preeminent authority on nothing less than the history of time.

Jeremy Squithers rose to speak. Placing his speech on the lectern, he put on his reading glasses, took out his pocket watch, flipped it open, and laid it beside his papers. He had *timed* the speech so he wouldn't run over his *time*, although it had occurred to him he could make a joke about what that would mean. He knew the first rule of show business is never to stay on the stage too long—get off while they're yelling for more. Juicing himself with adrenaline, he greeted his audience and introduced the title of his lecture: "'As *Time* Goes By: What Is *Time*? What *Time* Is It?'"

He grinned at his clever, yet profound, title and looked into the unresponsive faces of the crowd. Tough room, he thought. He started: "First I must talk about calendars, much on our minds these days. As you know, one millennium is ending and another is beginning. But, as some of you might not know, one is ending today and the other beginning tomorrow, not last year. What does that mean?

Not much really. This millennium thing is just a Christian idea, and a pretty vague one at that. For that matter, the very concept of 'year' is rather slippery, as we will see.

"Anyhow, Christians say they're counting the 2000 years from when Jesus was born. But nobody really knows exactly when that was. There wasn't a calendar in the manger. And nobody had even tried to determine the year of that birth until an enterprising medieval abbot named Dionysius Exiguus calculated that Jesus had been born exactly 525 years before Dionysus made the calculation, and he christened that The Year of Our Lord, *Anno Domini* in Latin, abbreviated as AD.

"Actually, Dionysus had not been looking for Jesus's birthday at all but was trying to fix dates for Easter, which Christians had celebrated for centuries, as they had not celebrated 'Christmas,' because they cared more about Jesus's resurrection than His birth. But they had never been sure quite when to schedule that celebration because, for various reasons, it was tied to cycles of the moon, and moon *time* doesn't fit sun *time*—of which much more later. Dionysius couldn't quite nail down Easter either, but his incidental notion of counting the years since the birth of Jesus stuck. Dating the years before that birth was another afterthought a couple of centuries later when the Venerable Bede here in England wrote a religious history using the AD scheme of Dionysius and traced that history back to the '*time* before the Lord's true incarnation.' This became Before Christ, BC. Tradition has followed both Dionysius and Bede, even though modern historians have put the birth of Jesus in the years 3 or 4 BC, a historical curiosity ignored because it would mess up the traditional chronology. And here's another wrinkle. Since neither AD nor BC had a year zero, the first millennium began in the year 1 AD. That's why we are here today to start ringing in the third millennium AD (or, as is becoming fashionable in our secular *times*, CE for Common Era), which truly begins at midnight tonight when we turn our calendars to January 1, 2001, not a year ago. You follow? Well, it gets worse."

Jeremy Squithers smiled a little and raised his eyes from the page he was reading to see the audience's response. He couldn't tell for sure what it was.

"You see," he went on, "before those medieval Christians, not many people had ever felt much need to count years from a single beginning of any kind. They had rather tended to count years by the reigns of their rulers, if they did it at all. The Roman Varro did try to figure out when Rome was founded in order to start the years from there, and Dionysius had used Varro's system in part to compute the year of Jesus's birth. But the Romans still generally relied on the regimes of their rulers to chart the years and let it go at that. And we must not forget the Hebrews. The Jewish calendar, which probably had sources going back to the Sumerians, counted years from the presumed Creation of the Garden of Eden, which they put at about 5500 years ago now. But even that chronology more or less gave way in *time* for practical purposes to the Christians calendar. The same could be said of the Muslim calendar, invented to mark the years after Muhammed's epochal departure from Mecca for Medina. The Christian *time*table eclipsed that too. In Asia, counting years took a different course. The Chinese started out counting them from their early emperors, but over *time* they developed a repetitive sixty-year cycle broken into sub-cycles of twelve years, each labeled by symbolic names of the zodiac and keyed to moon *time*. Hence, we are now in the year of the Dragon—an especially good year signifying adventure, romance, and royalty—which ends on January 23, to be followed by the Chinese New Year on the 24th that will usher in the year of the Snake—also a good year (all of them are really) symbolizing idealism, enthusiasm, and determination. You have to hand it to the Chinese. They showed that calendars can be fun. But even the Chinese now largely submit to the Christian system in the everyday conduct of life. I would say something about the Hindus and Buddhists, but with their infinite cosmic twists and turns on things, they came up with calendars too complicated to venture into here.

"At all events, anyone who looks very closely into this business of counting years sees that the ways we try to do that only arbitrarily mark the passage of historical *time*. Now we say we are at the beginning of a new millennium. That is in truth a Christian myth set in play by a resourceful monk. But that myth has pretty much taken over the world. And that's not a bad thing. It puts some order into *time*, which can be pretty messy, as I trust you are now discovering, if you did not know it already."

He peeped over his glasses and thought he saw a few assenting expressions.

"OK, moving on, just as counting *time* in years from the birth of Jesus is a useful myth, so are the ways we count days and months adding up to a year. But these didn't come from Christianity. They started with pagans, east and west, who tried to chart the passage of *time* in days and months as perceived in the cycles of the sun and the moon (many also broke months into what we call 'weeks,' but never mind that). But those cycles are not as regular at they might seem. *Time* in nature is trickier than our perceptions and calendars would lead us to believe. It doesn't fall into convenient pieces that we label days and months and years. This is because the sun and the moon and the earth all have different *times*. At least we say they do. Do they know what *time* it is? I don't think so."

He was sure he heard a few chuckles. That pleased him. He scanned the crowd for signs of mirth. Not finding any, he gave a conspicuous "ahem" to signal a change of direction and proceeded.

"Here we must take a quick look at what scientists tell us about counting years and days and so on. They say the earth rotates once every 86,400 seconds, more or less, which adds up to 1,440 minutes or twenty-four hours—that is in clock *time*, of course, which we will come to later. And they say, let's call it a 'day.' It takes 365 and roughly a quarter of those days for the earth to make a complete revolution around the sun. That's not tidy, but we call each revolution a 'year,' or a solar year. At the same *time*, the moon goes around the earth twenty-nine and a half *times* from full moon to full moon. That is a lunar 'month' as we see it. In fact, the moon takes only twenty-seven and a third days to circle the earth, but because the earth is also moving around the sun it takes the moon two days to catch up and make a lunar month. As you might suspect, fitting these irregular celestial movings about of the sun and moon into a consistent calendar of days and months in a year wasn't easy. But science didn't do it. Culture did, after a fashion.

"Many cultures just took the seemingly easy way of letting cycles of the moon mark the months. But it turned out that lunar months add up to about 354-and-one-third solar days, ten short of one revolution of the earth around the sun, or a year of 365-and-one-quarter solar days. That's why lunar calendars shift about each solar year, changing the dates of the Chinese New Year and Jewish holidays, as well as that of the Christian bugbear, Easter, which even now is still keyed to moon *time* and observed on the Sunday after the first full moon following the spring equinox. Hardly an orderly arrangement. But forget Easter. We have to go back to the imperious and ingenious Romans to find the first efforts to create calendars marking months and days in a year rationally. Well, if not altogether rationally, at least they invented a system that became the basis for the monthly and daily calendars we have today adding up to a year. The Egyptians had tried to do something like that when they adopted probably the first solar calendar about six thousand years ago, but it lost out to the Romans."

He glimpsed the audience again and found them rather impassive. It dawned on him that perhaps calendars were not as captivating to them as to him. But he was certain to change that. Raising the volume of his voice a bit to heighten attention, he resumed the theme.

"This Roman ingenuity started under Julius Caesar. His wise men fit the lunar months and solar year together by adding days in a relatively consistent way. This became the Julian calendar of months and days, and Julius got a month named for him, July. That calendar was far from precise, but it gave us the twelve months of irregular lengths that we now have, beginning with January, and it added a leap day to the unfairly short month of February in order to manage that pesky extra quarter of a day in the solar year (the Egyptians had struggled with this problem, too, in creative but not enduring ways). Julius's successor, Augustus, continued juggling, and he got a month named for him, too, August—the two powerful rulers getting their summer months of thirty-one days back to back, just like their reigns.

"But there was still a problem with that nettlesome leap day. The Julian calendar prescribed that it should come every four years in years divisible by four (although a miscalculation seems to have made it every three years for a while; ah, the difficulties of getting a hold on *time*). However, even this expedient had a flaw. The scheme for leap day didn't match solar *time* after all. In fact, it added *time* to the calendar year—about eleven minutes. Think of that. Adding *time* to the year."

Quickly surveying the audience, he was convinced by their silence that they were indeed with him.

"Finally," he went on, "Pope Gregory, who was still trying to settle exactly when to celebrate Easter, had that flaw in the Julian calendar fixed in 1582 through a rather arcane ingenuity. He and his wise men simply eliminated the leap day in any century year not divisible by four hundred. That oddity worked. The days of the sun and the days of the year now fit together—which, by the way, is why the year 2000 is a leap year but the year 1900 was not. But wouldn't you know, jolly old Protestant England, and some other countries, didn't want to go along with this clever Catholic calendar trick and stuck with the Julian version. That did not turn out well for them. Those eleven extra minutes each year kept adding up. After about two hundred years, England was living no less—or is it fewer? Oh, who cares?—than eleven days behind the continent. That wouldn't do. Bowing to the politics of *time*, to catch up England wiped out those eleven days overnight in 1752—stirring protests in the streets against the loss of English *time*. As well it should have. No one wants to lose *time*. Especially not a whole country."

He flashed a smile at his listeners to underscore his wit. He did not wait for the response.

"So it is," he continued, "that the Gregorian calendar is now the standard for the business of life around the globe—thanks to modern Western economic and political preeminence in this age of *time* on the mind—although some cultures still use their traditional calendars for dating rituals and festivals. It works, but it shows how nature's *time* is not quite ours. Our calendars are awkward human inventions to organize the passage of days, months, and years for human beings—again, I'm not even going to bother with the quirky notion of weeks. The trouble is, *time* slips away from anyone who tries to tie it down. But we keep trying."

He paused and took a sip of water from a glass placed for him beside the lectern. He did not detect eyes wandering.

"And so far I have barely mentioned clocks," he said with emphasis. "A very complicated subject. Measuring years, months, days was not enough. The *time* came when people wanted to break the days into hours, minutes, seconds, even fractions of seconds. Nowadays, we actually have atomic clocks that calculate those fractions with a precision well beyond human experience and causing some, shall I say 'temporal,' problems that I'll return to.

"OK. As you probably know, throughout most of history, measuring the passing of *time* during a day depended on nature itself, shadows cast by the sun, or water rising against a bank or pouring over a wheel, and the like. That was all rather ambiguous but it was sufficient for most purposes in traditional societies. It was not until the invention of mechanical clocks that people really started to know what *time* it is."

He looked up to see how that line had registered. He couldn't tell. He pushed on to the explanation, lapsing into a somewhat more professorial tone.

"In case you don't know, mechanical clocks originated in the late Middle Ages to help monks schedule the rituals of their days with regularly *timed* bells, and to help organize the routines of burgeoning urban life with clocks in towers rising above marketplaces—some of these marketplace clocks have become tourist attractions because of their elaborate figures that move around with the chiming of the hours. The heart of mechanical clocks is what is known as an escapement. That's a device—usually powered by a spring or a pendulum—with a spiked wheel that turns at regular intervals as each spike is caught and then released by—or escapes from—the prongs of a connected moving mechanism. This is why we wind mechanical clocks and they go tick tock, tick tock as the wheel turns and the spring winds down. Not long after the invention of mechanical clocks, Renaissance clockmakers went on to design elegant mechanical *time*pieces that could keep more accurate *time*, but they did this not so much to aid daily life as to display artistry in keeping *time*. The eighteenth century upped the accuracy by introducing tiny jewels into the escapement to reduce the friction in the moving parts caused by softer materials. From there on came more refinements. But, wonderful as mechanical clocks can be, in recent *times* they have largely yielded in everyday use to quartz clocks. These use vibrating crystals powered by batteries instead of mechanical escapements and springs."

Growing aware that these technical matters might not excite everyone as they did him, he left them and turned to a topic he thought surely would captivate every listener in the room.

"All right. I won't bother you with more of these details. Instead, let's come back to where we are right now. I mean at the very place that sets the world's *time* every day because of a particular clock invented in the eighteenth century. Namely, the clock that solved the historic problem of longitude. Some of you might know that story. It's fascinating. I'll summarize it."

He had another sip of water and peered over his glasses again at his listeners. He couldn't gauge their reaction but assumed they were curious.

He now tried to speak in a folksier tone. "First, I should define longitude, just so we all know what I'm talking about—I trust *I* do." He smirked and continued.

"In short, longitude is nothing but a way of marking distance east and west on the earth guided by imaginary lines running vertically north and south and meeting at the poles. These lines are called meridians, and each of them marks one degree of longitude, adding up to the earth's circumference of 360 degrees. I should also point out that the earth rotates fifteen degrees every hour, accounting for the distance between the lines of longitude you see on world maps and giving us the twenty-four hour solar day. Got that?"

He glanced up to underscore the question and proceeded.

"By the same token, latitude is a way of marking distance north and south guided by imaginary lines called parallels that encircle the globe horizontally from top to bottom and never meet. Each parallel marks one degree of latitude with ninety degrees above the equator and ninety below it. That sounds simple enough. But here's the thing.

"Seafarers for centuries had known how to find their latitude, or distance going north and south, by using the equator, or zero latitude, as the natural starting point for measurement and observing the sun and stars in relation to the horizon. But finding their longitude, or distance going east and west, was a mystery because it was so influenced by the earth's rotation and spherical shape, and there was no natural starting point like the equator to measure from. So, when European seafarers ventured far out on the ocean going west from Europe they kept getting lost, causing many shipwrecks, since they couldn't track their distance from home port. In other words, they had no way to determine their longitude.

"This got so distressing for the seagoing British Empire that in 1714 the government offered a reward of twenty-thousand pounds to anyone who could at last figure it out. Astronomers here at the

Royal Observatory took the bait first, claiming they could find true longitude by producing a complete map of the stars providing fixed east-west coordinates that sailors could follow anywhere. But—and now we return to *time*—surprise, surprise, a clockmaker beat them to the solution. As it happened, a chap named John Harrison believed he could solve the problem of longitude with a clock that would keep accurate *time* at sea. For this would enable sailors to know the actual *time* that had elapsed since their departure despite the rotation and shape of the earth, and then, by determining their own local *time* with celestial observations, they could compare the two *times* and calculate the distance traveled in degrees of longitude at whatever latitude they were sailing. At the equator, one degree of longitude is at its widest covering about sixty-nine miles—divided, I might add, into minutes and seconds for more precision, confusing as these words might be here. Therefore, at the equator every error of one hour in *time* that had accumulated over the course of a voyage west or east resulted in an error of one degree of space, or sixty-nine miles. That proved to be very perilous."

He raised his eyes to connect with his listeners but failed to detect some yawns and rapidly went on to wrap up his summary.

"I know that's a mouthful. But now the climax. Harrison, a carpenter by trade and an amateur clockmaker, won the contest in the 1760s while the astronomers were still scratching their heads. It had taken him some forty years—and he never got all the prize money because of jealous astronomers. He had first tried three pendulum clocks, which as you might imagine, can be unstable on the ocean, even though Harrison built ingenious counterbalances into them to roll with the sea. They were also very large and complicated. Finally, he shifted gears, so to speak, and came up with a marvelous jeweled *time*piece you could hold in your hand, and, more important—get this—it kept accurate *time* to within one minute over an ocean voyage of 4,700 miles and about a month from England to Jamaica, ticking away without a hitch, unaffected by ocean movements or the rotation of the earth. Amazing. You can see all of these won-derful clocks here in the museum."

He looked up, gave a slight smile, and pressed on.

"Well, that's the summary of the longitude problem. But it's far from the end of the story. And that's good. Because this British triumph with a clock would put here, at Greenwich, the starting point of longitude, zero degrees, or the Prime Meridian—that is, the imaginary line encircling the globe vertically that divides the eastern and western hemispheres into 180 degrees each and is the equivalent of the equator for latitude. An international commission formalized this in the 1880s. By putting the Prime Meridian of longitude here, the commission also made Greenwich the place that set the world's standard *time* with Greenwich Mean *Time*. After all, longitude and *time* go together. And to further organize *time*, the commission created *time* zones starting here and rolling westward around the world to coordinate what *time* it is everywhere as the world turns. They also established the International Date Line to mark where the earth's day officially begins and ends, exactly half way around the world from Greenwich at 180 degrees longitude. The pace and spread of modern commerce, communications, and transportation demanded these things. Nowadays we always have to know what *time* it is and be on *time* wherever we are. A very dizzying business. But it's all very important in the history of *time*."

He sipped a little more water as he surveyed the room expecting eager faces. He didn't find any but didn't look too closely. He cleared his throat and continued.

"But I must also mention that, complicating the keeping of *time* even more, the earth rotates at changing speeds. It might even be slowing down, dammit all. That could make for some very bad troubles ahead. Maybe everything will fall off. Not soon, but in *time*. We can't sense any of this in daily life, but it does have an effect on the precise measurement of *time*. Here's how. And this will wind up my concise history of counting *time* with calendars and clocks."

Again he glanced at the audience, and this time gave a reassuring nod.

"Remember those atomic clocks I mentioned and the problem with *time* they raise? Well, they keep a different *time* from other clocks. That's because they don't measure *time* by the sun and the earth's wobbly rotation—or even by the battery powered oscillations of crystals in quartz clocks. They rely on the virtually perfect regularity of the oscillations of atoms. Consequently, their *time* is slightly more accurate—and actually faster—than that of other clocks. What *time* is it, really? Scientists quarrel over that. Physicists want to follow precise atomic *time* because they deal with atoms and the inner workings of things. But astronomers want to follow solar or earth *time* because they study the heavens from the earth as it rotates. The astronomers have won so far. But this has made for a *time*keeping gimmick. To offset the disparity between atomic *time* and the earth's solar *time*, technicians have to, in effect, slow down atomic clocks. So they add a 'leap second' every now and then to what's called atomic Coordinated Universal *Time*, abbreviated as UTC. UTC has actually supplanted Greenwich Mean *Time*, or GMT, as the standard of *time* on earth because it's universal and not anchored to a particular place. But the two *times* really amount to the same thing because of that leap second. Isn't that a kick? Just like the Romans adding a leap day to the calendar to make it fit the year. What *time* is it, indeed?"

Jeremy Squithers paused, took more water, eyed the audience, passing over the wandering eyes and restlessness here and there, and mentally geared up for the best part of his lecture now to come. His own take on *time*.

"So, where does this little survey of *time* and its measurement leave us? What, after all, is *time*? Ask yourself, Does *time* exist outside our minds? The philosopher Immanuel Kant said it doesn't, as far as we know. *Time*, he said, is basically a way of thinking that we can't have any experience without. How could we live without *time*, at least in our minds? Now, ponder this: Could we even be conscious if there were no *time*? Doesn't consciousness depend on *time*? Try being conscious without it. But does *time* depend on our consciousness? What would *time* be if there were no consciousness of it? Nothing?

"Oh, my," he exclaimed with a grin. "*Time* raises so many questions. Go on to this one: does the universe know what *time* it is? Or care? The universe would have to be conscious to know what *time* it is or care, wouldn't it? Is the universe conscious of *time*? Did the universe begin without *time*, and when it ends will there be no *time*? What would that mean? Can *time* exist when nothing else does? In the end, who really knows what *time* it is, or what *time* is?

Restlessness widened in the audience as people looked quizzically at each other and at their watches. Jeremy Squithers continued.

"Now, I see by my watch that *time* is passing, to be sure. It is now nearly what we think of as 2:30 p.m., or 1430 hours. What does that mean? The designations a.m. and p.m. come from Latin terms for *ante meridian* and *post meridian*, or before and after the middle or mid-day. We use those designations with twelve-hour clocks. But 1430 hours tells us the *time* past midnight on twenty-four-hour clocks. Is that better? Of course, like so many things we say about *time*, these are both simply human abstractions marking the passage of *time* in the daily rotation of the earth. And yet, we all know that *time* is no mere abstraction in our lives. Because things change. We can see this happening. Things get old. They decay. That's *time* for you. What it does to you. You can't find *time* itself, but you can sure find the effects of *time*. *Time* takes a toll. On everything. That's how we know it's real. Maybe it's more real than anything else. Actually, we can say that everything is a clock, measuring *time*. Our bodies. Our buildings. Nature. Measuring *time* with decay.

"Yes, decay, or at least aging. Because nothing lasts. The very clocks invented to measure *time* with abstract numbers decay in *time* unless we prevent it. Even ideas get old. Plato was wrong. Ideas aren't eternal and changeless. They get old. They may not decay, but they get out of date, become clichés—dead clichés we call some of them—or they just get forgotten. Yes, even ideas get old and can die. But if we could stop that thing we call *time*—*temps, tempo, tiempo, Zeit*, and all the others—that is, if we could stop all change, we could escape *time*. And death. Couldn't we?"

Shuffling and some murmurs in the audience failed to catch his attention as he concentrated more intensely on his thoughts and words.

"Einstein proved it," he went on. "Making a hash of common sense, he said *time* is space and space is *time*. Granted, seafarers who use *time* to measure space or distance know something about this. Still, what does it all mean? *Time* and space and life? Einstein claimed that if you could go fast enough through space, the clocks with you—including your own body—would slow down relative to clocks where you left. So when you return, the people you left behind would be older than you are. That's a cosmic fountain of youth, isn't it? But Einstein's theory also indicated that as things go faster—I mean really, really fast, up to the speed of light, which is about 186,000 miles per second—their mass increases. And if you could reach the speed of light your mass would become infinite— that's a hell of a weight gain—then *time* would stand still. How about that? But it can't happen. Nature won't let it, or so Einstein believed. Because it would screw things up completely since everything would be a single mass and nothing more could happen. Of course, nobody knows for sure. Does nature know? All very strange. Very strange."

He shook his head with histrionic bewilderment.

"And there is this: we measure the very space or size of the universe itself by *time*, in light years, counting on light to travel at its fixed speed. Most astronomers say that the universe originated about thirteen billion solar years ago in a Big Bang that threw things outward, and they are still going, meaning the universe is expanding. Don't ask to where. So, if we could see light from the first stars formed by that Big Bang their light would be some thirteen billion of our years old traveling to get here at 186,000 miles per second across thirteen billion light years of space. That's all longer ago and farther away than we can really grasp. And by the *time* that light got here, the stars it came from could be gone, extinguished by old age and the assault of *time* itself. So we would be seeing light from nothing, stars that don't exist. Wow, talk about *time* going by. Space in *time*, *time* in space, all tangled up. Quite baffling, isn't it? That's *time* for you."

More shuffling in the audience. A few people in the back slipped out. Jeremy Squithers carried on without a pause.

"Well, let's leave the weird *time* and space of the universe and return to the clocks of our lives. They tick down, year by year, month by month, day by day, hour by hour, minute by minute, second by second, and we see this because our bodies age, and we are conscious of our lives passing and have memories of our past. That was Marcel Proust's whole point, wasn't it? Proust searched for lost *time*, not in the universe but in his life, or in his fictional character's life. We are *time* with a past. We are memory. As he wrote, 'The memory of a particular image is but regret for a particular moment; and houses, roads, avenues are as fugitive, alas, as the years.' Ah, yes, 'tis so. And as the song says, 'You must remember this, a kiss is just a kiss, a sigh is just a sigh . . . as *time* goes by.' So we should remember the kisses and the sighs before *time* takes them from us. Buddhists say our lives are nothing but a bridge of dreams from birth into nothingness. And it's all as fleeting as the Drake fly, which lives only hours and that etymologists label an ephemeroptera— isn't that a terrific word for ephemeral things? It is here, then not here. Come and gone. Moments in *time*. Then nothing. Like the vanished stars. Like us."

Puzzled whispers were running through the room. More people made their way out. Jeremy Squithers didn't notice.

"Or look at it all another way. Maybe *time* itself is an illusion. I mentioned Immanuel Kant's notion that *time* is in our heads. And think of Plato. He said *time* was an illusion of mortals in the lowly material world. True reality is transcendent, outside of *time*, changeless, eternal, like abstract ideas and the soul. I said he was wrong about ideas never getting old or dying. But that applies only to the material, mortal world where things do get old and die. Outside of that material world, maybe he was right. Nothing dies or even changes. Take the soul. After all, if the soul isn't immortal and eternal, what's it good for? And yet, we have to ask, does the immortal soul have to be changeless? Eternity is a long *time*. Why shouldn't the soul change through eternity? It'd be a very dull thing and hardly worth having if it didn't change, wouldn't it? But, if the soul changes in eternity, it is subject to *time*. So there you are. Either the soul experiences *time* and changes or it doesn't."

He raised his eyes for a moment, looking out over the audience rather than at them as if collecting his thoughts, then returned to his text.

"Now contemplate this. If the immortal soul knows *time* and changes, does it get old? Jonathan Swift conjured up a bunch of people in *Gulliver's Travels* who got their wish to live forever. They had triumphed over death. They were immortal. But they had neglected the passage of *time*. *Time* kept going for them. And they kept aging, getting older and more decrepit as *time* went by. They were miserable because they couldn't stop the ravages of *time*, and yet they couldn't die. *Time* had become an eternal curse. As Plato said, change is a defect in perfection. So *time* is a defect in existence. But what would existence be without it? One of the conundrums of *time*."

More of the audience departed, distracting Jeremy Squithers not at all.

"The Bible says God created the heavens and the earth in six days. What was a day? Did God have a calendar or a clock? Was there *time* in the Garden of Eden? Not likely. Adam and Eve weren't supposed to get old, were they? Aging was one of the punishments of getting thrown out of the Garden. That means human *time* started only after God got vexed over the incident of the apple.

But divine *time*, God's *time*, if He or She has any, must be something else. Saint Augustine said that God Himself is both *time* and *time*less, past, present, future, and eternity, all rolled into one at the same *time*. But this really doesn't make much sense. Either *time* goes by or it doesn't. Whoever God is. What would *time* be if it didn't go by? It can't really stand still, can it? 'The world will always welcome lovers, as *time* goes by,' and as *time* goes by it takes a toll on lovers, like everything else. Would a kiss still be a kiss, a sigh be a sigh if *time* didn't go by?"

Still more listeners left.

But Jeremy Squithers was riding high. He felt loquacious, eloquent, brilliant, completely dazzling as he wove together expertise and ingenuity, history and imagination, science and literature, philosophy and psychology, and more, demonstrating the illusory nature and fugitive wiles and the sweet and bitter consequences of *time*. He was not aware that *time* was flying and that the audience was diminishing. Nor did he see Algernon Mahoney fidgeting and then slipping a message to a staff member discreetly summoned from the wings. Finally, Mahoney got up and gently informed the professor that he was running over his time.

A trifle flustered by the interruption and the revelation that he had violated the rule of show business about getting off stage at the right *time*, Jeremy Squithers fumbled with his papers, collected himself, and finished with a flowery peroration on how *time* travel might come some *time*, if nature will let it, and then we will be able to turn our clocks backward and forward and go anywhere in *time* that we want to, and maybe we'll even be able to stop *time*, and then aging will end, and everything will last forever because nothing will change, nothing will happen, and then a kiss will not be just a kiss, a sigh will not be just a sigh, because *time* will not go by. He closed with the words, "But would we really want that? We'd have no memories, we'd have no consciousness. Maybe it's better to just let *time* go by. Now, what *time* is it?"

He eyed his watch, picked it up and shook it. It had stopped.

Had *time* stopped? What would happen now? Maybe he wouldn't have to get older. He'd be an ageless star. But, he remembered, he wouldn't be conscious of it. So, what would be the point?

Reflecting on that puzzle while gathering up his papers and envisioning his new renown, he had to concede that *time* was still going by despite his stopped watch. He sat down beside Algernon Mahoney, oblivious to the depleted audience and convinced that everyone had been stunned into silence by his genius. Mahoney stood up and thanked the professor and the remaining people in the room, remarking what an extraordinary presentation they had heard. Then he led Jeremy Squithers out to the grounds.

The drizzle had let up, and Jeremy Squithers smiled at the people who were posing for photos straddling the Prime Meridian, the line of zero longitude where Greenwich Mean Time started and the organization of time on earth with it. Presuming they had been in his audience, he thought proudly how much more they now knew about *time*. Others were pushing through the clock museum, and he was sure they had also been inspired by his words. How good he felt. This millennium thing has been good for England after all. And for him.

A pair of officious looking men came up the hill toward them. Mr. Mahoney excused himself and asked his guest to wait as he went to greet them. Jeremy Squithers concluded that news of his brilliant performance must have gotten out already and that they must want to arrange an interview with him, or maybe take him to a television studio. I am a star, he congratulated himself.

Algernon Mahoney brought the men over and introduced them as officials very interested in him and his welfare. He added: "Thank you again for your amazing talk here today, professor. Now these gentlemen will accompany you from here. I wish you well."

Jeremy Squithers stood tall and thought of the good things to come. One of the men took his arm. "Let us help you, professor," he said. "You are an important person, but you're not as young as you used to be."

"Very true," Jeremy Squithers replied. "Ah, the toll of *time*." He chuckled. "Where will we be going?" he asked brightly. "To a television station?"

"Well," the man answered, "it's kind of a surprise."

As they walked together down the hill, the men asked him his thoughts on living into a new millennium. Jeremy Squithers was pleased at the attention and offered a few pithy insights on the familiar subject. His anticipation of renown was soaring.

When they reached the bottom of the hill, a van was waiting for them. The professor liked that, too. A good sign. No ferry ride in anonymity. He was clearly a celebrity now. One of the men opened the door and the other helped him in. There sat a woman he vaguely recognized, maybe from television, he thought. She greeted him politely and patted him on the arm.

"Well, professor," she said, "I understand you've had quite a day."

He smiled broadly. "You've heard already?"

"Oh, yes indeed," she answered. "But you gave us quite a scare. You know you really mustn't go out by yourself like this. You can't just do anything you want to do anymore. It could be dangerous. We must take better care of you and watch over you more closely. You'll just have to get used to that, Professor. It's time."

Sunrise at Copacabana Beach with Sugarloaf Mountain in the left center, Rio de Janeiro, Brazil

Ciéla

It was after midnight on a warm December night when he slouched into the hotel on Copacabana Beach. The long day of meetings in São Paulo had dragged on through dinner. He'd decided to take the half-hour flight to Rio afterwards, whatever the time, just to escape the deadly corporate strategy sessions on how to build new markets for disposable diapers. Yes. Disposable diapers. He would be among the pioneers, he had been assured. South America was virgin territory for them, so the research department had claimed. Mothers there hardly knew what disposable diapers were. And once they found out, the VP of marketing had crowed, there'd be fortunes to be made. Especially in Brazil. The biggest market. But top management said they had to move fast. Competition would be ferocious. He carried a recent *Wall Street Journal* article making the case, distributed at the breakfast meeting: "South America's Emerging Markets Poised for Battle over Diapers."

But he didn't care. Not anymore. Professional ambition, and the zeal for marketing products like disposable diapers, had leaked out of him—he cringed at the thought. Even with fortunes to be made. Even if Cuddlies, Snugglies, Cozies, by whatever name—"Ickies," he called them—were the key to South America's economic and social future, the engine of development, the makings of utopia, a panacea for freedom and the good life, and all the rest of the humbug that the company philosophers high-mindedly puffed. He shuddered to think of the nonsense he'd heard colleagues say: "When Cuddlies are in every house and shack and shanty in Brazil you'll see a new country. A nation of energetic, productive people who feel good from day one of their lives! And they'll never go back. We'll have customers forever. We can diversify with a whole line of products. Cuddlies for infants in various weights and absorbancies. Then Cuddly underwear. Cuddly pacifiers. Cuddly pajamas. Maybe a movie tie-in. Remember Pocahontas underpants? Why not Cuddlies in Disney movies? Why not . . . ?"

He figured that a day in Rio de Janeiro would take him away from all that. Maybe give him a new start. He needed it. Before going home to the empty apartment in Manhattan where Natalie used to be waiting. That was six months ago, before she announced she was leaving him for her workout trainer at the gym who could do wonderful, profoundly moving things for her. What could those things be, he wondered? He guessed he would never know. She was gone. And he had nothing to go home to but diaper theory.

So Rio would be an escape. It wasn't like him to do that. But he did it anyway. And he felt good about it.

Once there in a hotel room, he emptied his pockets on a table, threw off his suit jacket, and stepped out onto the terrace. Seeing the arc of Copacabana Beach seven stories below, lit by the street lamps of Avenida Atlântica swooping in a great crescent from his hotel at one end of the beach around to the other where Sugarloaf Mountain rose prominently, he mentally patted himself on the back for coming. He absorbed the exhilarating sight and his own self-satisfaction for a few minutes, then splashed water on his face, changed into casual clothes, locked his valuables in the closet safe to protect them from the urchins he had been warned descend from shanties in the hills to pilfer from tourists, and, disregarding the late hour, headed down to the street for a drink at a sidewalk café along the broad seaside avenue.

The Avenida Atlântica was alive with *Cariocas*, locals, whose night had hardly begun, and with visitors, all enjoying the scene and eating and drinking and merry-making in the balmy southern summer night. He took an empty table in a nearby café spread along a stretch of the avenue. Bent on plumbing the adventure, he asked the waiter about the Brazilian drink specialty, *caipirinha*. The waiter, with arching eyebrows and animated hands, described it as a delicious Brazilian concoction of sugarcane liquor called cachaça, sugar, and lime juice that lifts the spirits like Carneval. That sounded just right. When it came, he sipped it timorously, then thirstily. Limeade, he said to himself, and soon ordered another, settling in to watch the parade of ambling passersby. Then she sat down.

"'Allo," a husky female voice said. Startled, he jerked his head around. There across the table sat a woman smiling at him. It was an easy smile, and it revealed a broken tooth she made no attempt to hide. Quite pretty, though, he thought. Large eyes. Strong features. Long dark hair. He could not tell her age for sure. The light was dim, and he suspected she wore a lot of makeup. Then studying her face a little, he detected enough lines around her mouth to show that youth had passed a while ago.

"Hello," he replied, uncertain if he should speak or ignore her or ask her to leave. Who was she? No tourist. A friendly *Carioca*? Possibly a prostitute? He'd been warned about them. They're legal in Rio, he remembered some guidebook had said, but that doesn't make 'em honest. He wasn't searching for that kind of escape anyway. Too dangerous.

"I am Ciéla," she said warmly.

"Nice name," he answered without thinking, hearing the melodic syllables, "See-ayy-la."

"I like eet. From my madre. She Argentinian. She love to look at the sky. Sun. Moon. Stars. The heaven. So she call me Ciéla. For the sky. The heaven." She gestured heavenward and widened her smile.

Kind of sweet, he said to himself.

"You American?" she asked.

"Yes."

"First time in Rio?"

"Yes. I just got here."

"You like?"

"I guess so. It's very nice out here."

"I luv eet. I leev heer all my life. Ees beee-yooo-teee-foool. Sometime rain. But every time beee-yooo-teee-foool." She flashed her broken-tooth smile again.

He returned a quick grin, and shifted his eyes to the street.

Her voice came back. "You beezness een Rio?"

He paused. "Not really," he said distractedly.

"How long you stay?"

"I leave tomorrow night."

"Ah," she replied with a slight air of disappointment.

Then for reasons he could not have explained, an irresistible curiosity came over him. And he asked nervously, "You, uh, work here?"

"Yayss," she answered pleasantly.

He pushed on, "Where?"

She shrugged, "At hotel."

"Oh. Which one?"

Casually, she opened her arms and reached out toward Copacabana. When she brought them back she nodded toward his hotel and said, "Mostly heer."

"Wha . . . what do you do?" he stammered almost involuntarily.

She looked at him and smiled warmly. "I make peepul happee."

He gazed at her. She *was* a prostitute. That's what she had meant wasn't it? No pretense. But she was softer than he had imagined someone like her would be here. Yes, even sweet. His curiosity grew. Feigning nonchalance, he asked, "Do you like it? Your work?" Stupid question! he scolded himself silently.

"Yays. I like," she said without hesitation.

No stopping now. "Why?" he blurted out.

"Ohhh, I like because ayvree day somtheen new. Deefrent. Adventure!" She said it with a laugh.

He didn't know whether to believe her or not. New? Adventure? Nonsense! She can't really think that. The happy, good-natured hooker? A cliché. An act. Phony.

She leaned toward him and spoke in a solemn tone. "My seester, Maria, she mareed. No good for her. Always unhappee. My life better."

"But," he said impulsively, "aren't some of the men you meet . . . aren't they, well, bad to you?"

"No. No," came the swift reply. "Oh, maybee one time or two. Not like Maria. Husband beet her manee time. I go only with men I like. And they like me. I make them happee. Ayvree time. Ayvree day! Some make me happee too." She grinned, and sat back, running a hand through her long black hair. The glare of a street light fell over her face, revealing more age than he had seen at first. He couldn't stop focusing on that broken tooth. She lit a cigarette and blew smoke into the faintly stirring night air. Then she leaned across the table again and whispered heartily, "And I luvvv sexx." Her laugh burst out once more. She tossed her head back, took another drag on the cigarette, and exhaled a cloud.

Part of him wanted to leave, but he couldn't. So what if she was just playing a role to lure a customer? She was good. Good at seeming both innocent and adventurous. Her word. Adventure. And likeable at that. He gulped down the rest of his second caipirinha, starting to feel its potently pleasant effects, and waved to the waiter. He ordered a third and bought one for her.

He blinked when he heard her say, "Your beezness, you like?"

He didn't answer at first. "Oh, I don't know," he muttered.

"Your beezness make peepul happee?"

He squinted at her. He'd never thought of it that way. There was the marketing hype, of course, all that stuff about changing peoples' lives with disposable diapers. "Sure," he sighed, "that's what we say."

"What you do, your beezness?"

He squirmed in his chair. No way was he going into that. Their drinks came and he downed a swallow. "Uh, children," he said groping. "I, uh, work with children. Clothes to, uh, keep them dry and, uh, warm." Clever, he thought, a marketer's ingenuity. He took a long drink to conceal his silly satisfaction.

"Ahh . . . Goood. Makes them happee. I have son," she said proudly. "Seex year old. Hee ees beee-yooo-teee-foool." Reaching into her purse, she withdrew a photograph and held it out to him. "Carlos," she beamed. Taking it carefully, he examined the picture. The boy stood on a beach in orange swimming trunks holding a volley ball against his hip. She was right. He was beautiful. Lean and slender. Olive skin, dark curly hair, big round melting eyes, and a wide bright smile.

"Yes, he is very handsome," he said returning the photograph.

"He veree happee. And make me happee. He ees smart too." She tapped her temple. "He go to school ayvree morning. Father ees American," she added emphatically to make a point.

Taking the bait, he asked, "The father . . . is a . . . ?"

"Yays. From Boston."

"You mean . . . Oh, I see. Does he . . . know . . . ?"

"Yays. He know. He come. But not now. Not anymore." She turned away, and he saw a hint of sadness flicker over her face in the streetlights. They sat without speaking, watching lovers strolling past, and the palms lining Avenida Atlântica wafting quietly, and the full moon hovering over the bay beaming a rippling white line across the black water into the shore. Time passed. Then her husky female voice said softly.

"You go weeth me now?"

He stared at her without answering. She wore her alluring expression, mingling innocence and adventurousness with that warm, broken-tooth smile. Maybe it was the caipirinhas, but, as if someone else were speaking, he heard himself hesitantly say, "OK."

He signaled the waiter and paid the check nervously. They got up and made their way through the tables to the sidewalk and on to his hotel. He didn't know quite what he was doing, and hoped no one would suspect, even though he knew it didn't matter here. Nervously averting his eyes from the hotel staff, he escorted her to the elevator and up to his room. But once they had shut the door behind them and lay on the bed, everything changed. For him.

Ciéla was tender. Loving. Joyous. He felt an unexpected desire he had never known. It started with delicious sensations, and deepened to where it lit a flame inside that spread heat throughout his body. And with that heat he found himself feeling a tenderness for her he had never imagined, wanting nothing so much as to give pleasure to her. He didn't know where it came from, this desire. It was simply a desire to please, to make her happy. And he went with it, bestowing on her every affection and delight he could discover to give. Some things he didn't know he could do. He'd never done them before. He'd never thought of doing them. Strange, he thought, as he gently caressed her, why should I care? Why did he want to make her happy? Why did he feel this warm ecstasy flow through him as he attended to her every loving sensation? And why her, this whore working the hotels of Copacabana, who claimed to like the "adventure" of her prostitute's life and to "luvvv sexx," and who hid her sadness behind an off-beat but winning smile? He stopped asking, and gave himself to it. To the feeling. To the night. To Ciéla.

The early gray light of dawn was ascending into the sky when he opened his eyes and peered over the bed and out through the translucent curtains fluttering at the open balcony doors. He yawned, rubbed his eyes, and stretched, feeling pangs of stiffness in his muscles and joints. Then he remembered where he was. With a pulse of surprise, he saw Ciéla lying next to him already awake. She rolled on her side and raised up. "*Bom dia*, good morning," she said, with a smile he thought too warm and full for the hour. But he had to admit that it cheerfully invited him into the day. And the broken tooth had become an emblem of her good nature.

"Good morning," he responded sleepily. She voicelessly traced the features of his face in the dawning light. "You nice," she whispered. "You make mee verree happee."

"I'm glad. You are nice, too."

"Your wife, shee veeerree luckee."

"I don't have a wife."

She paused. "Then girlfriend veree luckee."

"I don't have a girlfriend."

She lifted her fingers to her mouth and played with her lips as if coyly about to reveal a secret. "Then I eeven more luckee," she murmured, bending over to kiss him lightly. He gathered her in his arms and held her close.

She breathed into his ear words he could just barely make out: "Do not go yet. Pleez."

He drew back a little. "What do you mean?"

"Do not go home today."

He swallowed hard. "I . . . I have to."

They lay for a few moments in a quiet embrace. Then she released him and sat up slowly. He saw that her cheeks were damp with tears. She wiped them with the palm of her hand.

How strange, he said to himself again. It is all so very strange.

"Go some other day," she sniffled.

"I . . . can't. I'm sorry. I have to go today." He felt odd having this kind of a conversation with a prostitute in Rio de Janeiro. He added, partly to be polite, "But I'll be back."

"When?" she asked with a calm insistence that surprised him.

"Soon. Very soon," he answered awkwardly, not knowing quite what to say, or feel.

Ciéla sank silently back against the pillow. Through a window early daylight could be seen creeping above the horizon, whitening the wisps of clouds drifting across the morning sky. After a time, she said she had to leave to get Carlos ready for school at home where her mother watched over him at night. She pressed a kiss on his forehead, and slipped out of the bed. She washed in the bathroom, pulled on her clothes, combed her hair, dabbed on some makeup, and walked to the door. He threw on a robe, collected a wad of *reals* from his wallet, and held them out to her. Shyly she let him close them into her hand.

"Pleez come back," she said softly.

"I will. I promise. Soon. Maybe next month." Then an idea hit him. "Give me your address and your phone number. I'll write to you. I'll let you know when I'm coming. I promise." He went over to a table where he had dropped his newspaper earlier, tore off a corner, and handed it to her. She found a pen in her bag and, holding the paper to the wall, scrawled on it and gave it back. He read what was written on it: a street address and phone number and the words, "Ciéla Gesualdo, *com amor*." He stuffed it into the pocket of his robe.

"I like you very much," he said earnestly. "And I will come soon."

She gave him a half-smile and kissed him gently on the mouth. Then she stepped back and opened the door. "*Obrigado*," she said softly. "Thank you."

"*Obrigada*," he echoed, summoning his only Portuguese. "Thank you, Ciéla. I do want to see you soon."

She offered another half-smile with an ambiguous nod, turned around, passed through the doorway, and headed down the corridor. He watched her go. At the elevator she turned around again and softly blew him a kiss then stepped inside. He waved slightly as the doors closed. Slowly he backed into his room, shut the door, and stood leaning his against it. "How very strange," he repeated aloud, shaking his head. The room now felt warm and humid, and he wanted some fresh air. Seeing the curtains at the balcony shifting languorously in the sea breeze, he walked over, drew them aside and stepped out. The sun, nearing the horizon, was throwing a yellowish tint into the summer haze. Sugarloaf and the islands offshore in the distance were taking form in the eastern light. The sweeping arc of Copacabana still sparkled with street lamps just before the daylight fell upon them. Then in a stroke, they went off. He could make out a couple of runners jogging along the broad black-and-white swirling patterned sidewalk of Avenida Atlântica abutting the beach. And a group of adolescents was setting up a volley ball net on the sand to get in their play before the heat and crowds arrived.

Then he saw her. At least he thought he did. Walking away on the swirling pattern of the beach sidewalk. The first rays of the sun peeking over the horizon shot across the water and caught her in their beam. It was Ciéla. A wave of elation flowed through him, followed by an undertow of regret. He wondered what was going on in him? Was it the sight of the sunrise? The ocean? The beach? Rio? Or memories of that joyful night? Ciéla? Yes! Yes! Ciéla! "To hell with diapers and the rest of it!" he exulted. "I'll stay!"

Impulsively, he shouted, "Ciéla, wait! Ciéla!"

She walked on, oblivious to his call. His heart sank. Then he remembered. Shoving a hand into his pocket, he pulled out the crumpled piece of newspaper. Leaning forward against the balcony railing, he ironed out the wrinkles with his finger tips, and his eyes fell on the words, "Ciéla Gesualdo, *com amor.*"

A gust of wind suddenly whipped over the balcony. And like a mischievous child, it plucked the paper from his hand, blew it up and around in looping circles and out into the soft morning air. "Damn!!" he cursed, and reached out for it, leaning farther and farther over the railing with his arm flailing and fingers grasping for the elusive scrap, which bounced tauntingly on the playful breeze beyond his straining limbs.

Desperate, he lunged farther for the fugitive as it skipped mockingly away. For a moment he felt like he was flying toward it, riding a kindly swell of that jaunty breeze, as he fell from the balcony, crying her name, "Seeee-aayyyy-llllaaaaaaaa . . ."

Ciéla didn't hear. She had climbed into the bus for her early morning ride home to Carlos. Sitting at a window, she was telling herself that this nice man who had made her so happy would, after all, be just like the others. He wouldn't come back. Not to her. But that was all right. She had had a happy night. The bus moved off. Ciéla looked out at the palm trees flitting past, the wide velvety beach tapering into the surf, the ceaseless waves rolling rhythmically to crash in sparkling spray on the sand, the rising sun silhouetting Sugarloaf and the rocky islands and glistening over the water of the perfect bay, kissing Rio awake. She smiled to think this was hers. Every day. And every day, something new.

Hawaiian singers under the kiawe tree at the House Without a Key, Honolulu, Hawaii

Mr. Chan's Tea Time

You couldn't miss him. He sat alone at a table in the hotel's outdoor seaside restaurant near an arching coconut palm. The tables all around hummed with chattering tourists in flowered dresses or Hawaiian shirts enjoying their escape to the tropics, along with a few relaxing locals having lunch by the sea. A swath of manicured lawn led from the tables out to a hedge of hibiscus and a large, old, gnarled kiawe tree that rose high above, casting mottled shade over the grounds from its thin fluttering leaves. Beyond that, the ocean rolled off to the horizon, the crests of surf breaking toward the beach, carrying surfers who caught the waves and leaving others in its wake.

No, you couldn't miss him. There in the elegant hotel's casual restaurant beside the sea, he didn't quite fit in, even amid the cosmopolitan clientele. Japanese or Chinese, I figured, studying him from my own table a discreet distance away. That would hardly have made him unique in Honolulu, where Asian-Americans and Asian tourists abound. Except he was peculiar. He looked like an ancient coolie. Or a Taoist sage. The kind depicted in historic Chinese paintings and caricatured in cartoons. His face was thin and sallow. A wispy mustache drooped from the sides of his upper lip down to a few gray strands of beard that hung from his chin in a frizzy goatee. His head was nearly bald but for a crescent of thin, uncut hairs that fell over his ears and a tiny braid in the back. He wore a silky black long-sleeved shirt that rose up his throat in a Mandarin collar. Baggy black pants draped to his feet, bare but for wooden clogs. He leaned forward in his chair and poured tea from a small metal pot. Then he sat back and held the handleless cup with the bony fingers of both hands to sip. And he gazed out toward the ocean, as if seeing nothing around him, looking into the infinite or into the past, or into inscrutable mysteries. Or so I began to think.

A character right out of a Charlie Chan mystery, I fancied, letting my imagination play. Those tales, mingling Eastern intrigue with Hawaii's then-newly-fashionable tropicality and emergent commercialism, had originated right here in Waikiki during the 1920s. Chan's creator, Earl Derr Biggers, had visited Honolulu in those days and had stayed in one of the cottages that had long preceded the modern hotel on this site. And he had taken the title for his first Chan novel, *The House Without a Key,* from the houses around here at that time that hadn't troubled with keys. That title later gave the name to this very restaurant, said to be where the house in the novel had stood. I liked that. Yeah, I said to myself, this guy belongs in a novel of old Honolulu. A Honolulu that had existed long before statehood and the war and the commercial desecration of paradise, which Biggers had seen already happening. But who is this mysterious Asian? I asked myself as I sat nursing a Mai Tai in the salubrious late afternoon.

I had come to Hawaii to research a book on tourism. Prosaic stuff. But maybe, I thought, this peculiar person could provide a fresh angle on the subject.

I watched him sip his tea and nibble a cookie. Occasionally he would jot something down with a stubby pencil on a pad. Otherwise, he stared out to sea. Was he taking notes on the guests? Was he writing messages? Was he writing poetry?

Finally, he got up rather creakily, lifted a knotty walking stick that had been propped against the table, and, steadying himself with it, slowly shuffled out of the restaurant, gesturing vaguely to the waiter as he went. I kept wondering. Who is he? A tourist? Not likely. He must have a story to tell. My imagination began to work on that.

Perhaps he's a refugee from old Shanghai who had made millions before Communism and now lives in the luxurious anonymity of this hotel. Or maybe he's a fugitive from Singapore traveling in disguise on corrupt riches. Or possibly a drug dealer making a stop on his route across the Pacific. Or is he a sage on tour to promote a book? Or maybe he's recovering from tragic times that had taken everything from him—home, family, love, belongings—everything but the means of coming here for tea and cookies and memories.

He could be just about anything. Except ordinary. The possibilities absorbed me, if only as an imaginative diversion during a languid tropical afternoon of professional procrastination.

The next day, after a series of desultory interviews with business executives for the book, I returned to House Without a Key. And there he was. With tea and cookies. He poured and sipped. He nibbled. The same appearance. The same gestures. The same occasional jotting in a notebook. The same aimless stare into the distance. Like a ritual.

I observed him for an hour while snacking on coconut shrimp. The possibilities of his character multiplied in my mind. Was he a master Chinese spy who has the perfect cover in appearing too conspicuous to be taken for a spy? Or a detective trailing a suspect, a real Charlie Chan? Or maybe a writer of mysteries who steeps himself in mystery? Or a Chinese scholar doing research in a capitalist haven? Or even an actor who plays "Oriental" character parts, and pretends to live them? My fantasies played with each other. Then I watched him again gather himself up, finger his stick, and gingerly make his way out.

He was there again the next day. And the next. And so was I. The routine had become ours together. He was becoming my own personal mystery. My private preoccupation. I had to find out his story.

I could just go up and ask him. But that wouldn't very likely get at the truth. How could I believe what he said, even if he could speak English? If he was anywhere near as enigmatic as he appeared to be, he would refuse to answer, or evade, or prevaricate. So I decided to do some sleuthing.

The next day, after my now daily unspoken communion with him, I followed him. Idling behind at a cautious distance as he left and shuffled through the corridors past the hotel shops and out to the street, I trailed him to busy, overbuilt Kalākaua Avenue a block away. There I browsed in shop windows to conceal my skulking as he made his way along with his walking stick. He didn't really seem to need the stick. It was more of a stage prop. And he appeared rather disengaged from everything around. He must have been lost in whatever was hidden in his impenetrable mind. That made him more mysterious, and kind of suspicious.

Then he paused as if deciding where to go next. After a time, he moseyed on and wound up at a spot near the curb. It looked to me that he could have been waiting. For whom? A contact? A limousine? I loitered nearby. A city bus pulled up and he climbed inside and rode off. That was a surprise. Was this a guise to hide his tracks? Was he traveling to intrigues of the night? One thing was sure. He was no ordinary hotel guest.

That evening, I had dinner at House Without a Key, settling in to coconut shrimp and tuna poke while wondering about my mystery man, who did not venture here in the evening. It occurred to me he could be writing a novel about Hawaii, an exotic saga of passion and intrigue in this tropical paradise weaving together many cultures now transformed by war and greed and tourism into a cosmopolitan crossroads of multinational business and international anonymity, where people still search for a semblance of Edenic innocence, and where they rarely find it because it is all but gone. Or, he could, of course, be just writing a Hawaiian travel guide larded with impressions of Waikiki. But that would be disappointing. His story, I was sure, had to have more to it than that. And I let the skein of my thoughts wend off to more inviting plots.

The musings eventually dissipated as the strains of hula music lilted into the fragrant air. A trio of musicians picked guitars while a dancer swayed beneath the kiawe tree, silhouetted against ocean and the sky, her fluid hands coaxing timeless tales and ageless emotions from the undulating melodies. And when the sun started sinking beyond the horizon, and the Hawaiian sunset began throwing its kaleidoscope of roseate colors across the sky, I lost myself in the moment and a tropical indifference to all the rest of the world.

The next day, my pursuit resumed. I watched the mystery man through his regular routine at House Without a Key, the seemingly unbidden tea and cookies, the note pad, the vacant gaze. Afterwards, I tracked him again out to Kalākaua. This time he crossed the street and disappeared into a warren of open air shops and vendors under a large sign reading International Marketplace. My interest piqued, and not wanting to lose him, I followed again. There I found myself surrounded by stalls purveying all kinds of Hawaiian and tropical curios and artifacts. Shell and coral jewelry and pearls. Coconut trinkets. Aloha shirts and dresses. Pearl Harbor memorabilia. [All of that has since yielded to an upscale mall.] But I couldn't see my prey. Shouldering through the stalls and shoppers, I wound up at the trunk of an enormous Banyan tree whose canopy I now discovered spread over the entire marketplace, supported by half a dozen aerial roots that had become tree trunks themselves. The tree was a spectacle, and as I circled around taking in its vastness, I saw the little man in black. He was talking to a merchant at a stall displaying jewelry of some kind. But he didn't seem to be buying anything, only talking. Was this a secret contact? I stood at a nearby stall toying with some shells until he finished his clandestine business and scuffled away. He nodded greetings toward a few other merchants as he wandered back to the street. Clearly he was no stranger here. But why? Puzzling over this, I watched him once more board a bus and ride away. I was tempted to get on the bus myself but held back. For now. He surely had a dark mission. How would I discover it?

I picked an easy gambit. I would ask at the hotel. Someone there must know something about this unmistakable character who comes so often and receives such singular attention. The next afternoon I nonchalantly put the question to my waitress, as she served my usual afternoon Mai Tai.

"You see that peculiar old guy over there?" I whispered. "He seems to be here every day. Do you know who he is and why he's here?"

She glanced in his direction, "Oh, you mean Mr. Chan?"

"Mr. Chan?"

"That's what we call him. I don't know if that's his real name. The management just tells us to be nice to him and serve him tea and cookies without charge."

"Why?"

"I don't know. I've only been here a few months. You'd have to ask a manager. He's a sweet little man though. Very polite. But he doesn't say much."

"Where's the manager?"

"Try Mr. Wong, the assistant manager. He's on duty today. You'll find him over there." She pointed toward the service area under the eaves.

I thanked her, and she went to serve other tables. Mr. Chan, eh? I said to myself. So I was right. An enigma. An alias. A mystery. Out of the novels. I sat for a few minutes, then got up and strode casually to where the assistant manager was working over some receipts.

"Excuse me," I interrupted, "but could I trouble you for a question?"

He raised a finger to signal a moment needed to complete a calculation on the papers in front of him, then lowered it and raised his eyes to mine. "I'm sorry. Yes. What can I do for you?" he asked graciously.

"I don't mean to trouble you, but do you see that old gentleman over there? He comes in every day." I nodded in his direction. "I'm just curious, do you know who he is or why he comes here? The waitress said you might know."

"Ah, Mr. Chan. Yes, he's a regular. In fact, more than that. We extend our hospitality to him because, well, we always have, as far as I know. At least ever since I've been here, and that's nearly five years now."

"But why? Why do you accommodate him? Why is he here?"

"All I know is that management wants us to be nice to him. It goes back to a former general manager, I think."

Aha! I said to myself. A mystery with history. "Would anyone know about that?" I asked.

"You could ask the GM, he might have some idea," he said in a tone that suggested he had no curiosity about Mr. Chan. And that struck me as another oddity. Was this a cover for dark machinations?

"And who is the GM?" I asked, feigning nonchalance.

"Helmut Rolfsen. He's in the head office on the administrative floor of the hotel. But he will be gone by now."

I thanked him for his help and went back to the table to remain as long as my subject would be there. Then I tracked him again.

This time he walked along Kalākaua to the majestic Moana hotel, the oldest in Waikiki, its grandly columned porte-cochère welcoming guests since the turn of the twentieth century. There he passed through the historic open lobby to a veranda on the ocean side, where another huge Banyan tree sheltered restaurant tables arrayed around it to the beach. He took a cushioned chair on the veranda and gazed out at the sea. Surfers were riding the gentle Waikiki waves as they had done for a century, some performing acrobatics with children on their shoulders, and others gleefully sharing their boards with surf-seasoned dogs. He watched for a time, exchanged a few words with an employee who seemed to know him, and completed his daily routine with another bus ride, to where I did not know.

Yes, Mr. Chan was a mystery. A fixture of Waikiki, and particularly of House Without a Key. Perhaps he had won deference with some magnanimous deeds, or with a fortune, or with secrets that threatened someone. Ah, blackmail rooted in dark deeds or wicked money. Or he wielded influence with the tongs or mafiosi or some underworld network whose interests he sinisterly served or controlled while, at the hotel's expense, he innocently drank his tea and peered out to sea. The plot, I decided, must go beyond Mr. Chan himself. But if that was it, I would probably never find the truth by asking anyone. Would the GM reveal anything?

The receptionist appeared a bit nervous the next afternoon when I said I was a guest at the hotel and wanted to speak to the GM, with no appointment.

"Is there a problem?"

"No. Not at all. I'd just like to ask Mr. Rolfsen a few questions."

"Can I help you?"

"I don't think so. I was referred to him by the assistant manager at the House Without a Key. I . . . I'm writing a book on tourism and thought he might be able to help with some details."

Proud of the deception, I handed her my card identifying myself as an author. That quickened her interest. She excused herself and went into the general manager's office then returned and ushered me in. The GM politely rose to meet me.

"What can I do for you Mr. . . ." he said, looking down at my card. "Do sit down. So, you want to write something about the hotel?"

"Uh, perhaps," I answered, taking the chair offered me in front of his desk. "I am gathering material for a book on tourism, and I would like to ask you more about that later, if I may. What I would like at the moment is a bit of information that might be only indirectly related to the hotel and my book. It concerns one of your guests. Or rather someone who regularly visits the House Without a Key. He's an old Chinese gentleman who comes here every day and is taken care of at no charge. Then he sometimes goes elsewhere in Waikiki, where people seem to know him. My question is this: Who is he and why does he come here, and why do you take care of him? Can you tell me?"

Helmut Rolfsen sat back in his plush desk chair with no interpretable expression. "So that's it. Mr. Chan. May I ask why you are so curious about him?"

"It's a mystery that's got hold of me. I've got to solve it. I guess I can't help myself. A writer, you know. There's a good story in every mystery. And any good story must be told."

"I see. The writer's curiosity must be satisfied?"

"Something like that," I confessed.

"Well, to be frank with you, Mr. . . . I don't have anything very helpful to say about Chan. Don't read too much into that. You'll be disappointed."

"Oh? Please go on," I answered, feeling my adrenaline rise with a revelation about to break. Or a cover-up about to thicken into something worthy of a serious journalist's scrutiny. There is a secret here that no one seems to want to tell. I had to know why.

"The truth is, I don't even know the whole background myself. What I can say is that I am told my predecessor, who was a convivial Chinese-American, met Mr. Chan—that's what we call him, for Charlie Chan—at the House Without a Key one afternoon and shared tea and cookies with him. The GM evidently took a liking to him and invited him to come there for tea anytime as his guest. I think Mr. Chan was coming almost every day when I got here. Before that GM retired, he set aside a line in the manager's discretionary fund with a stipend for Mr. Chan. We've continued the hospitality ever since."

"So you give him free service, and it's just a tradition? That's all?"

"Not quite. The expense doesn't amount to much, and now he's sort of family, although he doesn't say much. But as my predecessor explained to me, Mr. Chan is also, well, good for business."

"What do you mean?"

"Local color. Honolulu today can, I admit, be very bland, very Miami Beach. Mr. Chan gives our guests a small but memorable image of an exotic Honolulu to talk about and take home. A bit of lost history. And a mystery at the House Without a Key. You can hear guests in the restaurant exchanging guesses about who he is. It costs us very little, and gives them good conversation and interesting stories to tell. I dare say he has had this effect on you."

A bit stunned, I stammered, "Really? That is a surprise. You mean to say . . . the tradition of accommodating him is . . . basically . . . marketing?"

"I'd call it Hawaiian hospitality. Like aloha. That's the business we're in. We host Mr. Chan, and he returns the favor."

"But . . . but what does he write in that little notebook every day?"

"I have no idea. We asked him to find something to do while he's here. Keeps him from being bored and makes him more intriguing, don't you think?"

I sat dumb for a moment, not certain whether to believe this disillusioning explanation or not. Then I had to ask: "But . . . do you even know who he is? Where he came from? What he does in life besides come here?"

"I understand that he lives with his son in Chinatown, where he used to have a shop that his son now runs. He just likes to spend his afternoons in Waikiki. Then he goes home. So, perhaps you have unraveled the mystery. Still, it's not much of a mystery. Mr. Chan is nobody to write about. There is really no story about him to tell."

I knew, of course, that faux exotica and ersatz local color had become a staple of tourist promotions in Hawaii and other places, but I would not have guessed that a luxury hotel would subsidize an old Chinese man to be an exotic attraction there by having afternoon tea every day in the seaside restaurant. This would add at least a novel anecdote to my book. And yet, there had to be more to the story.

I thanked the GM for his courtesy and for the information and went down to the House Without a Key and ordered a tall drink. Mr. Chan was there. Sipping tea and looking out to the sea with his notepad at the ready. I thought a minute then took out my own pad and wrote at the top of the page: "Mr. Chan's Tea Time." Beneath that I started: *"Sitting under a tall coconut palm in the mottled shade of a large kiawe tree in the seaside restaurant of an elegant hotel on the shores of Waikiki sat an old Chinese man who could have strayed from a Charlie Chan novel, like the one that gave the name to this restaurant, the House Without a Key. With a drooping mustache and frayed goatee, dressed all in black and wrapped in mystery, he sipped tea and gazed out toward the endless ocean in unfathomable contemplation and occasionally scrawled cryptic Chinese figures on a pad. He didn't fit in here. He must have had a past, and possibly a present, steeped in intrigue. His was a story that had to be told. But what was it?"*

I paused. Then I knew.

"It was raining in Shanghai when the ramshackle steamer and its secret cargo set sail under the fugitive Captain Chan. . . ."

The Pantheon entrance seen from the west, with a crone in the lower left poised for alms, Rome, Italy

Hadrian's Moon

I woke up smiling. It had happened again. The dream. In Rome. How many times? Over how many years? It had started one night right here.

Roused by the pleasing memory of that night, I wiped sleep from my eyes and could see gray light seeping through the tall thick wooden shutters that enclosed the windows and that had muffled, without silencing, the sounds from outside while we slept. The evening had run late, carried along by convivial voices resounding over the cobblestones and echoing off antique walls in the piazza outside our hotel. This piazza is noisier than many, attracting both tourists and local Romans to dine and socialize in its outdoor cafés and to lounge around the prominent fountain in the center. My husband George and I had wanted to stay here anyway, in an old hotel on the Piazza della Rotonda, just to look out the window at the most perfect building in the world. The Pantheon.

I got up and drew in the windows and pushed out the shutters. And there it was. The "rotunda." The Pantheon. Filling the far end of the piazza. Its magnificent colonnaded portico crowned by a pointed pediment, and its graceful dome rising above to the hole-in-the-top oculus, an eye open to the sky. Standing almost exactly as it has for almost two thousand years, ever since the emperor Hadrian had built it to honor the Roman gods. Hadrian, it had always pleased me to remember, was one of those five "good emperors" who Edward Gibbon said had presided over "the period in the history of the world during which the condition of the human race was most happy and prosperous." I knew things like that as a teacher of Roman history. And I had liked that about Hadrian. I liked Gibbon, too, for his exalted praise of the good emperors, and for reporting that he had decided to write of Rome's decline and fall one evening in the late eighteenth century while "musing amid the ruins" of the then half-buried Roman Forum as "barefoot friars were singing vespers in the temple of Jupiter." I could never visit Rome without picturing the melancholy Gibbon sitting "amid the ruins" listening to that evensong and resolving to tell the world how this greatest of all empires had crumbled, leaving its derelict capital to "barefoot friars."

But the Pantheon had survived. The impeccable, enduring Pantheon, the one unruined monument of ancient Rome, almost as perfect now as ever—probably because the Christians, like those singing friars in the Forum, had made a church of it. And yet, I also remembered that Hadrian had claimed no credit for building it. The bold Latin inscription across the pediment reads: "Marcus Agrippa, son of Lucius, Consul for the third time, built this." A historical red herring, I explained to my students. Once historical memory of the Pantheon's origins had been lost, history had understandably attributed the Pantheon to Agrippa, the renowned general who had defeated Marc Anthony and had become second-in-command to the first Roman emperor, Augustus, and who had erected a temple on this site a hundred years before Hadrian. Agrippa's temple didn't last. But Agrippa got credit for the Pantheon until the 1890s, when industrious archaeologists unearthed evidence that it had arisen during Hadrian's reign, and that the original inscription to Agrippa had been stuck in as an act of deference of a kind that Hadrian commonly observed. I liked this story of the good emperor too. An appealing Roman curiosity.

Rome brims with such historical oddities. It is a mongrel city, made of bits and pieces of history jumbled together in a dozen styles—like the fountain facing the Pantheon, installed in the sixteenth century, replacing a predecessor, and then recast and embellished a couple of centuries later with a soaring Egyptian obelisk surrounded at the base by sculpted dolphins. You never know what will turn up around the next corner. An ancient ruin. A solitary column. A medieval gargoyle. A Renaissance fountain. A Baroque church. A lively piazza. Mentally cataloguing the styles this morning, I noticed a banner hanging on a wire beside the Pantheon announcing festivities for the completion of a year-long restoration of the piazza. Surprisingly, the asphalt surface was being replaced by cobblestones, and restricted to pedestrians only, returning the Piazza della Rotonda to its more traditional character, before it had been given over to automobiles in a wayward act of modernization. Rome even goes forward to the past, sometimes, I thought. Very Roman.

The sun was rising now, its first rays grazing the rooftops. And sounds of sweeping and of water spraying against the cobblestones were readying the piazza for the day. The city was awakening.

I watched the piazza come to life. Workers collected yesterday's trash, news vendors opened their stands, waiters arranged tables and chairs at the outdoor cafés, delivery men hauled food from trucks parked in the narrow side streets. And sunlight began falling across the columns of the Pantheon from the side, touching each one with a thin band of light, then bathing the east-facing façades of the sixteenth-century buildings bordering the piazza and calling to life the colorful mural of a Madonna, or some other innocent, on the upper floor of one of those façades. I knew tourists would arrive soon, too, following their predictable path here from the large Piazza Navona a few streets to the west and then on to the cramped Fountain of Trevi close by on the east, reminding any Romanophile that much of the eternal city now seems to exist mainly for transients. One of many Roman ironies.

As I looked out over the awakening piazza to the Pantheon, musing on two thousand years of Roman history, I smiled again, recalling my dream and that other early morning here years ago on a previous trip when the prelude to that dream had begun. Those memories filled my mind.

I had been looking out of this same window back then in the dawning light when I had caught sight of a peculiar human figure barely visible in front of the Pantheon. The figure had appeared to me like an old woman cloaked in black, a cowl shrouding her head, and bent forward almost at a right angle, leaning on a cane. A crone preparing to beg, perhaps. But the hour had seemed too early for that. Why was she there?

Staring more intently, I had detected something at her feet. An animal. Then two. Then three. Ah, Roman cats. You can't be here long without seeing them. They slink along alleys, flash through entryways, doze in cafés. They're everywhere. Part of a mongrel city as hospitable to cats as it is to history and to history's remnants.

Before long, a cluster of these cats had entwined themselves around the feet of the crone as she stood before the Pantheon like a drooping specter, the cowl covering her face, one frail hand propping herself up with a cane, the other possibly poised to appeal for alms. The setting had struck me as quite picturesque, her spectral figure against the great pagan temple. Maybe, I had mused, she was actually a con artist with an act that she knew many tourists couldn't resist as she invited alms or posed for pictures for a fee. Who knows, I had said to myself, she might live in a comfortable house somewhere and travel here for her performance and livelihood.

With that disillusioning fantasy, I had turned from the crone and the window that morning to begin readying for a day of explorations. We were fairly young then, and George was always a willing, if slightly cynical, tourist. We had planned on that trip not to dwell on the usual "sights"—except for the Pantheon—and to find a different Rome. So we had strolled back streets that most visitors neglect and had walked along the Tiber River that wends through the city nearly hidden by its banks, a trickle that goes practically ignored compared to the Seine in Paris or the Thames in London. And we had wandered through Trastevere across the river, where working people live and few tourists go because it is a thriving part of Rome, not a ruin. We had wound up on the Aventine Hill in the south, where the Protestant or "English" cemetery nestles and where the poet John Keats rests under the epitaph "Here lies one whose name was writ in water"—"Evocative," George had said, "but what does it mean?"—and from whose crest you can see the sun set over the Tiber behind the Janiculum and the distant dome of St. Peter's.

Later that evening, we were back in the Piazza della Rotonda after dining not far away at Alfredo alla Scrofa, which boasts of inventing Fettuccine Alfredo and deserves the honor, whether the claim is true or not, for the sublime version it serves. In the piazza, we had then sat for a drink at a still busy café where seasoned waiters dressed in black, fronted with white aprons, scampered about exuding a charm fashioned to please patrons—and possibly to win the hearts of ladies visiting from the likes of Midwestern American towns who have dreamed of Roman romance, and who get just enough of it this way, a staged dose of solicitous Italian male attention that they can take home with them in memories of imagined raptures, and can invoke with faraway looks for inquisitive friends, and can thereafter savor sweetly and safely in their sleep. These are the guys who can do that.

"Ah, buono sera. Espresso? Cappuccino? Gelato?" Or something like that, I remember a waiter had asked us graciously. We had ordered espresso, biscotti, and sambuca, as I recall, delectations we often enjoyed here at night. With a friendly *"Mille grazi"* and a crisp approving bow, he had clicked his heels and glided briskly away. We had watched him go and followed the others with our eyes as they darted back and forth, with amiable salutations and ingratiating banter for customers. *"Bella notte, signorina."* "Ah, veree nice." "Splennndeedo." It was all Roman charm. The convivial piazza. The summer night. Safe romance. Eternal Rome.

Then through the bustling waiters and crowded tables, I had seen her again. The crone. She was still there in front of the Pantheon, now illuminated by lights aimed at it from around the square. She had hardly moved since morning as far as I could tell. But the Pantheon was now closed. Why would she be here at this hour? Maybe she did live in the streets, I had thought as I pointed her out to George. "From central casting," he had replied nonchalantly.

We had lingered a while relishing the Roman night, then polished off our drinks and returned to the hotel. Later that night, lying in bed, I had listened as the voices outside waned. Unable to sleep, I had gone to the window and watched the last few café patrons drift away. The waiters had started to stack their tables and chairs against the walls and to shutter the doors. The lights illuminating the Pantheon had gone dark, other lights around the piazza had flickered out, and the piazza had fallen silent. But the scene had remained unusually bright, the Pantheon standing in a soft luminescence. I remember leaning out the window and craning upwards. A radiant full moon had hung in a starless sky. It suffused the dome of the Pantheon and washed over the piazza with a radiance that picked out fanciful contours and threw weird shadows down from the rooflines and the fountain's serpentine forms, shadows that seemed to belong to such a night.

Absorbing the sight, I had seen a shadow move. It had passed in the moonlight from the front of the Pantheon to a narrow street running along the western side of the structure toward the back. A trail of creatures low to the ground moved with it. It wasn't just a shadow. It was the crone. And the cats. Or so I had concluded. This gets mysteriouser and mysteriouser, I had said to myself, like Alice in Wonderland.

Curiosity and the luminous night banished my timidity. Leaving George sleeping, I had slipped on some clothes and stolen out the door. Down two flights of stairs, I was outside in the quiet, deserted piazza. As if stalking a spy, I had sneaked through the shadows against the buildings toward where I had seen the mysterious entourage. I couldn't see them now, but I had pushed on, having no clear idea of why, or of what I expected to find.

When I had reached the spot by the Pantheon where they had been, I peered down the shadowy side street. Not a trace. Irresistibly, I had pressed ahead, driven by what I considered a youthful fascination and a trace of slightly dangerous excitement. Twinges of nervousness had pecked at my stomach as I left the open piazza behind for the uncertain path I was following. Firming my will, I had told myself that if I found nothing, I would continue on all around the Pantheon. Then I could at least go home with a story of a solitary moonlit walk in the deep of the night around the two-thousand-year-old Roman temple that is the most perfect building in the world. On through the semi-darkness I went, careful of my steps, which involuntarily grew quicker as I plunged into the night.

As I neared the rear corner of the temple, my nerves had tightened more. Moonlight falling on the ancient bricks of the temple's back wall were creating a weird patch-work of jagged surfaces and shadows. But no sign of the crone and her cats. They must've wandered off down one of the tangled medieval streets and alleys fanning out from here, I had decided. No point trying to guess which. Sensing how alone I was deep in the night of this foreign place, I had braced for the next stretch and headed swiftly along the narrow road behind the Pantheon toward the far side, glancing here and there for my prey. No trace. When I got to the far corner, I had relaxed a bit as I entered a small adjacent piazza brightened by the moon. There I had found a tall obelisk in the center standing on the back of a small sculpted elephant. I had seen it before and knew it to be by Bernini. But in the moonlight it had been even more odd and whimsical than in daylight, not at all an emblem of wisdom, as its inscription stated. Amused by this engaging Roman spectacle, I had forgotten for a moment why I was there, thinking how mongrel Rome keeps surprising and delighting you. After futilely scanning around for the crone, I had started back toward the hotel.

Hurrying along the street to the east of the Pantheon toward the Piazza della Rotonda, I had been eager to complete the adventure, and no longer concerned about why I had begun it. As I approached the piazza, the bright moonlight reflecting from the building façades in the wide open space had emboldened me again. The night had once more become too inviting for me to leave it just yet. I slowed my pace. Then it had occurred to me that on a night like this, the full moon shining down through the oculus in the roof of the Pantheon must look kind of magical. I had to see it, if I could. Maybe I could peek inside at the front doors.

Soon I had passed between the majestic columns at the front and through the dark portico to the massive bronze doors ascending twenty feet from the ground. There I had pressed my face to a thin open space separating them where they met.

I could barely see through. But enough. A column of moonlight was indeed pouring down through the oculus. My eyes had followed the beam to the floor, where it lit a circle in the middle like a theatrical spotlight. Then what I had seen so startled me that I bumped my head against the doors. In the center of the large oval spotlight was—the crone! Less crooked than before, she was swaying back and forth and waving her arms and tossing morsels in the air that momentarily caught the light as they fell. Surrounding her on the floor to the edge of the spotlight and into the darkness were—cats. Dozens. Scores of them. They jumped to catch what she tossed. They rolled. They ran. They tumbled. They stood on their hind legs. They batted the air with their paws. They had almost seemed to be dancing with the crone. But they had made no perceptible sound.

I had stared. How did they get in? A hidden passage? An underground conduit from a nearby ruin? That would be like Rome. But is this really happening? I had asked myself.

I had watched for five, ten, fifteen minutes. The crone and the cats frolicking, all as silent as the night, a mysterious performance in a heavenly light that had shined down on this stage every night of the full moon for close to two millennia. Tourists see the sunlight come through. But who sees the moonlight?

Maybe Hadrian knew, I had thought. The oculus lets in the moonlight as well as the sun. And even more dramatically. Here was the perfect Roman building, for sure. The perfect temple for worshiping all the gods of heaven, who had given the temple its name. The perfect stage for moonlit rituals. The perfect setting to celebrate the mysteries and magic of the night. The perfect place for congregations of Roman cats and a playful crone to cavort in the spotlight. Hadrian must have known.

Finally, a bit dizzied, I had eased away from the doors and found my way across the piazza to the hotel and up the stairs and into the room and under the sheets, and there I had dissolved at last into sleep. Then I had dreamed, for the first of unnumbered times to come, the dream of last night.

Had it all been just a dream? I had sometimes come to wonder. And yet, my late-night Roman adventure had been too real for a dream, even if seeming rather unreal. Either way, reality or dream, it would forever epitomize for me the Eternal City's wondrous history and eclectic character, its whimsical spirit and endless surprises. And I will always smile whenever, asleep or awake, I see again in my mind's eye that faceless crone and the cats of Rome silently dancing in the Pantheon under Hadrian's moon.

Chinese fishing nets on the bay at Cochin (Kochi), Kerala, India

And She Went to the Elephant Races

I hadn't seen Frank in quite a while. Now I'd bumped into him in a haunt where we'd shared drinks occasionally over the years. He was always easy to talk to, going back to our college days when we'd roomed together, half a lifetime ago. Not loquacious, but genial, intelligent, and sensitive. And a good listener. Becoming a corporate lawyer hadn't changed him much. He asked where I had been, and what I'd been doing since we'd last seen each other. He could tell I was down. And I was ready to talk. I started and kept going, pausing only for sips of scotch, egged on by the inquisitive comments he made. A good listener.

"Sandra left me," I began. "For a younger man. Or it could have been for another woman. That's how it goes nowadays, isn't it? Anyway, she said I was making her feel old. Hidebound, I think was the word she used. She said she was sorry. But she had to do it. To save her life. I didn't get it. Sure, she was younger than I was, but I had thought she was happy. I was happy. Not that I had thought much about it. I have my comfortable career as a college professor. The hours aren't bad. The money is OK. We had spent plenty of time together. Or I thought we had. We went out to dinner. We had friends. Traveled to Europe in the summers. A civilized life. Maybe Sandra wanted children. She'd said something about it a few times. Or did she really want something else? What did she want from a younger guy or from a woman? I don't know. Well, she left. Without more explanation. That's all.

"Her timing was painfully perfect. I was turning fifty. It felt like a double punch in the gut. Maybe the midlife thing. I didn't know what to do. I felt lost. So, I decided to run away, immature as that might have been. I told a travel agent that it didn't matter where. But it had to be far. And not familiar. Not Europe. So she told me of all kinds of exotic destinations. Bali and Kathmandu. Tahiti and Shanghai. Rio and Kyoto. While she was ticking them off, I caught sight of a calendar hanging on the wall behind her desk. The picture on it showed a beautiful sunset on the ocean through some spidery forms. 'Where's that?' I asked. She told me it was Cochin, or Kochi, India in Kerala down on the southwest Malabar Coast where the European spice trade had begun.

"'When you see the sun setting through the lacy Chinese fishing nets rising along the shore of the Laccadive Sea in the bay of Cochin,' she said, 'you know you're not in Kansas any more. It's enchanting. And exotic. And about as far away from here as you can go.'

"'That's it,' I told her. 'I'll go.'

"I had only a vague idea where it was, of course. I'd never cared to travel except to Europe, where you can drink the water and stay in reliable hotels and get along in English. But now I wasn't myself. Or I wanted to escape myself. Anyway, I went."

"I took a leave from the college and flew from New York to Mumbai, where I stayed overnight in an airport hotel, then flew from there to Cochin the next day. I was a bit numb when I arrived in the afternoon at the Malabar Hotel on Willingdon Island on the bay of Cochin. I had a bite to eat and slept a while. Then I got ready for the boat I had hired to take me out on the bay for the celebrated sunset beyond the Chinese fishing nets.

"Staggering up the gangplank, I discovered twenty seats on the open upper deck and another twenty below. I counted them. They were all empty. I was the only passenger. Just the boatman, a guide, and me. Now that's a change, I thought with pleasure. I have indeed left behind the world I knew. My travel agent had been even better than her word. As we sailed out, the boat swayed on the water, and others like it, crowded with tourists, churned past. Within fifteen or twenty minutes, we slowed near the mouth of the harbor to wait, rocking slightly on the wakes of harbor traffic. In another ten minutes the show began. As the sun descended to the horizon and started sinking beyond the sea, the sky ignited with bursts of sunset colors that spread on the wispy clouds overhead and deepened in tone moment by moment. And the array of Chinese fishing nets that hang on frames in picturesque rows at the mouth of Cochin bay stood out against the glow like silhouetted spider webs, or a string of vast gossamer hammocks. It was kind of dreamlike. Just as my travel agent had promised.

"I stayed out on the bay until the colors had faded into gray. Then I had the boatman take me back to the private dock at the Malabar Hotel. And I wandered through the gardens of palms and frangipani and wound up at a table on the fringe of the informal hotel restaurant outside by the water to have a drink and watch the lingering western light gradually fade into night. The air was moist and warm and fragrant.

"A few patrons were scattered at other outdoor tables. And I had felt quite good as I lifted a glass of Indian beer brought by an efficient soft-spoken waiter. Have I done it? I asked myself. Have I escaped halfway around the world just for a stunningly memorable sunset? But is that all? I still had plans for a car and driver to take me around old Cochin the next day, and then south to Alleppey the day after for a boat trip through the maze of inland waterways that the travel agent had insisted must be seen by anyone visiting Kerala. And I could watch the sunset here each night. After that, I was scheduled to fly north to Delhi and Agra and Varanasi and other stops on my escape into another world. But now that I had seen the sunset on Cochin bay, my depression was returning. I didn't really want to go anywhere. Or do much of anything. I sipped the beer and stared at the lights twinkling across the bay in old Cochin. My isolation was broken by a soft female voice saying, 'It is a marvelous place, isn't it?'

"I looked up to see a rather tall, slender woman in a long flowered dress standing near me, her pleasant smile and inviting eyes catching light from the waning dusk and a candle on the table.

"'Would you mind if I sit?' she asked politely while pointing, with what appeared to be a folded parasol, toward the empty chairs at my spacious table.

"The intrusion took me aback. I was not seeking company, much less conversation with a random stranger. But, not knowing what else to say, I replied haltingly, 'Of course.'"

"'Thank you,' she said, seating herself at a discrete distance with confident grace and hanging the parasol on the back of her chair. 'It is such a lovely view from here,' she added.

"'Yes, it is,' I answered vaguely, while I examined her for clues to the sort of person she was. Certainly not Indian. But not American either. Her English was distinctly but unobtrusively British. I could not determine her age. Her face had tiny lines at the mouth and the eyes that showed she had seen her share of summers—and had possibly basked in them. I could see this even in the candlelight. Some might say she was of *a certain age*. I could only say that she was of *un*certain age. And she was not unattractive. More agreeable than beautiful. I thought she could be a school teacher on vacation, traveling with a tour group to see remnants of the bygone Raj and to collect tidbits of exotica for the ladies' club back home. She seemed nice enough. I figured I might as well be cordial while I finished my beer. Then I would go to my room.

"'I do hope you will forgive me for intruding,' she apologized. 'My name is Alice Stilton. As in the cheese.' She smiled and continued. 'I am from England, as you can probably tell.' She extended her hand. I offered mine and mumbled that my name was Jack Drummond.

"'Ah, American,' she responded, as if a bit disappointed. 'And what brings you to Cochin, Mr. Drummond, if I may ask? I do prefer the old name of the town to the new Kochi, don't you?' A busy-body tourist? I groaned silently. Still, her manner was so civil that I could not fail to answer with some grace. I agreed with her about the city's name and told her the half-truth that I was on vacation, and had come for the sunset through the Chinese fishing nets.

"'Yes, of course. And so have I,' she said pleasantly. 'You might see equally grand colors elsewhere, perhaps, but nothing like this setting. The fishing nets against the sky and the open sea and the setting sun, palm trees wafting beside them, the sunlight glinting off the water of the bay, and the lights of old Cochin beginning to twinkle, with the fragrance of frangipani in the balmy air. Ah, India.' Her voice trailed off.

"I couldn't resist saying, with a hint of sarcasm, 'You must be a poet, Miss Stilton, or a travel agent.'

"'Oh, nothing like that,' she said with a soft chuckle. 'I only love beautiful places. And I like to talk about them. Have you been to India before, Mr. Drummond?'

"Her gentle civility. Her gracious poise. Her, well, serenity. They were starting to have a surprising effect on me. Almost beguiling.

"'No, never,' I answered. And, yielding to a rising curiosity in myself, I asked, 'Have you?'

"'Oh, yes, many times. I love India,' she said with a contented, if slightly longing, sigh.

"I thought she might go on with reminiscences of previous visits. But she simply gave me a small smile and silently faced the western sky and the lights of Cochin with a serene expression that seemed to come from memories of happy times. It was growing clear to me that she was no commonplace tourist on a quick trip abroad to collect anecdotes for the ladies' club at home. She had such an ingratiating manner and embracing sensibility. And, I guessed, an interesting a past. Now I wanted to probe.

"'And what brings you here this time, Ms. Stilton, if I may ask?'"

"She waited for a moment, glanced at me, and, without breaking her gaze into the west, said, 'Oh, I just wanted to come back to some of the places I have especially loved. My husband and I came here shortly after we were married in our youth. He died a few years ago. Now, I have come back to revisit some of my happiness.' She tilted her head toward me and smiled again. 'And to visit other places I have not seen before, or not seen enough of, and to gain more memories, and perhaps new happiness. There is so much in India. It would take a lifetime to absorb it. Or perhaps I should say, like a Hindu, it would take *many* lifetimes.' She chuckled as she had done before.

"An unusual woman, I said to myself. Serene yet adventurous. I started to feel that I was succumbing to her charm, in the original sense of *charm* as a magical power that sways like a spell. Yes, I was being *charmed*, falling under a spell. She wasn't trying to do this. It came naturally. And, after all, I was susceptible.

"'So, you believe in Hindu reincarnation?' I asked, gropingly.

"'Only as anyone might do—metaphorically,' she answered, as if meditating, 'to learn acceptance and renewal, peace and rebirth, in this life.' She turned toward me and smiled. 'We all need that, don't you think, Mr. Drummond?'

"I didn't know what to say. I'd never considered such things. But I answered, without truly understanding, 'Yes, I suppose.' And I thought, yes, I am being charmed. It actually felt good, a little like intoxication. Yielding to the mood—or her charm—I invited her to have a drink. She accepted with a hesitation that told me she had not intended this, but that she was happy enough to continue this minor adventure on this enchanting night beside the bay of Cochin, India, with the fragrance of frangipani in the air.

"'But I must confess to you Mr. Drummond,' she added with blithe candor, 'I am not staying here at the Malabar Hotel. I am staying at a small place over in the old city. Only a few rupees a night. I just came over to see the evening light from here. I hope I have not diminished its pleasures for you.'

"'No. No,' I stammered. 'Not at all. But,' I asked, 'are you not traveling with someone?'

"'Oh, no. I am traveling quite alone.'

"'Alone?' I said with astonishment. 'Really? For how long?'

"'I have been in India for a month now. I'm not sure how long I will stay. A few months perhaps. You see, if you travel by buses and trains and sleep in small hotels, you can stay in India for a long time on very little money.'

"I was dumbfounded. How incongruous. This calmly adventurous, serene British lady in a flowered dress, carrying a parasol, riding ramshackle Indian buses, and sleeping in decrepit hotels. 'You mean,' I exclaimed, 'you are traveling on trains and buses and staying in cheap hotels all over India by yourself?!'

"'Why not? You meet the most interesting people that way. And people here are very kind to a lady traveling alone. Perhaps it is the parasol.' She smiled genially and patted it hanging on her chair. It had a floral pattern not unlike her dress. 'It makes me seem ladylike, perhaps kind of quaint, and possibly even a bit dangerous, don't you think?' She laughed lightly. She sipped from the glass that the waiter had poured for her. 'How long will you be in Cochin, Mr. Drummond?'

"Still grappling with the incongruity of this tranquilly intrepid lady traveler, I told her it would be just a couple of days, and then I was flying north to Delhi and Agra and other cities and sights. I must have sounded unenthusiastic, because she looked at me intently and said, 'You do not seem very joyful to be on such a fine holiday. May I ask why?'

"I didn't answer right away. She pressed on.

"'I don't want to pry, Mr. Drummond. And I will surely understand if you do not wish to answer. But, why are you here, truly?'

"Again I was taken aback. She could tell? And she was confident, even brazen enough to ask. I could have shrugged her off. Or I could have invented something. But somehow, I felt myself wanting to tell her. It was that charm. I spoke tentatively.

"'You said you have come to revisit your happiness here. And to gain new happiness by seeing more of India. Well . . . I have come to escape my . . . unhappiness. My wife left me and I wanted to run away.'

"She pondered my words for a time and then with a kindly expression she said softly, 'I am sorry to hear that, Mr. Drummond. But, if I might say so, it appears that we are here for similar reasons.' She smiled gently.

"I stared at her. And this face of *uncertain age* became before me as beautiful as any face I had ever seen. Or was it just her charm? I burst out, 'Will you show me Cochin tomorrow?' I gulped at what I was saying.

"She looked at me thoughtfully for a moment then answered, 'I would be happy to share Cochin with you Mr. Drummond. And perhaps you will be able to share some of my happiness.'

"A quaint phrase—to *share* Cochin and her happiness. But then *she* was rather quaint, as she had said. Feminine and gracious, blithely self-confident and irrepressibly serene. It was all part of her natural charm.

"'How kind of you, Ms. Stilton,' I said, falling into her rather formal manner of speech. Collecting myself, I asked, 'Could I ask another favor?'

"'And what is that, Mr. Drummond?'

"'Could,' I said somewhat shyly, 'could we use first names? You can call me Jack.'

"She paused, before replying. 'You are indeed American,' she said with the hint of a smile. 'You Americans have such a fondness for familiarity. Very democratic, of course. But it makes everyone and everything quite the same, doesn't it? I suppose that is the intent. And yet, I suspect it often obscures proper differences and sometimes thwarts genuine intimacy. And it can cheat you of the gratification of discriminating among experiences. Don't you think so?'

"I probably should have expected such a reaction, but I didn't. And not knowing what to say, I answered with feigned formality, 'Alice Stilton, you are a not only a poet, you are a philosopher.'

"She laughed lightly again. 'And you, Mr. Drummond,' she said with her own gentle mockery, 'are a flatterer. You know what Dante did with flatterers.'

"I confessed I didn't, and I got a brief lecture on Dante's depiction of flattery as a despicable sin of deception, leading Dante to cast flatterers down near the bottom of Hell steeped in excrement, symbolizing what flattery is. I feared I had offended her and was about to apologize when she told me she had been a teacher, and that, although she had probably put that behind her, she could never resist a chance to *share* interesting bits of knowledge.

"That word again, I noted, *share*. I concluded that it expressed a generosity in her nature that went with her other manners. Then she asked as graciously as ever, 'Is Jack a nickname for John?'

"I told her it was, and she replied without hesitation. 'I must say, if we are to use first names, I prefer John. It has more dignity and character to it. Jacks are flighty.'

"I laughed nervously, resigning myself to her formality. She surprised me by adding, 'So, I will call you John, if you don't mind.'

Relived that I had not overstepped after all, I said, trying to make light of the situation, 'So, I guess you would be *Alice*, not Allie or Lisa or something flighty like that?'

"She tilted her head in assent. And with a soft smile she said, 'Yes, John, you *may* call me Alice,' subtly stressing the grammatically proper *may*.

"And with that she remarked the advancing hour and deepening darkness. She thanked me for the drink, rose up, plucked her parasol from the chair, and said genially that we should meet late the next morning in old Cochin at the St. Francis Church. I escorted her to the hotel entrance exchanging comments on the salubrious evening, and she assured me, as she put it, 'a happy day on the 'morrow.' We shook hands, and she left in a taxi, with a departing, 'Goodnight, *John*,' emphasizing the name to make her point. I went to my room a trifle baffled over this charming adventuress. And I went to sleep looking forward to the next day. Which would be an adventure for sure.

"A driver from the hotel named Rashmi took me over to the old town. There I met Alice at the St. Francis Church, where the pioneering Portuguese explorer Vasco da Gama had been buried—before his countrymen had ceremoniously removed his remains and reburied them with much ado in Lisbon. Her fresh floral dress shifting in the breeze and parasol in hand, she led me through the old city's historic sights, down its alleys of tiny craftsmen's shops and narrow lanes alive with vendors. Along the way we loitered here and there and drank from fresh green coconuts through straws poked in the tops, and she insisted we stop for chai and fried bananas in a musty dive strewn with half a dozen rickety tables and buzzing with flies.

"'Are you sure we won't get sick?' I inquired timidly as we entered.

"'Posh,' she answered emphatically. 'You should be more adventurous, John. Or you will miss life. Besides, they boil the water for chai.'

"Unable to reject the challenge and retain any semblance of manliness, I was soon choking down a greasy fried banana with sickly sweet chai, wondering what I had got myself into. If I die of dysentery, or worse, I told myself, I'll blame this charming lady of uncertain age, who seemed to fear nothing, and who was now making casual conversation with a scruffy, wizened guy at the next table.

"'He's been coming here for fifty years,' she turned toward me to say, 'and he's never been sick. So you see, John,' she said mockingly, 'you have nothing to worry about.' She flashed a beguiling smile. *Charm.* There is no other word for it, I thought. Irresistible, swaying charm. And I began to think she might well be a little dangerous, as she had hinted when explaining the parasol.

"The afternoon went like that, exploring places, examining local crafts and artworks, sampling food, subduing my nervousness, becoming comfortable together. By sunset, Rashmi had driven us back to my hotel for a drink and the view. After we toasted the sunset and the day that we both judged to be a *happy* one, she sat up and said, 'You know, John, you cannot come to Kerala and not see the Kathakali dancers.'

"'What are they?' I reacted, a bit embarrassed at my ignorance.

"'They act out the dramas of the *Mahābhārata* and *Ramayana* and other Hindu tales dressed in extravagant costumes and outlandish makeup. Men play all the roles with exaggerated theatrics. Slapstick and tragedy. Warfare and sentimentality. Performances can go on for hours. We can see one tonight, if you are game.'

"I could not have refused. Before long, Rashmi had driven us over to the new town of Ernakulam to a roomful of raucous patrons already watching Kathakali dancers. We couldn't follow the words, but the performance's melodramatic style had a certain universality that surpassed language. Alice laughed loudly at things I couldn't grasp. She seemed to know what was going on. Or maybe she just laughed instinctively. And her laugh was infectious. So I laughed, too, without knowing why. It was her charm.

"We left before the performance had ended because, she said, we had probably seen enough and who knew when it would end.

"'Thank you for the day,' I said to her, as Rashmi drove us away. 'You're a splendid guide.'

"'And you have survived all the local fare, culinary and artistic. I'm proud of you John.'

"I laughed a little. Then impulsively I blurted, 'Why don't you come with me tomorrow to Alleppey for a cruise up the waterways. You must have been there before, but come anyway. I'd like to *share* it with you, as you might say. Besides, the boat ride would be dull with no one to talk to but the guide. And you could continue to *enlighten* me in the ways of India and life.' I grinned for the first time since I had met her, and possibly for the first time in years.

"'There will be no one else? No other tourists?'

"'No. They told me the boat is mine alone. So I can invite anyone.'

"'That is unusual. I did go to Alleppey ten years ago,' she said pensively, 'with my husband. But I haven't been there since. The waterways are very lush and beautiful. I had planned to leave Cochin tomorrow. But I could stay another day. The elephant races aren't until Wednesday.'

"'Elephant races?'

"'Yes, I've never seen them. Sounds exciting. In a village up the coast near Tellicherry, what they now call Thalassery, but as with Cochin, I like the original better, probably because I am sentimentally British. The Raj and all that.'

"'Oh,' I said with a combination of puzzlement and distraction. My mind was on tomorrow. 'So you will come with me to Alleppey? We'll be back in time for the sunset in Cochin.'

"I could hardly believe that I was all but imploring this virtually unknown lady of uncertain age to stay and spend another day with me traveling into the backcountry of Kerala along the canals of Alleppey that my travel agent had promised would help satisfy my hunger for escape.

"And Alice came. With a floral dress and her parasol.

"The hour-and-a-half drive down the Malabar Coast was predictably harrowing, like every trip on the treacherous Indian highways. We nearly grazed every car racing toward us in the other lane, sometimes three of them abreast, all trying to pass each other as they bore down on us in our lane. Somehow we survived. And the boat ride was restoratively slow and lazy. We sat on the upper deck, just the two of us and the guide, among twenty or so empty chairs. She held her parasol to shield her from the sun that sporadically fell through the overhanging tress as the boat chugged up the river through the jungle. Alice said that this was kind of like sailing up the Congo into Conrad's *heart of darkness.* She had done that, she explained. Sailed up the Congo River into the heart of darkness. Not finding Conrad's Kurtz, she said with a wry smile, she had returned to civilization none the worse for wear. I pictured her sitting in her flowered dress under her parasol on the deck of a rusty steamer lumbering up the steamy, overgrown rivers of central Africa into she knew not what. I laughed to myself at the image. An image just like the person sitting beside me.

"I had read Conrad's novel in college but hadn't thought of it since. Our guide knew it, too. He was a school teacher who conducted tours for extra money. And he wanted to talk about Western literature. He said he especially liked Hemingway. I said I did too. Alice didn't share our opinion. She said Hemingway was an oaf who didn't know how to love. I asked her what she meant, and she explained that he was a narcissist always trying to prove his manhood, and that he viewed women pretty much the way he did animals, part of the adventure of *his* life, although he actually respected animals more. The guide and I questioned that, but I knew we were outmatched. She was, as always, serenely confident. And well educated. The conversation moved on. It was all kind of strange. There we were, in South India, drifting along through the maze of muggy inland waterways lined with dense jungle greenery, dotted with water hyacinths floating on the surface, and bordered by occasional grass huts tucked into the shore where peasants waist-deep in the water were washing clothes, and we were talking about Conrad and Hemingway and I don't remember what all. And there was Alice Stilton under her parasol cheerily leading a literary discussion.

"Eventually, the waterway flowed into a lake, and the unshaded sun now beat down hard while the humidity rose. But Alice never seemed discomfited in her own parasoled shade. An hour later we had crossed and disembarked at a lakeside hotel where the two of us had a leisurely late lunch of Kerala specialties on the veranda, conversing easily about India and literature and life. From there we returned to Cochin by car, first winding through forests of rubber trees then along another hair-raising highway. I wanted to get back for another cruise out on the bay to see the sunset again through the Chinese fishing nets and to dine outside by the bay again watching the sky's radiant colors dim into darkness. And I wanted to share it all with Alice Stilton and her parasol, because she had just plain charmed me.

"She agreed to join me for dinner and asked to be dropped at her hotel first to freshen up. I went on and arranged for Rashmi to go back to get her then booked a boat to take us to the sunset. She arrived a while later in another fresh floral dress, parasol in hand. Why she brought that thing in the evening I couldn't understand. But it had become an indelible part of her image in my mind's eye. In the two days I had known her, she had passed from being an eccentric lady of uncertain age to being a woman of invincible serenity and winsome warmth. And now I wanted to be close to her. She was changing me, or maybe unwittingly seducing me. With her irresistible charm. And as we watched the sunset that evening from a boat that we had all to ourselves, with only the boatman to accompany us, she let me come close. By the time the sun had sunk beyond the silhouetted fishing nets and disappeared into the Arabian Sea, I had emboldened myself to put my arm around her shoulder. She did not withdraw. As the boat began turning around for the ride back to the hotel, bewitched by the beautiful moment, I asked if I could kiss her on the cheek. She smiled and seemed to lean into me. I kissed her lightly.

"'Thank you,' I sighed, and said, 'It has been wonderful spending another day with you, Alice.'

"'Oh, thank you, John,' she responded warmly. 'You invited me and have been a splendid host.'

"Back at the hotel, we sat for dinner at the same table where I had met her two nights earlier. And we watched the same kind of evening light show on the bay as we had seen then. But this time it was different. We were not strangers now. After dark had long descended and we had seen the lights of old Cochin come up and twinkle across the bay and reflect off the water, and we had dined enjoying a wandering conversation and were now having an after-dinner drink, I stunned myself by asking impulsively and rather awkwardly, 'Alice, I don't want you to go. Would you, uh . . . stay with me tonight?'

"Where the courage to say that came from, I don't know. But I said it. Even though I wasn't entirely sure what I meant. Immediately I regretted it, fearing I had broken the spell, and that she might think me vulgar and rude. She didn't answer. She just gave me a sidelong look as though studying my character. Her face caught the soft light from the candle on the table and reflecting from the rippling water. The tiny lines of uncertain age, the irrepressible smile, the animated eyes, the invincible serenity, were all there. But now this was the face of someone I seemed to have known for years. And who had cast a spell over me. Still, I didn't know what she would say. Was she deciding how to decline in her own civilized manner? Was she framing her departing words? Or was she thinking of staying?

"I was about to apologize for my clumsy and brazen invitation when she sat back and smiled tenderly at me. 'You are very sweet, John,' she said in a soft tone I could not quite interpret but hoped was not condescension. She paused. I wondered what would come next. I braced for some civility to stroke me but put me in my place. At last, she said affably, 'You are a gentleman. And I have enjoyed being with you. You have given me new happiness. Yes, John, I will share the night with you. In my way.'

"That word again. *Share.* I was as much surprised as elated. Then I grew nervous. Had I really invited her to stay the night, and had she accepted? 'In my way,' she had said. What . . . ? How should I . . . ? I stammered to myself.

"As things turned out, I was naïve. She wasn't. It became a night I will never forget. She wasn't like any other woman I had known. I can't really describe it. It wasn't passionate. It was hardly physical at all. We just held each other and exchanged—no, *shared*—some very sweet, tender, loving caresses. And when morning came I knew that I didn't want to let her go. This breathtakingly free, unflappably serene, magnetically appealing, amiably warm woman, with her flowered dresses and her ever-present parasol, had me definitely under her spell.

"I ordered coffee and tea and pastries brought to the room for breakfast at the table by the window looking out over the manicured grounds of the hotel and the glistening waters of the bay and off toward the fishing nets barely visible in the daylight.

"'Alice,' I said earnestly, 'please, don't leave. I don't want to lose you. Come with me to Delhi and Agra and other places. It needn't cost you anything. We would have a fine time and, as you might say, find new happiness.'

"She raised her eyebrows with mild astonishment. 'Why, John,' she said, 'I do believe that is a proposal of some kind. How very dear you are.' My heart lifted. 'I thank you for the sentiment. And for the very lovely day and night. But, John,' she said with her quiet matter-of-factness, 'I couldn't possibly do that.'

"'Why? Why not,' I stuttered.

"'Because, John,' she answered, softly and yet firmly, implying that I should have known already, 'I would miss the elephant races.'

"I gaped. What? The elephant races? After last night?! But then, I should have known she would not respond in a predictable way.

"'And I must go very soon,' she added amiably, finishing her tea. 'I have stayed too long, and now I must not miss my bus to Tellicherry.'

"My balloon burst. Alice didn't really care about me after all. I was just part of her Indian adventure, her pursuit of happy memories and the making of new ones, 'in her way,' and she was ready to move on. She could tell I was bewildered and hurt. She smiled sweetly.

"'Oh John,' she said, 'you must not feel bad about it. You have been divine, and I have grown very fond of you. We have shared some lovely experiences. And you have given me a gift I will always treasure in fresh happy memories. But you see, John,' she said this with that unwavering serenity and calm confidence, 'if I went with you, I would miss too much. The elephant races, and my India. I must see it in my own way. On buses and trains and in cheap hotels. You meet the grandest people that way, and learn the most surprising things. I think this is not your way, John. And you must live your life in your way, just as I must live mine. So it is best that we just cherish our memories of the delightful time we have spent together. I am sure that if you think a little more about it you will agree.'

"I knew it was futile to protest. She was too composed. Too calmly certain. And, after thinking about it, I decided she was probably right. I couldn't endure her way of travel, or probably her way of life. I didn't actually understand her. Finally I nodded resignedly and said, 'Let me at least take you to the bus station.'

"'This I will happily accept,' she answered brightly, still smiling and placing a hand affectionately on my arm, as if to say something like, 'You are such a dear.'

"I called for the car, and Rashmi drove us to collect her things at her flea-bitten hotel in old Cochin and then on to the bus station in Ernakulam. There, a few minutes later she climbed into a crowded, dilapidated bus, her parasol protectively in hand. As the bus pulled slowly away, listing to one side under the unbalanced weight of late passengers clinging to the sides and baggage piled precariously on the roof, I saw her wave to me from the back window. I waved back sorrowfully and watched as the bus chugged onto the highway into the traffic and drove cumbersomely off toward Tellicherry. I kept my eyes on it as long as I could, the pile on top visible in sporadic bounces above other vehicles, until that, too, vanished in a stream of trucks and buses and clouds of dust.

"And so she went to the elephant races. And out of my life."

I stopped talking and downed the last of several drinks.

"That's the end?" Frank asked. "That's it?"

"Yeah. That's it. More or less. I went on to the other Indian cities, but they didn't do much for me. The thing is, I kept seeing the sunset in Cochin with the beguiling presence of Alice Stilton. She had helped me escape my life but had then sort of made it seem impossible to escape her. I went from India to Paris and London for a couple of weeks, just to put off returning home. It didn't help. Finally, I came back here and more or less picked up where I had left off. I didn't know what else to do. Except that one thing had changed."

'What's that?"

"The memories."

"So it wasn't a loss."

"No, but . . ."

"You regret letting her go?" Frank prodded. "But wasn't she right in what she said?"

"What do you mean?"

"That she had to go her way, and you had to let her go. That it was only a passing episode in your lives? That it had to end, and this was the best way to end it?"

I thought for a minute. "Maybe," I said. "Still," I went on, "there was another possible ending to this story. I've dreamed it many times, as vividly as if it had all happened. I wish it had."

"What's that?" he asked.

"It starts with what did happen."

"What was that?"

"Well, after her bus had disappeared, I asked Rashmi to take me back to the hotel so I could pack and check out then leave for my own departure from the airport.

"'Very nice lady,' he had said, as he gunned the car into the traffic. 'Very kind. Good. A strong spirit.'"

"'Yes," I had replied vaguely, looking blankly out the window. 'Yes, she is.'

"'Too bad to lose her,' I had heard him say. The remark had surprised me, but I let it pass.

"At the hotel, I had packed desultorily, unsure of why I was going to Delhi or anywhere else. After paying my bill, I got in the car and we set out for the airport. The going was slow because cars and buses and trucks clogged the road to the bridge from Willingdon Island. 'It will be better after the bridge,' Rashmi had assured me. 'Most of the traffic goes over the bridge to old Kochi on one side or to Ernakulam on the other. But we go the other way to the airport here on the island. Plenty of time.'

"While sitting there, inching along toward the bridge intersection, I had felt depressed and restless, maybe thinking about what Rashmi had said about Alice.

"So, that's what actually happened. Now, here is the part of the story I would change."

With a choke in my throat, I leaned across the table.

"As we finally get close to the bridge intersection, a sensation comes over me, dissipating the depression and blowing clouds from my mind. An urge moves me. I reach forward and grab Rashmi by the shoulder.

"'Rashmi,' I say firmly. He turns around, and his face lights up with a grin when I say, 'Never mind the airport. Do you think you can catch that bus to Tellicherry?'"

Sunset beyond an acacia tree, Okavango Delta, Botswana

Safari

Maun isn't much of a place from the air. An array of native huts and small boxy modern dwellings resembling trailer houses scattered on the sand amid a smattering of trees along the Thamalakane River in north-central Botswana. It used to be a Wild West town of cattle men, adventurers, and big game hunters. It's more settled now, thanks mainly to the tourist traffic of high-priced photographic safaris embarking from there into the vast Okavango Delta to the north and deeper into the Kalahari Desert to the south. But remnants of the Wild West spirit persist. Maun brims with testosterone.

At least that's what our guide, Granger, told the six of us as we met him there after our flight from Johannesburg, South Africa, for our safari into the delta. "It's loaded with guys trying to prove they're dominant males like lions in the bush," he said with a broken smile. "Tourists are prey here, and they'll believe anything that guides say about Africa and wildlife and their own exploits. Bragging and lying are currency, and turf wars among the guides are a way of life. But, of course, I'm different," he assured us. "You can trust everything I say." He gave us that broken smile again.

Who'd have guessed that tour guides competed for dominance like lions? Maybe Africa does that, I thought—brings out the animal instincts in humans. The heart of darkness and all that. But I couldn't see Granger succumbing. He was unusual in many ways. One member of our group had traveled with him on a previous safari and had lauded him when organizing this adventure, insisting that he be our guide from beginning to end. Ruddy-faced and weathered under his ever present Tilley hat, he spoke with a soft South-African English accent and displayed education, wit, and a social flair. He also proved to be a gifted photographer and patient instructor. He certainly didn't match the predatory, dominant male type he had described, even physically. And we were inclined to believe pretty much everything he told us.

Before long, to begin our safari we took flight in a puddle-jumper from Maun to the Duma Tau Camp a couple of hundred miles northeast. Below us we could see the Okavango Delta stretching out in an abstract patchwork of waterways, swamps, grasslands, and sandy islands sporting clumps of palms, acacias, Mangosteen, sycamore figs, and jackalberry, and providing watering holes for abundant wildlife, like the elephants we sighted lumbering along or gathered to drink. It was a remarkable sight, at once artful, fascinating, and desolate. It belongs, after all, to the Kalahari Desert.

The Kalahari Desert. A fabled, often forbidding, land idealized decades ago by Laurens van der Post in *The Lost World of the Kalahari* as a remote, largely inhospitable, habitat of Stone Age Bushmen living pure, pre-civilized human lives. Today the original Bushmen (or San) and their world, once far removed from the rest of us in time and space, no longer exist. Modernity and tourism have seen to that. But the Bushmen's isolated desert home was not the whole of the Kalahari either. Their piece of that austere yet varied terrain claims but a section of the vast Kalahari Basin, whose sands range over much of southern Africa from Zimbabwe in the east into Namibia in the west, from South Africa in the south to Angola and Zambia in the north. And almost wherever you go in landlocked Botswana (previously the British protectorate of Bechuanaland) you remain in the Kalahari, including the great Okavango Delta, where waters of the Okavango River flowing from Angola fan out to create the largest delta system in the world.

That delta is a maze of waterways that flood in the wet season and weave around sandy islands and broad plateaus where many species of animals live off the water and greenery and each other. The herbivores and omnivores—elephants, giraffes, zebras, wildebeests, buffalo, hippos, monkeys, warthogs, various antelopes known as lechwe, kudu, and tsessebe, and others—have it best. They munch on grasses and leafy trees, and they proliferate in herds. The carnivores—lions, leopards, cheetahs, hyenas, wild dogs, crocodiles, eagles, and more—have a harder life. Usually living in pairs or in small groups and dependent as they are on killing herbivores for food, carnivores find their mealtimes come irregularly, unpredictably, and dangerously. Herbivores often outrun them or collectively defend themselves with lethal hooves or horns. Not only that. Carnivores kill each other, too, to protect territory or to seize it for survival. So, heroic as they may be in the human imagination, their lives are short.

Not long ago, both the herbivores and carnivores here also had to fear hunters seeking trophies for their parlor walls. Ernest Hemingway exemplified the type, although he favored Kenya and Tanzania northeast of the Kalahari. He took great pride in the hunt. And he respected the honest courage of animals. But, like most hunters, he showed little real courage compared to the creatures he killed. Animals have to search for food and fight for survival every day.

Hunters just travel into the animal kingdom carrying high-powered weapons that snuff out animals' lives at a safe distance. Hemingway even confessed, recounting his safari days in *Green Hills of Africa,* "I like to hunt sitting on my tail. No sweat." Such courage. Shooting fish in a barrel or lions or elephants or other wild beasts at several hundred yards—like Hemingway's Francis Macomber, who finds courage only with a long-range rifle in his hands and lives his "short happy life" after wounding a water buffalo from a vehicle and then pumping more shells into it close up until it dies, moments before his wife fires a bullet into his own head. Anyhow, those hunting days in Africa are largely gone, except in restricted areas where shooting animals is still allowed, and, of course, for poachers who respect neither animals nor laws. Nowadays, the camps of the Okavango Delta greet only affluent tourists who come for photographic safaris led by guides mainly from that nondescript little town of Maun.

An hour and a half after taking off from Maun, we landed on a dusty strip in what appeared to be nowhere and were soon bouncing along a rutted path, not a road, in an aging Land Rover toward the camp through an arid and eerie landscape of nothing but dead and broken trees standing forlornly in the sand. It was a desolate terrain seemingly bereft of life. Puzzled by the lifelessness, we asked Granger about it. "Elephants," he said. They had over time broken the trees to get at the leaves and then stripped away the bark for food. "This," he went on, "is the kind of thing that has led ignorant critics to claim that there are too many elephants and so they should be culled. But what does 'too many' mean? 'Too many elephants' means only that humans have invaded the elephants' habitat and decided there are now 'too many' for human convenience or sensibility. But nature has its own ways of deciding whether there are too many animals in a habitat. Nature takes care of itself without us if we leave it alone. You might not like how it does this and want to intervene for some moral or sentimental reason, but what is morality or sentiment in nature?" Granger's words made us feel like interlopers in the strange landscape that elephants had created.

That landscape finally yielded to a cluster of green foliage where the camp lay. Among the trees, tented cottages perched on platforms ten feet from the ground were linked to each other by elevated wooden pathways. Why? we asked, and were told matter-of-factly, as though it should have been obvious, to allow animals to pass under unimpeded, and to let people go by without getting killed. An elephant stood lazily chomping from a tree near the central camp structure where meals would be served, and no one but us seemed to give the beast any notice. Granger explained the code: "Animals rule here, and you have to respect them and their space—for their sake, as well as yours. If you see an elephant or lion near the path when you come out of your tent, don't move, or slowly go back in. Someone will come get you. Otherwise you could be sorry."

We heeded the warning. After settling into our comfortable lodgings and having lunch overlooking a plain on the delta where red lechwe grazed, we climbed back into our three-tiered Land Rover and went off for a late afternoon game drive and sundown cocktails in the Savuti Channel, a valley-wide riverbed that, Granger told us, attracts many kinds of wildlife to its watering holes, and for food. First we wove through the forest surrounding the camp then on out to the channel. The landscape was greener and more inviting here than earlier on our way to the camp. Grasses grew in the channel, and palms, acacias, sycamores, and Mangosteen rose amid vegetation on both sides. A herd of elephants wandered through the trees on our left toward a watering hole not far away, prompting Granger to speed up and swing the Land Rover around to the far side of the hole to get in position for photographs when the elephants arrived. He was an adept stage director, finding just the right angle and lighting for the photo buffs to capture the scene. We sat with our cameras at the ready.

A soft rustling sound in the trees just behind us switched our eyes to the lanky forms of giraffes ambling along at the edge of the channel nibbling in the high leaves. They were in no hurry and seemingly had no fears. As they moved along, their long necks undulated gracefully and their bodies swayed like rocking chairs, making them look like fanciful beings of primordial times, or a filmmaker's invention. Before long, the elephants appeared and joined the giraffes beside the large water hole in front of us. The elephant herd had many young who waded into the water to drink. Granger pointed out one of them whose trunk was, well, truncated. "It probably got attacked by a crocodile," he said. "The poor thing won't survive to adulthood because an elephant needs its trunk to eat, and that trunk won't do the job."

It was sad to think of this child being marked for doom and nothing was to be done about it. "Couldn't a zoo take it, or something?" someone asked.

"That's not how nature works," Granger answered. "You can't save every threatened animal. Nature has its ways."

The sun now lay low in the sky, casting soft light and spreading long shadows on the ground that mirrored the distended forms of the elephants and giraffes. Cameras clicked, people sighed. This was the Africa we had imagined.

Suddenly, the idyllic scene was disrupted by a noise no animal could make. It was a Land Rover roaring down the channel toward us. We stared as the driver pulled up nearby. We could hear him telling his passengers how to get the best photographs. Several of the animals, unsettled, backed away from the pond and disappeared into the bush. Granger was not happy. But, gentleman that he was, instead of causing a row with the intruder, he just told us it was time for our sundown cocktails and drove off down the channel.

We came to a stop near a majestic umbrella acacia, the iconic tree of the African plain whose flat canopy spreads out a hundred feet or more. There we had cocktails, served by Granger with aplomb from the trunk of the Land Rover, and watched the sun set, lighting the sky in fiery colors and silhouetting the acacia in picture-postcard perfection. More elephants and giraffes passed by, trailed by kudu and wildebeests. We sipped our drinks and held the picturesque African moment.

As dusk descended and a chill drifted into the air, we climbed back into the Land Rover to search for creatures of the night on our way back to camp. Darkness came quickly, and we pulled padded parkas over our shoulders to warm us against the Kalahari's arid nighttime cold. Granger drove along one side of the channel near the foliage, adroitly steering with one hand while holding a spotlight with the other, shining it into the trees and around the channel, keeping up a steady stream of talk over his shoulder. It was a remarkable performance. He found owls perched on branches and bright unidentified eyes staring from dark brush. Out in the channel his light caught a bushy-tailed aardwolf on its nocturnal hunt for termites. The sight excited Granger, and we came to a stop. "It's not often you see one," he said. "They're very shy and hard to find." The aardwolf sat still in the grass, looking at us. Then it slunk away, and we drove on.

After a few minutes, Granger hit the brakes and turned off the headlights. Shining the spotlight beneath a tree, he turned and said softly, "Leopards." There were two of them on the ground at the edge of the forest, difficult to see with their mottled coats blending into the surroundings. "Male and female," Granger observed and inched the Land Rover forward to get a better view, directing the spotlight toward them briefly and then averting it to avoid frightening them. "Leopards are among the hardest animals to find," he said, almost in a whisper. "They're very nocturnal and there aren't many of them here. They protect their privacy and are easily spooked. Occasionally, you find one sleeping in a tree during the day. But to see a male and female out together at night is rare."

The leopards gathered themselves up, stretched, and started to leave the trees for the channel. As Granger cautiously shined the light around them, we could see that the male was distinctly larger than the female, but their faces looked very much the same and not the least wild. When someone mentioned that, Granger replied,

"All cats are wild. Even the ones you think of as pets. They're closer to leopards than you'd think."

While he said that, a pair of headlights showed up across the channel careening rapidly toward us. The leopards stood still. The headlights grew larger, glaring directly on the cats, who then darted from the channel and disappeared into the dark beneath the trees. "Christ," Granger grumbled. "That moron again." He shined his spotlight in the other driver's face and held it there to send a message. Then he backed the Land Rover up and we headed for the camp. The drive from there went swiftly. Granger kept shining the light into the trees and talking, still steering with one hand despite the rugged road and the speed he was going. We saw more owls and anonymous eyes that shined from the dark in the spotlight. But it was growing very cold in the desert night and we were ready for camp and dinner.

Dinner went convivially with chat about the afternoon. We asked Granger about the guide who had so rudely disrupted our peace at the watering hole and had scared off the leopards. He told us he knew him all too well. The guy had worked in several African countries and had come to Botswana from Zimbabwe a while ago after safari work there had dried up because of political turmoil. A tour company had given him a contract and he'd settled in Maun, where he liked to boast of how well he knew Africa and its wildlife. He wasn't making any friends among the other guides, who respect certain protocols toward each other in the field, whatever their competitive spirit. But he didn't seem to care. He figured he would be the Big Man in Maun and the Okavango and clients would come running. He evidently had a group of them now staying at another camp. Granger confided that he had himself had an altercation with the guy in a bar that had almost turned violent. But he wouldn't say just what had happened.

After dinner, Granger showed us some of his own nature photographs. He proved to be as much a photo tourist as anyone. But his pictures were professional. He was an artist. A lioness stretched out in midair leaping a stream, a cheetah racing on the attack, a sleeping leopard draped over the branch of a tree clutching the remains of a small antelope, an elephant chugging through the dust as if on some urgent mission, an eagle diving for a rodent, buffalo fending off an attacking lion with their horns. Granger had been in Africa all his life, and it was in his blood, giving him an unsentimental admiration for animals in the wild, a regard for the ways of nature, and a wariness of the ways of people. He was a civilized gentleman, but he also belonged to this world of nature, where he was very much at home, and which he clearly was not inclined to trade for the world of civilization.

The next day took us away from the Savuti Channel through another area of sandy desolation littered with dead trees twisting into the sky, until we reached wetter land and a grassy meadow surrounded by leafy greenery. There we found herds of giraffes and zebras mingling in photogenic pairings. The gangly, blotched-skinned giraffes fed from tall trees or awkwardly spread their long spindly front legs and stretched their necks down to reach nourishment on the ground. The neatly designed black-and-white striped zebras (each pattern slightly unique, Granger told us) stood still at first to watch us, some of them in rows as if at attention, their thick and evenly cropped manes rising on their necks like the crests of centurions' helmets. The young of both species followed close to their mothers, looking like children's toys. Groups of monkeys and baboons playfully swung in trees and scampered through the grass. A family of warthogs trundled speedily past on their little legs toward some insistent destination. The peaceful amicability of the scene was Edenic. No predators. No competition for survival. Just placid eating and quiet socializing among herbivores and their omnivore friends. We sat at a discreet distance, being eyed occasionally by curious and cautious zebras standing at attention.

Then the atmosphere changed. A vehicle burst into the meadow and rumbled toward us. Zebras jerked their heads around, giraffes froze. It was the same Land Rover we'd seen before. As it loudly advanced, the zebras closed ranks and trotted away, and the giraffes moseyed into the trees. Baboons and monkeys skittered nervously across the ground and into high branches. Granger cursed under his breath and snarled aloud, "Unbelievable. This guy hasn't a clue. But he's bragging that he can find more wildlife and get better pictures than anyone else." Granger pulled our Land Rover out of its spot and drove to the other end of the meadow and around a patch of bush to a space largely concealed from animals who were gradually moving in that direction. A mother giraffe and her bony offspring came by, the young propped up on wiry legs like stilts, followed by others sticking close to the trees and zebras grazing in the grass. A group of distant elephants crunched their way through the woods and the meadow.

Once again our peaceful viewing was shattered by the other Land Rover rolling toward us. "Are they following us?" someone asked.

"He doesn't know what he's doing," Granger responded, "so he tracks me and other guides. And he's getting worse."

"Isn't he violating the safari protocols you mentioned?" I asked.

"Yeah," he answered. "Guides might be rivals, but they should let each other know where good sightings are, and they're not sup-posed to crowd in. But he tells his clients he's the best there is. The clients don't know the difference."

"Can't anything be done about it?" I inquired. "Can you com-plain to the tour company?"

He paused. "We don't do that kind of thing out here," he said, as though I should have known. "He'll get his . . ." he muttered without finishing.

We left the meadow and drove on through another landscape of desiccated trees and termite mounds standing sometimes ten or twelve feet high as monuments to the industry of the insects. Mon-keys and baboons and warthogs scampered around. Eagles flew overhead or perched prominently on dead tree branches. In time, the desolation gave way to more wetlands. There a large herd of elephants was moving through a stream where the eyes of bathing hippos poked above the water and others stood chewing grass on the bank. Not far from the hippos, saddle-billed storks stood statuesquely, their black and white feathers and the bright orange saddles across their bills standing out against the greenery surrounding them. Tsessebe antelopes meandered in the background. As we watched and snapped pictures from our position near the stream, a huge bull elephant with six-foot tusks, bringing up the rear of the herd, stopped some thirty yards away, casting us a suspicious eye. Slowly he waved his massive ears. "That's a warning to us," Granger said. The elephant took a few heavy steps toward us and stood waving his ears.

"What's he going to do?" we asked Granger nervously.

"He's just telling us this is his herd and he doesn't like intruders," he replied.

The elephant pawed the ground with deliberate front footfalls and flapped his ears more vigorously. "Shouldn't we leave?" someone said nervously. "He could crush us."

"Don't worry," Granger replied. "He just showing off. And you can see he's proving his manhood by enlarging his genitals." The beast now came forward a few more steps displaying all his signs of masculine dominance.

"Yikes!" one of the women in the group exclaimed with theatrical wit and no fear. "If he's going to come after us I'm going to need some lubricant." The group erupted in relieved laughter. The elephant kept moving slowly toward us until he was only ten feet away. His tusks practically touched our headlights. We could see his six-inch eyelashes protruding over the eyes that glared at us. His ears flapped like flags in a breeze.

"Uh, Granger," someone said edgily, "Are you sure . . . ?"

Granger turned around and said firmly but good-naturedly, "Paranoia emanates from this vehicle. Relax. When he's made his point, he'll go away." We waited. The bull stood his ground. After seemingly a very long time, he took a few steps backward then turned and clumped off toward his herd.

"Why were you so sure he wouldn't attack?" we asked.

"They don't attack unless you get in their way or provoke them when they're hungry or protecting themselves against a threat. This was nothing like that. It was just territorial masculine authority. This is his herd. Once he had put us on notice and decided we weren't going to challenge him he calmed down." But, Granger warned, "We never pass in front of an elephant, if we can help it, even in the Land Rover. They can get alarmed and charge. And remember, you never get out of the vehicle when any animals are near. Elephants or lions might walk past within a couple of yards and disregard us because they sense that in the vehicle we are neither prey nor enemy. But a human on foot could be either."

Granger's explanation ended with the noisy appearance yet again of the pesky guide who was still on our trail. Granger just drove away, and we wended back to camp for lunch and rest and afternoon tea before going out for the next sundowner. As we lounged after lunch by the swimming pool, a lone elephant strolled past beyond the fence almost close enough to touch but indifferent to our presence. And we watched as he made his way to a distant rendezvous with another elephant under some palms near a group of hippos. It was again a picture of tranquil nature.

The tranquility continued through the sundowner that evening amid the elephants and giraffes and lechwes that had become our neighbors. And the dramatic sunset again turned Africa into an art form. The sole jarring note came from another entrance of the intrusive guide who, fortunately this time, only rumbled by and then parked farther down the channel. Granger said we'd be free of the pest tomorrow when we moved on to Duba Plains for the lions and buffalo. But first came the dogs.

Granger greeted everyone the next morning with boyish alacrity. A pack of wild dogs had been seen in the area, and he wanted to find them. We didn't understand why dogs should have animated him so much. After all, we have dogs at home. How could wild dogs be that much more exciting? "You seldom get to see a dog pack," he explained at breakfast, "and they are among the most fascinating creatures in nature. They're highly intelligent and thoroughly social. They hunt as a team with scouts, leaders, and soldiers. I hope we can see that." We took him at his word, as usual.

He drove back to the Savuti Channel well beyond where we had gone before. Eventually, we veered around a bend where Granger announced, "There they are." He pointed across the channel to a rise against the trees. We strained our eyes to see anything moving, but saw nothing. He headed cautiously across. As we drew near the other side, we could at last detect a dozen or so splotchy brown forms lying together blending into the ground. "Still sleeping," Granger observed, as he coasted the Land Rover to a stop. "We'll just wait until they get up." In ten minutes or so a couple of the dogs started stirring. One of them stood up, and one by one the others rose, stretched, and rather restlessly paced around. "They'll leave together then fan out when they begin the hunt," Granger said. "When the time comes, they'll surround their prey and attack."

We watched as a lead dog started out. The others followed. They loped on down the channel against the trees. We trailed them. Several hundred yards along, they slowed, gathered, and paused. We waited. Then, as if having consulted and decided on a course of action, they disappeared under the trees. Granger seemed to know where they were going and drove on down the channel to an opening that delivered us to another branch of the channel where we could see a herd of lechwe. Granger pointed out some of the dogs that were already circling widely around the lechwe. Others dogs waited under the trees. We waited, too. Then, as if on cue, from their appointed positions the dogs dashed toward one lechwe that had drifted slightly apart from the others and that the dogs had somehow collectively singled out. It bounded from its first pursuers. The herd took off. Other dogs rushed in from the side. Shifting direction, the lechwe met yet another attacker. A panicked turn took it to another. And another. One dog now got close enough to grab a rear leg. The lechwe struggled to break free but got seized by the other rear leg. The lechwe went down. It was over. The pack raced in and the lechwe was finished.

It was quite a drama. Granger was more excited than anybody. "They're remarkable, aren't they?" he effused. "You've had a treat." That wouldn't have been the word I'd have chosen, but the incident did give us all more respect for wild dogs.

While the dogs devoured the ill-fated lechwe, we turned back toward the camp. Re-entering the main part of the channel, we crossed paths with the other Land Rover, which was racing toward the dogs. Granger steered clear and shook his head slowly. It was a sign of contempt. But this time he had bested his rival without incident. And soon we would be far away at Duba Plains.

As the plane descended to the Duba Plains landing strip that afternoon, we could see that the delta below was more flooded than at Duma Tau. Granger explained that this was a marshier area and that the year had been unusually wet, making for some soggy travels on the ground. We soon learned what he meant. Going out for a sundowner later that day, our Land Rover crossed a bridge to a road that lay underwater. A foot of water. Then two feet. Then three. By the time we had ventured fifty yards toward an island that appeared quite far away, the hood of the vehicle was underwater. We plowed our way through, sending a wake into the marshes on both sides. Water washed through the vehicle covering Granger's legs and onto the floor of the lower seats where we had to lift our feet up to keep them dry.

"You ever get stuck out here?" someone asked, and Granger replied that it happens a lot, while he struggled to keep the vehicle on its underwater track. "What do you do?"

"Wait until we can get pulled out," he answered nonchalantly.

To our relief, we made it to dry land, where we had our sundowner in view of a band of baboons and monkeys cavorting in the acacias. We enjoyed another African sunset in the silence of isolation.

The next day, we went out before dawn for our first look at the lions and water buffalo. Shortly we found ourselves driving through water again up to the hood of the vehicle. For an hour or more, we were in and out of water as we passed from one small island to another. At last we rose onto a large plateau and drove along a relatively dry road until we reached a stand of trees where we encountered a pair of regal male lions sitting a few yards away. They gave us a lazy look and resumed their quiet gaze toward a herd of buffalo a couple of hundred yards beyond. Beneath another clump of trees three lionesses lolled with their cubs, who played like kittens. We commented on how domestic and familial they looked, the females attending to the children as the males sat proudly to command the scene. Granger disabused us.

"Domestic, perhaps," he said. "But the females are waiting for their chance. If a young buffalo strays, they'll prepare to attack. The older males wait for lunch to be served. By the drooping of their stomachs I'd say it's been quite a while since the family's eaten, so they're getting hungry. A good meal lasts them several days. But going after buffalo is no picnic. Buffalo protect each other, and they can send a lion flying with a well-placed kick, or skewer it on their horns. The lions have to be cautious and lucky."

Granger eased the Land Rover close to the females and their cubs so we could photograph the fun. The cubs frolicked, rolling and biting and scampering, and the adult females bathed them with affectionate tongues. This pride of lions had been in the area for a number of years, Granger told us, and the males were getting on in age—twelve years, he said, is a long time for a lion to survive in the wild. "Sooner or later," he went on, "young males from another pride will come in and force them out and take over. And they'll kill any cubs that are left. That's the ultimate turf war. Nature, red in tooth and claw, as Tennyson said."

Disregarding those cruel realities, we happily snapped photographs of the familial bliss. After a time, Granger pulled back and drove to get closer to the buffalo. They were munching grass and drifting slowly across the field, indifferent to both us and the lions. While we watched, two of the lionesses left the group and slunk out into the tall grass toward the buffalo. They crept almost indiscernibly, coming within twenty yards of the trailing members of the buffalo herd. They crouched to a stop with their eyes fixed on their prey. As the buffalo grazed along, a space opened between two young ones and the rest of the herd. The lionesses' inched forward. The young buffalo still appeared blind to their presence, thanks possibly to the light wind blowing in the lions' favor. We sat nearly as still as the lions. And waited. A little more distance opened between the herd and the two trailers. The lions crept still closer.

They sprang as one. In a flurry of dust, they vaulted toward the slighter of the two young buffalo, who took off toward the herd. The chase was on. The commotion startled the herd, but instead of running the buffalo pulled together, horns and hooves set for battle. The lions raced after the two fugitives, gaining ground fast.

At that moment a Land Rover came racing into the chase, engine roaring, gears grinding, wheels churning the ground. "What the . . . ?" Granger exclaimed. "Not him again! All the way from Duma Tau?" It was as though the guy was trying to horn in on Granger's turf, like the young lions taking over territory from the old ones. The lions slid to a halt. When the dust cleared we saw the buffalo herd standing at alert, the two strays now back in their midst, and the lions slumping back to the pride. The alien vehicle had pulled up very near the site of the aborted attack. "Unbelievable!" Granger exclaimed. "That SOB. You never interfere with a hunt. Now these lions probably won't eat today. I wish they'd make a meal of him."

The drama over, the female lions rejoined their brood, and the buffalo resumed their munching. Granger muttered that we might as well go back to the camp for lunch. We circled around past the female lions, now lolling with their cubs despite having lost a hunt, and on past the male lions, who had wandered away and were lounging on a knoll with a view of the plain, as impassive as if nothing had happened to disturb their regal calm, hungry as they might be. Granger paused for photographs.

"What would happen if we got out of the vehicle here?" someone asked.

Granger replied, still a bit agitated, "Remember what I said. You'd be their lunch."

"But they seem unthreatening."

"Don't kid yourself," Granger said a little edgily. "The males let the females do most of the work, like lots of guys. But you'd be much easier for any of them to catch than the buffalo."

With those cautionary words, Granger turned the vehicle around, and we made our watery way in the increasing heat of the day to the cool repose of the camp.

After our usual afternoon of leisure, Granger told us that we would now be going out to try to find a cheetah that had been reported in the grassland several miles away. The prospect excited us. We piled into the Land Rover and went off. In a while, we passed through marshy terrain and to an area of verdant grasses where lechwe and wildebeests grazed. It was all quite peaceful. Granger scanned the landscape with trained eyes while driving through the fields. Then, gesturing to us to be quiet, he slowed to a stop. He pointed to an area of tall grass ahead of us to the side maybe thirty yards away in the vicinity of some lechwe. "Cheetah," he said, "in the grass." We strained to see. Eventually, we found its pointed ears rising just above the grass. That he had detected it amazed us. As we peered intently, we could discern more of its form. It wasn't very large, but we could tell it was a handsome cat, with proper spots and a lean face, poised and alert. We couldn't get very close, Granger said, without scaring it off so we had to settle for distant photographs. We waited. And waited. Then came a burst of movement. The cheetah attacked in a blur, bounding and swishing in the grass. It happened so fast we almost missed it. A young lechwe had wandered a bit, and that was the end of it. The cheetah brought it to the ground in the flash of an eye.

Granger was as excited as anyone. "Africa is full of surprises," he exulted. "This is one not many people get to see. We were lucky this time." At that moment our luck changed.

A recognizable vehicle rumbled into the scene. We all knew what that meant. Granger growled that the bastard had at least missed the drama but was certain to disrupt the cheetah's dinner. Having no desire to see that, Granger drove away for our sundowner. Despite the intruder, we were still exhilarated by the cheetah. But Granger was a little more subdued than usual at cocktails and on the ride back to camp. His annoyance was evidently deepening.

The next morning brought a drive along a new route that abounded in wildlife. We saw hippos bathing and saddle-billed storks posing and wattled cranes nesting and egrets prancing and kingfishers fishing and eagles soaring and monkeys and baboons swinging in trees and kudu tussling playfully with their curly horns and crocodiles sunning and elephants chomping branches and a fox on the hunt and a hyena scavenging for someone else's lunch. No great drama, but it was Africa in its abundance. And everyone was contented. Even Granger, possibly because the intruder had left us alone.

Later during lunch, Granger told us he had just learned that a second group of lions was following a small herd of tsessebe not far from a neighboring camp. He explained that the space between the turf of this pride and that of the pride the previous day with the buffalo was sufficient to keep them apart, as long as they both got enough to eat. But when lions get hungry enough, he said, they will even go to a camp in search of food. So you don't like to see them too nearby. Anyway, he said we should go find this pride and the tsessebe and have our last sundowner at Duba Plains.

The drive was drier than that of yesterday to see the buffalo, although there was plenty of water around. Within about an hour we came upon three female lions leading three young ones who were cavorting through shallow water and reeds, while a pair of mature males brought up the rear. "They play like house cats," someone observed. "But water doesn't seem to bother them."

"They couldn't survive long here if it did bother them," Granger remarked. "And all the water this year makes it harder to hunt because their prey don't have to go to only a few water holes to get it. You can see that these lions are as hungry as those yesterday. A tsessebe would make a good dinner, if they can catch one."

Seeing the tsessebe in the distance, we drove slowly alongside the lions and stopped with them at a cluster of trees and bushes beside a large termite mound some ten feet high. A couple of the lions lay down with a view of the tsessebe feeding not far away. A male scratched a tree trunk like a house cat does to furniture. The cubs wrestled. One of the females climbed up the termite mound to perch on the top perhaps for a better view of the prey. Sitting there, with the sun now lowering to the horizon and coating everything in soft warm hues, she looked more like a statue than an animal on the lookout. Cameras clicked ferociously to capture the picturesque sight, another of Africa's stunningly scenic and tranquil moments.

The tranquility was broken yet again by a Land Rover rushing toward us. It pulled up in front to grab the view of the lioness with the sunset. She turned her head and climbed from the mound. The pride withdrew into the greenery. The tsessebe scampered.

"That's it," Granger said through clenched teeth. "This is intolerable." He went on to say there would be nothing more to see here tonight so we should go for our sundowner. We were all happy to do that, and we drove off to where a forest of palms stood against the setting sun. But Granger was distinctly out of sorts and quiet. And the return to camp went quickly as darkness fell and he drove faster than before, shining his spotlight around but catching only the eyes of some owls and small nocturnal creatures that vanished into the night. At dinner he also seemed preoccupied, not his usual loquacious and amusing self. Maybe he was tiring of us and the troubles with the obnoxious guide. But we had one more camp to go to after this, and it didn't seem like him to lose interest or energy. We hoped that this time the invasive guide wouldn't be there. Granger left dinner early pleading preparations to make and rest to get. I went to bed thinking of the hungry lions in the sunset, and wondering if they would eat tomorrow.

At breakfast the next day, Granger was much more lively than he had been last night. And, as we flew off for a short stay at Kwetsani Camp before our return to Maun, he cheerfully told us about the loveliness of the waterways we would be seeing and the other striking scenery dotted with wildlife that we would find.

Once at the new camp, our first foray took us out on the swampy water in mokoro, or dugout canoes, pushed along by oarsmen wielding poles that penetrated to the bottom of the shallow water. We drifted through vast patches of colorful waterlilies and bulrushes and stands of lacy papyri that arched elegantly out of the water, giving perches on their stems to tiny brightly colored frogs. After a while, we could see far away a pride of lions assembled on a knoll beyond the floodplain. It was all perfectly quiet but for the motion of the water against the mokoro and the poles that eased us along. It was the placid Africa again. And no one to spoil it. We wondered if that would last.

The pleasant morning exploration of the waterways led to another midday lunch, followed by time at the pool, a siesta, and tea service, before our last sundown game drive. Granger had regained his spirited, voluble self. He didn't say why. But we were glad to see it. The change made afternoon tea more enjoyable and promised a genial sundowner. When the time came, we climbed into the Range Rover with anticipation of a new sunset adventure and regret that it would be our last.

We saw more hippos and cranes and lechwe and other inhabitants of this majestic land- and waterscape. In time we also encountered the lions, who had traveled from where we had seen them that morning. The females and cubs were leading the way as usual through patches of water with the mature males ambling unhurriedly behind. They appeared better fed than the ones at Duba Plains, their stomachs not sagging from delayed meals. Granger suggested we go ahead of them to where we would get a good close-up view of their eyes in the sunlight as they came toward us. We did. As they drew near, their coats glistened and their yellow eyes shone bright, and the manes of the males matched their eyes in the late afternoon sun. We all snapped pictures as they strolled by treating us as though we were part of the scenery. We slowly followed them toward a large termite mound amid brush on a rise, and there they all lay down but for one male who climbed the mound and perched on it as the female lion had done back at Duba Plains. We eased near them. The sun was now at the horizon, and the scene was if anything the most picturesque yet. Palms and umbrella acacia trees stood silhouetted against the descending sun, and wisps of high clouds overhead lit up the sky in a diffuse light of radiant orange that the waterways reflected, creating a golden glow that enveloped everything. Pink lilies covering much of the water became almost orange, and the spidery sprays of the tall delicate papyri tendrils here and there glistened almost like a Fourth of July sparkler. The same radiance fell over the lions. The proud male sitting atop the termite mound was a monument to his species, his statuesque form and full mane burnished in the warm light, making him appear to be the king of beasts for sure, surveying his kingdom.

The spectacle gave us a feeling of déjà vu from last evening. That now seemed like a rehearsal for this one, which was perfect. And, as the sun sank beneath the horizon beyond the lions, giving the clouds overhead and the waterways nearby an even more intense celestial luminosity, we all had the feeling that this was the ideal finale before the curtain came down on the last act of our African adventure. It was Africa at its most magnificent and serene.

Eventually, someone broke the silence that had held us all for minutes. "This is the best night yet."

"And thank god that crummy guy didn't show up," someone added.

"He won't bother us or anybody anymore," Granger said calmly.

"Why not? How do you know?" I asked.

"I'll tell you at our sundowner," he answered and drove off to a spot where we could still see the lions and the termite mound across the water in a distant tableau against the sky. As he took up his usual bartending duties, he explained: "The manager told me he had got word this afternoon that the guy didn't come to breakfast at his camp this morning or show up for the game drive. He wasn't in his tent, either. So some of the crew went to search. They found what little remained of him out toward where we saw the lions last night. The lions lay nearby in the shade under some trees. They weren't hungry anymore." Granger seemed to try, without success, to suppress his distinctive smile.

"What happened?" we asked almost in unison. "How did he . . . ?"

"It's a mystery," Granger answered. "But the manager told me they suspected he got drunk, as he often did, and wandered out in the night."

"But could he have walked that far?" I pressed.

"I guess it wasn't all that far from his camp. As I told you, hungry lions can roam around camps and be very menacing. One of them could have jumped him and dragged him away. He was arrogant, reckless, and stupid. Something like that was bound to happen to him." Granger wore a peculiarly placid expression as he said that. It was as if this news had come as no surprise to him. It clearly pleased him.

Back at camp, Granger was full of life at dinner, telling stories of funny safaris and ridiculous clients and wayward guides. He was entertainer, philosopher, naturalist, and bon vivant. We had never seen him more spirited. Possibly it was a performance for the last night of our safari. But I couldn't help thinking there was more to it than that.

In the morning, after a leisurely breakfast, we gathered our things and took a midday plane back to Maun. From there the six of us would fly to Johannesburg then take our separate routes home. In the Maun airport we said our grateful farewells to Granger and tipped him generously. He accepted graciously, swung his backpack around his shoulder, and amiably saluted us goodbye. I watched him go out of the airport. For some reason, my eyes followed him as he crossed the street to a place with a weather-beaten sign reading Safari Bar. He pushed through the entrance. I figured the bar probably wasn't for tourists. It looked kind of forbidding. But curiosity seized me. I couldn't resist. I tailed him. As I approached the bar, I heard cheers from inside. Cautiously I went in and stood near the door in the semi-darkness. Rough-hewn and seedy, it looked like a suitable hangout for safari guides in Maun's testosterone culture. The light was dim, the air musty. Animal trophies adorned the walls, a few ramshackle tables and chairs were strewn around the dusty floor, and a bunch of rugged guys crowded the bar area. I couldn't see Granger at first, but I could tell he was being hailed for some accomplishment that they all seemed to know about. Rivalries aside, they had a certain camaraderie and admired manly acts.

A couple of them hefted Granger up on the bar. They all toasted him loudly: "To the man! The man who did it!"

Granger shrugged with a theatrically innocent expression and said, "I don't know what you're talking about."

"Who else could it be?" they shouted.

"You were there," one of them cried out, "and smart enough to pull it off."

"What do you mean?" he responded as unknowingly as before.

"Got the bastard drunk, of course," bellowed another guy, "and fed him to the lions."

"Oh," Granger replied, feigning surprise. "How would I know anything about that? All I know is that the lions were hungry." He flashed his broken smile.

"To the man!" They toasted again. "The winner! The safari king!"

Granger reluctantly joined the toast with a drink thrust into his hand.

I was stunned. Nature, red in tooth and claw. Granger actually lived it, for all of his civility. He had proved it by vanquishing an insufferable rival. But I was sure he had not done that for turf or dominance like the lions, or to demonstrate his testosterone for other guides. He'd done it to preserve the civility of safari protocols, paradoxical as that might be. That was Granger. And here he was being celebrated as the dominant male. The safari king. The biggest guy in the room. Even though he stood only four feet tall. A dwarf with a limp. I had long since ceased to notice.

Barroom anywhere

On Parole in Aspen

Aspen had been a rough-and-tumble town once, roiling with grizzled silver miners digging their way to imagined riches. And some had succeeded. Fifteen thousand people lived there by the 1890s. It had culture, too. An opera house and a grand hotel, both built by a founder of Macy's department store in New York, who had discovered Aspen not long after the first miners had staked their claims. During the silver rush, Oscar Wilde had visited the neighboring town of Leadville, teaching the miners aesthetics and galvanizing their spirits with tales of the rambunctious Renaissance artist and silversmith Benvenuto Cellini, prompting a barrage of pistol fire in Cellini's honor. But that Rocky Mountain glory had swiftly ended when the country went off silver in 1892, despite William Jennings Bryan's rousing protest to the Democratic Party convention that year against crucifying the country on "a cross of gold." Aspen pretty much died, like all Old West silver towns. Until it came to life again half a century later with the arrival of skiing and an infusion of new money and culture.

Within a few decades, Aspen became one of the glitziest vacation retreats in the world. Old Victorian houses once teetering toward collapse sold for fortunes. Movie stars and billionaires erected palaces on the mountainsides and up secluded valleys. In the ski season hotel rooms could practically cost blood, like silver in the old days. And glamorous parties lit the nights. In summer, visitors flooded to outdoor concerts, and the prestigious Aspen Institute drew notables to high-minded seminars and high-powered conferences at its campus on the outskirts of town. This was a place no socialite or celebrity or influence monger would wish to miss. A capital of the glitterati and the culturati and the oligarchy and policy makers, all together in a dolled-up Old West town surrounded by multi-million-dollar mountainside estates.

I had come to be with them. Well, not really. I had never cared much for that kind of thing. But I had been invited to participate in a conference on human rights at the Aspen Institute and figured it would be worthwhile. It was. Still, I found the socializing around the conference with movers and shakers of the world wearing thin pretty soon. At least for me. So, one evening I wandered into town looking for a more local experience. I passed trendy restaurants and fashionable boutiques and eventually ran across an old liquor store that appeared to have been there in times past and had a loyal clientele. I went in and asked the guy at the counter if there was a pub or something like that where locals go for relaxation and conviviality. He answered, "Harold's." It was owned, he told me, by a crusty family who viewed the modern Aspen renaissance with a jaundiced eye, and whose downtown property, worth millions, they clung to defiantly as a haunt for working people to escape the glitter and the culture that had engulfed the town. Sounded like the kind of place I wanted.

I tracked it down on a narrow street a few blocks away tucked into a line of gentrified vintage commercial buildings. It might have survived the silver mining days and its front been brushed up like its neighbors during Aspen's "restoration," but it had obviously been allowed to decline again into a more fitting rustic state. "Harold's" read a florescent sign over the door. Signs for Coors and Budweiser beer blinked in small windows on each side.

I pushed open the creaky door and met a haze of cigarette smoke. It struck me that the place could be violating ordinances against smoking in such establishments. But the smoke was a welcome throwback to the past in this ecology-health-culture-celebrity-obsessed town. Inside I paused to take in the scene. No beautiful or powerful people here.

The bar was lined with the denim- and leather-clad backs of gnarly guys and of a few hearty gals bellied up to pitchers of beer. Nearby other denizens gathered around pool tables in serious play. I made my way to a stool at the far end of the bar and ordered a pitcher of my own. After scanning my fellow barflies I swiveled to study the room. Many of the faces were worn, the clothes plain, the manners coarsely civil amidst the lively chatter. Workmen with calloused hands, cleaning people carrying the scent of bleach, hotel and restaurant laborers weary after long hours of serving the affluent, rugged ranch hands and other workers from outlying neighborhoods at home in this tavern where they could kick back and drink beer among their fellows who had never been in a movie or made a fortune or read Plato or adored Mozart or worried about global markets or philosophized about human rights. These were earthy people with their own stubborn pride and individuality and attachment to an Aspen of the past. They couldn't live in the town anymore because real estate, rents, and taxes had climbed too high, but they kept the town and environs running and would come here after work or from their modest homes down the valley or their trailers in a camp on Route 28. And here they could share camaraderie and tell tales of the fabled mining town and of their adventures in the mountain life, when they had time to live it.

The sounds of country music emanated from an antique juke-box, alternating between mournful anthems about the likes of lonely truck drivers on the road, loyal at heart but hungry for love, and angry songs assailing prissy elites and arrogant authorities. The songs did not sing of the Aspen of today. The pool tables lit by bright domed overhead lights hosted rounds of players who took their shots while their luck held then moseyed to a narrow shelf along the wall where their beer awaited. The clicking of pool balls punctuated the rough sociability of the room, and a curse would erupt from time to time when a pool shot went awry.

"Shit! A miscue!" The words burst from a hulking guy with a beard wearing a T-shirt emblazoned with the words Jiffy Lube as his cue ball made only a light click glancing off his target. How amusing, I thought. The refinement of "miscue," a tough guy's curse over a missed shot at the pool table. But that's exactly what it is isn't it? A cue that misses. A *miscue*. And a just cause for a curse.

Tough guys who commit miscues. And tough broads, too. A few of these women were sprinkled along the bar, and a whole bowling team of them surrounded a couple of pool tables. They were on their way, so I overheard, to a tournament at Miracle Bowl down the valley. They had matching leather jackets with metal studs spelling DTOM over an image of a coiled snake. And their own bowling balls in bags stamped with that moniker lined the floor along the wall beneath the shelf holding pitchers of beer and glasses. I watched as one of them, standing tall with wide shoulders, a pony tail, heavy eye shadow, tight jeans, and cowboy boots, took a gulp from her glass and then racked up the balls. She made a shot that hit the mark with a sharp *crack* as loud as gun fire. The balls scattered like buckshot. One dropped into a corner pocket. She cruised coolly around the table, lined up the cue, and smacked another into a side pocket. Again, with a surgeon's precision and a pugilist's punch, she deftly sent yet another down a pocket, then one more. But her next shot fell short. No cursed "miscue" though. She shrugged, ambled to the wall and refilled her glass. A heavy-set companion with her jacket off blew out a lungful of smoke, snuffed out her cigarette, flexed an arm tattoo, stepped up, and knocked a ball so hard into a corner pocket that it clattered all the way down to the rack below. She sniffed and swaggered to the next shot, which sent the remaining balls careening around the table, but none into a pocket. "Fuck," she mumbled, the "miscue" went without saying, and she sauntered to her pitcher. One after another the members of the team took their shots with the assurance and muscular bravado of their DTOM, Don't-Tread-On-Me style—which I gathered was the name of the team. Crack. Smack. Clunk. Clatter. They cleared the table with each pass through the team. I watched them for probably half an hour. Then, checking their time, they polished off their beer, cased their cues, donned their jackets, grabbed their bowling ball bags, called out "Yo!" to the female bartender, who responded with a robust: "Kick ass, girls!" and, with fists punching the air, they passed through the door to the street.

My gaze followed them then switched to the bartender. She looked as tough as they did. Not large but solid, with a voice like a bellows, a laugh like the mating call of a moose, a full head of fuzzy hair accentuating a face of imposing but not unattractive features that had weathered a lot of seasons and had no doubt intimidated many a mountain man. She could fill and top off a batch of mugs and pitchers with perfectly-timed pulls of the taps without a flicker of hesitation while carrying on conversations and sharing jokes with half-a-dozen customers. She seemed to know them all. A good-hearted soul who I figured must've been here for years. Maybe one of the owners. She could joke and curse and even flirt by instinct in her rugged way. And I suspected she brooked no disrespect or rowdiness. She'd refuse to serve and send packing anyone who couldn't handle their liquor or who misbehaved according to her rules.

"Don't Walk In If You Can't Walk Out!" announced one of the signs above the bar. And another: "Stay outta my face in my place." And "You fight, you're taillights." This was Aspen civility, old style. Hardly a lady's tea room, it was plenty boisterous. Just within the limits of the house and of the hardy hostess at the bar.

While eyeing her, I saw the door swing open and a guy come in, look around, and swagger to a vacant seat at the bar. He was husky but not very tall, unshaven for a while and wearing a plaid shirt and a cowboy hat like several others in the room. The bartender approached him with a pointed look and a casual, "What'll it be?" He obviously was not a regular. He ordered a pitcher of beer in a gruff voice that carried down to me. She took her time filling the pitcher and delivering it to him. The guy grumbled something and settled into his beer.

I worked on mine while watching more pool players and absorbing the atmosphere, a world away from the new Aspen. I drifted back in time to what the town might have been like in the early days. Yes, there was an opera house and a fancy hotel. But bars like this and the people in them were the real Aspen. The real West. Places that had true stories of real life to tell. Not like those melodramas in the opera house. I'd have liked to see Aspen in those days. But would I have wanted to live in such a place? I doubted it. I knew the idea of the Old West had more appeal than the reality would. I let myself get lost in that idea anyway.

Suddenly my reverie was broken by a noise near the other end of the bar. I strained to see what it was. A gravelly voice erupted above the occasional curses from pool tables and the contained conviviality of the room, "Don't mess with me!" A fist pounded the bar and glasses shook. It was the guy who had come in not long ago. He was face to face with the guy next to him, who had somehow caused offense.

The bartender stalked down to where they were sitting and told the loud guy to keep it down. This was her place and she makes the rules. He growled something. She leaned across the bar. "I don't know who you are fella," she snarled in a voice everyone could hear. "But watch your manners or you're outta here." He spat words back at her that I couldn't grasp. Without hesitation, she swung an open hand that smacked his cheek. The slap resounded to all ears. The place went quiet.

I stared. Stunned, the guy glowered at the bartender. Seconds passed in silence. Finally, collecting himself, he straightened up as tall as he could, squared his shoulders, and pushed back his hat. He threw a few bills down on the bar, swung off his stool, stood firm facing the bartender, and shouted, "I DON'T HAVE TO TAKE THIS SHIT!" He looked around pugnaciously at his listeners, then bellowed for all to hear, "I'M ON PAROLE!" Tossing his head back, he marched emphatically to the door, flung it open, and haughtily went out into the night.

The room burst into laughter. I laughed, too. In time, the commotion subsided and the patrons resumed their earthy conviviality. I finished my beer, paid my bill, and left.

But as I strolled back to my room at the Institute, the parting words of that gruff dude stayed with me, mingling with anticipation of the lofty discussions that I would have in the next few days among international notables on human rights policies to change the world. Everyone there would be important in some way, many self-important, all pleased with themselves and their work for humanity. Me too. But now I wondered who among us would feel more self-respect and a stronger sense of their own humanity than that little guy who had silenced the smoky saloon of hard-working, hard playing characters with that proudly defiant declaration of his achievement and worth: "I DON'T HAVE TO TAKE THIS SHIT! I'M ON PAROLE!"?

The Rue Catinat and the Hotel Continental c. 1925, Saigon, Vietnam
(vintage photo, Saigon Tourist Bureau)

Saigon Night and the Gentle Man from Laos

It wasn't nostalgia that had brought me back to Vietnam. I didn't have much of that. What Americans call the Vietnam War and the Vietnamese call the American War was nothing to be nostalgic about. But, as a journalist covering that war, I had always thought that despite two generations of war against foreigners from the West, the Vietnamese are an amiable people. Even warm. Actually rather lovable. And now that the victorious Communist regime had opened the doors to international trade and tourism, I wanted to see who the Vietnamese are today, and how the country had changed, and before it changed too much. I persuaded a magazine editor that an article on contemporary Saigon, triumphantly

261

renamed Ho Chi Minh City, twenty-five years after the war would be worth the trip.

I would be there for the Tet New Year, the weeklong Vietnamese celebration of the lunar New Year. That seemed an appropriate time to do a story on the new Vietnam. Americans know the Tet New Year mainly from the infamous "Tet Offensive" by the Viet Cong in 1968 that had caught the American military by surprise and, although it had cost the Viet Cong dearly, had turned American public opinion against the war for good. I would give American readers a new reason to remember the Tet New Year. Or so I had pitched the story to my editor.

Disembarking from my long flight at the Ho Chi Minh airport, I began to have doubts about my idea. The scene reminded me of the chaos engulfing the frenzied departure of the Americans in 1975. People were pushing about helter-skelter, and a cacophony of shouts filled the air. The passport clearance was mayhem as arriving passengers were told they had to supply additional photographs with our visa photos. I grumbled and filed into a crowd to get a second photograph taken. An hour later my passport got stamped. Then to the baggage claim. A maelstrom of tumbling luggage, shouting voices, and shoving arms. The end of the war all over again. Finally, I saw my bag, grasped it, and, rattled and exhausted, made my way through the gauntlet to the exit where another cluster of confusion clogged the doorway as harried officials demanded further identification forms, which everyone had to fumble through papers stamped by other officials to find. Then more turmoil outside, hoards of greeters crushing forward, waving and hollering to attract the attention of arriving travelers. I elbowed through, spurned the outstretched hands of soliciting taxi drivers, and was relieved to see at last an upraised hand holding a sign scrawled with the words: "Hardwick Hotel Continental."

I gestured vigorously to the man with the sign, and, after I identified myself as Mr. Hardwick,, he took my bags and led me to his car. Jangled, breathless, and sweltering from the heat, I climbed inside and wiped the sweat from my dripping face. He grinned into the rearview mirror and said, "Hotel now?"

"Yes. Yes," I answered as emphatically as I could, and we lurched away. Soon we were on a congested highway into the city.

As I watched the roadside and street scenes passing by out the window, they appeared both familiar and unlike what I had seen before. Dozens of construction cranes were bringing a modern cityscape to Ho Chi Minh City. But the streets themselves were still choked with bicycles and motorbikes and trishaws, while cars were scarce. Billboards advertised local products, not yet American fast food, but I knew that would come. Sidewalks spilled over with eateries and fix-it shops and what looked to be, but I suspected was not, piles of junk. A few signs of the war also showed up, including an armored tank and a downed American fighter plane standing outside a couple of government buildings as rusting monuments to victory. And there was colonial Saigon itself—even by name, I was told, since "Saigon" officially designates the central downtown of metropolitan Ho Chi Minh City and is still commonly used for all of it. Here wide boulevards shaded by trees lent grace to the old city. And the grand colonial Hotel Continental, my destination, was awaiting there, if not entirely its old self.

Built in the 1880s when Saigon was the burgeoning Paris of the East as capital of the fledgling French colony then called Cochinchina, the four-story Hotel Continental Palace, as it was originally named, became one of the grand hotels of Asia. It had provided opulent rooms for guests, a cool retreat for dining in the garden, and gracious conviviality in its sidewalk café, dubbed by foreigners the Continental Shelf, fronting the open Place Garnier, home of the colonial opera house along the fashionable rue Catinat. Colonial Saigon had revolved around the hotel. And it was said that the longtime owner, a French Corsican named Mathieu Franchini, reigned there over not only Saigon's *haute monde* but its *demi monde* as well. Hosting dignitaries and affluent travelers, the Continental had also shrouded the intrigues of spies, the transaction of drug traffickers, the assignations of fortune hunters, and the clandestine liaisons of lovers.

I had cherished this exotic colonial tradition. And I liked thinking of the writers traversing Asia who had brought literary luster to the Continental. Somerset Maugham had stopped there in the 1920s on a journey from Rangoon to Haiphong that he recorded in *The Gentleman in the Parlor*. Saigon, he said, "is a blithe and smiling little place," where "it is very agreeable to sit under the awning of the terrace of the Hotel Continental, an electric fan just above your head, and with an innocent drink before you 'taking in' the affairs of the Colony and the *fait divers* of the neighborhood." Near the same time André Malraux wrote of enjoying "drink time on the terrace of the Continental as the brief twilight descended on the carob trees and on the Victorias going up and down the rue Catinat to the jingle of bells." Those colonial idylls had come to an end, of course, with World War II and the subsequent decade-long struggle of the Vietnamese against French colonial rule. Graham Greene saw the next episode in Saigon's history beginning in the '50s. In *The Quiet American* he set subversive doings at the Continental and violence in Place Garnier portending the end of the French era, and, with the follies of a misguided American, he foreshadowed the ill-fated American entanglement to come.

During the American War, we journalists used to gather at the Continental Shelf to drink and share stories and observe wartime Saigon along the former rue Catinat, which, after the French, had become post-colonial Tu Do Street. The hotel was no longer Maugham's and Malraux's Continental, or even Greene's, but it was still at the center of Saigon's modern history. And I wanted to go back to it.

Disappointment greeted me as my cab pulled up in front. In some misbegotten renovation the Communists had eliminated the Continental Shelf, possibly to efface its associations with the colonial and American past—leaving the sidewalk barren of the café life that generations had taken pleasure in. And I found that a rather penumbral air had settled over the whole place. The furnishings of the public rooms were sparse, and the cavernous hallways languished in a musty dimness. The vast Continental Suite that I had reserved at the rate of about $100 a night, exuded the same sad air. But its rows of French doors opened onto balconies over the former Place Garnier, now Lam Son Square, offering a vista of the lively urban scene and the opera house that had become a municipal theater. Despite the decline of the Continental, I was glad I had come.

After catching some sleep during the scorching midday sun, I went out late in the afternoon to begin finding my story.

What used to be rue Catinat then Tu Do Street had been renamed, with revolutionary fervor, Dong Khoi, "Uprising Street." It was the place to start. Running from the gaudy French cathedral at one end down past the Continental to the lazy Saigon River at the other end just a mile or so away, as rue Catinat, it had been the fashionable heart of Saigon. There, besides the jingling Victorias Malraux had seen pass along, you could, said Maugham, "find Paris dresses from Marseilles and London hats from Lille" and see ladies "dressed in smart clothes" who "bring a cheerful air of sophistication to this far distant land." But after the French lost their Indochina War, it had in time descended from a chic and elegant Parisian boulevard into the boisterous main drag of another wartime Saigon, Tu Do Street. Sporting honky-tonks and brothels and the high-rise Caravelle Hotel, which had become the hub of wartime nightlife across the square from the Continental, Tu Do Street had beckoned soldiers with plenty of escapist pleasures. In those days, you could get almost anything on Tu Do Street, as its name suggested to the Americans. Drinks. Drugs. Girls. Anything to escape for a few hours from the futile war.

I decided to stroll down to the river and see what had become of Tu Do Street a generation later. I could tell right away that the honky-tonks and brothels were gone, and the Caravelle had been tamed. Despite its name as "Uprising Street," Dong Khoi had taken on a quiet local character, neither chic nor notably seedy but showing the neglect of lost cachet. Dusty stores purveyed curios and objects crafted in silver and lacquer. Crammed electronics and photo supply shops offered modern wares. A few nondescript eateries and refreshment parlors catered to locals. Some tourist offices were open for business. But nothing to evoke the fond words of Somerset Maugham. Here and there the concrete sidewalk was crumbling, and a scattering of beggars with missing limbs had positioned themselves to appeal for alms. It was actually a rather sad street. Not much rooted in its past and not sure of its future. If this was the new Saigon, I thought, it's not promising. But then, I had never cared much for the raucous wartime life of Tu Do Street either. And I knew the flowering of tourism would transform the street yet again.

By the time I reached the end of Dong Khoi at Ton Duc Thang Street, where the Saigon River wends past on its way to the South China Sea, I was ready for a rest. On the corner stood one of my occasional wartime haunts. The stately Majestic Hotel, boasting a roof garden restaurant that in the hotel's heyday after opening in 1925 had attracted cosmopolitan visitors for a view of the river and the lush lowlands on the other side and to while away warm languid nights with tall cooling drinks, candlelit dining, slow dancing, and convivial, sometimes world-weary, conversation. But all that had long gone when I had known the place as just a quiet, kind of sorry-looking reprieve from perpetual war.

I found the roof garden to be as quiet as I remembered it. That was a little unexpected just days before the festive Tet New Year. A few people were sipping drinks and idly watching boats and clumps of water hyacinths floating by on the river amid the lengthening shadows of the late afternoon sun. Dinner tables awaited the first arrivals. I had a drink while the sunlight was fading beyond the river over the delta. And I wondered how I was going to begin my piece on the new Saigon. What I had seen so far hadn't stirred inspiration. There was more of the old than the new. But it didn't seem to belong quite to the present either. Saigon lay in a kind of historical limbo. Still, I had a lot more to see. After leaving the Majestic, I meandered back toward the center of things. This time to the Rex Hotel at the spacious intersection of the broad, busy boulevards Le Loi and Nguyen Hue, a block west of sleepy Dong Khoi and the Continental.

I knew the Rex well. But not so much as a hotel. I knew it from its days as the American Culture Center, where daily press briefings were held during the war—the "Five O'Clock Follies," as journalists labeled them for their unwaveringly optimistic reports of military progress despite unrelenting Viet Cong attacks and mounting American losses. Built in the 1920s to house a French car dealership, it had been enlarged and renovated to become a hotel just as the American incursion in Vietnam was beginning—even providing space for the first contingent of American soldiers in 1961—and it had fully resumed that role only well after hostilities ended. Now that role was a lively one, so I had learned. The Rex still had a roof garden from the old days, too, which was bound to be more festive than that of the somnolent Majestic.

You could see the imposing façade, radiant in lights, shining from blocks away. And when I reached the roof garden I found none of the Majestic's quietude. The place was festooned with Chinese lanterns, and paper mâché dragons laced the air and looped along the railings, all preparing for the New Year. Rattan chairs and tables were arrayed around a central bar among potted palms and tropical plants, accommodating customers who merrily reveled in the holiday mood. I found an empty seat at the bar and sat down.

Glancing about, I saw a few Western faces, but mainly they were Asian. I figured some of them might be Saigon residents celebrating the New Year. Then my eyes fell on a threesome sitting at a table nor far from me. Two striking young women talking to a man with his back to me. The women appeared to be Vietnamese. And they were flashy. Heavy makeup. Stylized hair. Short skirts. Tight fitting tops. They had the brassy hard look of hookers.

"*Plus ça change, plus c'est la même chose*," I mumbled. The new Saigon is indeed still the old Saigon. The moralistic Communists haven't put an end to long-lasting ways. Or, I asked myself, is this part of the new Vietnamese commercialism? Hookers trawling the hotel trade, complete with their pimp to make deals and protect the merchandise. I had expected the survival of some prostitution on dark street corners, but brazenly in the roof garden of the Rex Hotel? The pimp must be a real hustler, I thought. One of those ruthless traffickers in flesh who've plied the ancient trade in seaports and big cities around the world for ages, preying on helpless girls fleeing from hopeless lives in forlorn places and servicing, or exploiting, lonely soldiers and randy travelers. I tried to get a glimpse of his face, but I could see only his full dark hair from behind as he sat in nonchalant dominion before them, while they smiled and sent come-hither looks at potential clients throughout the celebratory garden.

I eyed them periodically as I nursed a local beer. They shot ever more alluring invitations to passing men. But they had no takers. They cast beckoning glances at me too. But I ignored them. Finally, the pimp leaned toward them and said something I could not hear. They got up, surveyed the bustling scene, and sauntered to the corner of the rectangular bar on the far side from me, where they perched to better see and be seen. I imagined he must have sent them to work the room more conspicuously. Obviously, they had nothing to fear from public authorities. That in itself, it occurred to me, was something of a story. The pimp sat unmoving for a minute. Then he shifted in his chair and turned to case the crowd. His eyes caught mine. He got up, came to the bar, and took the seat beside me. So he's going to work on me directly, I told myself. Do I seem easy prey?

He ordered a drink and then casually said to me in accented English, evidently identifying me as an American: "Nice night for Tet." The voice had a surprising softness for a hardened trafficker in human flesh.

I turned my head slightly toward him and saw an unexpectedly pleasant, innocent-looking Southeast Asian face. I replied warily, "Yes, it is." I returned to my beer to discourage more conversation and his inevitable pitch.

"Many kinds of people here," he went on, undiscouraged by my indifference.

I waited, then responded offhandedly, "Yes, I suppose so."

"You American?"

Here it comes, I thought, anticipating that he was circling around to his play. He probably views Americans as good targets, when he can find them. Not wanting to encourage him, I answered with only a nod.

"On business?"

He was persistent but not pushy. I muttered, "More or less," being barely civil.

"What business, if I may ask?"

I considered rebuffing him by saying I just wanted to be alone, but I did have a rising curiosity about *his* business. I told him I was a journalist.

"You write about Saigon?"

Was he genuinely curious? Or was it a soft sell in an old business? Then an idea hit me. I could take this pimp as the peg for my story. The new Vietnam is just an updated version of the old. *Plus ça change.* . . . A good angle. How about "Saigon Pimp Wields Modern Marketing in Oldest Profession"? I decided to engage him and act naïve.

"Yes, probably."

"What will you write?"

"Well, I was here years ago, during the war," I replied, "and now I'd like to write about Saigon as it is today."

"I see," he said kind of reflectively. He waited a few moments then added almost furtively, "You see those girls?" He tilted his head toward the two he had been sitting with. I followed his eyes thinking, here it comes. "They talked to me. Do you know what they said? They asked me to go with them. To their room." He reported this with a hushed voice and a guilelessness that was almost believable. Almost. I played along.

"Oh? Why did they do that?" I responded with feigned ignorance.

"They . . . said they would make me . . . happy . . . in special ways. I think they wanted money." Again he spoke rather furtively. I suspected he was being adroitly abashed. But his face had an openness that belied, or perhaps facilitated, his profession. A good act at least. Still, an odd gambit for a pimp. Where would he go from here? Did he think I would pick up on his understated pitch and go with the girls myself? I decided to smoke him out.

"You mean you don't know them?"

His face took on a quizzical expression. "Oh, no, no," he said firmly, dropping his eyes and shaking his head. "I do not know them." Whether this was true or false, my curiosity swelled.

"So, if you do not know them, why did you stay with them?"

"They sat down with me. They were nice. And I do not know people here."

This was a twist. He was subtly trying to lure unsuspecting guys by pretending to be an unknowing stranger himself.

"You do not live in Saigon?" I probed to get more of his scheme.

"No. No. I live in Laos."

Laos? This is intriguing, I thought. Either he's lying to keep the ruse going, or he's a foreign entrepreneur who's brought his girls to ply the oldest trade amidst Saigon's new commercialism. Or is he part of the Southeast Asia mafia? Even better. If I could get him to tell me the whole story, I'd have a neat international angle for my article.

"From Laos? That's interesting," I said genially and offered to buy a round of drinks as I eased my notepad our of my pocket. He accepted the invitation, and I pushed on with casual determination. "So, you come to Saigon often?"

"No. I don't like Saigon, Ho Chi Minh City."

I didn't quite believe him. Puzzled and skeptical, I prodded. "You don't like Saigon? Why?"

"Too big. Too many people. Too much confusion. Too modern." He said this last word with a tone suggesting both bafflement and contempt.

"So, why are you here?" I asked, my curiosity following his lead.

He took a sip of his beer and said matter-of-factly, "I came for a conference on agriculture. In Laos I work for the government agriculture department. Sometimes I have to go away for meetings. But I prefer to stay home."

He's taking this charade pretty far, I told myself, or, could he be what he seems? "Is Laos very different from Vietnam?" I inquired.

"Oh, yes," he said almost cheerfully. "Laos is not all confusing. Not full of people. Not all busy, as you say in America. Not too modern. Even Vientiane, the capital, is small and easy. But I still prefer the countryside where I live. Laos is gentle. Not like Vietnam or America."

Laos is gentle? An appealing image. Could a pimp have come up with that? Why would he? Unless he's preparing to tell me that the two girls are actually Laotian and therefore more "gentle" than Vietnamese girls and have more to offer a customer. I studied his face more carefully. He must have been in his thirties. I had to admit that his features were, well, gentle. They were small and soft. The eyes warm and clear. There was a slightly smiling quality to it all. Could this be the face of a pimp? And his voice went with the features. Gentle. Even his hands, although he had evidently done outdoor work with them, suggested a gentle touch. Maybe he was what he said he was.

"I went to America once," he volunteered pleasantly. "Chicago. To visit my uncle. He said I should come to America to see the country and practice my English. But I did not like it. Noise. Cars. Buildings. Everyone in a hurry. I came back as soon as I could. Now I go home tomorrow."

"You have a family at home?" I asked, almost resigning myself to the truth of his story.

"Yes. A wife and son and daughter," he answered with a distinct smile. He pulled a photograph from his wallet and held it out toward me.

"Very nice," I said as I examined the happy faces of a young woman and two children about six or seven years old, all dressed in bright silks and standing in a tropical garden. I handed it back to him.

I gave in. He could not have made all this up. And he had said no more about the girls at the bar. I switched back to Laos. "Isn't Laos getting modern now too?"

"Not too much yet. I hope it never will. I want Laos to stay as it is. Life is better that way. But some people try to make big change. For 'progress' they say. I know better." He glanced around as if suspicious of something, then he leaned close to me and whispered, "I try to stop it."

"What?" I responded quizzically in the hushed voice he evidently desired, as though we were exchanging state secrets. "What do you mean? You try to stop Laos from change, from becoming too modern? How?"

With his voice still low, he said, "I help farmers and villages keep many of their old ways and to use new ways only when they cannot do better. I tell them what will happen if we change too much. Like Chicago. Like Saigon. Like those girls." He checked his surroundings again, seemingly wary of spies, and then confided, under his breath, that he had tried, behind the scenes, to stop industrial developments, and—here his voice became almost inaudible—he had even sabotaged some construction projects.

I stared, dumbfounded. I had been wrong. Very wrong. This was no sly and jaded Asian pimp. He was a gentle Laotian who was also an anti-modern Luddite. I groped for more details, but he evaded most of my questions. He had finished divulging his secrets. Or maybe he had made it all up to impress me. I would never know. He downed the last of his beer and said he was going to bed now because he was leaving for home early in the morning to be with his family for the rest of the New Year celebrations. He bid me goodnight. Just like that. I watched him go, politely weaving between other patrons and disappearing through the roof garden door.

I sat still trying to fathom his incredible story when I heedlessly looked over at the two girls sitting on their perches across the bar. Our eyes met. They must have been keeping tabs on me during my conversation. One of them slid off her stool and oozed toward me. Now I wondered if that guy had been a pimp after all and had told me all of that about the girls and Laos and himself just to throw me off course and soften me up, and that he had now sent them a sign I was ready game. Not knowing what to think, I focused on the glass in front of me. When the girl reached me she breathed a seductive, "Hello."

Irresistibly, I shifted my eyes from the glass. They fell on a pair of long bare legs rising up into a tiny shiny skirt. From there, as my head turned, my eyes moved on up to a glittering halter top and straight shoulder-length black hair framing a face that, beneath its bright red lips, rouged cheeks, and heavily shadowed eyes, probably belonged to a girl no more than twenty. She donned an alluring smile and sat next to me. Moments later her companion, possibly even a little younger, joined us and assumed her own winsome pose.

"You visit Saigon?" the first girl said in heavily accented English.

I nodded, not knowing how else to react. The second girl edged closer and said softly through puckered lips, "You want good time in Saigon tonight?"

"Extra good time," the other added cozily. "For New Year."

I looked directly at them and managed a small smile. "Thank you," I said cordially. "You are lovely ladies. But I can't." I shook my head to make the point and confirmed the refusal with, "I must go now."

"You sure?" the first one reacted, slowly licking her lips.

"I'm afraid so."

Then, seized by a nagging curiosity, I asked if they knew the man they had been sitting with earlier when I came in. They laughed slightly, shrugged, and said no, he was nobody. Their manner convinced me. But taking my question as a sign that I might still be won over, they renewed their overtures. When I resisted and requested my check, they gave up. A pout came over each face, banishing their seductive expressions, their pose of worldly sophistication, and their pretense of professional poise. They became adolescents made up to appear as adults, showing a child's disappointment that I would not play their game. They eyed each other briefly, and those faces of practiced allure and artificial maturity returned. With a touch of huffiness, they slithered away, casing the room and seeking other quarry as they returned to their seats at the bar. I tucked my blank notepad into my pocket and paid my bill. I glimpsed them working on a new guy as I made a circuitous route around the bar and left the roof garden.

While I walked back to the Continental in the warm February air, my mind tossed about the unexpected and perplexing incidents of the night. What was I to make of it all?

Back in my suite, I switched on a dim lamp, ordered something to eat, took a Vietnamese beer from the mini-bar, and settled as comfortably as I could into a polished but un-cushioned rosewood chair in the sitting room. I pulled my notepad from my pocket, thought for a minute, and started writing . . . what, I wasn't sure. It wouldn't be the in-depth article on the New Saigon that I had originally planned. That would have to wait. It would instead be something about this Saigon night. Yes, it would tell of my stroll from the fabled but rather forlorn Continental down sad Dong Khoi to the somnolent Majestic at sunset and back up to the festive roof garden at the Rex celebrating the Tet New Year. Those girls would be in it too. It might become a kind of parable of history and modernity in this resilient city of war and peace, past and present, memories and idiosyncrasies. One thing was sure. It would tell a story of the gentle man from Laos.

Hawaiian pineapples

Livin' the Dream

Jonathan and I had grown up together in a Midwestern town where as boys we could run free and play imaginative games in the fields. We would often invent tales of good guys and bad guys drawn from comic books or movies or television. Sometimes we were cowboys, sometimes aliens, sometimes cops and robbers, sometimes spies, and the like. We would sort of take turns playing the good guy and the bad guy. I liked playing the bad guy because then I could do anything. Jonathan happily let me do that because he was a good guy through and through and didn't know how to think like a bad guy. He always wanted to save the world from evil, or at least to do good.

One bond we wholly shared was a dislike of cold weather. We reveled in summer and lamented the signs of impending autumn with its encroaching chill in the air. And when the snow came, and the wind blew hard across the plains, we shuddered and took our games inside as best we could. We could have gone out and romped in the snow, but neither of us had a yen for that. It was too cold.

When we grew out of our boyish games, Jonathan took up student politics. He still wanted to do good and got elected student-body president in high school. I wasn't as gregarious as he was, or as idealistic. Our paths started to diverge. He went away to college with political ambitions, and I went off with more academic aims. Ironically, a cruel fate sent us both to college in cold weather places.

We kept in touch occasionally and saw each other at home on holidays. We would talk about what we were doing in school and our plans for the future and such things. He was majoring in political science and I was in history. On one of those holiday visits, in our second year of college, he told me he was thinking of becoming a socialist. It was the only truly humane system of society. The inequalities, social and economic, in America riled him. "How can we live contentedly in a society that cares so little for so many of its people?" he complained. And he planned to do something about it. Politically. He needled me for wanting to become a historian. "I love you, Joey," he'd say, "but you're one of those people who, as Marx said, wants to understand the world. 'The point, however, is to change it.' I'm with him." Jonathan was right about both of us.

When we met the next time I asked how his campaign for social justice was going. He said he was still committed to it but was changing his strategy. He had continued to engage in college student government, and he had volunteered on some professional political campaigns. But he had begun to feel differently about the political life than before. It turned out he had no stomach for what politicians have to do much of the time to gain power and keep it. For one thing, he complained, professional politicians have to raise money all the time, and they have to shade the truth, if not tell outright lies, to placate various groups with conflicting interests. And they have to deal with other politicians who have no genuine interest in anything but themselves. He still wanted to be the good guy and save the world, but he was thinking that maybe being a politician wasn't the best way for him to do it.

"Economics," he announced. "That's the way for me to go. Not just to understand how the economy works but to change the world economically and help everybody flourish. I'll create sound, socially beneficial economic policy for everyone and let the politicians do the dirty work."

Buoyed by these ideals, Jonathan prepared to go to graduate school in economics, while I stuck to history. When we got together before embarking on our separate professional courses—he was headed for the University of Chicago and I was going to Columbia—we laughed over how we couldn't seem to leave winter behind, but we vowed to meet in the sun somewhere sometime.

When we saw each other a year or so later, Jonathan had revised his vision again. "Socialism won't work," he declared with the certainty that had led him to embrace socialism in the first place. "Not in this country, or probably any other. It's a good idea socially, but not economically. Too much management and not enough economic productivity. It can't generate the resources to uplift everyone and instead lowers everyone to the same base level. We've got to make the economy work better on its own for everyone, without government trying to manage everything. Capitalism might not be the ideal economic system, but it's probably the best we're going to get. We just have to make sure that it works at its best and helps everybody. 'Supply-side economics' is the key."

I said I wasn't surprised that he had switched from socialism to supply-side capitalism at the University of Chicago. "That's the favorite theory there isn't it? You know, don't mess with the free market. Make stuff and people will buy it. And as the rich get richer some of their wealth will dribble down to those below. So all boats will float, although some more reliably than others. But that has never really happened, has it? Supply-side economics has created the very inequalities you used to rail against."

"Well," he said "that might be true of capitalism in the past, but it doesn't have to be in the future. I'll find a way so that everyone can win."

"You're such an idealist, Jonathan," I said. "Still going to change the world. Good luck with that."

After graduate school, I got a teaching position in New York, and Jonathan got a job in Washington, DC, in the office of the President's economic advisor, directed by a former professor of his. He would be in just the kind of position he had yearned for. When I heard of this, I sent him congratulations and wished him well, holding my historian's cynicism in check. We didn't see much of each other while he was in Washington, but when we did I always asked him how his crusade for economic justice was going, and he always replied with a smile that he was working on it.

When his government job was about to end with a change of administrations in Washington, we ran into each other on a visit home and I asked him what he planned to do now. Stay in government? Become a consultant? Or a professor? Go into business? He looked at me with a rather wan smile and said he wasn't sure. Not government work. That had become frustrating. Politics invaded everything, limiting how much he could affect policy. Not consulting or teaching either. Too passive. Business? He couldn't see it. He still wanted to change the world. But he admitted to being a little disillusioned. Maybe he couldn't change the world, after all. Still, he remained determined to do good. At least to make peoples' lives better. Somehow.

Over the next few years we didn't see much of each other because Jonathan had taken up doing projects of one kind or another in far-flung places. Eventually, I kind of lost track of him. Meanwhile, I got married and plodded along in my career doing what historians do—teaching, giving papers, publishing articles, and so on. One day I received an invitation to be a visiting professor for the spring semester at the University of Hawaii. I'd never been to the islands, and, disliking winter so much, I jumped at it.

My wife and I left New York on a wintry December day. It was a long flight, but we landed under blue skies in radiant late-afternoon sunshine. We walked off the plane in Honolulu into soft warm air, and I thought, yes, this will do. As the taxi drove us toward our rented lodgings near the university, we saw verdant mountains rising into pillowy clouds as a backdrop to the city strung along the coastline. We also saw, to our surprise, many signs of the Christmas holiday season. The former royal palace downtown was festooned with Christmas lights, and nearby a huge figure of Santa Claus and Mrs. Claus, together with reindeer and elves and strings of Christmas lights, filled the grounds of what the driver told us was City Hall. Houses here and there were also decorated with similar paraphernalia. It all seemed quite odd in the summary weather. But our driver explained that holidays are a big deal in Honolulu. Folks love to celebrate. And the Christmas season starts right after Halloween. "It's a holiday place," he said with a laugh.

Finally, we rode up a winding street on a steep hillside packed with houses close together to the residence arranged for us. We stepped out of the cab and cast our eyes around. The houses were closer together than one might desire, but anyone could see why people chose to live up there. The view of the city below and the ocean beyond ranged almost 180 degrees from the west, where the driver told us Pearl Harbor lay, and identified the Waianae Mountains beyond, to the east, where the emblematic Diamond Head crater stood out prominently at the end of Waikiki beach. It was quite a sight. I embraced my wife and said, "This will be fun."

Having a couple of weeks before classes would begin, I completed arrangements at the university, and then my wife and I explored the island. Relishing the salubrious winter weather, which occasionally brought clouds and some rain, but never cold, we did what tourists do. We didn't much like the look of Waikiki at a distance below our residence because it was just a mass of high-rise buildings—which did, however, add glitter to the nighttime panorama. We later found that Waikiki does indeed have its charms, but the beach there couldn't compare in size and quality to many others around the world or even several elsewhere on Oahu. Still, none anywhere exceeds it in renown, going back to the early twentieth-century romantic days before modern construction started blighting Waikiki. Our favorite diversion was to leave Honolulu and drive around to the windward side of the island. There developers have been held at bay for the most part by restrictive zoning, and by lots of rain. Except for a couple of towns, a few small villages, and a couple of relatively unobtrusive military installations, the windward side is pristine. The green volcanic mountains rise dramatically three thousand feet high or more, and much nearer the shore than in Honolulu, their precipitous walls striated from waterfalls that come with the rain, and lush tropical growth abounds everywhere. The windward drive gave us the Bali Hai experience. Too bad, I thought as we drove along the ocean under overhanging foliage, that I would soon have to spend my days teaching subjects I knew too well and, I admitted to myself, had grown pretty stale for me. I had also been warned that most of the students at the university would rather be surfing or otherwise enjoying the island life than attending classes and pursuing knowledge. I couldn't honestly say I blamed them. I had encountered this type of student before, of course, but not with the enticements of nearly constant sunshine, luscious warm air, and an azure, rolling, endless sea. Pondering these things, I found myself wondering how my old pal Jonathan would like it here. The weather for sure. What had become of him? Surely he'd surface one of these days.

My reprieve from academic chores was about to end when my wife suggested that we go to the large Saturday morning farmer's market she had heard about. It was held at the back end of Diamond Head and was said to brim with produce grown by farmers all over Hawaii, as well as freshly prepared foods ready to eat. It sounded like something we should do.

We drove over early to beat the crowds we'd been warned about. It was getting busy all the same, especially Japanese tourists arriving by the busload. The market had clearly been discovered by travel agents. Rows of stalls were arrayed amidst trees offering a cornucopia of fruits and vegetables and even flowers, along with vendors peddling hot cooked items. We wended around lines of Japanese people awaiting the likes of fresh abalone, fried green tomatoes, Portuguese sausages, and kalua pork, and strolled past stands selling pineapples, coconuts, bananas, oranges, mangoes, papayas, dragon fruit, kimchi, bok choy, sugarcane, ginger, orchids, Bird of Paradise, varieties of Hawaiian honey, and much more. We approached a crowd gathered at one vendor who apparently sold fresh pineapple juice and bite-sized chunks of the fruit—some given as samples—as well as pineapples of many sizes from piles under a canopy. Half a dozen young people raced about getting juice and fruit for customers. Figuring this must be a good place to get pineapple, we wove through the convivial hubbub. Standing in front of a large display of the fruit in several sizes, we asked a young seller to select one for us. She responded brightly and said they were all good. I prodded for more assistance, and she said she would get the boss. She ran back to an open-ended truck half full of pineapples and spoke to a guy sitting beside it under an umbrella. He had a full beard and was wearing a flowered Hawaiian shirt and a broad plantation hat. Evidently, he was enjoying himself and his crew liked him. She pointed us out and he came toward us. Before he reached us he called out my name. I stared as he neared. Now in spite of the beard I thought I recognized him.

"Jonathan?!" I exclaimed.

"The same!" he replied and embraced me. I introduced him to my wife, and he warmly invited us to "come on over to my office."

He led us through the crowd and boxes and piles of pineapples to the truck and set a couple of folding chairs next to his. As we sat down I remained a little stunned. We exchanged exclamations on how good it was to see each other after so long, and how time had changed us but not unrecognizably, and what a surprise it was to meet again—especially like this. He asked if we were tourists, and we told him we were, sort of, but that I was here as a visiting professor at the university.

"Still pursuing the academic life, eh? Trying to understand the world." He smiled easily.

"Well," I responded, "I wouldn't put it that way. But," I stammered, still taken aback at seeing him here, "what in god's name are you doing here? Why? How did . . . ?"

His smile broadened, and his answer went like this.

Dissatisfied with politics and government for their distasteful machinations and bureaucratic frustrations, and with economic theory and policy for their removal from everyday life, but still imbued with idealism, he had hit the road to find some way of putting his idealism to work. He had wanted more than ever to do something good for real people, not just frame policy at large. So he had helped a village in Uganda get loans for a clean water supply. He had showed some young men in central India how to set up, finance, and manage a couple of small businesses on their own. He had worked with communities in several developing countries on projects to stimulate economic activity. And so on. But he had also seen, or learned, that many of these projects had later fallen victim to greed and ineptitude or into the maw of endemic political exploitation and financial corruption. Eventually, he had grown discouraged trying to change the world that way too.

Adrift again, he had strayed to Hawaii. Here the natural beauty and the prevailing civility, and, of course, the warm weather, had gotten to him. And—he stressed this—he loved the pineapples, unlike any on the mainland. But he had discovered that the pineapple business in Hawaii was struggling. Most of the large companies were closing down or shifting their operations to Central America for the plentiful and cheap labor, even though there they couldn't grow pineapples nearly as tasty as those in Hawaii. He had thought that was sad.

Then an idea had come to him. Instead of trying to help other people make their way economically, he would go into business himself. What better than to produce the best Hawaiian pineapples money could buy? He had set out to learn all he could about making that happen. Soon, though, he had found out how difficult pineapple farming is. There are many varieties suited to different places, and each fruit has to be planted and harvested by hand, and, not only that, they take about two years to grow to maturity. Nevertheless, that didn't daunt him. He had persuaded a bank to back him, leased some land in the center of the island formerly used by a mainland pineapple producer, hired some workers, and started. After several experiments crossing one kind of pineapple with another, he had managed to produce what he wanted. A super sweet, juicy, and low acid type superior to any other. They were the best. Restaurants featured them. And he was proud of the accomplishment. Most of all, he loved producing them himself. It was real economics for real people, he said, not abstract, theoretical, speculative ideas. He had become a farmer raising a special fruit that employed lots of workers and that people flocked to buy.

"Just look at all these folks," he said gesturing toward the crowd around his stand. "What do you see? They're eating freshly cut pineapples and drinking the juice and buying the fruit to take home. They're loving it. What more could I ask? Never mind that there's not much money in it for me. I create the supply, and it creates the demand. You remember. Perfect economics. It's all good and everyone's happy. Besides," he said with a hearty chuckle, "it's always warm here." A grin spread across his face as he leaned back and surveyed the market, then stretched his arms out wide, seemingly embracing everything around, "At last, Joey," he said through the grin, "Livin' the dream. Livin' the dream."

The Hemingway House, Key West, Florida

Hemingway's Ghost

"*But this is how Paris was in the early days when we were very poor and very happy.*"

The book flapped shut, and Burton Sharp let it drop on his stomach as he lay in bed beside his sleeping wife, Sylvia. His head sank back into the pillow. He switched off the bedside lamp. His eyes blankly fixed on the lazy rotations of the ceiling fan in the dim moonlight, filtering in the night air through gauzy curtains at the window. What a soft sentiment in those words, he said to himself. Nostalgia? Regret? This from Ernest Hemingway, the tough-guy writer who loved to kill as much as he loved to live? Whose life as a big-game hunter and deep-sea fisherman, bullying boxer and bullfighting aficionado, two-fisted drinker and intrepid war correspondent was as famous as his books? To live such a life! Free.

Adventurous. Literary. How many young men have yearned for it? Or used to. Me, too, Burton admitted. Me, too.

Then it hit him. Maybe Hemingway didn't get what he wanted, after all. Why the nostalgia, even regrets, at the end, in that last line of the last book, *A Moveable Feast?* A memoir, no less. But not about the legendary life and the stellar literary career. Instead it's about the beginning, before all of that. Why did Hemingway look back over the years of adventure and fame and seem almost sorry, as if he had lost something? What was it? Paris? The '20s? Youth? But that's probably how most lives work out, Burton ruminated, sleepily following the hypnotic circles of the fan. A trail of incidents, people, places, events that we leave behind, a trail that leads us to where we are, but that we can't see clearly until we look back, for then some incidents that had hardly caught our eye at the time have become landmarks, and others that once jolted us have left barely a trace. Neurosis comes from this, of course, Burton reminded himself, when we secretly cling to some moments so tightly that we cannot move on. But it's not neurotic to remember. Or to regret.

Burton Sharp could feel himself swimming in a stream now, as he tended to do late at night, hoping it would carry him, like free association in psychoanalysis, to undiscovered places and unexpected truths. The next words came to him as an echo: *"The memory of a particular image is but regret for a particular moment, and houses, roads, avenues are as fugitive, alas, as the years."* The end of *Swann's Way.* Proust meets Hemingway. Burton smiled at the pairing. The wan, loquacious novelist of the French Belle Époque's lustrous social world, who wrote in bed all day breathing the thick unchanging air of his cork-lined room, here together with the hardy he-man writer who whittled literary language to the bone and wrote of cold heroics and emotional desolation and lonely death, and who boasted that he'd choose action over fiction any day. Yet, here they were partners in images of memory and regret, in a Paris of long ago.

Pleased with himself, Burton Sharp closed his drooping eyelids and allowed the stream to ebb away into the rhythmic lapping of shallow waves on the beach below the open window. He liked tropical nights. Key West was a good place to enjoy them. Easy to get to. No customs to go through. And a hospitably historical town. He had come here years earlier researching his first Hemingway book. But that seemed a lifetime away. Before he had met Sylvia.

Burton and Sylvia had been married for nearly twenty-five years now. Before they met, Burton had written some short stories, and published a couple of them that nobody read in obscure literary quarterlies. And he had finished a novel that no one would publish. That's when he had settled on becoming a professor of literature. He had resented the clichéd come-down, and chafed at the prosaic demands of academia. But he had submitted to those demands, teaching pedestrian students and grinding out scholarly articles and a couple of critical books on American literature. And he had married Sylvia, a younger colleague at their small New England college. Now he was writing a new Hemingway biography, to put in the pulse of life that others had left out. Or so Burton told everyone. Sylvia kidded him that he was just sublimating his desire to *be* Hemingway. But that's OK, she would say, because sublimation is safe adventure; it can feel as good as the real thing without the troubles. He admitted to himself that she was probably right.

Burton and Sylvia had arrived in Key West that afternoon for the spring semester break and a reprieve from the northern chill. Burton was also tracking down some fugitive details for the book. And he was trying to decide what to do about Paula.

Paula, a graduate student with irrepressible allure, who had fluttered on the periphery of his consciousness through a class he had taught on the Lost Generation, until one day she had flown right into the center. She had come to his office for advice on research topics about Hemingway. Heaving with adulation, she had asked "Professor Sharp" if she could work with him on her Master's thesis because "you know all the interesting things about literature" and "are sooo exciting to talk to." Then she came again. And again. And again. She had wanted more than advice. Burton could see that. Why else would she keep coming so often and keep asking these unnecessary questions, and dress like *that*, and heave, and adulate, and linger? Yet, Burton was yielding. He knew that, too.

Burton loved Sylvia, or he had loved her long enough that he didn't think about it anymore. But deep in middle age and feeling that he was losing a little more of himself each day, he could not resist the attraction of . . . what? Was it Paula's seductiveness that made his blood rush and his head fizz and his knees go rubbery? Or was it Paula's adulation of him? Burton was honest enough to make the distinction. But he could not make it now.

He was glad to get away. He wanted to sort out his feelings and weigh what kind of life was left to him, and to Sylvia. Sylvia, admirable Sylvia. She never pretended to be what she wasn't, or to know what she didn't know. But she always seemed to know the important things. Sylvia had discrimination, and modesty, and integrity, and what Burton publicly praised as her Buddhist virtue of detachment. Rare qualities in academia, he would say. Her colleagues agreed. Admirable Sylvia. Paula was different. Young and spirited, she lacked discrimination. She winked at modesty. She blinked at integrity. She could never be detached. She heaved and adulated. And this got her into Burton's mind. He knew better, but he couldn't get her out. He wanted her. But he wanted at least to absolve himself first. Somehow, he hoped, Key West would help.

Voices of late-night passersby talking and laughing in the street pulled Burton back from the edge of sleep. He heard the roar of a motorcycle gunning its engine nearby. Probably heading for Sloppy Joe's, he guessed. He pictured that cavernous bar on Duval Street, famous for the drinking bouts and boxing matches Hemingway had held there to prove his prowess against the kind of ruffians who had given Key West its original character as a scar-faced seaman's hangout, and whose tradition lives on in burly bikers wearing leather skull-and-crossbones jackets who still gather in packs there to drink. Burton took himself back through time to the story of how Sloppy

Joe's original owner, Joe Russell, Hemingway's boozing and fishing pal, had moved his establishment one night to Duval Street from its cramped location up Greene Street not long after Hemingway had met the young journalist Martha Gellhorn at the bar there on a summer afternoon in 1936, and he had made her his third wife four years later and left for Cuba, and how that was twelve years after he had first arrived in Key West flushed with youthful renown as the author of tough short stories and *The Sun Also Rises* and newly married to his second wife, Pauline, who had taken him from his first wife, Hadley. One new wife and new life after another. A trail through wives and places and exploits and books and honors. And then at the end . . . regrets?

Enough! Burton pushed the meandering skein from his mind, rolled over, and burrowed his head under a pillow. He willed himself to sleep. But his sleep was not easy. It swarmed with restive dreams.

Burton saw himself in Paris long ago, before he had ever been there. In the working-class neighborhood up behind the Pantheon he was entering the diminutive Place de la Contrescarpe, bordered by dusty shops, weather-beaten apartment houses, and a couple of nondescript cafés, where a quaint fountain in the center splashed under a ring of shady trees. He recognized the spot. It was only steps from the bathroomless third-floor flat on the rue du Cardinal Lemoine where Hemingway and Hadley and their infant son nicknamed Bumby had lived at the beginning, when they were *very poor and very happy*. Here, Hemingway had said, he would walk home through the leaves that blew off the trees in the wind, and the rain would pelt the apartment windows when the bad weather came in autumn.

Next Burton saw *him*. Sitting at an outdoor café in the square. Young, husky, dark-haired, clean-shaven except for a black mustache, a coffee cup and a glass of wine at his elbow, bent over a notebook, rapidly scrawling. Hemingway, and a story *"writing itself,"* as he said stories sometimes did. That is the life, the dreaming

Burton said aloud to no one. Writing literature in Parisian cafés. Talented and free, creating a myth, and living it. Burton wanted to speak to him, to ask about his life, about Paris, about writing, about anything. Burton walked across the square under the trees and around the fountain. But when he reached the outer tables of the café, Hemingway had disappeared. No cup, no glass, no notebook. The dreamer could only stand there watching leaves scatter through the empty chairs.

The scene dissolved, and Burton found himself in another, larger Paris square. The bustling Place Saint-Michel on the Seine. Rain was falling lightly. There, through the windows of another café he saw Hemingway again, hunched over his notebook at a table, with a coffee cup and a half-filled glass at the ready. Writing about Michigan, the dreamer suspected, because Hemingway had said he did that one rainy autumn day while drinking a Rum St. James in *"a good café on the Place Saint-Michel"* when Michigan was far away. The dreamer opened the café door and went inside. He turned toward the table at the window. It was vacant. No cup. No glass. No notebook. Nobody.

The dream went on, hazy and vivid, tantalizing and real. To the Closerie des Lilas at the other end of the boulevard Saint-Michel, where it intersects with the boulevard du Montparnasse, and where Hemingway often went to write, he said, like *"a blind pig"* or with *"the air of a man alone in the jungle,"* after he and Hadley and Bumby had moved to the adjacent rue Notre-Dame-des-Champs in 1923, where they continued to be *"very poor and very happy."* And there he was. Writing fervently at a table outside on a sunny day under the sheltering trees. And then he wasn't.

Again and again the dreamer found Hemingway at the cafés where he wrote and ate and drank and socialized, mainly along the boulevard du Montparnasse—the Dome, the Select, the Negre de Toulouse, and the unnamed—and then found him close by at 27 rue de Fleurus, where Hemingway visited Gertrude Stein in her longtime home while he was shaping the literary style that became his own and that Gertrude Stein claimed credit for teaching him, and to whom, like most other writers, he was not as gracious in his memoir as he might have been. Hemingway was everywhere. Then he wasn't.

The dream gathered speed as Burton tracked Hemingway from Paris to Spain for the running of the bulls in Pamplona and for the Spanish Civil War, then to the Serengeti Plain in Africa for safaris, and on to the commodious residence outside Havana where Hemingway lived for twenty years after Key West, and back to wartime Europe for real-life heroics, then to Sun Valley and the house in neighboring Ketchum that he shared with his fourth wife, Mary, where in the fall of 1960 he put the final touches on *A Moveable Feast*, and early one morning the next July put a shotgun to his head and pulled the trigger three weeks before his sixty-second birthday.

The gunshot woke Burton with a start. He sat up and pushed a trembling hand through his thinning hair. Where did all that come from? It was really no mystery. He had been trailing Hemingway for years. It was his profession. And his hobby. Sylvia said it bordered on obsession. And being here in Key West and reading the memoir for maybe the fifth time, and puzzling over its elegiac tone, how could he not dream some such dream?

Burton slumped back on the pillow. The questions intruded again. Not that Hemingway's suicide troubled him. That was an honest act, Burton had always thought, because Hemingway was in decline and ill. But what about Paris? What about the nostalgia in the last book finished before the suicide? Was the tone just a *topos*, a literary mood struck for effect? That wouldn't be like Hemingway, Burton insisted. Hemingway despised mere effects. *"Write one true sentence."* That was Hemingway's creed. He'd repeated it in that last book. But what about the hints of sentimentality? Could true sentences be sentimental? *True sentimentality?* Not possible. Sentimentality is a false emotion. So, what was Hemingway's *true* emotion in those last lines of regret that sounded almost sentimental? Burton asked himself. And what about the bitterness in that book before the regrets?

Bitterness over *"the rich,"* as Hemingway scornfully labeled them. Once *"you have the rich,"* he had snarled, *"nothing is ever as it was again."* He had meant Pauline, the second wife, the wife of the Key West years, and her wealthy crowd, who came into his life with success. Bitterness and regret? And nostalgia? Had Hemingway let his life slip away from him? What had he lost? What had he wanted?

Stop! Burton scolded himself once more. This is just a preoccupation of the night. Let it go. Besides, perhaps tomorrow there'll be clues at Hemingway's house. Burton rolled onto his side. One hand fell against Sylvia's, resting on her pillow. She didn't flinch. Sleeps like she's hibernating, he said mentally. Nothing disturbs her. Lucky Sylvia. Good Sylvia. He drew his hand away and turned over. Closing his eyes tight, he concentrated on the soft tropical sounds of the sifting palms and the lapping surf outside, and eventually he floated off on imagined waves of an infinite sea to beckoning images of Paula.

The next morning Burton groggily bemoaned the restless night as he and Sylvia had breakfast on the back porch of their bed-and-breakfast overlooking the ocean on the Atlantic side of the island away from the hubbub at the western end of town. It was known as the Dewey House, named for the philosopher John Dewey, who had vacationed in it during his later years. Burton and Sylvia liked the intellectual pedigree. And Burton had mentally invented a scene of Dewey and Hemingway meeting at Sloppy Joe's in the 1930s—Hemingway, the young buck flexing his muscles and his fresh reputation as the rough, plain-spoken, all-American writer, and Dewey, the grand old man of American philosophy, admired worldwide for his down-home pragmatism and high-minded democratic principles—both toasting to plain honesty and earthiness, the American style, in philosophy, in literature, in life. Now, Burton remarked, the Dewey House is just a modest B-and-B. And Hemingway's house is a major tourist attraction, a shrine. Fiction had in a sense eclipsed philosophy.

Burton and Sylvia bantered through breakfast, enjoying the

ocean glistening in the morning sunlight under a pale blue cloudless sky and sailboats bobbing against the azure backdrop as if in an Impressionist painting. Afterwards they set out for the shrine.

The walk from South Street along Whitehead Street took them past nondescript bungalows and a few pretty, two-story "conch" houses, some a hundred years old, enduring emblems of historic Key West charm, quaintly mingling Victorian fussiness and French-New Orleans grace, their wrap-around porches and balconies lined by filigreed railings evoking languorous evenings with tall cool drinks and breezy relief from tropical heat. When they reached the Hemingway House at the corner of Whitehead and Olivia—across from the towering lighthouse oddly out of place here, practically in the middle of town—tourists were lined up at the entrance in the six-foot high brick wall encircling the property. Burton grumbled while they waited, but he paid the fee and they went through.

A jungle of trees and plants almost hid the grandiose conch house, twice the size of any other in town and largely built of stone, not wood. It could have presided over a lavish plantation in the South Seas. Its yellow walls and green porch and balcony running around the two floors blended into the jungle and the verdant, penumbral grounds. Walking down a winding footpath, Burton pointed out the smaller mansard-roofed cottage behind the main house where Hemingway would go to write in the upstairs studio. And there were cats. Inconspicuous at first, they were soon everywhere. Dozens of them, lazing on the porch, munching from bowls of food, crawling through the bushes, curled up under trees.

"Six-toed, many of them," Burton explained. "Scruffy mongrels descended from Hemingway's own. Cats evidently could do no wrong for Hemingway. They were probably the only animals he wouldn't kill. He shot dogs to protect 'em. Key West is a haven for cats now. They're everyplace."

"Why the attachment?" Sylvia asked.

"Could be because they're always a bit feral, untrainable. Hemingway liked that in animals."

Burton and Sylvia loitered among the cats in the yard and sat in a couple of garden chairs studying the handsome house and watching tourists milling about. They could overhear tour guides telling how Hemingway and Pauline had bought the house in 1931 with a gift of eight thousand dollars from her rich, generous uncle, and how Hemingway had written great literature in it, and how he had left permanently in 1940 for Cuba with Martha Gellhorn, and how the house had been sold in the 1950s with the furnishings still in it after Pauline died. Burton had seen and heard it all before. On an earlier quest years ago for Hemingwayana. But this time was different. He didn't like it.

"It's wrong," he muttered to Sylvia. "A theme park. A circus. Tourists traipsing all over, gawking and craving cheap anecdotes to tell back home. False. Phony. Un-Hemingway."

"Don't be so supercilious, Bertie," Sylvia chided him. "You're a tourist, too, you know."

"Oh, that hurts. Isn't this research?"

"Well, if you want it to be, you'll have to do more than complain. Let's go inside."

"With all of *them*?"

"You can do it. Hemingway would expect courage." She smiled.

Taking her muttering husband's hand, Sylvia led Burton into the throng pouring through the house. Inside, tour guides were purveying their pat histories in every room. Burton tugged Sylvia aside through a brief opening in the mass, and urged her up a stairway. At the top, skirting another clutch of visitors, they ducked into a temporarily unpeopled room. It was spacious and spare, with a large, ornate iron bed cordoned off against one wall. On the bed, a plump orange tabby cat sprawled, blissfully asleep, oblivious to any intrusion.

"Hemingway's bedroom," Burton tersely observed.

"He might not like the circus atmosphere," Sylvia said, "but he would like the integrity of the cat, wouldn't he? Or is it a prop?"

"The 'integrity of the cat'?" Burton replied approvingly. "Nice.

Yes, it's the 'truest' thing here." He reached over the cordon and grazed the cat's fur with his finger tips. The creature languidly stretched out its legs, splayed its paws, and contentedly slept on. "No prop," he assured her.

Voices swelled near the doorway, and the room began filling with murmuring visitors in loud clothes. "This was Ernest and Pauline's bedroom," the guide announced to his ogling flock.

Burton and Sylvia withdrew through a door at the opposite end of the room and hastened down a corridor to an outside exit that opened onto the front balcony. From there, through the lush foliage, they could see a river of people gushing through the front gate from tour buses on the street.

"Yuck!" Burton grouched. "But can you imagine what it must have been like here in the '30s? The tropical grandeur of it. The serenity. No tourists."

"No air-conditioning," Sylvia quipped.

"But that's the point," he said. "It would have been so natural, authentic, quiet, steamy, languorous." Then he heard an inner voice say, *What would Paula be like on a steamy, languorous night?* A thrilling sensation coursed through him. Impulsively, he turned away from Sylvia, ignoring her comic retort about air-conditioning. Recovering himself and wheeling around, he said with mock ominousness, "If we don't go now we might never get out. We'll get caught in the crush and left as bony remains, like the great fish in *The Old Man and the Sea* after the sharks got him."

Sylvia groaned at the ungainly allusion. "Bertie, your literary humor can be about as deadly as a shark. Just not as cutting."

"Thanks. How deft. I'll remember that when I need it."

They elbowed their way back to the stairs and down through an ascending tide of bodies. Outside again, they wedged through the incoming visitors and squeezed out through the gate. Taking a deep breath, they charted a course for a quiet place by the shore where they could sit and have a snack and take in the beneficent serenity of the ocean. Strolling up Duval Street, they passed an unbroken row of cafés, boutiques, T-shirt stores, souvenir shops, and the other usual fare of resort towns. But one thing wasn't usual. That was Hemingway. His face was everywhere. Not the younger man of his Key West days, but the familiar Papa Hemingway, aging, handsomely bearded, his white hair combed onto his forehead. It was a logo. In advertising. On building signs. T-shirts. Jackets. Curios. Glassware. Dinner plates.

"Hemingway is as big here as Shakespeare is in Stratford-upon-Avon," Sylvia exclaimed.

"Probably bigger," Burton responded. "He's got American consumerism going for him. And it's gotten a lot worse since I was here before."

Approaching Sloppy Joe's, they saw a string of shiny motorcycles lining the curb outside. A cacophony of voices backed by the pulsing beat of an old jukebox reverberated from inside through the open window walls out into the street. In the capacious, rustic interior, they could see scarred wooden tables and banged up chairs jammed with midday revelers. Leather jackets and flowered shirts, macho guys and matching molls, boisterous college kids and novelty-seeking tourists, all drinking and inhaling the musty atmosphere, watched over by a gigantic smiling face of Papa Hemingway extending across a wall behind the bandstand.

"Hemingway votaries in the temple," Sylvia jibed. "Do you suppose they all read him?"

"Do they read at all?"

"You're such a snob."

Jabbing each other genially, Burton and Sylvia left the votaries at Sloppy Joe's and went up Green Street where they paused beneath a sign at Captain Tony's depicting a rugged seaman boasting that this was "The Original Sloppy Joe's." From the sidewalk, they peered into a smaller, darker, nearly deserted bar, every surface seemingly cluttered with tacked-on mementos of patrons past, and proudly exuding the grimy patina of reverential age.

"They're probably preserving Hemingway's and Martha Gellhorn's fingerprints on the bar where they met," Burton said sarcastically.

"Such a respect for history," Sylvia joked.

They moved on to Front Street accompanied by the thunder of more motorcycles gunning their way to Sloppy Joe's, or just calling attention to themselves, and by tourists disgorging from the waterside hotels. As they reached the end of the street near the shoreline restaurants, Sylvia took hold of Burton's arm and slowed to a stop. "Bertie," she said reflectively, "have you noticed anything unusual about a lot of the men here?"

"What do you mean?"

"Something odd about their appearance." She said this with a wry smile.

Burton studied the pedestrians and the motorcyclists coming and going. He began to see a pattern.

"Hey, you're right," he said. "Older guys. Cropped white hair. Trimmed gray beards. Hemingway look-alikes!"

"One or two you wouldn't notice," Sylvia remarked. "But ten, twenty, maybe more. What a spectacle. What do you think it means?"

"Oh, I don't know. They do actually hold a Hemingway look-alike contest here every year. They advertise it in tourist brochures. But that's not now."

"So is it about pretending to be someone you're not? To have a more interesting life than you have?"

"I suppose," Burton replied rather distractedly. "You know, it's really very ironic when you think about it. Hemingway being honored by mass imitations of his appearance."

Sylvia cocked her head slightly and threw Burton a quizzical glance.

"What's that expression for?" he asked.

She chuckled softly, affectionately brushed his whiskered cheek with her hand, and linked her arm in his. "Time for that drink," she said. Minutes later they were seated at a café on the water ordering drinks and a light lunch.

"The Hemingway look-alikes," Sylvia picked up the subject again, "do you think they're doing the same thing as Elvis imitators?"

Burton hesitated. "In part, perhaps, but not entirely," he began. "The Elvis guys are at least acting out fantasies that fit Elvis. He was a creature of the entertainment culture that depends on the mass media and marketing and publicity and the fawning identification with 'celebrities.' Can you imagine, say, Moses look-alikes trekking the hills of Judea, or even little Napoleon look-alikes glowering from horseback around Europe? You need our crass modernity for that. But Elvis imitators are just like him. Entertainers, antic pretenders, show biz fabrications. The Hemingway imitators belong to that culture, too. But Hemingway didn't. Hemingway was no Elvis. He'd hate it."

"Are you sure?" Sylvia prodded. "Hemingway liked fame, didn't he? And he got a lot of 'celebrity' from magazines and from movies of his books, and he fraternized with movie stars."

"OK. His bestselling novels and the movies made from them, and some of his stories and the magazine spreads about him, along with receiving a Pulitzer and the Nobel Prize all certainly brought him fame. But it wasn't mere 'celebrity.' I mean, Hemingway wasn't just a creature of publicity. He had genuine 'fame' for doing something significant. And he would have despised a world that confuses celebrity with achievement, fantasy with reality, and that doesn't care about the difference, and that lives for the theme park version of reality, pretending all the time."

"He wouldn't have just laughed it off?"

"Nah. Hemingway didn't laugh that way. Not the frivolous laughter that accepts anything as long as it's amusing or entertaining. Elvis look-alikes, bad TV, that kind of stuff. Grinning with a trophy of the hunt, yes. Guffawing with buddies over drinks, yes. But not casually laughing things off, or spewing the phony social mirth of cocktail parties that people use nowadays to take the place of words. Anyway, there's not much wit or humor in Hemingway's books. A bit of satire, but it's usually biting, deriding people he knew, or writers he wanted to send up—especially in *The Torrents of Spring*, but who reads it?"

"You figure Ernest was too earnest for comedy?" Sylvia teased.

"Ugh! And you complain about my humor! But you're right. His version of the importance of being earnest wasn't Oscar Wilde's. Hemingway would never celebrate being trivial. He saw life as struggle, a contest of wills. The hunter and the hunted. The drama of war and death. Noble. Tragic. His idea of a good time was to carouse or fight or kill. He'd never be a mere tourist. Never just sight-see or sit on a beach. And never just pretend. 'Write one true sentence.' That's what he believed. And that's the irony of this town. It's all about tourism and frivolity and pretense. And Hemingway's in the middle of it! If he were to see it today, he'd be repelled and run away again."

Sylvia held her eyes on Burton for a time without speaking. "Bertie," she began tentatively, "I don't know Hemingway the way you do, but I suspect you're idealizing him. He was, I'd bet, closer to his imitators than you say. Didn't he brag about everything he did, and about things he didn't do? And wasn't he always brazenly acting out his myth of himself as a heroic, honest guy, trying to prove something to himself and others? Didn't he pretend, after all?"

Taken aback at Sylvia's uncharacteristic critical intensity, Burton sat in silence. Maybe Sylvia was right again, as her judgment usually was. Hemingway was proud, and a braggart, and he could be vain. But was he false, or pretending, or self-deceived—as when he persistently plied the Gulf of Mexico from Cuba during World War II hunting Nazi submarines to no avail? Burton began feeling discomfited. He didn't know why. And he didn't want to argue.

"Well," he said distractedly, skirting the subject, "maybe so. Maybe so."

"That's a pretty tepid response," Sylvia said. "I don't think you believe it. You know, Bertie," she went on reflectively after a moment, "you seem a bit preoccupied and on edge lately. Anything wrong?"

"No," he feigned. "Just tired. Food will help."

They lunched and idled through the balmy afternoon gazing at cruise ships coming in, at sailboats skiffing away, and at parasailors under brightly colored parachutes tethered to speed boats towing them back and forth out beyond the harbor, where, as Burton said to himself in a kind of Hemingwayese, they were buoyantly riding high across the far wide sky. Then Burton and Sylvia browsed curiosity shops—a huge seashell emporium offering decorative crustaceans of every shape, a couple of cat-themed boutiques selling objects celebrating Key West's patron pet, and the Key Lime Pie Company purveying every confectional use of key limes known to humankind. The rest of the afternoon passed pleasantly like that. When the late-day shadows began to lengthen, they wandered back to the shore and the town's seaside gathering place, Mallory Square. "We have to see the sunset from here," Burton said. "Otherwise we'll have missed the full experience of Key West."

They were not alone. Hundreds of people were sauntering into the square. And jugglers, mimes, musicians, fire-eaters, and other performers were preparing their acts to entertain the crowds and pick up a few bucks. Burton and Sylvia found a spot near the water. By the time the sun had lowered to the horizon, the entire square was filled, and music, laughter, and bursts of clapping were resounding in the air. Then, as if on cue, the sun, poised against the crimson sky, inched downward, growing larger and in color a duskier orange as it descended beyond the glassy waters, silhouetting sailboats against its fire. Approving oohs and ahhs rippled through the crowd. When the sun's quivering crest slipped out of sight, a radiant array of colors washed up into the sky. And the audience erupted in sustained applause. Burton and Sylvia looked at each other and shared a muffled laugh. The show was over. The sunset was an entertainment, along with the jugglers and mimes and musicians and fire-eaters.

"Well done, sun!" Burton cracked, and they ambled off through town past the crammed cafés and rowdy bars, the T-shirt boutiques and curio shops, to the Atlantic side for dinner—and for another slice of key lime pie, Sylvia bent on finding the Platonic version of this indigenous dessert. Later, sated and tired, they settled back into their philosopher's bedroom at the end of their Key West day.

Sylvia fell asleep almost as soon as she wrapped herself in the sheets. Burton lifted a book from the stack on his nightstand. *To Have and Have Not.* Another of Hemingway's titles borrowed from venerable literary phrases that Burton had sometimes complained about. Not exactly "true sentences" of his own, were they? Was that pretense? This was not a very good novel, either. But it was written here in Key West, and set in and around the island. You have to read it if you go, Burton had instructed friends. For the flavor, if nothing else. He started reading it for the third or fourth time, but he couldn't get into it. He dozed and tried again. No use. Something was pulling at him. The town? Last night's dream? The agitation he had felt at the Hemingway House? Some other restless feeling? Whatever it was, he decided he had to go back to the house. Without the tourists. A crazy idea. But it grabbed him.

He waited a while, indifferently reading and fitfully dozing. Once assured that Sylvia was sleeping soundly, he eased out of bed, slipped on slacks and a shirt and sandals, and slinked out the door. It was well after midnight. Padding along the streets, he passed loving couples in tight embrace and party-goers straggling home in this ever-reveling town. When he got to his destination, he dallied along the walled yard, letting a car come and go. At last, seeing he was alone, he found a foothold in the craggy bricks of the wall and hefted himself up and over the top.

He dropped to the ground on the other side, crumpling to his knees among the foliage. It was easier than he'd expected. Only a scuff or two to show for it. Now, not a sound, except for his restrained breathing. Glad Hemingway liked cats, not dogs, he thought, standing up to case the scene. The nearly full moon in the clear sky cast a bright night light down through the trees, falling in patches on the grass like camouflage. The moonlight was so bright it reminded Burton of movies that have night scenes filmed in daytime with the camera lens tightened to make the foreground dark, while daylight still shines in the background. It's artificial night once you see it. This moonlight glared almost like that. But, Burton said to himself, this was an honest night.

He surveyed the house. Most of it lay in deep shadows. But the portions of the walls that caught the moonlight gleamed in an eerie yellow-green. Great place for a Halloween party, it occurred to him. And much better than earlier in the day. No circus. Quiet. Authentic. True.

He stepped cautiously through the shadows across the lawn. Remembering the chairs where he and Sylvia had sat that morning, he groped toward them where he could sit and have a good view of the house. He lowered himself into a chair. A screeching yowl tore the silence like a banshee in attack. Leaping up, he saw a small black form bound into the gloom. A cat. He'd sat on a cat. Shaken, he warily sat down again. When he regained his composure, he detected other cats lying on the chairs, beneath the chairs, on the grass, beside tree trunks, against the house. It was their place now. Hemingway would like that, Burton speculated. Let the cats have it. They don't pretend. They're just themselves.

Facing the house, Burton envisioned Hemingway here. He had done some good writing in this house, or in that cottage out back. Not as much as the tour guides claim, but enough. *A Farewell to Arms* had come just before he settled here. And *For Whom the Bell Tolls* had come after he'd left and switched his affections to Cuba and to Martha Gellhorn. But there was the first bullfight book. The first Africa book. Some of the best short stories. True, the one novel he wrote start to finish while living in the house, *To Have . . .* , wasn't very successful. He must have been too close to Key West to write about it well. He usually wrote about things better when they were past and distant. Hemingway had acknowledged that. *"Transplanting yourself,"* he described it when he told of writing about Michigan while sitting in that *"good café in the Place Saint-Michel."* He had to go to Paris to write about Michigan. And to Key West and Cuba and Idaho to write about Europe and Africa. He did write *The Sun Also Rises* close to its subject in Paris and Spain. But, Burton remembered, Hemingway had then revised it in Austria that winter of 1926 when he had fallen in love with Pauline, and *"the rich"* had come into his life. And everything after that had been different.

Hemingway's memories of Pauline and her ilk weren't happy. So he couldn't have been very contented here. The Key West novel wasn't happy. But, Burton asked himself, what did Hemingway write that was happy? "The Short Happy Life of Francis Macomber" was about as far as Hemingway could go. He wrote it here after the first trip to Africa. Francis Macomber is happy for about one minute while shooting a water buffalo on safari, just before a bullet from his wife's rifle kills him.

Burton liked this tidy insight. Of course, he conceded, "happy" was probably too "domestic" a term for Hemingway—despite the memory of a fleeting time "in the early days" when he was "very happy," which closes the memoir. Hemingway never cared for domestic life, or for women, either, at heart. He needed female affection. But that's not the same thing. He had to be active, manly. Was that pretense? When he lived here he was usually alone, writing about masculine action or fishing in the Gulf with Joe Russell or drinking at Sloppy Joe's, or he was far away. He traveled more and more during the '30s. Africa. The Spanish Civil War. Lengthening stays in Cuba. Then he left Key West for good. The second marriage was over. The third was beginning. And with it came *For Whom the Bell Tolls* and new acclaim, then a good war in Europe that he relished playing what Burton recognized was a rather contrived part in, down to "liberating" the Ritz Hotel in Paris. But the World War II novel didn't work. The trite title hinted at that: *Across the River and into the Trees.* A Hemingway parody. The third marriage didn't work, either. How could it have with a wife like Martha Gellhorn, that resolutely independent woman who couldn't live in Hemingway's shadow or abide his histrionics? And then—*The Old Man and the Sea*. Perhaps his best. On his mind for fifteen years. It brought a Pulitzer. And clinched the Nobel Prize. But after that, for the last ten years, almost nothing. Or nothing that he finished or was working into something memorable. Except the memoir. Why?

Burton left the question hanging and took in the moonlight playing among the shadows of the evocative scene. From the corner of his eye, he vaguely discerned the cats lying next to him. He came back to them again. The honorable nature of animals. None of the self-consciousness that makes people pretend and prevaricate. Just honest instincts. Hemingway admired them for that. Burton's mind returned to *The Old Man and the Sea*. All *true* sentences. Crystal clear. But, it now struck him, wasn't that story about loss, too? Hemingway had believed he was writing about the old man's courage and manliness and endurance, and about the noble fish's beauty and strength and valor, and all of that Hemingway morality. But in the end, the story turns out to be about loss. The old man kills the valiant fish that he has come to love. *"I love you fish,"* he says, *"but I must kill you."* To prove his manhood, to test himself against nature. Then he loses the fish, his victory, his triumph, his honor, to the sharks, bite by bite, as he hauls it toward shore, and he winds up with nothing but a skeleton and with regrets for having taken the great free fish from the sea, depriving it of its splendid life—for nothing. And he goes home to bed sad, and he dreams of lions that he had once seen roaming free in Africa. Loss and regret and dreams of happier days. And so the story closes: *"The old man was dreaming of the lions."* Wasn't that Hemingway himself? Burton asked in a flash of discovery. Wasn't he, too, dreaming of the lions at the end? *"But this is how Paris was in the early days when . . ."*

Holding the image, Burton scanned the moonlit yard. The shroud of shadows was drawing back as the moon passed to the west, bringing the front corner of the house into the light. Very grand. And spooky. Burton's curious eyes played along the lower porch railing and up the moonlit corner column to the second floor balcony. He blinked. His head jerked back. He blinked again. He squinted. Was that a figure standing at the railing in what was now bright moonlight? He closed his eyes and shook his head. He opened them again and focused on the balcony. The figure was still there. Burton leaned forward, his hands on his knees. He gaped. Was it really . . . ?

The Papa figure of legend. Older than when he had lived here. Bulky chest, safari shirt, khaki shorts, cropped white beard, short white hair. Gazing motionless toward the moon.

Burton sat breathless for what seemed like minutes. Was this more of last night's dream? Again? He tried to wake up. But he couldn't. Then, as in that dream, an urge came over him. Slowly, he stood up. Quietly, he crept through the shadows to get closer, fixing his eyes on the figure above. He stopped near the front of the house beneath the balcony. This time, unlike the dream, Hemingway didn't vanish. He was still there at the railing. Burton could now see that he seemed to be holding a piece of paper in one hand while cradling something in his arms. As Burton watched, after a few moments the figure laid the paper on the railing and began lightly stroking what lay in his arms. A cat. The hands that loved to kill were caressing a cat with the tenderness of a mother fondling a child. Out of character. Or was it?

Burton craned to scrutinize the face. He couldn't tell for sure, but the features, although aged and bearded, appeared almost soft, kindly. This was not the hearty face of the photographs. The boyishly grinning hunter and fisherman. The ruddy pugilist. The champion drinker. The fervent writer. This face wore the lines of time and had about it a contemplative aura, as though the figure were summoning images from the past. The eyes seemed to glint in the light. It wasn't a sparkle. That face could not have sparkling eyes. They were more likely rheumy with premature age, reflecting the moonlight that they searched into. And except for the fingers stroking the cat, the figure remained unearthly still, leaning against the railing, looking off into the night.

Burton didn't move. The two of them were locked in a tableau. For how long, Burton couldn't tell. Finally, the figure above shifted slightly, stepped back from the railing, paused briefly in the light, and disappeared into the shadows.

Burton stared. Was it the dream? Or a dream within a dream? Or . . . ? Baffled and disoriented, doubting his senses but unwilling to deny them, he thought he saw a feathery object wafting in the moonlight down from the balcony. He watched it come to rest near the ground on the branches of a bush. He looked up again. No one. Irresistibly drawn, Burton stole toward the object. He leaned down and plucked it from the branches. An ordinary sheet of paper. Bringing it up in the light, he could just make out a page of faintly typed words. He brought it close to read. Three disconnected lines came out to him: *"I wished I had died before I ever loved anyone but her. . . . Paris was never to be the same again. . . . But this is how Paris was in the early days when we were very poor and very happy."*

The paper dropped from Burton's fingers. He froze. He trembled. Gradually he raised his eyes once more to the balcony above. Empty. He brought them down and nervously glanced around. Nothing but the shadows and the moonlight and the weird nighttime forms. Breathing haltingly, he bent down and picked up the paper and read it again. And a strangely benign yet slightly melancholy sensation began rising within him. Soon it enfolded him in a kind of spell.

Without thinking, he moved, as if levitating, to the front steps of the house and up onto the porch. Peering through the glass window of the front door he could see only the silent night of a haunted house. No one. Only darkness broken by patches of moonlight falling through a few windows. Glancing at the sheet of paper still in his hand, he considered sliding it under the door. But he didn't do it. Instead, he backed down the steps and made his way through the moonlight and the shadows across the grass to the wall. After a last gaze at the vacant balcony, bathed in the eerie yellow-green light, he hoisted himself up and over the wall. Somnambulistically, he walked the deserted streets to the Dewey House, where Sylvia breathed heavily in unrufflable sleep as he crawled into bed beside her and left the mystifying night behind.

When Burton Sharp awoke, it was late morning. It took him some time to grasp that. He sat up and rubbed his bleary eyes, coaxing consciousness into his befogged mind. Encountering the day, he fragmentarily recalled the night. A vague feeling of calm amidst turbulence passed over him. He didn't want to analyze it. He clambered out of bed and staggered to the window. Sylvia was outside reading in a chaise lounge under a broad umbrella on the private beach. He pulled on shorts and a shirt and wobbled downstairs to her.

"Well, you must've had a bad night," she said sympathetically.

He shrugged.

"I was starting to worry. Anything wrong?"

He ordered coffee and juice and a croissant. And he told her the story. About the first dream. And about the second—but no, it wasn't a dream. He told her about going out in the night to the house. And about the ghostly figure. And the floating page. Where was it? He couldn't remember what he had done with it.

He fumbled back upstairs to get it. He couldn't find it. Anywhere. Had he imagined it, after all? Unsettled, he returned to Sylvia and confessed his failure.

"Well, my dear," she said sweetly, "either your imagination is getting the better of you or maybe you've just spent too much time with Hemingway."

"Thanks for the confidence." He winked at her. "But, truth or illusion, at least I now understand something better than I used to."

"What's that?"

"What happened to Hemingway. Why it ended as it did. Not the suicide. That had more causes than it needed. But the regrets. The nostalgia. For the early days. The adventure and the bravado and the books and the fame all seemed to fall away at the end. And, like his old man of the sea, he went back to dreaming of the lions. Yearning for the lost time when he had been very poor and very happy at the beginning."

"I'm not sure I follow you, but it sounds like you've found Hemingway's 'rosebud.' The clue to a lost happiness."

He smiled slightly at her sympathetic ingenuity. "Sort of, I guess. Hemingway had a love in his first marriage that he lost, or let go, and whose happiness he would never know again. Maybe that love reminded him of the nurse he had wanted to marry in the Italian hospital during World War I, who broke his heart after he got well and whom he wrote about so heartbreakingly in *A Farewell to Arms*, just after he had left his first wife, Hadley. Anyway, the end of that marriage came to trouble and sadden him. But I think there was more to his regrets and nostalgia than the loss of an early love. He probably longed as much for Wordsworth's rosebuds as for Charles Foster Kane's."

"Wordsworth's rosebuds?"

"Yeah. The youthful feeling, or usually it's youthful, of . . . how does it go? . . . the feeling of *'something evermore about to be'* that makes us *'set the budding rose above the rose full blown.'* You know how it is. In the beginning we have the optimism of 'something ever more about to be.' Later, our lives usually let us down. We lose ourselves in our successes as well as in our failures. We can even, unknowingly, become people we would not have wanted to be. Then, when we look back, our lives appear very different from what we had seen at the beginning, or what we had wanted to see. In Paris with Hadley and Bumby and the notebooks and the cafés, Hemingway had his budding rose. A life buoyant with expectations of the future. Later he got what he wanted, or what he had thought he wanted, and he became someone else. And he gave up a happiness he would remember with sorrow. He had lost the beginning. But he couldn't see any of this until the end."

"A rose is a rose is a rose." Sylvia recited jocularly.

Burton shot her a mildly pained expression.

"Forgive me, Bertie. I didn't mean to be dismissive. But you sound so grave. Could there be more to this than Hemingway? You want to tell me about it?"

Burton didn't know what to say. He didn't know what he felt. He couldn't say anything about Paula. And it dawned on him that he hadn't even thought of her much lately. That ambiguous feeling of calm amidst turbulence was stirring inside him again. "It's nothing," he lied, and looked blankly through her.

"Well, c'mon," she said cheerfully, "before you lapse into hopeless melancholy. We can take a walk with what's left of the day, have a drink and an early dinner, maybe go to a cabaret—they must have something like that here. Forget Hemingway for a while. It'll clear your head. How about it?"

Burton shrugged compliantly.

They changed clothes and dawdled through the afternoon, exploring the town's cemetery for its witty epitaphs, touring the Truman White House for its reassuring Americana, and roving aimlessly until they settled into an oceanside café near Mallory Square. There they again watched the sailboats skimming over the water and the parasailors flying high across the blue sky. In time, people began drifting toward the square for the nightly performances and the sunset. Burton again felt that uncertain sensation of earlier welling up inside him where it had been percolating all day. But this time it brought agitation. Abruptly he blurted: "Let's get out of here."

"What do you mean? Don't you want dinner? Where do you want to go?"

"I mean leave Key West. Now."

"What?! Now? Why?"

"I'm not sure. I just want to get out of here. Do you mind? We can get a car and take our time driving through the other Keys. It could be relaxing and fun. Then fly home from Miami."

Sylvia assented without understanding. She perceived more than a whim at work. He had been behaving strangely since they had arrived. But she knew how to pick her battles, as well as how win without fighting.

They took a taxi back to their room. Burton rearranged the flight plans and reserved a car. A convertible, Sylvia had suggested, to make the most of the trip. While she started packing, Burton went into the bathroom for a quick shower. Toweling off afterwards, he stood before the mirror. "My God!" he gasped. "What the . . . ? Who . . . ? His eyes bulged. His mouth fell open. His heart pounded. A faintly recognizable old man looked out at him. The man had a cropped white beard and thinning white hair arranged to cover encroaching baldness. Burton's hands rose impulsively and pressed against his cheeks. Then with groping fingers he slathered foam over the beard. "One true sentence. One true sentence. Bullshit!" he hissed between gritted teeth as he swiped and hacked with the razor, back and forth, up and down. When he rinsed off, the beard was gone, and blood oozed from half a dozen nicks. He pushed the white hair back from his forehead, exposing a deeply receding hairline habitually concealed by a studied comb-over. "To hell with Hemingway!" he growled under his breath. "And . . . adulation! And . . . Paula! All of that."

Grabbing his toiletries, he marched into the bedroom.

"Whaaaaat's this?" Sylvia exclaimed, catching sight of his face.

"You have to ask?" he mumbled, stuffing clothes into his suitcase.

"Ooohhh kayyy," she said, dropping the question, but suspecting something about the answer. She came over and kissed him on the cheek. He paused and turned toward her

"You're a bloody mess, you know, Bertie," she said affectionately, dabbing his face with a tissue.

"So are you, Sylvie," he whispered with the hint of a smile, lifting the tissue from her fingers and lightly wiping a smudge of his blood from under her lip. He kissed her fondly on the forehead.

They finished packing and, bags in hand, headed out the door. Sylvia let Burton go in front as she stayed at the threshold to check the room, routinely guarding against misplaced things. Noticing the night table, she called out as he got to the bottom of the stairs, "Hey, Bertie, you forgot your books."

"No I didn't," he shouted back and kept going.

Sylvia stood puzzling over that. An intuition began rising. Her eyebrows arched and her lips curled up at the corners. She nodded to herself and pulled the door closed behind her.

They paid the bill, with apologies and a penalty for the early departure. And, after a short taxi ride to the airport to get the car, they drove off, top down. Traffic coming into Key West clogged the causeway linking this westernmost Key to the other Keys along narrow Route 1 leading to the mainland 160 miles away. But no traffic was going in their direction at this hour. They were going out, due east on an open road.

Warm tropical air flowed over them. Burton at the wheel turned the radio up to listen to the music above the hum of the road and the whoosh of oncoming traffic. The cracking voice of an elderly Frank Sinatra was finishing a Sondheim song: *"Send in the clowns. . . . There ought to be clowns. . . . Don't bother. . . . They're here."* Burton and Sylvia exchanged slow smiles that grew into warm laughter. He reached for her hand and took it in his and squeezed it hard. He said nothing. He didn't need to. Sylvia knew. They were going back to the beginning.

Burton pressed down on the gas pedal. The wind rushed against their faces and flapped their hair. Overhead, wisps of high cirrus clouds were brightening with rays of gold and pink and lavender. Behind, the wide western sky was a swirl of deepening orange and magenta and purple. In Mallory Square, the crowd was applauding the sunset. And at the Hemingway House, the day's last tourists had departed, leaving its walled-in grounds to the countless cats for another quiet night of moonlight and shadows.

www.ingramcontent.com/pod-product-compliance
Lightning Source LLC
Chambersburg PA
CBHW061116100726
47911CB00013B/565